SHADOWBORN

MAREN ALDER

Paradigm Publishing
www.paradigmpublishing.info

Ordering Information:
For details, contact info@paradigmpublisher.com

Hardcover ISBN: 978-1-7368432-4-6
eBook ISBN: 978-1-7368432-1-5

Printed in the United States of America on SFI Certified paper.

First Edition

Typesetting by Crystal Peake Type

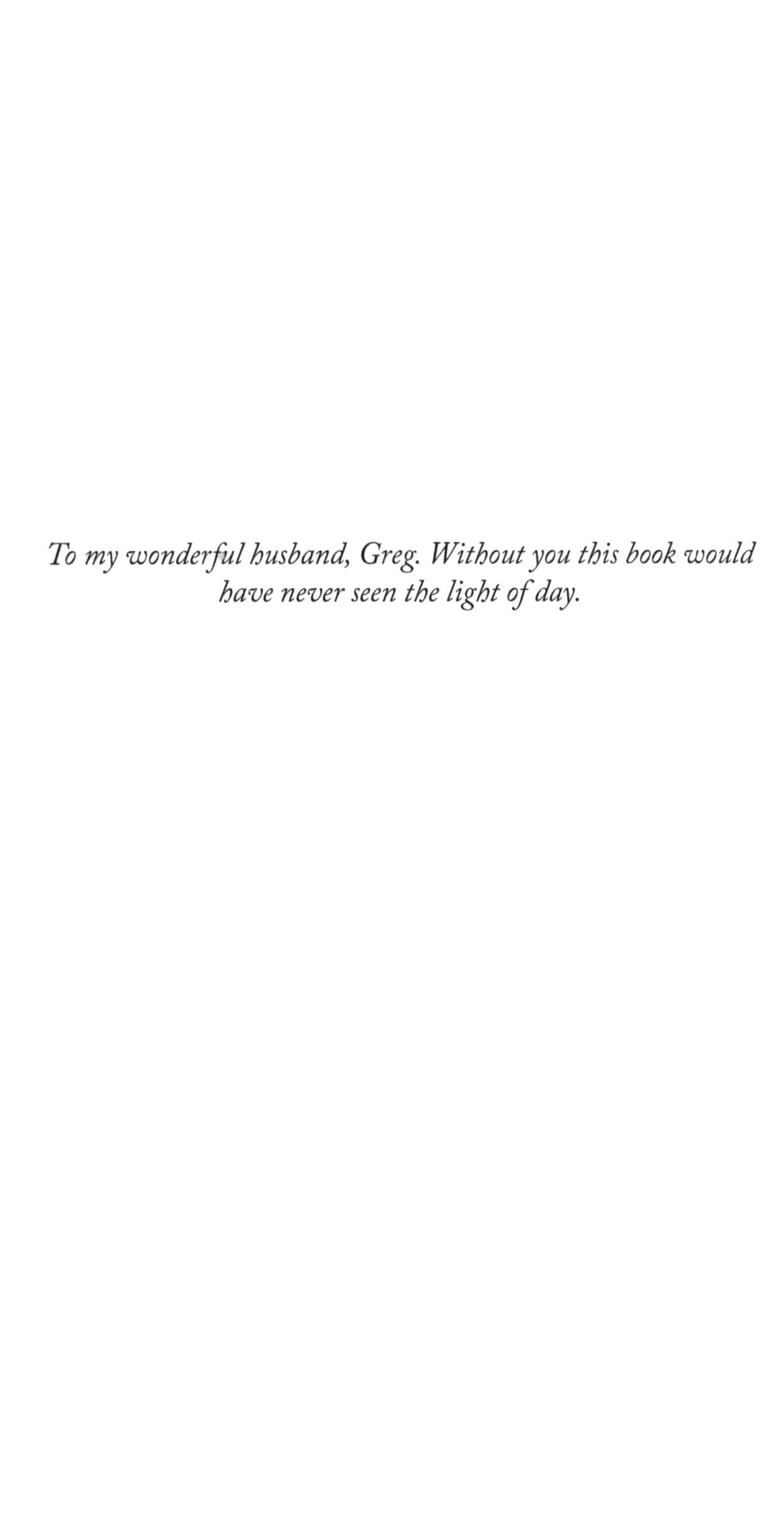

To my wonderful husband, Greg. Without you this book would have never seen the light of day.

CHAPTER 1

I was born on Friday the thirteenth on the wrong side of the bed, and it just went downhill from there. It shouldn't have surprised me when my day ended with my probable death, but bad luck isn't something you ever really get used to.

Butchering my audition was just the precursor to the worst day of my life. Now there was the rain, the hard kind that bounced when it hit the pavement and stung my skin.

The blouse I'd handpicked for the casting session clung to me in a damp embrace as I pushed the twenty-dollar bike I'd purchased from Goodwill at a frantic clip. The tire had gone flat and the chain now dragged on the ground somewhere next to my soul.

I glanced at my cellphone for the hundredth time, insides sinking a little at the lack of missed calls. Mom was probably too hung-over to even notice that her precious seventeen-year-old daughter had gone AWOL. I scoffed at myself. From the way I was acting, you'd almost think I cared.

To my right, several balconies stuffed with trash clung to an endless row of apartment buildings. The windows all had bars on the outside that dripped with the unseasonable moisture. My GPS app told me that I was still a good four miles from the dumpy hostel I'd been staying in since arriving in LA a week and a half ago. I took a deep breath, inhaling rain as well as the wet strands of hair that insisted on sticking to my face. I'd better get on with it.

Picking up my pace, I lifted my chin in an attempt to look determined and—

Slammed into something.

Both my bike and myself went sprawling in different directions, while my poor cellphone flew in a perfect arc, straight into a puddle. I pulled myself off the sidewalk and looked around, heart thudding behind my ribcage. There was nothing but another mile or so of warped sidewalk in front of me. What could I have possibly hit? That's when I noticed the rain next to my fallen bike. As it neared the ground it flared out as if it were falling over something. Something I couldn't see.

I bit the inside of my cheek and reached my trembling hand forward. My fingers made contact, and what I saw made me scream. A boy materialized beneath my touch. He couldn't have been any older than me but had hair as silver as a quarter. His startled blue eyes were the only splash of color in this rainy afternoon world.

I drew back from him, another scream lodged in my throat as he faded in and out of sight like a flickering light bulb. Slowly, he rose to his feet, clutching something to his chest. He limped a few paces, then gained momentum and ran.

The world seemed to sway around me. A ghost, he had to be a ghost. But as I looked down at the sidewalk, I noticed a thin trail of red soaking into the already wet cement. Could ghosts bleed?

Trembling, I lunged for my submerged cellphone. The cheap screen had blacked out. Too bad I had never saved enough money to purchase a waterproof one. I shoved the useless device into my back pocket and picked up my ruined bike. Surely by now I was too old to just start having paranormal experiences. Maybe all the disappointments of the last week and a half were driving me crazy instead. With my mom's track record of manic depression and alcoholism, it's not like mental illness didn't run in the family.

I closed my eyes like I always did when I needed a break from reality, and searched my mind for a character I could inhabit until I was back in control. I thought of the monologue I'd performed at the audition just fifteen minutes earlier, and suddenly, I was no longer Teylin Walker. I was Kathy from Singin' in the Rain, which was only appropriate considering the current weather conditions. I began to recite the lines of Kathy's unconventional meeting with Don Lockwood, trying to make up for the fact that I'd massacred them at the audition. My free hand gesticulated to thin air and my voice gained volume as I continued my trek down the sidewalk.

A hand on my shoulder snapped me back into myself. Gasping in surprise, I spun around and came face to face with a tall African American woman.

"'Scuse me, hon," she said. "Did you see a boy come this way?"

Heat filled my cheeks as I struggled to form words. "H-huh?"

Next to the woman, a Hispanic man dressed in an unbuttoned suit cleared his throat. "He'd be sorta odd-looking," he said. "Very thin. Hair, this color." He reached into his pocket and pulled out a small handful of nickels and dimes.

"Why are you looking for him?" I asked.

The woman gave me a tight smile. Probably in her late twenties, her black tank top showed off the sculpted muscles of her arms. "The dear little waif is in trouble. If we don't find him, he could injure himself worse."

I nodded and took a breath. "I did see someone like that.

This is going to sound crazy, but he…" My voice cracked.

The woman leaned forward. "It's OK, hon. You can tell us." She put her hand on my shoulder and squeezed.

"He sort of vanished. Like a ghost or something." I twisted a strand of my long wet hair around my index finger. "Sorry. Been a rough day. I'm probably just seeing things."

Neither of them laughed at me. "Not a ghost," said the man. "But he's going to be soon if we don't find him. Which way did he go?"

I pointed.

He wiped the rain out of his eyes and nodded. "Thanks. You should ride on home before this weather turns into a real storm."

"Yeah," I said. "Working on that." Never mind that my real home was over a thousand miles away, and my current residence happened to be a dingy hostel I could barely afford to stay in anymore. I glanced down at my flattened bike tire.

The woman grabbed the man's arm before he could take off. "Ricky, that was insensitive. She's got a flat." She gave him an intense look.

He glanced at my bike, then at me. "Sorry 'bout that. Need some money for a cab?"

With my track record of failed auditions, money was exactly what I needed, but what kind of person accepted it from a random stranger? "Oh no, that's OK," I said. "I'm from Washington—near the coast—so I'm used to this weather."

"Good luck, then," the man called Ricky said. He patted my shoulder and turned away. "Let's go, Nina."

Nina turned to give me one last glance as the pair of them took off down the sidewalk. Before long, they were lost from my view.

Squeak. Squeak. Squeak.

My bike seemed abnormally loud after the strange encounter, and all my senses were on full alert. I kept pushing robotically, but my eyes were on the shiny trail of blood that the rain was quickly dissolving on the sidewalk. If the boy wasn't a ghost, then how could he vanish like that?

I was so lost in thought that I was nearly run over by an SUV before I realized that the sidewalk had ended and I was now walking in the middle of the road. After several angry honks, I sprinted back to the safety of the curb and tried to get my bearings. Nothing looked familiar, and, with my phone dead, I had no GPS to guide me back.

A distant sound sent chills up my spine. At first, I thought it was the wind, but the air was too still for that to be true. Someone was screaming.

The only human visible was an old homeless man standing under an overpass, and the haunting voice didn't match his grizzled exterior. I heard it again, and this time, I was able to locate where it came from. There was a narrow space between two apartment complexes around the corner. I jogged to it. With a pounding heart, I peered around the edge and looked into the darkness.

Nina and Ricky were there, and they'd cornered the strange boy I'd seen earlier. He cowered against the bricks of the complex, clutching a cloth sack to his chest.

"How long did you think you could last out here?" asked Nina. "You have no chance away from the islands without us. Your ability barely works anymore."

Ricky took the boy by the chin and examined his face. "He's already got the shakes. Soon, the symptoms will hit hard." He leaned forward to be eye level with the boy. "You're lucky we found you in time."

The boy struggled out of Ricky's grip. He tried to run but

Nina blocked his way and shoved him back against the wall. I gasped as Ricky's fist slammed into his stomach. The boy dropped to the ground and the sack fell from his hands. Large silvery rocks spilled into the muddy alleyway.

"Well look here," said Nina. "Our runaway is a thief as well."

Ricky kicked him in the ribs and the boy writhed in the mud. "Think you would get away with stealing from me? Huh?" He kicked him again. "Do you know how much money I paid for you?"

Nina scooped the rocks back into the sack and held them at arm's length like the contents were repulsive. "Enough, Ricky. Let's get him back to the warehouse before he's too damaged to work."

"He won't be working for me anymore," said Ricky. "When you go back to Los Sueños you're taking him with you and handing him over to Antonio. He'll knock some sense into this disobedient waif."

"Fine, just get him up." She glanced back in my direction and I quickly withdrew, hoping she hadn't seen me watching. "Let's get outa here."

I heard a sharp cry as Ricky dragged the boy to his feet and then footsteps coming toward me. I abandoned my bike against the wall and made a run for it. I had just ducked around the next corner when they emerged from the alley, hauling the boy between them.

Breathing hard, I watched as they walked in the direction I had come. My head was a wasp's nest of questions. What was going to happen to that boy? And how could he…do what he did? I squeezed my eyes shut as premature regret slithered into me.

This is wrong, Tey. You're just going to get yourself in more trouble.

But I had to know.

Leaving my bike where it was, I found myself following Nina and Ricky and their mysterious captive as if I thought I were Nancy Drew, or maybe Dana Scully.

They didn't go far. After a few blocks, the row of buildings tapered off into a spacious industrial area next to a large transit garage. The sidewalk was replaced by wet gravel that slipped under the boy's feet as he continued to struggle in Nina and Ricky's grip. I walked as quietly as I could and kept myself in the shadow of the garage's wall.

This was only going to end badly. Everything I did ended badly, and yet, I still couldn't stop myself.

Ricky approached a warehouse riddled with No Trespassing signs. He looked in both directions then dialed something into a keypad on the side of a wide metal door. The door slid open to reveal a dimly lit interior, and the look of horror on the boy's face made me bite my tongue. Ricky and Nina forced the boy through the opening and I stood, frozen, as the door began to automatically shut behind them.

I had seconds to make a decision. I didn't see another way into the building, so I dashed forward and slipped through the crack, just before the electric door closed all the way.

A wave of pressure washed over me, halting me in my tracks. Nina and Ricky were too preoccupied with the boy to notice my entrance, and I immediately ducked behind a rusty generator.

Sweat beaded on my forehead. The air in the warehouse felt too thick to breathe, and the floor seemed to tip back and forth in dizzying waves.

Through squinted eyes, I examined my new surroundings. Flickering lights hung low to illuminate what looked like a small factory. Vats of silvery liquid sat on large burners. They glowed so bright they hurt my eyes if I looked too long.

Next to the vats stood a dozen children, all with silver hair and sky blue eyes like the boy who could turn invisible. My heart gave a little stutter when I noticed the chains around their ankles. The metal clinked as they worked to extract the glowing liquid and distribute it into tubes, which flowed into a large machine in the center of the room. The tubular mechanism reminded me a little of the enormous telescope I'd seen at the Griffith Park Observatory (one of the only touristy places I'd visited since coming to LA).

The longer I stared at it, the less benign it appeared. Electric wires connected to it, sparking whenever one of the strange children got too near. It suddenly occurred to me that this could be some kind of radioactive weapons manufacturing plant. I had to get out of here; tell the police.

I stood up, but the movement was too fast. My brain felt like a lemon in a vise as the pressure in the room squeezed the blood from it. I teetered forward and fell with a crash, knocking over a barrel filled with the same type of silvery rocks the boy had been carrying.

Nina and Ricky spun around and I knew it was too late to run.

"How did you get in here?" asked Nina. Her face was soaked in sweat, like the pressure of the room was getting to her too, but strangely none of the children appeared affected. Nina let go of the boy and stumbled over to me.

I tried to crawl backward to get to the door and run, but my limbs trembled and gave out. "Sorry," I grunted. I didn't know what else to say.

Nina turned to Ricky. "She followed us."

Ricky cursed and lowered the boy against the wall, then

came and squatted next to me. His oily black hair fell into his eyes as he peered down. "Just what were you thinking? This place is dangerous. Did you want to get yourself killed?"

Nausea gripped my stomach as the reality of my situation overwhelmed me. "N-no," I said, but it was pointless. I'd seen something I wasn't supposed to see. Now I would pay for it.

Ricky looked at Nina with a resolved expression. "You know what we have to do."

"But she's just a teenager."

"Would you rather go to prison? Or get this whole place shut down? Get her up."

Nina pulled me to my feet.

Black spots obscured my vision and I swayed, seconds from passing out. "Are you going to kill me?" I croaked.

"It's nothing personal, hon," she said with a tight frown.

"I suppose promising not to tell won't do any good at this point," I said, too sick and disoriented to feel the fear that should have gripped my heart. But with my eyes, I still searched desperately for a way out.

"What good's a promise from a stranger?" said Ricky.

Nina held me at arm's length. "Seems kinda a waste," she said to Ricky. "A healthy girl like her. And she's got a nice look to her. Could be worth somethin'."

Ricky pulled a pistol from the inside pocket of his suit coat. "That means nothing if it's at our own expense. Now, hold her still."

Despite the strange pressure in the room, my instinct for self-preservation kicked in. I jerked to my right and twisted out of Nina's grasp. I dashed to the door and pawed at the keypad that operated it, but it was useless without a code. I banged against the door and scrambled for a handhold.

The silver-haired children stood frozen, staring at me like

a herd of deer in an open field. Even if I could convince them to help me, they wouldn't be able to do much with chained feet. I looked toward the boy from earlier, but he had toppled over on the floor, unconscious.

Ricky raised his gun and fired. The bullet dented the metal of the door half an inch from my shoulder. I dove behind another barrel of the weird rocks and crouched low. My breath heaved like no matter how much oxygen I sucked in, it would never be enough. Peering, around the side, I searched for another way out.

The warehouse was windowless and I didn't see any other doors. I stood on shaking legs and reached into the barrel. My hand connected with one of the rocks and I felt a little shock, like a spark of static electricity.

Ricky advanced on me, finger still on the trigger. I hefted the rock behind my shoulder and threw it toward him with all my remaining strength. He easily dodged to the side, and my rock went spiraling behind him, right into the machine in the center of the room.

Both Ricky and Nina gasped, and then there was a sound like a small explosion as the rock tore through some of the wiring. The pressure in the room suddenly became a tourniquet around my whole body. I saw a white light, brighter than anything I'd ever seen before. It came from the end of the telescope-like tube that I now was certain was a weapon. And it headed straight for me.

My senses were too foggy to react fast enough. There was the sensation of burning pain as it struck my chest, and then darkness so complete I was sure I'd never wake again.

Just when I thought my day couldn't get any worse.

CHAPTER 2

I wasn't dead.

I became more and more aware of that fact the longer I felt the wild throb in my chest and the burn of acid at my throat. Around me, the world swayed in an unnatural rhythm, insisting that something was wrong. I struggled to open my eyes, but it was like two weights hung from my lids.

The movement continued to rock—up and down, back and forth, like the cradle of a giant. Los Angeles was known for its earthquakes. Could one be happening now?

Finally, footsteps, and the click of a door lock. The door creaked open and light blossomed outside my eyelids. I twitched, and life returned to my body in an eruption of needlepoint tingles. I turned onto my side and hugged my shoulders as the person moved closer.

At last, the weights dropped away, and my lids flew open to meet the strange stare of the boy I'd seen in the rain.

"Where am I?" I croaked. I clung to the wall as I rose to a sitting position, my head swimming.

He didn't answer.

"Can't you talk?" The room was small and white, and the cot I sat on had only one blanket. This was not the warehouse where Ricky had nearly put a bullet through my head. This was...

I turned and located a small, round window. With a hammering heart, I rose to my knees and peered out. The view outside explained why everything swayed. I was in the middle of the ocean. Dark clouds hung over heaving waves for as far as I could see.

I was not one for fainting when afraid, but in that moment, a lightness washed over me and evaporated my strength. My ragdoll body sank into my bunk and one arm dangled off the side.

"You're supposed to eat something," said the boy in a soft voice.

So he wasn't a mute.

I noticed there was a tray in his hands and the aroma of fried seafood and mashed potatoes drifted to my nostrils, a full assault on my heaving stomach.

I shook my head and looked up at him. "I'm not supposed to be here." For a moment I was taken aback by his peculiar features. Even his eyelashes were silver, encircling those strange eyes like a feathery metal frame.

He set the tray on my bed and turned away.

"Wait," I said, kneading my temples. "Maybe we can help each other."

He didn't answer as he limped to the door.

I slid off the bed, pulse galloping. "At least tell me where they're taking me." I tried to rush forward and grab his arm, but a sharp pain blossomed in my chest, right where that pillar of light had struck me. It was so intense that a cry burst from my throat and I felt my body slam into the floor. I twitched as something like an electric current ran through me.

The boy kneeled next to me and his cool hands held me down. As I looked up at him, he seemed to change, distorting into something that couldn't possibly be real. His pale face became frigid and demonic like it was carved from ice, and his blue eyes blackened into pools of endless night. I screamed and tried to drag myself away. My back slammed into the side of my bed and I pawed the mattress until I found the tray of food. I flung it at him, scattering the contents all over the small cabin.

The door flew open and another demon entered. This one was tall and dark, with wild hair that crackled with black flames. "What's going on here?" it asked in a female voice. I recognized the sound of it. Nina.

The monster changed. Nina stood in its place with her muscular arms outstretched toward me. Next to her stood the boy, no longer demonic, just thin and frightened like the moment I'd run into him with my bike.

I cowered on the floor, every muscle trembling.

"Teylin?" Nina said. She crouched next to me on the floor. "Can you hear me, hon?"

"How do you know my name?" My voice came in shuddering sobs.

"Found one of your headshots folded up in your pocket. Nice acting resume, by the way."

She put her arm around me and helped to lift me onto the cot. "I wanted to be an actor once too, ya know. That was before I met Ricky."

"Where am…?" I tried to ask.

"I know you're confused, hon, but now's a bad time for chit chat. Just know you're onboard La Ventura. It's a very reliable ship. You're going to be fine."

As my head fell onto the pillow her face warped again. She seemed to grow three feet, and broaden into a bestial form with jagged teeth.

I cried out and covered my head with my arms. Her claw-like hands came down on me and pinned my arms to my sides. I thrashed back and forth as I tried to escape her, but she was too strong.

"Hey," she said, her mouth close enough for me to feel her steamy breath on my ear. "Look at me, hon. You're hallucinating. What you see? It's not real."

"Get away from me!" I howled, unable to accept what my eyes couldn't. "Get away!"

Nina turned to the boy. "Stay with her. Let me know if there's any change." I heard the door slam as she left the room.

I kept my eyes squeezed shut, unwilling to look at the boy, terrified he'd change again into the cold demonic prince. Whatever was going to happen to me now, there was no escape. The ever-present movement of the ship reminded me of that. I pulled my knees to my chest and felt my consciousness drift away as each roll of the waves carried me deeper into their wilderness.

* * *

Waking dreams washed over me, as prolific as the waves outside my window. The worse ones were nightmares about my mom. She'd been in one of her rages the night I'd run away. Now I relived it over and over again in a horrifying time loop. I heard the sound of her screaming voice; felt the sting of her palm on my cheek.

"You think you know everything, don't you? Well let me be the first to tell you, you're as stupid as your traitor father. A stupid, little slut!"

Her words reverberated in my skull.

Running away wasn't uncommon for me. I often took off after her episodes. It was good for both of us not to be under the same roof for a while, and I knew she came to expect my departures with the confidence that I'd always come back. After all, with no dad or siblings in the picture, she was all I had.

I usually didn't go farther than a couple towns over. This time had been different. It was my first time going to Los Angeles; quite a bus ride from my small hometown of Millbrook, Washington. It was also the first time I had no intention of turning back.

I was determined to become an actor someone who flowed seamlessly from one character to the next; pretending to be anyone other than the unlucky girl who bore my birth name. I'd always been good at doing that.

Something touched my face and my eyelids flickered. I saw the strange boy leaning over me, but I wasn't sure if he was real or only imagined. I closed my eyes and was swallowed up again.

The dreams became less cohesive then: Indigenous albinos chanted in circles; shadows peeled off the walls and danced. In a stone room overgrown with flowering plants, veiled women slept side by side. There were sparkling balls of light and silver pools that flowed in vein-like channels deep into the earth.

I was a baby again, wailing in my mother's arms. I was old with white hair and withered hands. I was the sky, then the sea. I was darkness itself, sinking deeper and deeper into nothing.

An eternity passed before a light appeared; small and frail in the overwhelming void. Step by step, I followed it through a doorway and back into myself.

When I opened my eyes, I saw only the whitewashed wall of my tiny cabin and felt only the rock of the ship. My muscles felt limp, and sweat coated every inch of me.

I blinked, expecting the room to shift into another hallucination, but this time it stayed put. Slowly, I swiveled my bare feet around to meet the cold floor. I stood, one hand on the wall for support. In my weakness, just getting to the door was a struggle, but I managed. I rattled the handle, but it was locked. I stumbled back to my bed and attempted to piece together what had happened to me.

It's not like I didn't expect everything in my life to always go wrong, but getting shot by a mysterious weapon and taken on a ship that was currently in the middle of the ocean, deserved the highest spot on my growing list of Tey's Top Ten Worst Situations, which was saying something.

The sound of a key rattled in my door lock. The door opened and Nina walked in, curly black hair slicked back from her face in a high ponytail. Her lips tightened when she saw me sitting up.

"So, you're still alive."

"Disappointed?" I croaked.

She walked over to my cot and I drew back against the wall. "I'm not a monster, hon. 'Course I'm not disappointed you're alive. Ricky, though, won't be so happy to hear the good news."

"Is he on board?"

"Nah. He had some business to wrap up in LA. Lucky for you."

"I won't tell anyone what I saw."

"But how can he trust you? He's built an empire on dishonesty. He'll never believe someone like you is capable of keeping their word. Not without something valuable to hold over your head."

"So if he wants me dead, then why go through the trouble of kidnapping me? Don't tell me he ran out of bullets."

"He saw your mistake as an opportunity. Until you came along, our little machine hadn't been tested yet on humans.

Ricky wanted to know what it would do to you; how long it would take for you to die."

"What was that thing?" I looked down at my chest and glimpsed a circular red mark right below my collarbone. It still prickled with pain.

"Something that might come in handy in the future, but we've still got a long way to go. In the meantime, what am I going to do with you?"

"You could let me go home," I suggested.

Nina laughed. "And risk you spoiling Ricky's plans? Not going to happen."

I shrugged. "It was worth a shot."

"Besides," said Nina. "We're almost to Los Sueños now."

"Where?"

"Los Sueños. It's a tiny archipelago halfway across the Pacific. Very beautiful. You're going to like it there."

"Halfway across the Pacific? How long have I been on board?"

"Almost two weeks. You weren't very lucid for most of it."

I felt my pulse pick up speed and tried to breathe normally as the reality of my situation finally hit home.

Nina tucked a strand of my hair behind my ear and lifted my chin. "You have a nice look. I bet Arun Gheisari would like it."

I pulled away, suddenly cold. "Who's that?"

"One of the most powerful Coterie chiefs in Los Sueños, and he's got a weakness for pretty young things. I bet he'd give me a good price for you."

"Price? You mean, you're thinking of selling me to him? Like a slave?"

"We prefer the term 'pleasure mate'." She gave me a half-smile. "Well don't be so dramatic. Such things aren't so unusual on the islands. And I'm afraid the alternative is death, hon. In Gheisari's care, at least you'd be safe, and unable to blab to anyone who might disapprove of Ricky's practices. And I'm sure in time, you'll learn what it takes to keep a powerful man like him happy."

I couldn't believe how well I kept it together. Inside, every cell screamed like my body was on fire. This was really happening to me. All those terrible news articles I'd skimmed over about things that only happened to girls in foreign countries. Now I'd be that black-and-white photo on the grocery store wall where they pegged up missing people. People who would most likely never be found.

I swung around to face her. Maybe I could take her by surprise and get to a lifeboat. Some lifeboats were pretty high tech. One might even have a radio.

Out of nowhere, a gun appeared in Nina's hand. She fiddled with it casually, but I got the message. I turned around again and watched the waves crash against my porthole window as I clenched my jaw tighter and tighter.

"Please," I said, trying to sound young and innocent. "Put yourself in my place. It could be you."

Nina turned away from me and didn't look back as she walked out the door. "It was me. For a long time." Then she shut the door.

CHAPTER 3

My first glimpse of Los Sueños was at eight o'clock in the morning, three days since waking up. Nina had let me out of my cabin so I could witness our arrival, but a dense fog hung over the ocean, nearly obscuring the large island coming into view.

For the first time since running away, I missed my mom. It wasn't because she'd been any good at taking care of me. It was because I felt bad for her, and suddenly, I'd much rather deal with her drunken tirades than the reality that gripped me now.

Tears came to my eyes before I could call them back. I'd never been much of a crier, but no one was watching, so I let my misery flow.

Perhaps if my dad hadn't left when Mom was still pregnant with me, things would have been different. We would have had a real family. Maybe I'd have a brother. A sister? Maybe I'd have actually liked the girl I'd turned out to be, instead of being so desperate to escape her.

"So what do you think of Los Sueños?"

Startled, I looked up to see Nina. She had an amused expression on her face as if the fact I was crying was some kind of joke. I could feel my tears retreating into the well behind my eyes where they screamed for a release I no longer allowed. I wiped my face and sniffed.

"It must be a tiny archipelago."

Nina shrugged. "I suppose. But the islands are crammed full of cities and people and jungle."

"Why haven't I seen it on a map, or heard about it in school?"

"It's a private nation, and there are special charters that protect it. The monarchy doesn't want outsiders to become too interested."

"A private nation? How did you get there, then?"

"I was taken by the Coterie."

Nina had mentioned that word before. "Are they some kind of criminal organization?"

She nodded. "They're the ones who really rule Los Sueños."

"And Arun Gheisari?" I asked. "He's one of them?"

"One of their leaders."

"What's he like?"

Nina shrugged. "He's a Coterie chief. You don't get to that level without a lot of heads on your plate first."

Her words floated around me as I gripped the rail and gazed at what was to be my new home. My prison.

The closer we got, the more I could hear the chattering of thousands of birds coming from the bits of jungle poking through the mist. I caught a whiff of wild gardenias, strong and distinct. It overpowered the smell of the ocean, which I'd grown accustomed to in the past couple days, but did nothing to relax my nerves.

Nina leaned next to me and took a deep breath. "Beautiful, isn't it?"

I nodded, shielding my eyes against the stabbing sunlight. Other islands dotted the horizon, some too small for much more than a cottage, others massive mist-shrouded silhouettes sparkling with distant lights.

"The islands are all named after saints," Nina said. "The big one is Santa Delphina. It's where we're headed."

As we rounded the larger landmass she had pointed out, the jungle slowly disappeared, making way for a bustling city.

"Welcome to Cosmar," said Nina, motioning toward the city. "You'll see it's home to lots of wayward types. It's kinda like a beach after a shipwreck. You never know who will wash up here."

La Ventura arrived at a busy port. Looking around, I could see dozens of other ships next to us. Some were similar to our boxy mercantile vessel, but others looked like old galleons from pirate movies.

When the ship was fully secured at a dock, Nina gripped my arm. "Time to go, Tey." She didn't handcuff me, but several of her men surrounded me, making an escape attempt useless. I'd hoped that the silver-haired boy would be with us when we left the ship. I hadn't seen him since recovering from my hallucinations and couldn't help wondering what had happened to him. If he was still around, he was making good use of his ability to turn invisible. An ability I envied more than anything right now.

As Nina led me down the gangplank, my heart started to go haywire. We'd arrived. I swallowed a dry lump in my throat and tried to focus on my surroundings, looking for anything, or anyone that might help me escape.

There were people everywhere, mostly Asian or Hispanic, or a mix of unidentifiable races. I was glad my hair was brown instead of blonde or red. I didn't want to stand out more than I already did.

I smelled fish and smoke from the outdoor seafood market directly next to the port. Men in bandannas gutted fish and rolled them in newspaper, shouting back and forth in an

Asian language I couldn't identify.

Nina and her men maintained a fast pace as we went through the wharf, stepping over puddles from a recent rainstorm. She paused on a curb and looked around with a grimace. "The car's not here." She folded her arms and turned to the man next to her. "If you're looking for a new gig, a driver position just opened up."

I only spotted three other cars on the road. Come to think of it, the normal gasoline stench I'd come to associate with cities wasn't there, nor was the sound of honking horns or squealing breaks.

Before long, a skinny black man on a bike towing a bright yellow bicycle cab stopped in front of us. "Hey pretty lady," he called to Nina, his curly hair bouncing like thousands of tiny springs. "Need a lift somewhere? Sammy's real fast and gives a good price."

Nina eyed him suspiciously.

"Come on," he said. "Rain's coming back soon. Sammy will get you to your destination before it starts raining or no charge."

She looked at the sky. It was thick with dark clouds. "Fine." She sighed and pulled me into the cab alongside her. She took out her gun and put it on her lap where I could see it.

"That's good, lady," Sammy said. "Sammy will take you wherever you want to go in half the time of other cabbies. Sammy's fast as a horse."

Nina gave him a card. "Can you find this address?"

He smiled. "Sammy knows every avenue and alley of Cosmar as good as any map." He started to pedal.

Nina turned in the seat and looked back at her men who still stood on the curb. "Wait for me at Club Adder. I'll meet you there after I finish this transaction. Oh, and if you happen to run into my driver before that, tell him he's fired."

The men nodded and walked more casually in the other direction.

"Remember," Nina whispered into my ear, "I'm only doing this to give you a chance like Ricky gave me when I was brought here. But one wrong move and that chance will be over. I won't hesitate to kill you." She was silent for the rest of the ride, her face tight and her back rigid. She seemed worried about something and I didn't want to tip her over the edge. Instead, I wallowed in my dread. What was coming at the end of this ride was more terrible than anything I had ever imagined could happen to me. I felt the blood recede from my arms and face, almost as if it were seeping out of me from a gaping wound.

I thought of all the movies I'd seen with characters in similar situations. They all had people who cared about them. People who could afford to hire action heroes to rescue them. I had no one like that, and in this strange and secretive country, I couldn't count on help from the US government. To the people back home, it would look like I'd vanished into thin air.

CHAPTER 4

The narrow streets of the city gave way to neighborhoods of enormous villas with immaculate gardens. None of the mansions I'd driven by in LA could rival these impressive structures. Instead of picturing them occupied by celebrities and royalty, all I could imagine were the menacing faces of criminals, and attics full of girls like me.

After the dazzling streets, the city started to thin out. It regressed into smaller homes, then jungly hovels, and finally tapered off into muddy dirt roads leading into the trees. Sammy panted as he pedaled through the mud and then skidded to a stop at a gate covered with large vines. The jungle grew thick on either side, and the sounds of birds and the hoots of small animals surrounded us.

Beyond it, I glimpsed the sections of a grand house that weren't obscured by trees and foliage. I could see a stone tower with a tiled roof peeking out of one side, and an image of myself trapped inside flashed through my mind. I shook it away. I wasn't some sort of princess from a fairy tale, and the chances of a happily ever after were disappearing every second.

"Here's your stop, lady," said our driver, motioning to the gate. "Told you Sammy would make it before the rain."

"You sure about that?" said Nina holding out her hand. "I thought I felt a few drops."

Sammy looked at the sky. "That was just moisture from the leaves. But, tell you what. Sammy won't take your money if you'll give him your number. How's that for a deal?" He put on a lopsided grin.

Nina pretended to consider for a moment and then shook her head. "No deal I'm afraid." She pushed a few bills into his hand. "That's for getting us here fast." She hesitated, looking at him again, this time cocking her head to the side and lifting the corner of her mouth. She handed him more money. "And that's for waiting for me. I won't be long."

Nina dialed a number on a keypad and the gate swung open, revealing a paved driveway that led to the mansion. A fusion between a Spanish villa and French chateau, it was the kind of house I would have itched to explore, had the situation been different. I knew that houses so close to the shore probably wouldn't have a basement, so my eyes went to the second-story windows, gauging their height and scanning for trellises to climb down. There were some ragged vines and overgrown foliage, but nothing that looked strong enough to hold me. The jungle had overtaken the yard, and yet, not one tree was close enough to provide an escape route. Such was my luck.

I pulled back as Nina led me through the gate, prepared to scream for Sammy to help and make a run for it. I tried to turn, but Nina's strong arms yanked me forward. Then I felt the barrel of her gun in my back and knew she hadn't been lying when she said she'd kill me.

"Move," she said.

I stayed where I was, unable to make my feet obey her.

"All right, fine." She gripped my wrist and forced me to spread out my fingers. "You don't need your thumbs to make Gheisari happy." She pressed the gun into the base of my right thumb and put her finger on the trigger.

"Wait," I gasped, horror welling in my throat.

She saw that she had won and pushed me the rest of the way through the gate, her gun making a small round indent in the bottom of my hand.

I looked behind me as the gate slowly closed. The squeal of rusty hinges sang to me of hopelessness.

My chest constricted as we approached the door, and the sweat on my forehead had nothing to do with the humidity. Nina rang the buzzer and we waited in silence until a male voice came from an intercom next to the door.

"Name?"

"Nina Morlock."

A short Hispanic man opened the door. He was dressed in a suit and had the flair of an old-timey butler. His eyes passed over me, becoming grim, and he waved for us to come inside.

We followed him into a luxurious entryway. Nina pushed me forward. "This is Teylin. Think your master would be interested?"

The man circled me like a vulture and stared at me in uncomfortable places. "I'm a bit… underwhelmed, but that doesn't mean Mr. Gheisari would wholly disapprove. How much were you expecting to get for her?"

"The usual price, plus a little extra for travel expenses."

He scratched his chin. "I suppose her face is pretty enough. But Mr. Gheisari gets bored easily. You know that better than anyone, Nina."

Nina frowned. "Which is why you should trust my judgment. She's young, and she's an actress. She'll eventually learn what it takes to make Arun happy."

"And you guarantee she's not local?"

"I picked her up in Los Angeles. No one will come looking

for her here."

His face lifted. "Good."

A middle-aged woman with black hair and olive skin came down the staircase and put her arm around me. "Why don't you come with me, dear, and I'll get you a refreshment."

I looked at Nina warily, and she nodded at me. I didn't know whether to be relieved to get away from her or more afraid. I hated her in so many ways, but a part of me didn't want her to go. She was the only link I had to my old life.

I submitted to the other woman and she led me into another room. I could still hear Nina arguing faintly in the background but could no longer make out her words. I sat in an armchair in front of an empty fireplace and the woman brought me a tray of cheese and crackers and a cup of some sort of sweet-smelling liquid. I was parched but took the cup warily.

"What is this?" I asked.

"Guava juice," the woman said. "Go ahead, try some."

I took a cautious sip. It was very sweet, but I was so nervous I could barely register the taste. My sandpaper throat got the better of me and I swallowed more in a long gulp.

My mind went quiet as all my fear drained out of me. I could hardly remember why I'd been so upset. Maybe it had been stupid to follow Ricky and Nina into that warehouse, but I'd run away from my mom, hadn't I? I'd longed for a different life. This could be my chance to start over; to become someone new. My thoughts floated away as my head became warm and light. A bubble of laugher threatened to escape my throat but I choked it back. Something about this feeling was wrong.

I looked at the woman with wide eyes but she just smiled and encouraged me to drink more of the juice. I jumped to my feet and the whole room swam like I was back on La Ventura. I clung to the side of the chair and tried to keep myself lucid. It was no use. I heard a whacking sound as my body hit the floor, but was unconscious before I could feel any pain.

* * *

I smelled flowers and spices. Slender hands rubbed my arms. My eyes blinked open. Two girls hovered over me. They had long silver hair and sky blue eyes like the boy in the rain. Their hands were cold as they massaged scented oil into my skin. I craned my neck and looked at myself. I was dressed in nothing but scarlet lingerie and was lying on an enormous bed with sheets of the same color. All my insides knotted up, but I couldn't get my body to respond. I was weak and tired, but at the same time, all my worst fears were coming to a head.

"Help me," I said, not managing more than a whisper. "Please."

"Stay calm," whispered one of the girls. "He'll hurt you if you struggle." Her cold fingers threaded flowers into my hair.

"Please," I repeated, a tear trailing down my cheek.

"Shh," said the other into my ear. "Recover your strength. Arun will be here soon."

"You're prisoners too, aren't you?" I asked. "We can help each other get home."

Their blank expressions reminded me of cats. "This is our home," said the girl, drawing away. She wiped her hands on a towel then waved them in front of the fireplace. A fire instantly sprang to life as if it had sprouted from her fingertips, but the flames were as silver as her hair.

"How did you do that?" I croaked.

The girl smiled and led the other one to the door. "We'll

see you again," she said. "Please ask if you need anything."

I did need something. I needed to get away. I let my head fall hard against the pillow, tears swimming in my eyes. There had to be a way out of this.

I forced myself to sit up, my head swirling. I swung my bare feet over the bed and stood, arms around the bedpost. I looked for my clothes, but they weren't in this dark and lavish room.

I stumbled toward the door. It was locked—not that I had expected anything different—and there were no windows.

My pounding head forced me to sit back on the bed, and before I knew it, I had tipped onto my side.

"Don't fall asleep, don't fall asleep," I chanted. But the repetitive words only lulled me closer toward the inevitable. My drugged stupor pulled hard and darkness blanketed me.

CHAPTER 5

When I opened my eyes, I saw a man wearing a scarlet robe sitting in a chair near the bed. Muscular and middle-aged, he was casually sipping wine. And watching me.

A glacier formed inside my stomach. Was I finally meeting Arun Gheisari?

I still felt weak but was much more clear-minded than before. When I sat up the room didn't tilt, and I could see the fine details in the furniture more clearly. The scent of Arun's cologne was strong enough to strike my nose from his distance—sharp and cold like pine and mint aimed to cover the scent of cigar smoke.

Every muscle in my body tensed. Should I try to make a break for the door? Maybe. Would he try to stop me? Not sure. Would he have left it unlocked? Not likely.

He poured another glass of wine and offered it to me. I shook my head. While the alcohol could help take my mind away from whatever he was going to do to me, I wanted to remember everything about him so when I went to the police, I wouldn't miss a single detail.

"Very well," he said, downing the glass himself in a few gulps. The smell of the alcohol cut through everything else, bringing with it dozens of bitter memories of my mom and the reason I'd left home in the first place.

Arun sighed and stared at me for a long moment. "What is

your name?" he asked.

I didn't answer.

"Your name. What is it?"

His voice was commanding, with a Middle Eastern accent. I was afraid not to answer him this time.

"Tey," I whispered.

He set down the glass and stood.

I couldn't hold back a whimper of fear. This was it. This was why I'd been brought here.

I scrambled backward, but he caught hold of my foot and dragged me toward him. Tears overflowed from my eyes as he reached for my arms and hauled me to my feet. He squeezed my shoulders and pressed his lips against my neck. I gasped and sobbed, but this seemed to encourage him. He pressed his lips harder as he worked his way toward my mouth, leaving a trail of wetness across my neck.

His breathing became more rapid, and so did my own, but for a totally different reason. He let go of me, hands going to the tie on his robe.

No, I thought. Not now. Not like this.

The tie started to come loose and I looked away, holding my breath.

Something slammed against the door. I whipped my head around and searched for the source of the noise. There were shouts, then gunshots. Something shattered and there was the sound of a body dropping to the ground. A moment of silence followed, and then the crash of a fist on the door.

"Arun Gheisari," shouted a male voice from the other side. "We know you're in there. Come out on your own and we'll take you peacefully; put up a fight, and I'm afraid we'll have to fight back."

Arun yanked his robe closed and ran to a dresser, pulling

out a pistol. He aimed it at the door just as it was knocked open, revealing a young, brown-haired man and a tall Asian woman, both armed. They ducked back around the door-frame, but Arun fired rapidly and grazed the young man on the side of his right arm. The man immediately fired back, getting Arun straight through the shoulder. Arun's gun clattered to the floor as he gasped in pain, and the woman immediately seized it and pointed it back at Arun in addition to her original firearm.

The young man casually wiped blood from his grazed arm with one finger and examined it. "I go against the great Arun Gheisari, and this is all I have to show for it? What will they think of you back at the Agency?"

A muscular black man plowed into the room and latched onto Arun's injured shoulder. He pulled back so hard that Arun struggled and cried out in pain.

"Saints! Hold still, man," he said as he forced both of Arun's wrists behind his back and fitted them with handcuffs. "A guy has to know when he's beaten."

"You won't get out of this house alive," Arun screamed. "My security—"

"Are all down," said the young man. "Do you think we'd come straight for you without stunning your guards first? We're not that stupid. You, on the other hand—"

Arun spit, hitting him in the face. The young man wiped it away as casually as he did the blood. "Keeping it classy, as always." He rubbed his spit-soiled hand on his jacket. "Your pretty little wife tipped us off, Arun. Guess she's not as open to your promiscuous habits as you thought."

He waved his hand and Arun was dragged back by his restrainer. The young man approached me. I pulled the sheets over my shoulders and backed away.

"It's all right," he said, fixing me with a steady brown-eyed gaze. He couldn't have been more than a few years older than me but had a confidence about him I was still decades from obtaining. "I'm not gonna hurt you. My name's Rob Stryker, and I'm a fugitive recovery agent. This is my team." He gestured behind him at his two companions, who didn't seem much older than him. "That blockhead with the shaved head over there is Damion Hart," he said, pointing to the man holding Arun. Damion wore a silver cross around his neck and a sleeveless shirt that revealed dark-skinned arms muscular enough to snap Arun's neck. Since his hands were both occupied, he greeted me with a wink.

"And that's Xia Wang." Rob waved at the Asian woman who was almost as tall as he was. She acknowledged him with a frown. I noticed that her shoulder-length black hair was streaked with red highlights that perfectly matched her lipstick. "Xi, find the lady something to wear."

Xia muttered under her breath and opened the closet door.

Rob turned back to me. "Did the old bastard hurt you?"

I shook my head, unable to believe someone was saving me. Or were they? All at once, my shoulders started to shake with long contained sobs but no tears came, and it was difficult to breathe. Rob touched my arm and I pulled away. Could I trust him? Could I trust anyone?

"Are you from around here?" he asked.

"No," I said, my mouth barely able to form words. "Nina… she took me from Los Angeles. There was this weapon—"

Rob held up his hands. "Wait, stop right there. Did you just say Nina? As in Nina Morlock?"

I nodded, breath shaking.

Rob looked back at his companions. "She's one of Nina's."

"Sweet salvation!" said Damion. "That's the best news we've

had all year."

Xia threw me a long man's shirt. "Put this on. We'll get you something better at the Agency."

I complied, buttoning the shirt over the lacy lingerie. It was long enough to reach mid-thigh, which was a good thing because Xia didn't offer any pants to go with it.

She eyed me coldly. "What's your name?"

I finished the last button. "Teylin Walker. Most people just call me Tey."

"All right, Tey. Let's get you out of here."

Could my luck be changing? Or were these dangerous saviors only leading me into another sort of danger? With the way my life was going, I put my money on the latter.

CHAPTER 6

Xia stabbed Arun's arm with a syringe and his thrashing calmed. Once he was placid, we walked into the hall. The bodies of several security guards twitched on the ground as if they'd been electrocuted.

Downstairs, signs of shattered glass and tipped-over furniture signified that the struggle had been a lengthy one. The only one still conscious was the woman who had drugged me. She knelt in the parlor sobbing hysterically, and I wondered if she was the wife who had tipped off Rob's team. Had she known Rob was on his way when she'd given me that drink?

Rob ignored her completely and walked out the open door toward the now broken gate. I wasn't wearing shoes, but a thick layer of leaves protected my feet.

On the road were three of the strangest bicycles I'd ever seen. One of them was black with golden spokes, another, dark blue, with a tiny sidecar attached like a motorcycle. The third was maroon and gold with a sea chest strapped to the back.

The pedals on them connected to a network of gears partway hidden by sleek colored panels. Each had speed dials on the handlebars and padded leather seats, long enough to fit at least two people.

Damion and Xia loaded Mr. Ghesari into the sidecar of the blue bike and secured his handcuffs to a metal loop connecting the front of the car. Then, Damion hopped onto the bicycle seat and started to pedal.

"See ya at the Agency," he called back. The gears made puttering sounds as the pedals wound them. After a short distance down the road, Damion released the pedals and the bicycle wheels kept turning on their own, propelled by the gears.

Xia mounted the black bike and was soon right on his tail.

"Come on," said Rob, hopping onto the maroon bike.

"Where are we going?" I asked.

"Somewhere safe. I promise." His voice was gentle yet direct. I wanted to trust him.

He held out his hand and helped me sit behind him. Like Damion, he pedaled rapidly then released, letting the gears carry us along the road. The gears kept the wheels turning at a swift pace for about five minutes before Rob had to pedal for another minute to recharge. Again, I wondered at the strange shortage of cars in Los Sueños.

We rode back into the city to a district predominated by tall stone buildings. The cobbled roads were cleaner and were framed by gushing canals and small footbridges. Seagulls were everywhere, nibbling at trash in the gutters.

Everything was much calmer than the wharf had been, except for the howls of merchants selling fried seafood kabobs from corner stands. The people on the streets moved briskly and wore professional-looking attire.

We followed a row of tidy offices to an out-of-place building on the corner. It was seven stories high with a large clock over the doors.

Part wood, part brick, various floors stuck out at varying amounts from the original structure, and the windows followed no particular size requirement. It was as if each story had been designed by a different architect.

"Here we are," said Rob. "Seventh floor belongs to Christopher Corpus's Agency for Fugitive Recovery, or just the Agency."

Damion and Xia were already unloading Gheisari at the door. Rob pulled up next to them and I slipped off the bike. As soon as Rob dismounted, a valet boy hurried to take the bikes away.

Xia pushed some buttons and the glass doors unlocked with an electric click. We filed into a small lobby. The floor was polished wood and lined with three old-fashioned elevators. Rob pushed the up button and we waited for an elevator to open.

I studied Gheisari, feeling my skin flush with anger. He wasn't putting up much of a fight. I guessed that whatever drug Xia had injected into him was pretty powerful, or else he knew he didn't stand a chance against three seasoned fighters.

My pulse hammered in my ears. I hoped they locked him up for the rest of his life. No. I hoped they killed him. Looking at him and thinking about what he almost did to me made my stomach burn. My fingers itched to pry his eyes out so he could never look at another woman again. I wanted to hurt him. I wanted to—

The elevator dinged and the door came open. We walked inside, and Rob pressed the button for the seventh floor. I moved as far away from Gheisari as possible. The back of the elevator had only a grate, allowing me to see the pulleys and gears that lifted the mechanism up and down. I focused on them as we rose to the top of the building.

The door opened to a chaotic office. All the desks were made of dark cherry wood, and the chairs were high-backed, with quality leather. Doors leading to private rooms lined the walls with shiny gold nameplates.

"Think our team ranking will go up after this?" asked Damion, looking at Arun.

"We're already ranked number one, you idiot," said Xia.

"Yeah, but Corpus should factor our continued wins into the score chart. Then it will be that much harder for the other teams to catch up."

"No one's ever going to catch up," said Rob. "Not while I'm team leader. I believe I told you two to take our man to the holding cell. He's a criminal genius. You'd better hurry before the Supplicant wears off and he cooks up a plan to escape."

CHAPTER 7

As Xia and Damion dragged Gheisari to a makeshift prison cell at the west side of the office, Rob led me deeper inside. I pulled on the hem of the man's shirt I wore and hoped it was long enough to cover everything.

The Agency was bustling. We passed small groups of men and women with gun harnesses strapped to their waists crowded around wheeled chalkboards that were scribbled with diagrams. They reminded me of sports teams, planning out their next move. Several people were having serious conversations on outdated rotary phones, while others sat at desks clicking away at computers old enough to be relics.

Rob led me to a door at the corner of the room with Rob Stryker engraved on a nameplate. When we went inside, I instantly noticed the walls. They were plastered with black and white wanted posters. Some were hand drawn, while others looked like covert photos snapped from behind bushes. Classic mug shots were also scattered in the mix. As my gaze panned across them, I noticed that many had red Xs drawn over them.

"Have a seat," said Rob, motioning to a black couch.

My knees gave out and I plopped onto the soft leather. I turned to look out the window that took up the entire far wall. It was made of maybe twenty or so glass panels that gave it a checkerboard appearance.

Rob took out a notepad and pen and sat in a high-backed chair, resting his feet on the head of the wooden table in the center of the room. He tipped his chair partway back and chewed on his pen cap.

"OK, Tey, I need as many details as you can remember of everything that happened from the time you met Nina until the two of you parted ways."

"Are you going to send me back to California?" I asked.

He took a deep breath. "You're gonna be fine, I promise, but first there's some stuff I have to know."

I felt the hysterics creeping back up my throat but managed to push them down and take a deep breath. "No, first tell me what's going to happen to me. How can you expect me to say anything until I know I'm not gonna be handed over to someone just like Arun Gheisari?"

Rob blew out his breath and removed his feet from the table. He scooted the chair around to face me, hands folded in his lap. "Listen, we work to take down men like Gheisari. There's no way we'd sell you out. We may seem to you like a crude group of bounty hunters, but members of the Agency run by a higher code."

"But if you're bounty hunters—"

"Did I say bounty hunters? We prefer the term 'fugitive recovery agents'."

"Either way, it's all for the money, right? And you could get a big price for me, just like Nina."

Rob scrubbed his fingers through his hair. "I don't work like that. I'm a monarchist. The reason I'm here, doing this job right now, is to take down the Coterie. We're one of the few factions in Los Sueños outside of the King's circles who have openly declared our opposition to them. Sure, the money helps, but I'm not using it to get rich."

"The Coterie. Arun was a member?"

Rob nodded. "It's the criminal organization that rules the underground of Los Sueños. The founders came here over a century ago running from the law. They were pirates who gradually rose in power, even establishing their own chiefdoms, and appointing key enforcers we call guns. They have no legitimate political power, but some would say their influence is greater than the king's."

"Is that true?"

"Well, I'll say this. The Coterie has a lot of unwritten laws, and it's those suggestions people tend to follow more closely than anything the king ever tried to enforce. It's amazing how persuasive a little fear can be."

"And Arun Gheisari?"

"Gheisari was one of their High Six—the most powerful Coterie chiefs in Cosmar. We'd have probably never found him without his wife's tip. When it comes to crime, you can always uncover someone with a weak conscious. It's our job to fume them out."

"If you want to get rid of the Coterie, why do it this way? Why not become a police officer or something?"

Rob snorted and went to the window. He waved for me to join him and I did.

"See that man down there?" He pointed at a tall figure on the street corner dressed in an official-looking red jacket. He stood out against the gray backdrop of the city. "He's a member of the kingsguard. I guess they're the closest thing to police we have on the islands, but they're way too obvious. They go prancing along their assigned routes in those obnoxious red jackets, waving their firearms, and thinking they're gonna catch themselves a Coterie gun. That won't work at all. You have to be slippery, like the Coterie."

He went back to his chair. "Agents like me don't have to stick to any rules of the trade. We can do whatever it takes to catch us a gun. The kingsguard turn their backs on our operations because they need us. The Coterie would have probably taken over the monarchy years ago if not for our efforts. Besides, it's cheaper for the king to pay us bounties than to employ a full-fledged force."

Kings. Coterie. Bounty Hunters. What kind of country was this? I needed to get away from here before my life got any worse. "Will you help me get home?"

He gave me a long look. "I'm afraid that's impossible."

CHAPTER 8

I stood straighter. "What?"

"You can't go home, Tey. I'm sorry."

I got to my feet. "But, you told me everything was going to be fine."

"It is. You'll be fine here. Might even come to like it."

"If you think for one minute I'm not going to do everything I can to get off this demented island, you're gonna be really disappointed."

"I'm sure you will. In fact, I'm counting on it. The sooner you find out the truth for yourself, the faster you'll come to accept it. There is no way off of Los Sueños."

The room seemed to tilt and I fell back on the couch. "What do you mean?"

"Oh, I suppose there's always a way, but the king's exit laws have the country on lockdown, so you're outta luck with anything traditional. Your best bet is to join the Coterie. Laws don't stop them from coming and going as they please, and guns don't either. Might take about ten years though to work your way up in their favor, or cozy up to a chief long enough for one of them to entrust you with an overseas mission."

"There has to be another option," I said.

"You could marry one of the king's officials and get him to put you on a royal supply vessel. Those are the only ships that leave the islands legally. Thing is, all officials live on Santa Isidore, three islands northwest of here. Might make scoring a date with one a little hard. You might be able to bribe a sailor for their spot on one of them, but you'd need about twenty thousand dollars for that to happen, and then you'd have to know how to cover their ship duties or you'd get found out. Don't even think about stowing away. You'd be shot in the head the moment you were caught. I guess the last option would be to make a raft out of reeds and set sail. That might be the fastest way if you're in a hurry."

I blinked. "Is there a phone where I can call my mom?"

He shook his head. "Sorry, our phones won't work for you. You can make local calls, but no communication is allowed to leave Los Sueños. We're a little behind the times."

Like a hundred years behind the times. "An email then?"

"Unfortunately, that won't work either. The king blocked off any non-local email servers. He doesn't want information about Los Sueños getting into the hands of the wrong people, namely those overseas who he'd rather not take an interest in this place."

Nausea flooded my stomach. "Then I'm guessing sending a letter would be out of the question too." How could a country possibly hide itself like this?

The door swung open and Xia and Damion walked in, huge smiles on their faces. Damion was holding up a check. "Corpus actually paid us on delivery. Ten thousand big ones." He kissed the silver cross around his neck and danced around the room before falling onto the couch next to me and sliding his arm around my shoulders. His smile faded when he saw my expression. "Saints, what's wrong with you?" He quickly removed his arm.

What was wrong with me? Really? I scowled, and he scooted away a few inches. He probably would have moved to the other side of the couch if Xia hadn't chosen that moment to flop down in the remaining space. She threw me a women's t-shirt and pair of shorts.

"Don't worry; they're clean. You can have my sneakers too."

I looked around the room, hesitating. "Is there a bathroom I can change in?"

Xia groaned. "It's not like we haven't all seen you in those lacy panties before."

Damion barked a laugh, and my scowl deepened.

I shimmied into the shorts and then turned toward the wall as I unbuttoned the shirt and pulled the other one over my head. It felt good to be in real clothes again. I rolled Gheisari's shirt into a ball and chucked it in the wastebasket.

"Sweet Salvation," said Damion, fishing it out. "That's Egyptian cotton. Can't let a beauty like that go to waste."

"You're just going to ruin it by tearing the sleeves off," said Xia.

Damion looked affronted. "You can't expect me to keep deltoids like mine covered? That would be a cruel disservice to all the women of this city. We don't want them picketing in front of the Agency."

"Take it as a thank you gift," I said, pulling the sneakers over my dirty feet. They were a bit tight but better than nothing.

"She told you all the specs on Nina yet?" asked Damion, holding the shirt up to his chest. "'Cause if that feline's back in Cosmar, we gotta act fast."

"Just give her a sec, OK?" said Rob. "She's had a rough day."

I snorted. That was an understatement.

"Yeah," said Xia, picking at a split end, "I bet the poor thing's traumatized."

I didn't like how she called me a 'poor thing,' like I was a lost puppy or something. "Would it help if I curled up in a ball and whimpered?" I asked.

"Only if you want to stop Damion from pestering you."

Damion didn't seem to hear the comment. He rifled through a pile of papers and threw one at me. It was a wanted poster for Nina. "Look familiar?"

I nodded. Her face would be burned into my memory for the rest of my life.

"Good. I wanted to make sure we were talking about the same Nina. Wouldn't want to be chasing after the wrong woman." He took the picture back and examined it closely. "Saints! Why does she have to be so damn cute? Maybe once we find her hideout, I can go in undercover. You know, like a gigolo or something. I'll seduce her, then cuff her to the bed." He stroked his chin with a smirk on his face, obviously lost in that thought.

"You're disgusting," said Xia, ripping the paper out of his hands and crumpling it up.

"What? Like you've never crushed on any of these low-lifes." He motioned at the wall of wanted posters. "Some of 'em ain't half bad to look at. With so many faces starin' at ya all day, you're bound to fall for one of them."

"Yeah, OK, I spend all day having romantic fantasies about the people responsible for murdering my sisters and burning down my house, because that's what normal human beings do. Some of us are here for bigger things, Damion."

"I've got my beef as well. Doesn't mean it extends to all of them. And I'm here for something bigger too. The cash reward."

Xia groaned. "I think we should just forget Nina and turn you in instead. I bet you're worth a pretty penny after hiding out all these years. I doubt your precious chief posted that bounty so he could welcome you back with open arms."

Damion's back went rigid. "You know he's not my chief, hasn't been since I left the Coterie four years ago. Why do you think I joined the Agency? For the good company?"

I turned to him. "There's a bounty on your head?"

Damion opened his mouth to speak, but Xia cut in. "Psychotic, isn't it? That we'd let a former member of the Coterie on our team? Coterie chiefs don't allow their underlings to abandon ship the way he did, and they post bounties just as often as the king. Damion's price goes up every year. I don't know why Rob puts up with him."

"You both know Agency rules don't allow us to collect bounties from the Coterie," said Rob. "Besides, we'd never have come this far without Damion's expertise." He sighed. "Why don't you both go home? We'll call it a night and come back here first thing in the morning. I think Tey could use some rest before we start picking her brain. And I've got a feeling we all need a break before we go full force after Nina."

"I won't argue when it comes to breaks," said Damion.

"Then you guys take off," Rob said, "but be back here no later than eight a.m. tomorrow."

"And her?" Xia stuck her chin out at me.

"She can stay at the Castillo with me," Rob said, then he looked at me. "Unless you've got somewhere better to go, Tey?"

I shook my head. "What's the Castillo?"

"Not much I'm afraid, but spending the night there is a hell of a lot better than the streets, where you'd be begging to be back in a chief's bed."

He slapped his teammates on the shoulders as they said their goodbyes, then tugged my arm and guided me out of the office.

CHAPTER 9

I hopped onto the bike behind Rob and we cruised through throngs of people back toward the wharf. It was golden hour, and vendors found any excuse to get in our faces before they had to close up shop. Most people were dressed in what looked like vintage clothing and wore various fedoras, newsboys, and bowler hats. Some of the women wore corsets; others long trench coats over striped dress suits. Now and again a child scampered through the crowd wearing surf shorts or a sport's jersey to remind me that I was still in the twenty-first century, not some time warp that couldn't make up its mind what decade it wanted to be.

Rob put his feet down and skidded to a stop next to a dock post.

"I need to pick up a few things while we're here. Will you wait with the bike?" I nodded and he disappeared into the crowd.

I turned to face the ship at the dock and froze. La Ventura was still there. On board, I spotted two unfamiliar silver-haired children watching me from the rail. A boy and a girl. They must have boarded recently since I had definitely not seen them while I was a passenger.

A chill ran down my spine and my mind went instantly to the boy I'd nearly run over in the rain. These two were much younger, and so frail they shivered in the mild ocean breeze. A man on deck shouted at them and they quickly ran into one of the cabin doors and out of sight.

That's when a thought occurred to me. Would La Ventura be sailing back to California? Maybe I should talk to one of the sailors and explain my situation. Perhaps—

A hand touched my arm. I spun around. Rob was back, carrying two brown paper sacks full of food. My stomach growled and I realized for the first time how hungry I was.

He laughed—a warm effortless sound. "Here," he said, pulling a roll from one of the bags. "This should take the edge off until we reach the Castillo."

I devoured the roll, and he stuffed the bags into the sea chest strapped to the back of the bike and buckled it shut. Our journey through the city continued.

Men in safari hats waved flyers from the sides of the streets, advertising jungle tours, and others called for us to view the exotic birds they were selling or to sample rare spices.

Despite my horror at being stuck in a foreign country, I noticed a strange energy in the air that made my heart pump faster; not with fear, but with excitement. I wanted to explore everything and sample all the new things around me.

The city was every time and every culture—a strange yet beautiful fusion of the world combined to create something new. And yet here I was, feeling so out of place despite the mishmash of trends. I didn't belong here any more than a house cat belonged in a refuge for endangered animals. No matter what Rob said, I couldn't possibly stay here forever.

I wouldn't.

Bit by bit we made our way through the main part of the city, along the edge of the poor sector Rob called the skids, and to the outskirts. As the world around me quieted, I leaned over Rob's shoulder so he could hear me. "Who are those weird kids I keep seeing?"

"Which ones?"

"The ones with the silver hair and creepy eyes."

Rob pulled on the brake and turned to face me. "You've seen shadowborn?"

"Shadow-what?"

He laughed. "We call them shadowborn because no one knows where they came from. They don't even know themselves. It's like they were birthed from the shadows."

"Way to be cryptic."

"Wish I could tell you more. They started popping up about five or six years ago. The king wants them all eradicated."

My shoulders tensed. "Why?"

He started to pedal again. "Because of what they can do. They're extremely dangerous."

"What do you mean?" I asked. Did they all have the ability to turn invisible?

He sighed. "Coming from America, this might be hard for you to believe."

"Unlikely," I said. "I had a pretty crazy experience with one already."

"They're all different. Their abilities and the extent of them vary. Some can jump from high buildings and hit the ground as lightly as a feather. Some can see into your mind and know the next thing you'll do. The really scary ones can stop your heart with the wave of a hand. The king hired a group of top-notch scientists from China to study them, but so far, nothing's been discovered as far as where they came from or how they can do what they do. The king passed a law requiring all shadowborn to be turned in to authorities for execution."

A cold breeze swept through my heart. "I just saw two on the deck of the ship I came on. Do you think they were being taken away to be killed?”

“Not likely. You were on a Coterie ship. The Coterie offer money for shadowborn. The amount can be pretty high depending on their physical condition and abilities. A shadowborn with an ability that could aid in crime is gold if turned in to the Coterie. That’s why you need to tell me if you ever see one again.”

“I thought you said Agency rules don’t allow you to collect bounties from the Coterie.”

“Shadowborn are the exception since they have no affiliation with the Coterie or Monarchy. We could turn them in to either faction, but I’d rather spare the kids from execution and get some extra cash besides.”

“But you said you became an agent to get rid of the Coterie, not help them.”

He shrugged. “Some money is too good to say no to.”

I frowned. Rob’s morality didn’t seem much better than Nina’s—who had sold me for the same reason. But despite everything, I was still going along with him. I had no one else, and nowhere else to go. But once I found something—a rumor, a lead, an offer of help—Coterie or not, I’d take off so fast my memory of Los Sueños would be as the island’s Spanish name suggested. Just a dream. A bad one.

The Castillo was located on a road more jungle-covered than the one Gheisari lived on, and full of mud puddles and rocks. Rob peddled through a rusty gate overgrown by weeds. We dismounted and pushed the bike up a hill that led to a dilapidated mansion. At least five stories of mossy gray stone and long arching windows, it looked like something Count Dracula would live in.

“Welcome to the Castillo Paraiso,” said Rob, making a wide swoop with his arm to showcase the property.

I raised my eyebrows.

"What?" He lifted the corner of his mouth.

"Nothing. I'm just wondering if I would have been better off with Arun Gheisari. At least he wasn't going to suck my blood."

Rob laughed. "OK, so it's a little spooky, I'll admit. But try to imagine what it used to be back in its heyday. Musta been pretty grand. Perfectly trimmed gardenia bushes, big parties with people in tuxedos and ball gowns, fancy cars, valets. Wish I could've seen that."

"Me too," I agreed, scanning the overgrown entryway.

"It used to belong to a celebrity couple from America, but loads of people left Cosmar in a hurry twenty years ago. Their mass departure was one of the reasons the king felt the need to impose the strict exit laws we have today."

"Why'd they leave?"

"The Coterie tried to start a civil war and turn people against the king. It was a failed effort, but it sure scared away a lot of rich people. Some just left their mansions abandoned. This one was a lucky find for me."

He took the sack of groceries from the sea chest and led the way inside the door. I barely had time to glimpse a long, curving staircase before a pack of children ran down it and swarmed Rob.

"Rob! Rob's back!" they cried all at once.

"What's in the bag, Rob?"

"What'd you bring us?"

"Got any food?"

Doors flew open and other children spilled out, joining the bouncing crowd. There were probably about thirty of them in all, some only toddlers, others as old as maybe thirteen.

Rob clutched the bag to his chest and laughed. "Calm

down, everyone. Let me at least get it to the dining room." He plowed through the crowd and was treated like a hero, with kids holding doors open for him, and clearing any obstacles strewn across his path.

We made our way to a spacious but derelict room at the back of the house. There was an enormous wooden table in the middle with rusted candlesticks placed at intervals along a moth-eaten runner.

Rob hobbled to the table and threw down his sack, fending off eager kids as he unloaded the contents—long loaves of red-colored bread, tubes of fish paste, and a wheel of pock-marked cheese. There were also some strange fruits about the size of apples but with hairy brown skin like kiwis.

"Ichiro, go get me a knife, will you?" said Rob to a little Japanese boy who then scampered off to do Rob's bidding. Ichiro came back holding what looked more like a dagger, but Rob accepted it and drove it into the bread, dividing the loaf into equal portions. All the kids grabbed for the food.

He waved a hand, putting a halt to their efforts. "I haven't even added the best part yet."

They retreated, but were taut with anticipation, legs like loaded springs, ready to pounce when the pickings were good.

He squeezed fish paste onto the bread and topped each piece with a slab of cheese. "Get it while it's hot," he said with a chuckle. The kids didn't waste any time. They attacked the table and claimed each portion of bread like a prisoner of war. Wolfing the food down, they licked their fingers and looked around for more. I wondered if this was the only thing they'd eaten all day.

Rob handed me a portion of the meal that he'd managed to save before the attack. I felt bad taking it, but I knew if I offered it to one child, the rest would never forgive me. And the roll from earlier hadn't exactly filled me up.

Now I understood what he meant by 'some money is too good to say no to.' With so many kids to take care of, he must feel like he has no choice.

I studied his face. Intense brown eyes, dark brows covered by loose curls. He looked direct and sincere. Once again, I felt a nudge inside of me, as if something were pushing me to trust him. I wanted so badly for there to be someone I could trust here.

He pulled several fruits from his bag and cut into them, dividing up the pieces the same way as the bread.

No one noticed me until the food was gone. Then a little Chinese girl, probably five or six, pulled on my shirt and looked at me with eyes knit together. "Who are you?"

The room went silent. Everyone turned to me at once, licking their fingers for any remnants of their dinner.

"Kids, this is my friend, Tey. She's gonna be staying with us for a while."

"How long's a while?" asked the girl.

"I don't know, maybe forever." He smiled at me, begging me to play along, though the word 'forever' made me want to scream.

I heard some of the other kids muttering: "I hope she doesn't try to sleep in my room," and "I wonder how much food she eats."

The little girl took hold of my hand and watched me, her face stone cold. I smiled at her. "What's your name?"

"Lei," she said in barely a whisper.

"Lei? That's pretty. It rhymes with my name."

Her expression didn't change, but she squeezed my hand a little tighter.

CHAPTER 10

"There are dozens of rooms," said Rob. "You can take your pick of any that aren't already occupied. I bet you're exhausted."

I was exhausted. Mentally and physically. I longed to curl up in a dark hole and disappear, but that had never worked before.

"We have electricity and running water sometimes," Rob continued. "Not sure how. I certainly haven't paid any utility bills on this place. But it comes and goes, so don't get caught in the shower with soap in your hair when the water shuts off. Best thing to do is take a bucket to the stream out back and dump it over your head. Most refreshing way to start the day, if you ask me."

He opened a closet door and took out candles and a small matchbox. "When the electricity is on, it usually doesn't last more than ten minutes or so, so you'll probably need these." He shoved them in my direction. "Batteries aren't cheap, so I prefer the old fashioned way." I took them from him and held them awkwardly with one hand, my other hand still captive in Lei's grip. He reached in the closet again and emerged with some folded sheets and blankets, which he piled over one of my shoulders.

"If you need anything, just ask. We don't have much, and I can't promise it straight away, but I eventually come around.

Don't I, Lei?"

The little girl nodded.

I could think of dozens of things I needed—a new wardrobe, a toothbrush, a ticket home—but all that came out of my mouth was, "Thanks; I'm fine for now."

"All right," he said. "I'll be awake for a while if you change your mind. Lei, you can let go of her hand. She's gonna go upstairs now."

"Oh, it's OK," I started to say, but Lei immediately let go, cheeks flushing, and ran off. "Lei!" I called after her, but she was already gone.

Rob just smiled and shook his head. "Kid's had it rough ever since her parents abandoned her at the docks. She seems to like you; just don't expect to get a smile out of her."

"I've never been good with children," I said. "Where'd you find them all?"

His face tightened. "An orphanage in Cosmar went bankrupt. The kids would have all been on the street if I hadn't interceded, and it's not as if I didn't have space." He motioned to the interior, looking at home in the cavernous entry hall.

I was suddenly very curious about him. "And you were just living in this abandoned place, alone?"

"What can I say? I'm a crazy recluse."

"Don't you have any family around?"

He looked away from me and became interested in a loose string on his shirt. "Nah. I was raised in New York City. Any relatives I have would still be over there."

"Do your parents know where you are?"

"They might, if you believe in the whole afterlife—Mom and Dad watching over me sort of thing."

"So they're dead."

"Yeah, pretty dead. Let's see, I was, fourt—fifteen, when a

Coterie chief named Apollo convinced them to come to Los Sueños. The bastard conned them out of nearly everything they had and then shot them when their backs were turned. I was hiding in a closet of their beach house at the time, the door was ajar just enough for me to see the whole thing."

I felt the blood drain from my face. "And the Agency?"

"I was recruited soon after. Once I'd set up camp in the Castillo, I knew I had to find some sort of work. Being young and idiotic, I thought I could go after bounties on my own, you know, for revenge and all that. Let's just say it didn't work out so well at first. Lucky for me, I was saved by an Agency team going after the same bounty. They brought me to the office, treated my wounds, and then Mr. Corpus—he's head of the Agency—offered me a place with them."

"Rob, I'm so sorry. I can see why you want to take out the Coterie so bad."

"Yeah," he said, and I detected deep sadness in his tone, but then he shrugged. "It was six years ago."

He was fifteen, six years ago. That made him twenty-one.

For a moment, I felt the urge to hug him, but I ignored it. "Would you ever want to go back? To New York?"

He shrugged and then smiled, his sadness disappearing in a flash. "Can't tell you how long I searched for a way. I considered everything. Stowing away, joining the Coterie undercover, stealing enough money for a bribe. But now I couldn't leave. Not with these kids; they need me. I don't know what I'd do in the States anyway. Los Sueños has become my home, and I'd give my life to save it."

I took a breath. "Is there really no chance for me?"

He moved in close enough for me to feel heat radiating off him and bent down. "There might be. But you have to be patient. The things I have planned could change this place forever. But first, we have a lot of work to do. Helping us find Nina is a promising first step."

I nodded weakly, my breath catching in my chest.

"Go upstairs, Tey. You'll want to find a room before it gets too dark."

I took the creaking staircase to the next floor. The mansion was five stories high; it would take hours to explore. Right now, sleep was the only thing on my mind. I needed to find a room. Fast.

I opened the first door at the top of the stairs, revealing a couple of shirtless boys playing jacks on the floor.

"Hey!" one of them said. "This is our room. Girls aren't allowed." The other one jumped to his feet and slammed the door shut.

Two girls and a boy ran past me, each going into a separate room.

"This one's mine!"

"Don't come in here!"

"I had it first!" They all cried at the same time before I could peek inside any of the doors.

I decided this floor was probably out of the question. The next floor was also at capacity, but the fourth level was quieter. The halls were narrower and the floors creaked.

I opened a door in the middle of the hall and found a small empty room. A window looked over the jungle toward the ocean. Most of the glass was still intact, although brown vines snaked over half of it. The bed in the corner had a tattered canopy and a box spring mattress that didn't look too dirty.

On the wall hung a black and white photograph of a young woman, probably around my age, with long dark hair and darker eyes.

"Do you mind if we share the room?" I asked her. The light

of the setting sun glinted off the tarnished metal of her frame.

I sat at her vanity table, my face divided in the middle by a large crack through the mirror. I hadn't seen myself since before the drugs knocked me out at Gheisari's chateau. Lavish makeup covered my face, some of it smudged and creating morbid shadows beneath my eyes. My long brown hair had been styled into loose curls that were coming out from the jungle's humidity and starting to tangle.

There was a metal comb on the vanity and a few old hairpins. I wiped the dust off them with the end of my shirt and pulled the comb through my hair. The curls came the rest of the way out as I combed, and my feathery hair fell loose around my shoulders.

There was no air-conditioning in the Castillo, and the heat had risen to the upper levels. Sweat already dotted my forehead and trickled down my neck. Without thinking, I took my hair and braided it in a circle around my head, the way my grandmother used to on hot summer days when she was still alive.

I secured it with the hairpins then looked through the small drawers of the vanity. They were empty except for one on the far right, which held a teardrop pendant hanging on a blackened chain. It was silver, with the sheen of a dozen different colors. I put it around my neck and wondered if it had once belonged to the girl on the wall. I looked toward her picture. "Can I borrow this for a while?"

I wasn't a big jewelry wearer, but mostly because the gaudy rhinestones the other girls at school wore seemed fake and ostentatious. This was something older, with a symmetrical simplicity that spoke of a classy time that no longer existed, one I had always longed to inhabit.

I turned away from the mirror, my eyes set on the bed.

The room was orange from the setting sun, and the light was fading fast. I quickly beat the dust from the mattress and made the bed before the last of it faded over the horizon. The darkness only amplified chitters and squawks from the jungle creatures and chirping insects harmonizing in the night air. With no electricity and nothing else to do, sleep was my only option.

I closed my eyes and let my mind be overwhelmed by the sounds of the night.

CHAPTER 11

I dreamed of the girl in the photograph. Her hair was done up like a debutant and she wore a silk gown that flared out like a rose. Around her neck was the same pendant I still wore in my sleep.

A handsome young gentleman, who reminded me of Rob, escorted her into the Castillo Paraiso and led her to a grand ballroom filled with dozens of other dancers. The Castillo was full of expensive furniture and lights that reflected off crystal vases and fine china. Live music played and people twirled in an elegant dance. Their laughter echoed off the high ceilings, at one with the music that whirled through my mind.

When I awoke the next morning, a wave of longing swept through me. I felt like I had been there—another dancer in that glorious scene, each face distinct, and each note of music clear. I could still smell the mix of perfumes the women wore.

Outside, the sun was rising and the air was already sultry. I went to the vanity and checked my hair in the mirror. The braids around my head had somehow endured the night, and I only had to adjust two of the pins to accommodate the few strands that had fallen out while I slept.

I wiggled into Xia's sneakers and made my way down the three flights of stairs toward the dining room. Rob sat alone at the huge table where he sliced blood-red fruits the size of cantaloupes. His curly hair was wet, like he really had gone to the stream he'd mentioned and dumped water over it.

"Hi," he said with a smile I couldn't help but return. "Did you have any trouble finding a room?"

I sat in one of the chairs. "I had to fight for one, but I eventually won it with my brute strength."

He laughed. "Those little devils will defend their space to the death. Did you at least sleep well?"

"Even deeper than I expected."

"Glad to hear it." He nodded at the pendant. "That's a pretty necklace. Where'd you get it?"

I looked down at the silvery teardrop that I had forgotten was still around my neck. "Oh. I found it in a drawer. I hope it doesn't belong to anyone."

"Doubtful," he said. "Probably just another abandoned trinket from the past."

I was quiet as I recalled my dream. "Rob? Does the Castillo have a ballroom?"

He laughed. "Why? Would you like a dance?" He stood up and bowed to me like the gentleman from my dream.

I held back a laugh of my own as I stood and curtsied. "With all your talk of parties and the way things used to be, I just wanted to get a better picture."

"There is a ballroom," he said. "Want to see it?" He waved his hand for me to follow and I trailed him eagerly. He led me through some fancy double doors to a wide-open space with gold trim along the walls and ceiling.

Other than the obvious decay, it was exactly the room from my dream. My breath quickened at the memory of the graceful dancers and flowing violin music.

Rob laughed at me again. "Glad to see something about this dump impresses you."

"I...I dreamt about this room," I said. "Every detail of it.

Only it was full of dancers and musicians like I was seeing back in time."

Rob nodded in a way that said he knew exactly what I meant. "They say the islands speak to people through their dreams and unveil their secrets. That why the first settlers named it Los Sueños."

"You make it seem like they're alive."

He shrugged. "Some people think so. There's even an order of nuns on the isle of Santa Eurosia that drink a special dream serum. It allows them to remain permanently asleep except for one hour at dawn when they rise to take nourishment. They believe they can enter the archipelago's dreams and discover what it wants."

"Why does it matter?"

"Los Sueños is their goddess. To them, dreams are sacred visions and must be adhered to as if the islands themselves were commanding them."

I laughed. "How do they follow the commands if they're asleep all the time?"

"Some believe they work by sending dreams of influence to those who can change things. Some people travel to the sanctuary looking for answers, but I'm not sure what they find."

He led me deeper into the room and stopped next to a cobwebby chandelier that had fallen and smashed ages ago. We were silent for a moment, and then I thought he was humming. As the tune gained volume, it reminded me of a Beethoven waltz. "My lady!" Rob said with a flourish. "Wouldst thou honor me with a dance?"

I snorted. "Right now?"

"If the islands can make your dream a reality, so can I." He grabbed my hand and spun me into his arms.

My left hand gripped his shoulder and his right found

my waist. Then he was sweeping me around the room, all the while humming in perfect time. We must have made a funny sight, he in an unbuttoned flannel with bare feet, me in Xia's old clothes and sneakers. Nothing like the glorious partygoers from my dream.

His feet moved through complicated steps as mine stumbled to keep up. Then he twirled me, transitioning effortlessly into a type of dance I didn't recognize. One two three jump, one two three jump, one two three jump, switch directions.

Just when I thought I was too out of breath to keep moving, he leaned me into a gigantic dip until my head was inches from the floor, then brought me up again as his humming reached a final crescendo.

Chest heaving, I stepped away from him, dizzy and full of laughter. "That was…that was…"

"Magnificent? Refined? The best moment of your life?" He grinned in a teasing way.

"Well, it was something," I said, and suddenly felt the same longing ache as when I'd woken from my dream. I didn't care that my body was exhausted. I didn't want to stop dancing with him. But it was clear Rob was finished.

His lips brushed my hand in a light kiss, then he walked toward the double doors. I was left with one question. How did a bounty hunter get to be such a magnificent dancer?

* * *

We rode toward the Agency after a breakfast of the red fruit. Giagons, Rob had called them. They were tart with loads of seeds but still tasty enough for me to want seconds.

"What do the children do when you're gone?" I asked Rob as the wind whipped strands of my hair free.

"They usually go into the jungle and gather as much fruit as they can find. Some walk to Cosmar and beg for money. The younger ones aren't supposed to leave the yard, but it's not uncommon for some to wander off and get lost. They're not used to being told what to do."

"Do they usually find their way back?"

He shook his head. "Not always. I've spent days searching for some of them, but the jungle is thick and there are plenty of poisonous things that could…well, you know. There's only so much I can do to protect them. The rest is up to them."

Rob took a detour onto a dirt road parallel to the shore. The smell of the ocean reminded me of my days aboard La Ventura. I looked across the water and shielded my eyes as the rising sun dazzled them. I could see another landmass in the distance connected by a long bridge.

I pointed. "Is that another island?"

Rob followed my gaze and nodded. "It's called Santa Arcadia. It's smaller than Santa Delphina, and way less populated. Most people say it's because it's cursed, but I know the real reason."

I leaned forward. "Oh yeah?"

"Lepers."

"There are leopards here?"

"No. Lepers. Like the disease. The king sent all the lepers from Los Sueños there ages ago. They've built a colony for themselves and don't like anyone crossing their turf. I believe they are responsible for the island's cryptic reputation, and are known to play cruel tricks on outsiders. Now, most people tend to stay away because they're afraid of ghosts or monsters in the dark, or of waking up dangling upside down from a tree."

"Guess I didn't realize leprosy was still a thing."

He looked toward the island wistfully. "I still like to get up early and go on rides across the bridge. It's the longest bridge in Los Sueños, and I rarely meet another soul on it. Santa Arcadia looks beautiful. Has that untouched feel, ya know? Still, it's probably not a good idea to venture inland, just to be safe. I've never actually set foot on shore."

I watched the island fade from my line of sight as we peddled the rest of the way to the business district of Cosmar.

We reached the Agency's office building and took the elevator to the seventh floor. Other agents glanced up from their desks as we passed. A few of them looked like the leather-clad, tattooed bounty hunters from action movies, but most were clean-cut and well dressed. From the diagrams I could see on their wheeled chalkboards, they were well versed in math and statistics, too. Perhaps the Agency required employees to follow certain standards.

Many of them perused a newspaper called the Beacon. I'd seen it at many stands in the Wharf, and assumed it was Cosmar's main source of news. Rob nabbed an abandoned copy from somebody's desk and walked the rest of the way to his office.

He opened the door. Inside a sleepy-eyed Xia sipped tea while Damion snored on the couch, feet dangling over the armrest.

Rob rolled up his newspaper and launched it at Damion. There was a whack as it hit him in the face.

Damion bolted upright. "Sweet salvation! Where's the fire?" He was squinty-eyed and obviously hung over.

"Wake up," said Rob. "Tey's the biggest lead we've had in ages. Let's get to work."

He wheeled the blackboard close to him and turned to me. "The spotlight's on you, Tey. Let's hear how you met Nina."

My insides sunk as I thought back to the ruinous encounter. "She approached me on a sidewalk in LA. She was looking for a runaway shadowborn boy who I'd bumped into earlier."

My eyes grew distant as I recalled the whole scenario. I'd been so stupid to follow people who were clearly dangerous. Only days ago I'd been in the city of angels, finally free of my mom and eager to begin my acting career. Now I was cut off from everything familiar. Trapped. Any dreams I once had were meaningless if I didn't escape.

I took a deep breath and recounted the rest of my time with Nina, holding back frustrated tears. Now that I'd given Rob the information he needed, I wanted him to smile and tell me that what he'd said in the office yesterday was just a joke. That he'd personally book me passage back to California.

"Nina likes working alone," he said. "That's why she's so hard to track." He'd been writing key details on the blackboard and made a white chalk streak across his face when he rubbed his chin. "The fact that she was helping to build a weapon in California has me worried that the Coterie plan on infiltrating other countries."

"Another reason I need to get back there. I know where the warehouse is. I can warn the police—"

"I get it," said Rob. "But one step at a time, OK? What was the name of the ship you came in on?"

"La Ventura," I said. "It was still in the harbor yesterday. I could show it to you."

"We could question the sailors," said Xia. "Nina might have said something to one of them."

"They're Coterie too. There's no way they'll help us." Rob turned back to me. "You didn't happen to overhear what she was planning on doing after she left you in Arun's care?"

My conversations with Nina blurred inside my memory. "She was supposed to meet some of her crew after. I can't remember where. A restaurant or maybe a club. She was pretty pissed that her driver never showed up and we had to take a bicycle cab." Suddenly an image of Sammy burst into my mind.

"Wait a sec," I said. "Maybe…"

"What is it? Asked Rob.

"That bicycle cabbie. He would have taken her to her next stop." I explained how Nina had paid him extra to wait for her while she took me inside Arun's mansion. "If we could find him, he might remember me. I could ask him about Nina."

Rob leaned back and considered. "You'd want to keep helping us?"

"Of course. Nina sold me into slavery. I want her taken in even more than you do."

"Did you happen to get this cabbie's name?" asked Damion. "Cause, there's like a bazillion bicycle cabs in Cosmar."

"Sammy." I remembered his habit of speaking of himself in third person. "Not sure about a last name."

"That narrows it down a little," Rob said, "but still not much to go on."

"Are all bicycle cabbies in Cosmar independent contractors, or do they work for the same company?" I asked.

"I think it goes both ways," said Xia, scratching at where her red nail polish was peeling off. "Was there any sort of logo on the cab?"

I thought back to my ride with Nina. I'd been too afraid and overwhelmed to pick out fine details. "Not sure about a logo, but the cab was bright yellow. I remember seeing lots of other yellow ones, so I'm guessing those must belong to the same faction."

Rob scratched his chin. "That could help if we can find out which company he works for. Drivers tend to go after people just coming into Cosmar. Let's go ride around the wharf and see if we spot any." He scooted his chair back and stood. "Meet at the elevators in five minutes?"

We nodded, and Rob and Damion left the room.

Xia motioned for me to hang back, and handed me a bag. I looked inside. It was full of a couple of changes of clothes, some toiletries, and a pair of leather boots.

I was speechless. "Thank you," I said. "If I ever get the chance to pay you back—"

She held up a hand to cut me off. "There's something else at the bottom."

I fished through the bag until I felt something hard. "Oh," I said as I lifted out a tiny pistol about the size of my hand.

"If you're gonna stick around Cosmar for more than a day, you're gonna want to have something to protect yourself with."

"I don't think you gave me anything with pockets to carry it in," I said, searching through the clothes.

"Come on, Tey. I expected you to be more creative than that." Without warning, she took the gun and shoved it down the front of my shirt into my bra, then stepped back to admire her handiwork. "Carry it like that and no one will suspect."

I nodded, face flushed. "Thanks."

"All right. Now hurry and get changed into something better and meet us up front." She left the office, letting me change in privacy this time.

I figured I'd have a better chance of garnering Sammy's sympathy if I looked as benign as possible, so I picked a dark-blue sundress, the only thing that didn't look like it was made for a jungle safari.

I didn't have any nice shoes, but the boots didn't look too bad and weren't as tight as the sneakers. I put them on and laced them to mid-calf, then stuffed the bag and the rest of its contents under the couch.

The group waited for me by the elevator.

Damion gave a low whistle when he saw me. "Crazy what a change of clothes can do to a girl." He laughed. "That your doing, Xi?"

Xia whacked him on the side of the head and walked into the elevator.

CHAPTER 12

There were bicycle cabs of every color of the rainbow zigzagging through the wharf. Many were decorated with graffiti art or neon lights. Others had frilly parasols to keep the sun off passengers.

"Do you see your friend?" Rob asked in my ear.

I shook my head.

It was twenty minutes before we spotted a solid yellow cab. The driver was a Hispanic guy who didn't know anything about Sammy or the other drivers, but he did tell us he worked for a company called Quinto's Transpo, which had a small office a quarter mile down the wharf.

The office was easy to spot, as it was painted the same bright yellow as the cabs, and had a large fenced-in lot behind it where the off-duty cabs were stored. Inside was Mr. Quinto himself, skinny and snakelike with oiled black hair. He lounged at a messy desk and listened to Hawaiian music from a radio.

"Can I help you folks?" he asked in a traveling salesman voice. "Need a lift somewhere?"

"We were wondering if you have an employee named Sammy?" said Rob.

"Sammy? Hmm, Sammy?" He rubbed his chin. "Is there a last name that goes with that?"

"We don't know," said Rob.

Mr. Quinto rifled through some papers and then looked up. "Ah, Sammy! Now I remember. Friendly fellow. Tall and skinny."

Rob looked at me and I nodded.

"Do you have a complaint to report about my driver, sir? Was he too slow? Did he overcharge?"

"No, nothing like that," said Rob. "We were just wondering where we could find him. Last time he gave us a lift we sort of ran out of money before we could tip him. It was easily one hundred degrees and he'd towed us for miles, so you see why I feel so terrible about it. The guy was a saint about the whole thing and said it had been his pleasure to give us a lift. Now that I have the money I want to give him what he deserves."

So, I wasn't the only actor in this group.

"No problemo," said Quinto. "You can leave the money here and I'll see that it reaches him when he turns in tonight."

"We were hoping to give him the money ourselves so we could thank him in person. If you know any way of reaching him, it would be greatly appreciated."

Quinto continued to rub his chin for a few moments before he sighed and pulled off a paper tacked to the wall. It had long columns of names with numbers listed next to them. He scrolled with his index finger until he found Sammy, and then he dialed the corresponding number into a device resembling a walkie-talkie.

There was the sound of static. Quinto pushed a button and spoke into it. "Yo, Sammy! You there, amigo? This is Quinto here at headquarters."

More static, then Sammy's distinct voice. "That you, boss?"

"Are you on a job right now?"

"Just finishing," said Sammy. "You need something?"

Quinto eyed us suspiciously. "Got some folks here who

want to give you something. Can you swing by before you pick up any more pasajeros?"

"Sure thing, boss," said Sammy. "Be there in fifteen."

Quinto put down the receiver and looked at Rob. "You folks want a cold beverage while you wait?"

Quinto's version of a cold beverage was fruit-flavored, carbonated water in glass bottles. The purple label read Cosmar Cola. Not exactly a Coke. I realized I hadn't seen any of the brands I was used to since coming to Cosmar, or food chains for that matter. Not even a McDonalds had managed to sneak in between the cracks.

We opted to wait outside for Sammy so we could talk in private. We stood on the landing and sipped our Colas until we heard a dinging bicycle bell. I saw Sammy pumping his pedals down the street. He waved and skidded to a stop in front of me.

"Sammy knows you, lady," he said, his smile revealing large white teeth. "You're Nina's friend."

Perfect segue. "Yes, I am," I said, returning his smile. "I was wondering if you knew where I could find her."

"Did you tell the boss to call Sammy here?"

"I did, and I apologize for the trouble, but I haven't been able to get a hold of Nina, and I'm worried about her. Could you tell me where you took her after you dropped me off?"

"Don't worry about Nina," said Sammy. "That lady could take down a charging rhino with her bare hands."

"That's true, but I still need to find her. Can you help me out?"

"Sure, sure. You see, Sammy and Nina have a date tomorrow night."

My eyes widened. "She actually gave you her number?"

"Sammy has a way with the ladies." He laughed.

"Where are you going?"

"A big party. Sammy gets to get all dressed up and everything. Can you imagine him in a fancy costume? Ha!"

"Where's the party?"

"Club Adder. Ten o'clock. But please don't butt in on Sammy's date. This is his big chance with a hot lady."

Club Adder. Of course. Now that I heard the name again, I remembered Nina telling her men to meet her there after she dropped me off.

"Don't worry, Sammy," I said. "I'll try to catch her after."

CHAPTER 13

"You're under no obligation to attend the party at the Adder," Rob told me when we were back at the Agency. "Nina is one of the smartest Coterie guns. It's gonna be very dangerous."

"At the same time," said Damion, "Tey's the only one here to have ever seen Nina in real life. She could help us identify her. A wanted poster can only go so far."

Rob nodded. "That's true. But you've already been through enough danger, Tey. I'm not gonna ask you to risk your life on our behalf."

I wanted to go. I craved the distraction, and something about Rob made me want to impress him. I wasn't going to let him think I was afraid. "If you think I can increase your chances of success, then there's no way I'd sit out. Not when we're so close to finding her. I want her to pay for what she did to me."

Damion rubbed his hands together. "Vengeance. I like it! Best motivator, if you ask me."

"No one's asking you," said Xia.

Damion braced himself for one of her head-whacks. When it didn't come, he added, "Don't even try to tell me you're not here for that exact same reason."

"I didn't say I wasn't," said Xia. "But vengeance isn't going to help Tey get home."

"Still, she's got a right to it," said Damion.

One of Rob's cheeks dimpled as he smiled at me in silent thanks. "What are we sitting around for? Party starts in an hour." He stood up and turned to Xia. "Would you mind lending Tey something a bit fancier to wear? We don't exactly have time to go gown shopping."

"I guess I don't have a choice." She looked at me. "Just don't get any blood on my clothes tonight."

Damion snorted. "She's just trying to scare you out of coming," he told me. "You'll be fine. We do this kind of thing all the time. Besides, you'll have Pricilla and Antoinette to protect you."

I raised one eyebrow. "Pricilla and Antoinette?"

He flexed both biceps.

"You've got to be kidding me?" said Xia. "You really named them?"

"Bet you wish Pricilla was wrapped around you right now," said Damion. "You can touch her if you want."

Xia got to her feet, her mouth a thin white line. She tugged on my arm. "Let's go before I chop Pricilla off."

"So, I'm coming home with you then?" I asked.

"I'm not going to trek all the way to the Castillo with dress options." She turned to Rob. "How about we meet at my place? It's closest to the Adder anyway."

"I'll be over as soon as I get changed," said Rob. He followed us out the door.

I turned and caught one last glimpse of Antoinette as Damion gave me a wave goodbye.

CHAPTER 14

I followed Xia into the street as she filled me in on Cosmar's night scene.

"Parties happen here almost every night, but they aren't just the suit and cocktail dress kind," she said. "Rich people usually wear lavish costumes or masks. It's a tradition that comes from the Coterie's desire to keep a low profile while wandering in social spheres."

Her apartment was within walking distance of the Agency. A baby wailed from a distant room and various occupants of the building chattered through the thin walls as we made our way up the stairwell to the third floor.

Xia unlocked and opened the door. The inside was small and dark. "It's me, Ma," Xia said as she motioned me inside.

A middle-aged woman stood from the couch. Half her face was covered in shiny pink burn scars and both of her eyes were a sightless milky white. She stumbled over to Xia and took hold of her hands. "I saved you some supper." She had a hoarse voice, as if her vocal cords had also been damaged in the fire that ruined her face.

"No time," said Xia. "I'm just here to get changed. Me and my co-workers are going to a party tonight."

"A party? Are you celebrating something?"

"Someone got a big promotion." She shrugged at me.

"How nice," the woman cooed. "Soon, it will be you they

are celebrating. With your education, I'm surprised you're not an executive by now."

Xia snorted. "I'm just a secretary. Secretaries tend to stay where they are. Unnoticed." I looked at her, surprised at her lie. Her mother had no idea where she went every day and what she really did. What would happen if something went wrong and she got hurt, or worse?

Xia pushed me forward. "This is Tey, one of my coworkers. We're going to get ready together."

Her mother's face lit up and she put her hands on my arm. "Are you a secretary too?"

Xia gave me a look, urging me to play along.

"Y-yes," I said. "But I'm not half as efficient as Xia. She'll get promoted long before I ever do."

"So nice of you to come," she said, patting my shoulder.

"Wish we could chat more," said Xia, pulling me away. "But we're running late."

"It was nice to meet you," I said over my shoulder as Xia herded me to her bedroom.

Like the apartment, Xia's bedroom was clean and bare. Her closet was another story. She flung open the door revealing a space so stuffed with clothes, I was afraid one wrong move would trigger an explosion.

"Formal dresses are to the left," she said. "Take your pick." She began to rifle through the hangars until she came across a red ball gown. "Aha. That's where you were hiding," she said to the dress, holding it up to her. She pulled the dress out of the closet and pushed me in.

I dug into the mass of dresses. How could I ever choose?

"No time to be particular," Xia said, stepping into the red gown and fiddling for the zipper. "We've still got hair and makeup to do."

"Where'd you get all these?" I asked, pulling out a long violet dress with flowing layers of sheer material.

Xia shrugged. "With a job like mine, it helps to have a stock of disguises on hand."

I smiled. In spite of everything, a tingle raced down my spine. For a moment I felt like I was in my drama teacher's wardrobe room. Even the smell was the same. But this wasn't a play, I reminded myself. This was real life. Someone could get hurt.

"What do you think?" I asked, holding up the violet dress to my chest.

Xia pursed her lips in thought. "That was one of my pricier buys. But the color goes well with your skin tone. It'll work."

When we were both in our dresses, she guided me to a small bathroom where she removed an enormous case of cosmetics from a cupboard under the sink. I reached for the eyeliner but she stopped me.

"I'll do it," she said, grabbing a tube of liquid liner and tipping my chin up to study my face. "No sense going overboard, you'll be wearing a mask. But a few touches here and there could go a long way with you. She worked on my face with the delicacy of a professional painter. When she was finished, the makeup was only slightly visible, and yet I barely recognized myself.

"Now for the hair," she said, pulling the pins out of my braids. The style had kinked my hair into waves, which Xia combed out, then wound into a stylish bun below my left ear.

I watched her work in the mirror, trying to memorize her finger movements so I could repeat the look again. After tonight I'd never go back to the raccoon-eyed makeup, and lazy ponytail I'd worn to high school for the last three years.

There was a knock at the door.

"That'd be the boys," said Xia. "Would you mind answering it? I've still got me to do."

I gave my reflection one last glance and then went to the door. Mrs. Wang was making her way to it, hands outstretched. I grabbed her elbow.

"I'll get it," I said, guiding her back to the couch.

She nodded at me gratefully and sat down.

Rob pushed the door open and strode inside. He was dressed in a long blue coat with wide silver cuffs. A top hat was on his head, peacock feathers adorning one side. His brown hair was combed beneath it, except for a few curls that had come loose over the side of his forehead. He was…stunning.

I opened my mouth to say something, but nothing came out. I closed it, then opened it again. Still nothing.

Rob laughed. "Aren't you going to let me in?"

I stepped aside and held the door open.

He entered the apartment, eyes never leaving me. "You look really beautiful," he said.

I took a deep breath, praying he couldn't see the blood filling my cheeks. "It's all thanks to Xia," I said gesturing at the long dress and elegant hairstyle she'd skillfully given me. "You look pretty great too."

He grinned, whisking off the top hat with a flourish. "Think Nina would spare me a dance?"

"She'd be stupid not to." I sat stiffly on the couch.

Damion plowed through the door, out of breath. He spotted me on the couch and flopped down next to me, sliding Pricilla around my shoulder. Or was it Antoinette?

"Hello, good-looking," he teased. "Tonight's gonna be even more fun than I thought."

He was dressed like a pirate with a flowing white shirt that hung open to reveal his pecks. A scarlet sash was tied around his waist, and he wore high leather boots and a swooping hat with red feathery plumes.

He turned to Xia's mother. "Nice to see you again, Mrs. Wang," he said, reaching out to pat her arm. "Wish you could come to the party with us."

"Are you the one getting the promotion?" she asked in her hoarse voice.

"Promotion? Saints no. I'm just going along for the ride. And the ladies." He rubbed his shoulder into me then leaned back. "Almost done in there, Xi?" he called toward the bathroom.

"Don't rush an artist while she's working," Xia called back.

Damion laughed, but when Xia finally stepped out, I could see that she wasn't joking. Her makeup was indeed the work of a master artist. Her face was painted white, with swirling eye makeup only the steadiest of hands could have managed, and I noticed that her elegant red gown perfectly matched the scarlet highlights in her hair.

Damion let out a low whistle. "Saints and angels, the wait was totally worth it."

Xia didn't acknowledge him. She went back into her room and brought out a large trunk. "I'm guessing you all need masks?" At Rob's nod, she plunked the trunk down in front of us.

Rob lifted the lid and took out a silver and purple mask. He held it up to his face. "What do you think?"

"Very mysterious," I said with a smirk.

He set it to the side and rifled through the contents again, this time bringing out a birdlike mask with peacock plumes sticking out the top. He held it up to my face. "Perfect. Now you'll match me."

Damion eyed Xia's red dress, then pulled out a mask of the same color covered in decorative dragon scales.

"You're kidding, right?" Xia said, scowling. She didn't need a mask. The makeup rendered her unrecognizable.

"Sorry to pair you with that scalawag," Rob said to her. "But Tey and I already had practice dancing." He grinned at me, and my heart suddenly felt like a sponge soaking up warm apple cider. I pictured the way he'd twirled me around the Castillo's crumbling ballroom and had to brace myself on the side of the couch as a light feeling rushed through me.

"Well," said Damion, stretching to better showcase his muscles, "looks like we're ready to go." He went to Xia and gave her a flourish. "Your carriage awaits, milady."

Xia frowned and strode past him out the door.

"Saints, Xi!" he called after her. "You're not gonna act this way at the party, are you?" He ran to catch up with her.

Rob held out one arm, and I took it unsteadily, feeling the heat of him through his coat. "Xia will get over it," he said with a short laugh. "I'm not about to let you out of my sight."

He turned to Xia's mother. "I'll make sure your daughter makes it home safe, Mrs. Wang," he said. "You don't have to stay up worrying for her."

Mrs. Wang reached for a basket of knitting and began to wind yarn around her fingers. "I'll do it anyway. It's a mother's duty."

Rob nodded, even though she couldn't see it, and escorted me out the door.

Instead of riding our bikes, Rob had hired two bicycle cabs from Quinto's Transpo. It was only appropriate.

Rob put his arm around me and it took all my effort not to make my back rigid as nervousness and excitement coursed down my spine. Hoping he wouldn't notice my reaction to his closeness, I said, "Do you think Sammy picked up Nina in his cab?"

Rob laughed. "If anything, she was the one who picked him up. Nina's rich enough to own a real car, which is saying something."

"Why is that? Most people own cars back in the states."

"Gasoline doesn't cost fifty bucks a gallon back in the states."

I gave a low whistle. "Fifty bucks a gallon! Who could ever justify that?"

"The king doesn't do trade deals with outsiders, so any gas in this country has been smuggled in, making it a valuable resource."

We passed a group of colorful people dressed in striped jester outfits and bulbous checkered gowns. They tottered around, off-balance, as they yelled drunken nonsense at the tops of their lungs. In the distance were more people in incredibly detailed animal costumes—posing as long feathered birds, circus bears, and pink poodles. The city of Cosmar had been transformed from a chaotic shopping center to a laughing dreamland of adult trick-or-treaters.

"Don't be fooled by their silly costumes," Rob whispered into my ear, sending two identical shivers racing up the backs of my arms. "Many Coterie use the charade as a way to get away with crime. Trust me when I say, you do not want to get caught alone on the streets of Cosmar after dusk."

I shivered and glanced behind my back before I could stop myself.

Rob laughed and squeezed my arm, his touch electric. "You're not alone, Tey."

If only he knew how aware of that I was.

The Adder was located in the outer city, near the rich sector. The black building sported a blue neon sign made of cursive letters that connected to form a snake. We joined a group of people wearing wigs made entirely of elegant curled paper as they filed into the nightclub.

Inside, the music was loud and reedy. People flirted over drinks and others twirled on the dance floor, chatting softly. Rob let out a breath. "This will be tough with all the costumes, but let's split off in pairs and look for anyone who may resemble Nina."

Xia's eye twitched as she clung stiffly to Damion's arm. Damion pulled her away from us and the two disappeared into the crowd.

I scanned the dance floor, searching for anything that might give Nina away—her lean muscled arms, curly black hair, chocolate skin—but with so many obscure costumes, I soon grew frustrated.

Rob slid his hand around my waist. "Come on, let's get closer." He escorted me onto the dance floor and soon we were gliding among the other dancers. Their costumes were a sparkling blur of color as we whirled by. I was once again reminded of my dream, but with all these strange creatures around me, this seemed like a greater illusion.

"Much more appropriate than our first dance, don't you think?" said Rob with a smirk.

"I think I liked our first one better," I said. It had been spontaneous and unexpected. This had an artificial feeling to it. We were playing two parts in a drama out of necessity, not because we wanted to.

Our dance ended abruptly when Rob spotted Damion and Xia at the bar. He pulled me toward them, mouth curving into a frown.

"I hope those drinks aren't alcoholic," he said. "It's not like we're about to face one of the most wanted Coterie guns or anything."

Damion downed the rest of his drink in one gulp as Xia set hers aside, lips tightening. "How else am I supposed to pretend to be this lout's date?" she said.

"Hey," said Damion, chewing on an ice cube from his glass, "I don't like this arrangement any more than you. Do you know how many looks I've gotten from other babes tonight?"

"Be quiet," said Rob. "I need you two to stay focused." He ripped the glass out of Damion's hand and chucked it into a wastebasket where I heard it shatter.

"Hey, there was good ice in that," said Damion with a downturned lip.

"I picked you both to be on my team because I thought you were the best, but I'm not sure you take it as seriously as—"

My gaze connected with a dancer in the distance. He wore a golden coat and pants made out of real animal fur, and a mane-like headdress that couldn't quite cover all his tiny black curls.

"Rob!" I slapped his shoulder.

He turned to look at me. "What?"

I pointed at the man dressed like a lion. He turned, revealing his face. It was definitely Sammy, and when he spun his partner around, I was struck with a jolt of electricity. With him on the dance floor was a woman who could only be Nina.

CHAPTER 15

"At least one of us is paying attention," Rob said. "Good work, Tey."

We observed Sammy for a long moment. His partner was dressed as a leopard in a form-fitting dress covered in patterned black spots. Her face was half concealed by what looked like an actual leopard head with holes for her eyes. Only her blood-red lips showed underneath the muzzle.

"That her?" Damion asked. "Saints! She would choose a leopard." He gave a feline growl.

"I didn't make memorizing her lips a priority," I said, watching for anything that might give her away. "But it has to be her, right? She's Sammy's date. Do we butt in after all?"

"Not so fast," said Rob. "Let's get in there. I want you to be absolutely sure." He turned to Xia and Damion. "You two get on the other side and at least pretend to like each other so we don't attract attention. If our suspicions are correct, I'll signal you to get ready."

He held out his arm to me and smiled, instantly transforming into a gentleman courting a young lady, not an undercover bounty hunter. I took it, and let him guide me back to the dance floor.

Rob led me through a few steps, and his firm hand steadied me each time my feet faltered. He was wearing a cologne that enhanced his natural scent. It reminded me of a forest. I pressed my body even closer to him, muscles relaxing despite the danger that was so close.

Every twirl brought us closer to Sammy and the leopard.

Across from us, Xia was rigid in Damion's arms, her mouth a tight frown. Damion was at least trying to follow Rob's advice, but his wide smile contrasted so much with Xia's expression that the charade looked ridiculous. Luckily, everyone seemed too absorbed in their own partners to give the other dancers much notice.

I was almost shoulder-to-shoulder with Sammy. I pivoted my eyes without turning my head, examining his dance partner at close quarters. Her disguise was excellent, covering her hair and most of her face. But now that I was so close, I could tell she was Nina's height, and the small amount of exposed skin surrounding her lips was the same coffee shade.

She moved with a dangerous grace, her body feminine but powerful like the leopard she imitated. It was Nina. I was sure of it.

For a moment, her dark eyes flickered away from Sammy and toward me. I glanced at the ground, grateful for the mask concealing my face. Still, I wondered if she'd glimpsed anything familiar.

I wrapped my arms around Rob's neck and leaned in close, pretending to be overwhelmed with feeling. I moved my mouth as little as possible as I whispered in his ear. "It's her."

Rob's lips turned up ever so slightly. He looked at Damion, who was sweating as Xia dug her red nails into his shoulder, and gave him a nod. Damion slowed his dance. One hand released Xia's and reached for the gun hidden in his gaudy costume.

Rob twirled me in front of Sammy and Nina. With a flourish, he tapped Sammy on the shoulder. "Care to swap partners for one dance? The lady has been eyeing you all night."

I hoped my mask hid my blush as I forced myself to remain calm and play along. This wasn't real. It was all just an elaborate set, and I, just an actor.

Sammy gave me a stunned look, then his face softened. "It would be my pleasure." He took my arm and led me to the middle of the dance floor.

I took a deep breath and forced my muscles to relax. I smiled and leaned into Sammy, but my heart was out of control and my eyes were on Rob.

Rob took Nina's hand, positioning himself for a dance. His feet moved in rhythm with the music and I saw his lips move. He was talking to her.

"Sammy came only expecting one partner tonight," said Sammy. "Never thought he'd get so lucky. What's your name, pretty lady?"

His words jumbled in my mind as Nina drew back from Rob, looking startled. One of Rob's hands gripped her tighter. The other slipped into his pocket.

Damion and Xia were behind Nina, blocking her off. Both had guns in their hands.

Rob pressed his gun into Nina's chest. She gasped and stood frozen in the middle of the floor as Rob leaned over and whispered something inaudible in her ear.

I stiffened. Would Rob need my help? Or should I focus on keeping Sammy occupied?

Sammy followed my gaze before I could decide what to do. He yanked me over to Rob, refusing to release me. "Hey, man, what's your problem?" I felt bad for him in a way, but a nice guy like him shouldn't be getting mixed up with someone like Nina anyway.

Damion and Xia pointed their guns at Sammy's head, forcing him to halt. People around us screamed, but they sounded like they were coming from underwater.

Sammy ripped a long knife from the breast of his lion suit. Before I could react, the knife was at my throat, close enough to draw blood.

"Let me through or I'll cut her," he hissed. I was afraid if I breathed too deeply, the knife would slice my skin.

Sammy looked at Rob, who still had his gun bored into Nina's back.

"You hurt her and I'll fire," Rob said.

Sammy shrugged. "Go right ahead. I met the woman less than an hour ago." He was no longer referring to himself in the third person, and there was something different about his voice.

Rob's face paled. He tore off the woman's headdress. The face underneath was about ten years older than Nina's, with large almond eyes.

For a split second, Rob's eyes found mine. Lost, disappointed. Then the connection was severed. He pushed the woman away and she fell to the floor with a sob of relief. He held up his gun.

"Let the girl go," he said, sweat dripping from his mask in shiny trails.

Sammy's grip on me tightened. I could hear a low laugh from deep in his throat. Black shadows moved at the sides of my vision and I looked to see five gigantic men closing in on us.

"Rob, watch out!" I screamed.

Rob turned just in time to duck as a bouncer's gigantic fist hurtled toward him. He grabbed the man's wrist, yanked him forward, and slammed his skull into his forehead. The man dropped like a sandbag and struggled to come to his senses.

Rob kicked him in the stomach and then raised his arm to guard his face as another man launched a blow at his nose.

Xia and Damion sprang into action, guns in both hands as they tried to keep the other bouncers off Rob. One of Xia's guns went off but I didn't see anything get hit. One of the men struck her wrist, knocking the weapon to the ground. Without hesitation, she brought up her knee into his groin and pushed him back.

All around me there were screams from the onlookers. At the sound of Xia's gun, many in the crowd raced for the exit. Damion brought up his gun and guarded Xia as more men dressed in black weaved through the maelstrom of fleeing people and surrounded them. He couldn't risk shooting with so many civilians.

"Now," said Sammy to me in his new, more cryptic voice. "You're gonna come on a little trip with me."

With the knife still at my throat, he dragged me up the balcony stairs.

"Tey!" It was Rob who screamed my name as he pushed against the crowd. One of the bouncers grabbed his coat from behind and yanked him back. Rob slid out of the coat and grabbed for his top hat, which had fallen from his head. With a flick of the wrist, he spun the stiff brim into his attacker's eyes. The big man sprawled backward and lost his balance. Rob twirled his hat back onto his head as he ran after me.

There was a door hidden behind a black curtain. Sammy pulled me inside and threw me to the floor. He turned to shove the door closed.

Rob was there before it was fully shut. His shoulder wedged inside and stopped Sammy from slamming it all the way. For a moment, he struggled against the other man, as he pushed for entry.

I came to my senses and lunged at Sammy. I dug my nails into his arm and yanked it back.

Rob burst inside and plowed Sammy over. But Sammy was strong. With a growl, he flipped Rob onto his back and slammed his head into the floor.

Rob tried to sit up but his head lolled backward. Gritting his teeth, he rammed his knee into Sammy's gut. Sammy drew back with a grunt, and Rob had enough time to roll out of his grip. Sammy came at him immediately and pushed him into the wall.

I looked around for something I could hurt Sammy with, but except for a leather couch, the room was bare. Besides, the two men were so tightly locked in combat, it would be impossible to come between them without getting hurt myself.

I remembered the tiny gun that was still secured in my bra. I'd never fired one before, and if I pulled the trigger, I'd risk hitting Rob.

Sammy's hands gripped either side of Rob's head and bashed his skull into the wall. Rob's eyes found mine as if to say, "I'm sorry," as the light drained out of them. He toppled to the floor.

Sammy was on me before I could get at my gun. He pulled a cord out of his pocket and tied my wrists together in front of me. I strained to look at Rob, to see if his chest was rising and falling. I screamed his name, but he lay unmoving, face pallid.

I shouldn't have come tonight. Not with luck as bad as mine. Now Rob was hurt; possibly dead. Why had I been so selfish?

Sammy slid the couch aside to reveal a trapdoor. He flung it open, grabbed the back of my dress, and pushed me down a narrow flight of stairs. I fought against him and continued to call Rob's name.

Sammy dug his fingers into my arms with bruising strength. "Shut up or I'll put my knife through his chest. Then he'll be dead for sure."

The stairs led to a garage with a sleek black car. He threw me into the back seat and started the engine. I clawed desperately for the door latch. "Sit still," he said. "I don't want to damage you."

"Where are you taking me?" I screamed. "What are those men going to do with my friends?"

He clicked something and the garage door lifted. The road beyond was dark and empty. He pressed his foot on the pedal and the car lurched.

I sprang. My bound arms arched over his head and pulled back on his throat. He gasped and choked as the car swerved in crazy directions. He slammed on the brakes and my body flew forward, giving him enough leeway to duck out of my chokehold.

"I didn't want to do this," he said and swung his fist. I tried to throw myself to the side but wasn't fast enough. His knuckles got me in the temple and it was like a light switch turned off the world.

* * *

The pounding in my head pulled me from oblivion. The air was stale and cool. I lay on what felt like hundreds of gritty stones, hands still tied together. Voices echoed as they came closer, and I wondered if I was inside a cavern or tunnel.

"Were they kingsguard?" I didn't need to open my eyes to know it was Nina. The real Nina.

"No. Kingsguard don't go undercover," came Sammy's answer. "They were the ones with the girl at Quinto's."

"Bounty hunters," Nina spat. "Did they see you leave?"

"Your security took care of them, and I slipped out the balcony exit. There's no way they followed me."

"Good." I could hear Nina pacing.

"I brought you what you wanted," said Sammy. "Am I initiated?"

"You'll be closely monitored for a trial period. If you mess up, there's no going back. You are aware of the consequences?"

"Yes."

"Then consider yourself the Coterie's newest trainee. And don't forget, you belong to me."

"Do I get a tattoo or something?"

"I could brand you like a bull, but then if you do something stupid, everyone will be able to trace you back to me. I can't risk you ruining my reputation. Your biggest test will come next week."

"Next week?"

"I'm returning to California with another shipment. That means you'll have to take care of mining operations while I'm gone."

My chest tightened. California.

Footsteps crunched as someone else approached. I opened my eyes a slit and saw a stocky man with thick black hair and dark shadows under his eyes. He was dressed in a suit and black shoes that squeaked when he walked. The area around me looked like a mine tunnel. Lanterns flickered on hooks, creating monstrous shadows with every movement.

Nina stiffened as she watched the man come closer. "You're earlier than I expected."

"Is that a problem?" His voice was as gravelly as the ground.

Nina's breath quickened. "No, not at all. Sammy, give Mr.

Santos his vials."

Sammy handed him a suitcase, and the other man popped it open to examine its contents. He nodded. A pearly glow illuminated his face. He turned to Nina. "You said you had other things, as well?"

She walked out of my line of sight and I heard her shuffle around. Someone gasped in pain. Nina pushed forward a shadowborn boy.

A fist gripped my heart. It was the boy who could turn invisible!

"This one needs reforming." Nina's smile was pitiless. "Ricky said you could help with that."

The boy trembled. He was so skinny that I could see his ribs through the grey material of his shirt.

The man loomed over him like a mountain, his frown deepening. "Ricky knows me well. Reforming disobedient shadowborn is a specialty of mine." He swung his fist and struck the boy in the stomach. I flinched as the boy gasped in pain and fell to his knees. The man's foot came at him and the boy was knocked onto his side. He curled up and tried to make himself as small as possible as the foot returned again and again.

It took all my control not to jump to my feet and pull him away, but it wouldn't do any good. I'd probably just get the same treatment.

I saw Sammy look away, but Nina watched with no expression. "If the ability we bought him for worked, he wouldn't have been stupid enough to get himself caught after trying to run away. Not that he'd have lived long on the streets of LA."

"A runaway, huh?" said the man with one more savage kick to the side of the boy's head. "He must be useful if you still want to keep him alive."

"Invisibility is an extraordinary gift," said Nina. "None of the others can do it, so he'd be invaluable if you think you can fix him. There'd be nothing he couldn't steal. No one he couldn't kill."

"We'll see," said Santos. He kicked again and the boy stopped moving.

Sammy stooped over him to check if he was still breathing. "He won't wake any time soon. You'll have to carry him out."

Nina gave Sammy a threatening look, but the other man's face didn't change. "No, you'll have to carry him out."

Sammy just shrugged. "The kid probably weighs as much as a sack of feathers."

"Is that everything, Nina?" asked the man.

"One more thing," she said. She turned to face me and I clamped my eyes shut. "On the off chance you want to do more business, I have this girl. Picked her up on my last run to California. She's fresh on the market and I can give you a good price. She was meant for Arun, before…everything happened."

I felt like a pig at the fair.

I could sense the man stooping over me. His thick fingers brushed my arm, and I had to tense every muscle not to flinch. "Is she healthy?"

"The peak of health."

The man snorted. "Then it looks like your friend has two loads to carry out."

"Not at all," said Nina. "The girl's awake. She's been listening to us this whole time."

CHAPTER 16

My heart leaped and my eyes flew open.

The man standing over me gave an amused grunt and nodded.

Nina yanked me to my feet and brushed the gravel off my violet dress.

"Don't count on anyone saving you this time, hon. You only get that lucky once."

Lucky. If only she knew.

My fingers twitched, itching to slap her, but my wrists were still bound tight with Sammy's cord. I scowled at her with all the hatred I could muster.

"Be good to Mr. Santos and you could go places."

I tried to shout at her, but my throat was so parched my voice cracked.

She handed me a water bottle, then forced me to walk.

Sammy stooped to lift the unconscious shadowborn boy over his shoulder, and the two men followed us toward the mine's entrance.

Outside, morning sunlight was just breaking through the trees in golden beams, but the heat in the air was already almost suffocating.

We were taken through the jungle to a dirt road where an old black and grey Chevy Nomad waited. The car reminded me of a hearse.

Sammy dropped the boy onto the back seat and Nina shoved me in next to him. The man she called Mr. Santos locked our doors, and then got in front and turned the ignition. The engine whined before choking to life.

As the car bumped along the road, I forced myself to commit every strange-looking tree and pothole in the road to memory. When I led Rob's team back here, I wanted to know exactly where to take them.

If they were still alive.

I dug my nails into my hands and tried not to think about that. They were fine. They had to be. It was me I had to worry about.

My heart thrummed against the small gun that was still tucked under my shirt undiscovered by both Sammy and Nina. Mr. Santos probably had one too, one much larger than mine; I just had to be smarter than him. And I had to wait for the right time. We were in the middle of nowhere, and it would be stupid to make a move so far from civilization. Getting stuck in the jungle alone could be just as deadly.

I licked my lips, parched throat burning. I fiddled with the water bottle with my bound hands until I finally got the lid off and tipped it to my lips. The cold, metallic liquid flowed down my throat in a reviving waterfall.

I stopped short when the boy next to me stirred. He gave a low moan and blinked.

His eyes were the color of a morning sky. The outer corners were slightly upturned, like he was a quarter Asian or something, which would have been pretty if they weren't ringed with purple bruises. He squinted at me as if I were out of focus.

I couldn't take my eyes off him. Rob had said no one knew where the shadowborn came from, not even themselves. The thought made me shiver even though the car was getting steadily hotter.

I wanted to ask the boy to untie my wrists, but Mr. Santos kept glancing back at us in the rearview mirror every ten seconds or so.

The boy's lips were dry and cracked. He had to be twice as thirsty as I was. I looked at the rest of the water in the bottle, licking my lips again, and handed it to him before I could change my mind.

His hand came forward to take the bottle and I flinched when his cold fingers brushed mine. With shaking hands, he brought the bottle to his mouth. From the way his throat moved, his ravenous thirst was obvious, but he only took a few sips before handing the bottle back.

I shook my head and signaled for him to finish it. He needed it more than I did. He hesitated a moment, and then gulped down the rest, breathing hard after dropping the bottle on the seat. He tried to lift himself into a sitting position, but his elbows buckled and his head knocked against the door as he passed out all over again.

I tugged his body into a more comfortable position, resting his head against the window. He didn't stir again. Despite the way Mr. Santos treated him, maybe it was better the boy lived with him. I recalled the king's extermination order. At least the Coterie would keep him hidden. What other sort of life could he have?

Santos drove for what felt like an hour before I saw something I recognized. The gate to Gheisari's mansion. We were close to the city… close to the Agency.

I let Santos drive another five minutes, trying to get up the nerve to do what I was about to do. I used the area where my wrists met to ease the gun through my neckline. I let it fall into my lap and quickly wrapped it in the folds of my dress as Santos adjusted his rearview mirror.

I grasped the gun between my knees and my shaking hands crept toward the door lock. I was grateful the car was too old to have child locks. Still, Santos's lack of security surprised me. Weren't villains supposed to have cars with doors that could only be opened from the outside? Then again, he hadn't come to Nina's mine expecting to purchase me. Perhaps this was the car he used for casual business, and he had a more secure vehicle for captives.

I held my breath, then grabbed the handle and pulled sharply. The door unlocked with a pop.

Santos had his gun out in a second, but he was too late. I threw myself against the door. It came open and I rolled out of the car. Santos wasn't driving fast; still, it hurt more than I'd expected when I hit the uneven road and rolled to a stop.

The Chevy Nomad's brakes screeched, and Santos whipped the car around, tires going off the road, digging up foliage.

I struggled to get hold of my gun and push myself to my feet with my bound hands. Blood dripped down my knee from one of the many scrapes the road had given me.

The car headed straight for me. The window rolled down and the muzzle of Santos's gun jutted out, aimed at my chest.

I ran, ignoring the pain of my bleeding knee.

The car sped up, wheels squealing like dying hogs. Santos was either going to shoot me or run me over. As I ran toward the jungle, I twisted just enough to fire my gun at the oncoming vehicle. By some miracle, my bullet hit the front tire.

Santos just missed me as the tire blew. He swerved off the road and collided into a tree. I looked back as I fled into the underbrush and saw smoke erupting from his engine. The front of the car was smashed. I hoped the crash hadn't hurt the boy, but there wasn't time to find out.

Santos cursed as he forced open his door and fired at me.

I used the trees as my shield as I ripped through the scrub. I heard him shout, followed by rasping breaths as he pursued me. Thorns and branches sliced my skin and tore at my dress, but adrenaline protected me from pain. I pivoted once and fired the remaining bullets from my gun. There weren't many, and none of them did any good.

I kept on running, sweat soaking my skin until I got tunnel vision. I stopped short, gasping for air.

A branch snapped. I turned my head to the left and my eyes locked with Santos's gaze.

I didn't have the breath to scream.

He fired his pistol as he advanced. His face was covered in sweat and blood. My gun made snapping sounds as I tried to fire back, but the cartridge was empty.

I hurled the useless weapon at him but just missed his head. As the tiny firearm disappeared into the underbrush, I spun around, feet sliding in mud. I grabbed onto a tree and barely kept my balance as I clung to it for protection. I moved on to another tree, ducking behind it the moment a bullet skimmed the trunk.

"I'm going to kill you, you little whore!" came Santos's rasping voice from a few paces away.

Risking everything, I pushed my body into a run and bolted for a vine-covered mass straight ahead. But my foot connected with something hard and I went down. I heard him chuckle as I lay sprawled out on the jungle floor.

It was all over. I was dead. The thought didn't come as too much of a shock, considering the recent direction my life had taken, but it still smarted.

I looked back at the thing that had sentenced me to death.

It was a rock, and not even a large one. Figures.

I pried it out of the ground, prepared to launch it at Santos in a final effort to defend myself.

His eyes never left me, which is why he never saw the patch of mud that had almost taken me down. For a moment, his body glided unnaturally across the turf, and then he was on his back, too.

I scrambled to my feet and hurled my rock at his face. It struck his left eye and knocked his head back into the mud. I didn't wait to see if he was still conscious. I took off.

I wasn't sure how long I kept at it or how far I went, but when I looked behind me, I was alone, and nothing stirred in the underbrush.

Lungs heaving, I clung to a tree until I no longer felt like I'd pass out. My head pounded and I could barely stand the humid heat of the jungle any longer. But I had to keep moving. Santos was still out there, and I needed to get to the Agency fast.

CHAPTER 17

My heart melted in relief when I saw a tower peeking through the trees. It belonged to one of the mansions from the rich sector of Cosmar. I stumbled on until I reached the road, the cobblestones a welcome change from the dense underbrush. I knew it wasn't smart to stay in the open, so I walked the edge of the forest in the shadows. Santos would not be stupid enough to backtrack all the way to Nina's mine, which meant he'd make for the city whether he stayed on my trail or not.

I wondered if he'd take the shadowborn boy with him and prayed my reckless actions hadn't hurt the kid worse.

I booked it through the rich sector and then kept to the sidelines as I made my way around the busy wharf. I buried my bound hands in a bunched-up section of my skirt that I held in front of me. I didn't want to draw any unnecessary attention to myself or have anyone ask questions.

Various bicycle cabbies rode alongside me, offering me rides. I turned them down. I had no money, and after Sammy's trick I'd never trust one of them again.

By the time I reached the business sector, I was so exhausted I was limping. I spotted a copy of the Beacon in a gutter and stooped to pick it up. On the front page was a picture of Sammy dragging me away, my face still covered by my peacock-plumed mask. The headline read: Knifeman Vanishes

After Party at The Adder Goes Awry. Three Masked Gunmen Make Escape. Kingsguard Suspect Coterie Feud.

A mountain lifted off my chest. Three masked gunmen. Did that mean Rob was still alive and had gotten away with Xia and Damion? I couldn't help smiling. Next thing I knew, they'd all have wanted posters of their own.

I knew I looked terrible as I entered the Agency office building and rode the elevator to the seventh floor, but I made no move to fix my hair or brush the dirt off my skin. Instead, I clasped my hands together as hard as I could, willing them to stop shaking. They were warm and solid, and I was still alive. Somehow.

The elevator door dinged open. I stumbled out, ignoring the stunned looks from the other agents as I made my way to Rob's door. I flung it open and hobbled inside. Rob was sitting on the couch next to Xia, an icepack pressed against the back of his head. My heart swelled at the sight of him and I let out a sob of relief.

Xia and Damion froze when they saw me, like they were looking at a zombie, which wasn't far off from how I felt.

Rob's eyes bore into me as though to make sure I was really there. I walked toward him and he jumped into action. He took a pocketknife from the inside of his jacket and sawed the cords around my wrists. When I was free, I hobbled to the table and sat, suddenly feeling all my scrapes and bruises.

"Go get a med kit," Rob said, and Damion hurried out the door. Rob knelt beside me. "Are you injured?"

"Just some bad scrapes," I said.

"You ruined my dress," said Xia. She spun a gun around in her hands, then rubbed it with a blackened cloth.

Rob gave her a look as if she'd just made a death threat. But I could tell from the way she cocked her head that it was her straight-faced way of teasing me.

"We have to hurry," I said, words coming out like shudders. "I know where Nina is. If we go right now we—"

"We're not going anywhere until we get you patched up," said Rob. He looked at my arm where the skin had been torn from my leap out of Santos's car.

Damion came through the door carrying a black bag. He tossed it on the table and handed me a water bottle. I finished it in a matter of seconds. He opened his bag and cleaned off the wounds, then applied a green paste over the exposed skin. It was probably some sort of herbal remedy. It felt tingly and smelled like sage.

"Not exactly Neosporin," I said.

"Is that an American brand?" he asked.

"Yeah, an antibiotic ointment."

"Too bad you didn't bring any with you. Antibiotics are worth more than gold in Cosmar."

"Remind me never to get sick or hurt again," I said, feeling my stomach clench.

"No kidding." He wound white bandage over the really bad cuts then pulled back. "Did I miss any spots?"

I shook my head.

"Good, keep those clean and covered. If anything looks like it might be getting infected, come see one of us, stat."

I nodded again and Damion patted my shoulder. "Glad to have you back with us."

Rob turned on me, eyes full of questions. Xia was already staring at me, as though afraid to ask what she was desperate to know. I decided to make things easier for them and launched into an explanation of everything that had happened since my abduction from the Adder. When I got to the part about Mr. Santos, they all sat up straighter.

"Santos, as in Antonio Santos?" Xia asked, eyes wide.

"Nina never mentioned his first name," I said.

Rob rifled through the hundreds of wanted posters on the wall and ripped one off. He looked at it a moment, then handed it to me. "That the guy?"

It was unmistakable. "That's him. Is he special or something?"

I heard Damion choke. "Special? He's only the cousin of Ricardo Santos, high chief of the Coterie. Do you know how much this man is worth?"

"More importantly," said Xia, aiming her gun at the poster and closing one eye, "if we catch him, it will severely wound his dear cousin. Maybe we could leech a clue out of him concerning Ricardo's whereabouts."

"Not likely," said Damion, running a hand over his shaved head. "Do you know how much torture training these guys have to go through to get to their level? Antonio will never cave. But his capture will certainly stir things up a bit. Might be the opening we need to hit the Coterie where it counts."

Rob sat down and leaned forward. "Antonio might still be out there with an injured shadowborn slowing him down. For all we know, he could be on the road right now. We play our cards right, we could walk home today with three bounties. Two top Coterie, one shadowborn."

Xia leaped to her feet and fastened her gun onto her belt. "Then let's get the hell out of here."

When I stood, Rob put his hand on my shoulder. "Tey, you've been through a lot. Stay here. I'll fix you something to help you sleep, and we'll be back before you wake up."

"No," I said, standing up again despite the trembling in my limbs. "Nina's mine is well hidden. I can help you find it." The idea of going back there should have freaked me out, but after my stunt with Santos, my emotions floated around me like a cloud, whispering for me to be afraid, but not triggering a response.

"And risk having you recaptured? What kind of man do you think I am?"

"Someone who has no control over what I do. Just because you rescued me from Gheisari doesn't mean you own me. If I can help you succeed, I'd be a coward to stay back."

Rob tugged on my arm, his eyes begging me to reconsider, just as a perfect gentleman should. But underneath I could tell he wanted me to come. I had the information he needed, and he hungered for it.

I pulled out of his grip. "I'll be fine. Just let me get cleaned up a little."

"I'm afraid I didn't bring extra clothes this time," Xia said, eyeing my torn dress.

"That's OK," I said, stooping to pull the bag she'd given me the day before out from under the couch. "I never had a chance to take these back to the Castillo."

I went into the bathroom where I tried not to shudder at my appearance. I looked like someone who'd been lost in the jungle for weeks—bits of foliage were stuck in my hair, scratches and dirt lined my face, and my wrists had purple rings from where they'd been tied together. I scrubbed my hands and face and did my best to weave my tangled hair back into its braids.

When I was clean, I changed into a simple tee shirt and cargo pants then went to rejoin the others.

"Tey," said Rob as we rode the elevator down. "Nina and Antonio are some of the most dangerous guns in the history of the Coterie. They're not gonna go down easy."

"I know the risks," I said. "If there's the smallest chance I might make a difference, I want to help."

"She's got a right," said Damion. "Nina and Antonio aren't gonna let her off just because she got away. If we don't get to them first, they'll be coming after her."

"Damion, you don't need to give her extra worries right now," said Rob, pressing a hand against his temple.

"She should know. She needs to be cautious."

"Thank you," I said. "At least someone isn't treating me like a child."

"Just promise me," said Rob, "if there's even a hint of danger, you'll forget the three of us and start running as fast as you can."

"I'm not stupid. I was planning on doing that anyway," I said.

We got on the bikes and rode toward the jungle. I scanned the foliage as we coasted by, looking for any sign of Santos. Now I was back on the road, terror settled in. Santos could surprise us, or a spy could be warning Nina right now. Every fluttering bird and every falling stick became a gunshot in my mind. I grasped Rob's waist tighter.

"Tey," he said. "I can't breathe."

Heat filled my face and I loosened my grip. "Sorry."

"Your hands are shaking. Are you OK?"

"Yeah, fine." But I wasn't really, and the truth must have shown on my face.

Rob put his feet down and skidded to a stop. "That's it. I'm taking you back."

"No, there's no time. And I'm all right. Promise."

He turned to look at me, face inches from my own. "Tell me honestly. Are you OK?"

"Yes," I said, lifting my eyes to meet his gaze. I held it for a moment, heart skipping around in my chest, then pushed on his shoulders. "Now hurry. Damion and Xia are waiting for us up ahead."

We caught up and everyone continued to follow my directions. We finally reached Santos's wrecked car and surrounded the vehicle. Damion motioned with his gun to the ruined tire.

"Nice work," he said, flashing his white teeth at me. "That was an impressive shot!"

Rob signaled for Damion to keep his voice down. He drew his gun and motioned at the car. Xia flung open the door, revealing an empty back seat. The shadowborn boy was gone, which meant he had either escaped, or Santos had come back for him. I couldn't decide which was better.

"We should steal the gas," said Damion. "Bet this thing has at least six gallons left. We could make a quick three hundred."

"Let's worry about that later," said Rob. "Tey, show us where you entered the jungle."

"Already found it," said Xia, motioning to an obvious opening in the jungle's thick underbrush. "She wasn't exactly discreet."

My path was easy to follow. I'd pretty much torn apart everything in my way. We quickly identified my footprints as well as the large ones made by Santos's squeaky black shoes. There was a third pair, smaller than Santos's and barefooted. The shadowborn boy. We found where Antonio's footprints backtracked to his car to retrieve him, and then where they returned with his injured companion.

We continued to follow their tracks until the jungle opened to the streets of Cosmar. They had made it all the way to the city and could be anywhere.

"We'll take a vote," said Rob. "We can keep going, see if

anyone saw Santos and try to get a lead, or we can go after Nina. My gut tells me Santos kept to the shadows and has made it to a Coterie safe house by now. He'd be stupid to stay in the open with a shadowborn in tow."

Damion wiped sweat off his brow. "Agreed. We have a more reliable lead on Nina. Let's strike before she realizes we're on her scent."

"We better go fast then," said Xia, fingers caressing her gun. "Once she finds out Tey escaped, she'll make a run for it. She has to assume Tey will give away her location."

"On that note," said Rob, turning back on the way we'd come. "Let's move."

CHAPTER 18

The late afternoon sun was strong by the time we reached the mine, and I was grateful for the tree cover. Sweat covered every inch of my body, and the humidity was so thick I could see it.

We hid on a tree-covered hill as we examined the entrance. A large metal door now blocked the mine with several No Trespassing signs plastered over the front.

"Do you think it's locked?" Damion whispered.

"Since when were locked doors a problem?" Xia asked, brandishing her gun.

Rob leaned over my shoulder and spoke into my ear. "Did you see anyone else inside?"

"Just Nina and Sammy. But I was only in the entrance; there might have been more people deeper in."

"Let's shoot down the door and be done with it," said Damion, tensing Pricilla and Antoinette until they looked hard enough to crack walnuts.

"It's too risky," Rob said. "Things may have changed since Tey was there."

"We didn't pass any other cars," said Damion. "And we know Nina likes to work alone."

"Doesn't mean she can always afford that luxury."

Xia rubbed her eyes. "So, are we just going to wait here all day until someone shows up?"

"Maybe," said Rob, "unless you have a better idea."

"We should send Tey down there," said Xia, and I turned to look at her in surprise. "She could pretend to beg Nina for help. That'll force Nina to open the door so we can see what we're up against."

"Absolutely not!" Rob shook his head and gave Xia an incredulous look.

"Actually, it's a pretty good idea," Damion said. "Nina will recognize Tey's voice, and she would be stupid to kill her."

"Exactly," said Xia. "She's kept her alive this long. She must have a plan for her. Tey's worth money, and Nina's way too greedy to let that go to waste."

I pushed back the fear in my voice with the same technique I'd used to disguise stage fright during school plays. "As long as you guys have my back, I say it's worth a shot."

"No," said Rob. "Too many things could go wrong."

Xia frowned. "If we don't act fast, Nina will find a way to slip through our fingers. She always does. You know that better than anyone, Rob."

"We'd be feeding Tey to the wolves." Rob turned to me. "You're insane for wanting to go along with this."

I nodded. "Probably. But maybe that's a good thing." It felt so good to be needed that for a moment, my fear was forgotten as I stood and started walking down the hill.

"Wait!" Rob rushed after me and yanked my wrist. "There's gotta be another way."

"As I see it," I said, "the mine has only one entrance." I was proud of myself for keeping my voice so steady. All those acting summer camps were finally paying off.

Rob made a sound of pure frustration. "If you get hurt…if you get killed…"

"Then you'll have one less mouth to feed," I said, twisting my arm away from him. "And like Damion and Xia said, there's no way Nina's going to kill me. I'm valuable. This is our best chance."

He let me go, eyes watching me like a caged puppy as I walked down the hill.

Acid burned my stomach when I tried the door. It was indeed locked, leaving me with one option. I knocked hard.

"Nina!" I called. "Mr. Santos crashed his car and sent me to get help. I think his leg's broken." There was no response, so I kept going. "Please, we wrecked in the middle of nowhere. I don't know where else to go."

I knocked again and this time heard the metallic scraping sound of a bolt being pulled from the inside. I braced for impact.

The door cracked opened to reveal Sammy's confused face.

"Tey? What are you doing here, girl?" He opened the door wider.

I gave a little sob. "Please, is Nina, here? I'm turning myself in. It's better than dying in the jungle."

"She's here, but she won't be happy to see you."

"Got that right," said Nina, stepping into the shaft of sunlight shining through the open door. She poked her head outside and then withdrew. "Who came with you?"

"I'm alone, I swear. We crashed. I came to get help—"

Her arm locked around me and she pulled me inside the entrance. I felt the cold barrel of a gun against my temple. "You have potential, hon, but you've a long way to go before you're an A-list actor. I know those new clothes didn't come from Antonio's glove box."

She pushed me out the door and into the open. "You better come out," she called into the trees. "This girl has caused me more trouble than she's worth. I won't hesitate to blow her head off."

I could hear cursing from the bushes and the whispers of an argument. Slowly, Rob emerged, hands in the air. "No need to panic. Can we talk this out?"

She looked past him, into the jungle. "All of you!"

Rob turned, nodding to where Xia and Damion were hiding. They came down the hill and out into the open, weapons in hand.

"Put your guns down," said Nina, digging her gun deeper into the side of my head. I winced and Rob frowned. "Now!"

Three guns fell to the ground.

"Step away and get inside the mine," she said, pulling me back so there'd be room for them to get through. One by one, they walked inside.

Sammy slid the door closed and locked it behind him. "I keep running into you people," he said. "I should have killed you when I had the chance." He raised his gun. "Better late than never."

"Wait," said Nina, pushing me forward. "Take her." She handed me over to Sammy, and he restrained me with both arms. I tried to duck out of his grip, but he held firm, squeezing the breath from my diaphragm. His gun rammed into the back of my neck.

Nina studied Rob's team with an amused expression. She approached Damion, fingers tickling his exposed arms. "Be a shame to kill this one before we've had some fun."

"Looks like you'll be getting your wish after all," Rob whispered to Damion.

"Not funny," grunted Xia.

"Shoot the others," said Nina. "The fewer bounty hunters in Cosmar, the better."

"We prefer to be called fugitive recovery agents," Rob said.

"Bounty hunter sounds a little Wild West, don't you think?"

"Keep your mouth shut," said Sammy, removing his gun from my neck and pointing it at Rob. I clawed at his arm, doing all I could to ruin his aim, but he just gripped me tighter. He closed one eye as his finger moved to the trigger.

"Hang on," said Nina, pulling his wrist down. "I'll do it. Ricky says I'm going soft. You can be my witness to the contrary."

She lifted her pistol and pointed it at Rob's forehead. She hesitated and then lowered her aim to his chest. "Wouldn't want to mar that pretty face," she explained.

"You don't want to mar any of him," said Damion. "Trust me. He's worth more than you and I put together, but only undamaged."

Nina snorted. "Nice try, hot sauce."

"He's telling the truth," said Xia. "Most of us got into the business because of the bounties on our heads. Rob's no exception."

I didn't hear anything else. Heart pounding, I dug my nails into Sammy's arm and yanked it forward so his gun was angled at his foot. He struggled, finger still on the trigger as his other arm tightened around my neck.

There was no way I could get the gun through force, but that didn't matter. I focused all my effort on reaching his trigger finger. When I found it, I pushed down. The gun went off and Sammy yelped as a bullet shot into his foot. He dropped the weapon and fell to one knee, releasing me as pain weakened him. I lunged for the gun, but Nina swung around, her pistol aimed at my chest.

"I don't want to kill you, Tey," she said. "But if you think for a second you can save your friends—"

Damion tackled her to the ground, getting his arm around

her neck while Rob and Xia searched for potential weapons. Damion smiled wide at Nina. "You're a lot softer than I imagined. It's nice."

Nina twisted in Damion's grip and pinned his arm to the ground. She must have hit a nerve because he cried out in pain and immediately released her. She leaped to her feet, shielding her escape down the narrow mine tunnel with gunfire. Everyone ducked for cover and covered their ears from the sounds of the deafening gunshots that were amplified by the rock walls.

I grabbed Sammy's gun and took aim. I knew Rob needed Nina alive to get the full bounty so I pointed the gun at her leg.

Someone grabbed me from behind, hands latching around my throat.

"Give me the gun," Sammy hissed in my ear as his fingers squeezed harder.

I couldn't breathe. Black spots swam in front of my vision, but I held the gun tight and tried to get my finger on the trigger.

Xia ran to me and reached for the gun. "Allow me," she said.

I relaxed my hand and the weapon slipped through my sweaty palm into hers.

"You try anything and I'll snap her neck," howled Sammy.

Xia's lips tightened. Before Sammy could react, she raised the gun and shot him in the head.

His fingers went limp as he fell back. Xia grabbed me to keep me from tumbling on top of him as I sucked in air, coughing and fingering my throat. I didn't look back as Sammy's body slid to the floor. The last thing I needed was that image haunting my dreams. Instead, I fell to my knees, gaping at Xia.

Unperturbed, she ran after Nina.

Nina bolted deeper into the mine, shooting backward. I dropped to the ground and crawled behind an outcropping of rock, but Xia fired after her, bullets missing and ricocheting off the cavern walls.

The echoing shots tapered off as Nina disappeared into the tunnel.

"Oh no you don't," said Rob, jumping up from where he'd taken shelter behind a barrel. He grabbed a lantern from the wall and ran after Nina.

CHAPTER 19

Forgotten, I hung back as Xia, Damion, and Rob vanished into the darkness.

I pressed into the cavern wall and let the cold stone chill my body. Sammy's corpse was visible from the corner of my eye. I couldn't stay there alone with that. I couldn't stay and wait for someone else to die.

Looking down the mine, I watched Rob's bouncing light get smaller and smaller. My area seemed to grow darker the more alone I became. Something flickered on the edge of my vision and I turned sharply but found nothing there. My recent trauma had me jumping at shadows. I looked back down the tunnel and this time had to muffle a cry. There was the girl from the photograph on the wall of the Castillo. She was standing there, smiling at me.

I sucked in a breath and closed my eyes. She was gone when I reopened them, but as I stared down that dark tunnel, my skin tingled with thousands of pinpricks. Shadows danced on the walls around me, and when I glanced back at the opening, I thought I heard a soft clanging sound. Were more Coterie members coming? Would they find me all alone here? But no one was there.

The walls seemed unsteady as I took a few steps into the tunnel, and paranoia swelled inside my chest. It had finally happened; I'd gone completely crazy. I took a few more steps, then my walk turned into a run. Soon I was deep inside the mine.

I inhaled, but the air was as heavy as liquid, and I couldn't get a full breath. I heard tittering voices around me, too quiet for me to make out any words, like hearing voices through walls.

As quietly as I could, I ran to catch up with Rob and his team who had slowed to a walk. No one said anything. Even Rob seemed too focused on the single path ahead to notice me, or maybe something else was distracting him. His face was tight, and the lantern rattled in his hand like a jar of nails. Maybe he heard the voices too.

Next to me, Xia's head twitched from side to side. She blinked much too rapidly and hugged her arms around her trembling body.

I nearly tripped over her when she collapsed to the ground and curled into a fetal position. Her hands clamped over her ears and she muttered indecipherable words, adding her voice to the ones in the walls.

Damion kneeled beside her and leaned close. "Xi? What's the matter? Saints, talk to me, girl."

"I feel it too," said Rob. "Something's not right. I keep seeing things that can't be real." He prodded the bump on his head, as if it could be the reason.

"Yeah, no kidding," said Damion, looking around, his brow furrowed. "Maybe we should get outta here. This is doing nothing for my claustrophobia."

"Not when we're this close," Rob said through clenched teeth. His left hand curled into a fist. "Let's keep going."

"But what about her?" Damion motioned to the still muttering Xia.

"We'll come back for her." Rob unwound Xia's fingers from

Sammy's gun and shoved it into his pocket. It was the only weapon we had, and we'd need it if we caught up with our target. He grabbed Damion's arm and hefted him to his feet. "Come on; we have to keep moving."

"Wait," said Damion. "Let me take her outside. I don't feel right leaving her alone without a weapon, and—like this."

"No time," Rob hissed. He clenched his eyes shut for a moment and rubbed them hard. "I need you. And if there are any other Coterie in here, they'll be deeper in. She's safer than any of us."

Damion pulled back, arms sagging as we continued deeper underground. "Hang in there, Xi," he called over his shoulder. "We'll nab that bitch and be back before you miss us. I promise."

Because of the danger, I should have volunteered to stay with Xia. But now the team was down by one, and something about the way Xia muttered to herself sent chills down my spine. I was glad Rob didn't forbid me from following.

"What kind of mine is this?" I asked, flinching as my voice echoed back in loud reverberations.

Damion looked back at me, acknowledging my presence for the first time. "Whatever it is, I'm not sure I can handle much more of it." He took a shaking breath, eyes darting. "Saints and angels, Rob, you know what happens when I stay in enclosed places too long!"

"Just a little longer, Damion," said Rob, holding up the gun he'd taken from Xia and clenching it hard to keep it from falling out of his trembling hand.

I expected the air to grow colder the deeper we went. Instead, it heated up. Fresh sweat broke across my forehead and trickled down my cheeks like tears.

Finally, after the longest half hour of my life, we came to

an enormous opening. Below was a deep cavern surrounded by several mincarts and illuminated by a silvery glow. The air vibrated like I was inside a subwoofer, and every time my arm brushed against someone, there was a shock of static electricity.

Rob went to one of the minecarts and picked out a lopsided stone. It had a silver color, but with a rainbow sheen, like opal or mother of pearl. It reminded me of the strange rocks I'd seen in the warehouse where Ricky and Nina had kidnapped me. "Solidified Earthblood," he said, dropping it like a hot potato. "That explains the hallucinations."

"What is it?" I asked.

"A rare metal native to Los Sueños."

"Is it radioactive or something?"

"We don't know," said Damion. "No one can survive long enough to study it, let alone mine it."

I flinched at his words, suddenly wishing I'd stayed back.

Rob squeezed his eyes shut. "Prolonged exposure is known to cause delirium, madness, even death."

I nodded, remembering the dizzying pressure I'd felt when entering Nina and Ricky's warehouse in LA.

"Seems like Nina is managing just fine," said Damion, sweat streaming down his face.

The sound of gunfire brought me back to reality. A bullet whizzed by Rob, nicking the side of his ear and ricocheting off the wall behind him. I saw Nina crouch behind a metal crate, gun arched against the side. Rob advanced, firing warning shots, but Nina had the advantage. She was shooting to kill, while Rob only wanted to wound her.

Creeping forward, Rob motioned for Damion to get on Nina's other side while he distracted her.

"You're outnumbered," Rob called out to her. "If you drop

your gun, I won't hurt you." He dashed to another minecart and pushed it forward, using it as a shield while Nina continued to fire.

Damion shoved me behind the first minecart, then bent low and scurried to Rob's side.

With no other weapons available, I picked up one of the earthblood rocks and flinched as a shock went through my skin. The rock was warm and heavy, and I could have sworn it vibrated. The mark under my collarbone ached as the memory of being cornered in Ricky's warehouse flashed through my mind. I stood up and hurled the rock at Nina. Sparks flew as it struck the steel crate in front of her, sending Nina jumping back. She ducked and sprinted into a metal lift next to the wide cavern in the ground. Getting inside, she pulled a lever and the contraption dropped with the squeal of old pulleys.

Rob didn't waste any time. He ran after her and jumped onto the roof of the lift. Damion joined him, surprisingly agile for all his bulk, and landed with a thunk.

I didn't hesitate either. I had no gun, but three people would look more intimidating than two. Whether I could help or not, I had to try. And I didn't want to get left alone in this horrible place.

Heart skipping in my chest, I ran forward. The lift was a couple of meters below me, illuminated by the silvery glow from the cavern floor. I leaped and hit the metal roof hard, smacking into Rob, who clung to the edges the way a cat clings to a tree trunk.

"You shouldn't have followed," he said through clenched teeth. "I can't afford to watch out for you, Tey. Not when I'm this close."

"Then don't," I said, focusing all my efforts on not falling off. Rob and Damion seemed to be having more trouble than me. Their heads drooped and their shoulders quivered like they felt sick.

The lift jerked to an abrupt halt, nearly throwing the three of us off. On the floor of the cavern was a pool of what looked like liquid opals. I knew it was a liquefied version of the earthblood rocks. I felt heat radiating from it, even from my distance.

Rob fell flat on his stomach, gun pointed down.

With the screech of metal, Nina forced open the door of the lift and darted out before Rob could react. Rob's movements were much slower than normal, and I was afraid he was going to pass out, but Nina was still quick.

"Maybe frequent exposure made Nina immune," said Damion, perplexed.

I looked at the pool that was the cause of their weakness, and my mind grasped for something it knew to be true but hadn't formed yet into an idea I could compute. Then it hit me. "She knew we'd be at our most vulnerable down here. It's a trap."

Rob nodded, face pinched. "We have one gun, but there are three of us, so we still have the advantage."

We slid off the lift. When we hit the ground, Damion's knees gave out and he toppled to the rough earth. He clasped his hands around his middle and puked. I thought Rob might do the same; instead, he stumbled forward with the limp of a zombie.

My chest continued to throb in the spot where Ricky and Nina's strange weapon had struck me, but I didn't feel nearly as bad as Damion and Rob looked, or even how I had felt when I entered the secret warehouse in LA. Perhaps getting hit by that weapon had done something to me that made me more resistant.

"Rob, give me the gun," I said.

"Stay back, Tey," he demanded through gritted teeth. As he walked, he swatted nonexistent insects out of his way.

I wanted to run to him, but Nina was directly in his path, and I had nothing to protect myself from her bullets.

Nina let Rob come to her as she caught her breath, her face all too confident. When he was close enough for her to get a direct hit, she raised her gun. I screamed for Rob to fire, but his trembling fingers couldn't find the trigger. Nina pulled her trigger instead.

Click. Click. Click.

Her face tightened into a feline growl at the realization that her cylinder was empty.

Rob kept trying to bring his gun up, but his hand quivered so badly it was a wonder he was still holding it.

Nina threw her gun. It hit Rob in the wrist and his weapon fell to the ground, skittering behind him. He made no attempt to retrieve it. Instead, he fell onto Nina and pinned her to the ground. He tried to hold her arms down with his greater weight, but she sent a knee sharply into his stomach before he could close the gap between them.

Crying out, I tried to go to him, but my chest flared with a pain so awful that I stumbled to the ground.

Breath knocked out, Rob loosened his grip, allowing Nina to twist away and leap to her feet. He sluggishly reached for her legs, but she was too fast. She kicked him in the side of the head, knocking him onto his back. Her foot didn't stop there. It came forward again, this time bashing into his chest, then his side, then his stomach.

Rob groaned in pain and made another grab for Nina's leg. She tripped, shuddering as she hit the ground. Rob split open her lip with his fist, then fell back to catch his breath, weakened by the violent movement. Nina took the opportunity to descend on him once more.

Scrambling to my knees, I looked over at Damion. He was slumped against the cavern wall, only semi-conscious and babbling at shadows. He'd be no help here.

To my right was a large manual crane secured through a looped rope. When operational, the crane was set to pivot over the pool, probably to extract the strange fluid. The arm was low to the ground, its head only a few paces away from me. Ignoring the grunts and cries from Nina and Rob's struggle, I put one trembling hand in front of the other.

By the time I reached the head of the crane, the pain in my chest had died to a dull ache that throbbed with each heartbeat. I grasped onto the arm and pulled myself to a standing position. Clinging to the arm, I worked my way to where the head was secured against the cavern wall.

Next to the pool, Nina reached for Rob's gun and grasped it. Rob kicked her in the leg, but she only stumbled a little before catching herself and pointing the weapon at his chest. Her lips curled into a smile of triumph.

Taking a deep breath, I lifted the crane out of the loop and pushed it toward Nina.

It swung forward way faster than I expected, as if its pivot had been freshly oiled. Nina didn't have time to duck as it swooshed toward her. If she had been just a little shorter, it might have decapitated her. Instead, it struck her upper back with a crack.

Her scream echoed off the cavern walls as she was flung into the pool.

CHAPTER 20

Breathing hard, I forced myself to remain standing, half relieved, half horrified.

The pool bubbled where Nina had fallen in. The liquid inside looked as thick as molten metal. Rob lifted his head and blinked groggily in its iridescent light.

Using the arm of the crane as my support, I walked toward him. We needed to get out of this mine before it killed us. Or drove us completely crazy.

Rob struggled to his knees, but before he could get up, Nina's hand shot out of the pool and grabbed the edge. Her head followed and she gasped for a breath of air. Her hair and skin were covered in the silvery liquid, but despite the heat radiating from the pool, she didn't appear burned.

"Rob, watch out!" I cried.

He woke up a little. Scrambling backward, he looked around for the gun, but it had gone with Nina into the pool.

Nina dragged herself onto the gravelly ground, but she made no move to attack. Her body shook violently, eyes wide, limbs flailing.

"Pale faces, there!" she screamed. "Get away. It's all wrong!" Her eyes closed and her head twitched back and forth. Drool dripped down her chin. "So much blood, you poor wounded thing." The earthblood slid off her in heavy droplets, leaving her completely dry. It amalgamated around her body, then glided back into the pool like mercury on a slope.

I reached Rob's side and helped him stand. Dark circles ringed his eyes and an enormous bruise was forming on his cheek. "Help me," he said, only managing a rasp. "We need to take her away."

Slowly, I bent over Nina and reached out to her. Her hand clamped down on my wrist.

"Tey, Tey, Tey," she chanted my name with wide, hollow eyes. "You have to stay, stay, stay. You have to—"

"Why?" I shouted at her, the heat of my emotions overwhelming my exhaustion.

She looked toward the pool, then back at me, her face the face of a small child. "She wants to find you!"

"Who?"

Nina focused on something over my shoulder and took shuddering breaths. "They're coming back! No, no! Get away!" She batted at things in the air that weren't there.

I wanted to kick her, to punish her for bringing me here, but then I felt Rob's hand on my shoulder.

"Let's get her out of here," he said, reaching for her hand.

Together we lifted Nina's arms around our shoulders. Step by step, we dragged her away. She continued to shake and wail, and gave no signs that she even recognized me anymore.

Rob opened the lift grate and we dumped Nina inside, then went to retrieve Damion who struggled weakly and shouted something about the walls caving in. When we were all on board, I pulled the lever and the lift went up.

By the time we reached the top, Rob and Damion seemed a little stronger.

We found Xia slumped against the tunnel wall. Her lids were closed, and she breathed rapidly. Damion picked her up and carried her the rest of the way to the exit.

Rob and I continued to drag Nina, who kept spouting off nonsense. At one moment she locked eyes on me, and I wondered if there was still a spark of her old self somewhere deep inside. "This is wrong," she said. "You have no idea what you're doing; what's going to happen here!"

"What do you mean?"

"Help! The pale faces are everywhere. Everywhere."

"Will she recover?" I asked Rob.

"Doubtful," he said. "No one has walked away from a full submersion in earthblood with their mind intact. The stuff gets into your pores and goes inside of you. She'll only get worse as it eats away at her brain."

I shuddered.

When we made it outside, I felt a shift in the air, like a weight was lifted off me.

Next to me, Rob stood straighter and wiped sweat from his forehead. Whatever that earthblood stuff was, I hoped I'd never need to get near it again.

Xia's eyes shot open and she was suddenly lucid. "Ouch! Put me down." She pounded her fists against Damion's back until he set her on the ground. She looked around and frowned. "You caught Nina? What happened?"

"You were just a little more sensitive to earthblood than the rest of us," said Damion, stretching his arms above his head. "But it's all good; Tey covered for you."

I gaped at his casual tone. After what had just happened, I could barely get my mouth to work at all.

"And she rocked it!" he said, cuffing me in the shoulder. "Saints and angels, I don't know what we'd have done without you."

Xia's lips tightened and I focused on trying to keep blood from filling my cheeks.

"I think whatever Nina's weapon did to me in LA made me more resistant than most people. When I first encountered earthblood I could barely stay conscious."

Rob furrowed his brow. "Interesting theory. I wish I could have seen the weapon. If that's what it was."

"What else could it be?"

He shrugged. "I guess we won't know now." His eyes pivoted to Nina who continued to babble. Each of her eyes looked in a different direction.

Nina's power was gone, but Ricky was still out there, and who knew what he intended to do with that thing.

We hiked back to the road without speaking. I guess no one was in the mood to recount the fact we'd all almost died. But back at our bike, Rob whispered into my ear, "thank you."

"For what?"

"Saving my life."

I looked up into his face, some of the tension leaving me. "Still wish I'd stayed behind?"

"Definitely. But I am grateful to be alive."

Despite my exhaustion, I smiled.

* * *

It was night when Rob and I returned to the Castillo, but a few lights came from the upstairs rooms and foyer, which meant we were lucky enough to have temporary electricity.

My head floated above my body. The events from the last three days hadn't happened. They had to be a dream. A hallucination. Any minute I was going to wake up at my mom's house to the squawk of my alarm.

Children surrounded Rob and me as we went through the door, faces searching us for food.

No luck, kids.

Rob stopped to engage them but I just floated by, feeling no more substantial than a ghost.

When I made it to the bathroom, I was relieved to find that the water was working. The shower was freezing cold, but I welcomed the shock of it against my skin as a reminder that everything that had just happened had been real. I huddled in the tub and let the water pound against my back until it shut off with a stuttering finality.

Afterward, I went to my room and curled under the rotting canopy of my bed. The sounds of the jungle filled my mind. I'd spent my entire childhood wishing I could escape my mom. Now I wondered if she had filed a missing person report yet. Or if she had even realized I was gone. There was pressure behind my eyes, like the buildup of tears. I blinked, willing them to overflow, but they didn't. Instead, the hurt sank deeper, burying itself in the pit of my stomach.

Someone knocked on my door, interrupting my thoughts.

I got out of bed, legs shaking as I walked to the door and pulled it open. There was Lei, dressed in an oversized tee-shirt, hair messy from sleep.

"Lei," I said, relieved at the distraction. "Are you OK?"

She shook her head and looked at the floor.

"What's wrong?"

"Bad dream," she muttered.

I sighed and held out my hand. "Wanna come in?"

She nodded, still not looking at me.

I guided her into my room and was surprised when she climbed into my bed and lay down. I sat on the edge of the bed but she pulled back the blankets and scooted to one side so there was room for me to join her. Gingerly, I lay down beside her. Lei huddled close and I drew the covers over both of us.

"What was your dream about?" I whispered, wrapping an arm around her thin shoulders.

She shivered but didn't answer me, and I didn't press her further. She had no idea she was comforting me too.

I continued to hold her until we both fell asleep.

CHAPTER 21

When I opened my eyes, Lei's warm body was still curled next to mine. I slipped out from under the covers and tucked the blankets back around her.

I changed into another one of the outfits Xia had given me and padded downstairs, hoping I could forage for breakfast. I passed the dining room and stopped. There was Rob in his usual spot, cutting fruit for a few whining kids I was sure I hadn't seen before. He looked tired, and there were dark bruises around both eyes.

He caught my gaze and held it before I could look away.

"You're up early," I said.

"After yesterday, I couldn't sleep. I went for a ride across the bridge to Santa Arcadia. I even did some walking about the island, but then I got spotted by a few of the lepers. They fired some shots into the air to scare me and I took off quickly. I needed to come back to feed these tyrants anyway." His knife whopped against the table as it sliced through a thick giagon. He handed slices to grubby hands, and children took off, guarding their portions. He held out a piece in my direction. "Want some?"

I took it gingerly and leaned against the wall, not eating.

He set the fruit down and steadied himself on the table. "Everything that happened, I'm so sorry. If I could go back in time, I'd never have let you come to the Adder, I—"

"Rob, it was my choice and I don't regret it. I'm glad I could do something."

"I was hoping you would say that," he said with a weary half-smile. "I want you to know, you're one of the bravest girls I've ever met. If you agree, I would like you to join my team as an official Agency trainee."

I met his eyes, stunned. Me, become a member of the Agency? I'd helped Rob get one bounty, but could I handle more missions?

"Most prospective agents have to pass a test and then an initiation period before we even let them enter training. It's very selective. But you've already proven yourself. Without you, we'd have never captured Nina. We'd probably all be dead. With my reference, Corpus will waive the niceties."

"Rob—" I started and then cleared my throat. "I don't think I can." I felt that if I joined his team, I'd be accepting my fate. I'd be stuck in Los Sueños in a job. A very unusual job, granted, but I'd still be working to earn a living instead of spending my time trying to find a way out of this mess. And now that Nina was behind bars, I never wanted to put myself in another dangerous situation again.

"Just think about it, OK?" he asked, drawing closer to me.

I held still.

He coughed. "You probably don't feel ready, and you'd have to work really hard, but after what I saw, I know you have it in you to become one of our best agents."

I hugged my middle. "Wouldn't you want someone more experienced? I've done nothing really until—"

"Nothing? You escaped from Antonio Santos. You led us to Nina's mine and were brave enough to get us inside. The earthblood was driving us all to the brink, and you still found a way to take out Nina. You think fast, and outside the box.

We need someone like that."

He was almost close enough to touch me. I felt goose-bumps cobble my skin, but resisted the urge to back away. I shook my head. "I'm not sure."

He sighed. "I know you could use the money. It can be temporary, and in the meantime, you have my word that I'll do whatever I can to help you find a way back to California."

I squinted, looking for any sign of a charade. His face was as honest-looking as ever, but that didn't mean he wasn't a good pretender.

"Take your time to decide. I have to get to the Agency, but I'm sure the kids would love your company for the day."

I nodded.

"One more thing," he said, pushing a thick envelope into my hand.

I lifted my eyes. "What's this?"

"Your portion of Nina's bounty. It's only a trainee's sum, but I spoke with Xia and Damion when we dropped off Nina. We all agreed you earned it." He walked past me toward the door. As he pulled it open, he faced me one last time. "Who knows? Maybe with enough bounties, you'll get the money you need to get home on your own. Even the impossible can be achieved at the right price." He winked and closed the door behind him.

I stared into the envelope. There had to be at least a few thousand dollars inside. It was more money than I'd ever owned in my life.

A small hand grabbed the end of my shirt. Lei. I hadn't heard her come down the stairs.

"Are you gonna marry Rob?" she asked just as a group of other kids invaded the dining room in search of leftovers. They all turned to me at the question.

I snorted. "No. I barely know him."

Blank stares.

"A lot of things have to happen before you marry some-one."

Lei's face drooped. "Like what?"

"Like dating for a long time, falling in love."

"I'd like it if you and Rob fell in love."

I could see why. Lei saw Rob as a father figure. Now she wanted to add a mother to the picture. The thought almost made me cry. I exhaled loudly and pulled away from her grip, not looking at her hopeful face. I couldn't get attached. I wouldn't. I didn't want anything keeping me here.

I sat at the table and nibbled a scrap of leftover fruit. The other children eyed me suspiciously. This was the first time I'd been here without Rob, and they didn't know how to react to me on my own. I smiled at them, but they just stared back.

Feeling awkward, I decided to move on. I hadn't even seen the whole Castillo yet, and had the entire day ahead of me to mull over Rob's offer. My chair squeaked as I pushed it back.

"Where are you going?" asked a familiar Japanese boy who was probably nine or ten. I remembered Rob calling him Ichiro.

"Thought I'd do some exploring," I said. "Unless one of you wants to give me a tour?"

Ichiro gave an adult sigh. "I'll do it," he said, like I'd just suggested he wash dishes. "Come on."

Lei clung to me as I followed Ichiro down an empty wing on the ground floor. The other children tagged along, skipping ahead and making ghostly hollers down the dark hall to creep out the younger kids. The power was off again, but sections of dappled sunlight came through the windows to light our way in long dust-filled patches.

Ichiro opened a wooden door at the end of the hall, releasing a burst of cool air and a moldy smell. A staircase led from the opening into pitch darkness.

"Down there's the cellar," he said. "There's lots of weird junk stored there, and it's pretty creepy. I wouldn't go down there unless the lights are working." He shut the door.

Toward the back of the house was an enormous porch. Once surrounded by glass panels that now lay broken all around it, it was covered in dried leaves and overgrown plants. Just beyond were the remains of an old aviary with dozens of empty cages overrun by flowering vines.

There were multiple kitchens. One that looked like it came from the 1990s, but from the state it was in, I guessed it hadn't been used since the Castillo's original owners had taken off.

The other kitchen looked like it came straight from a Victorian drama. It was filled with dirty pots and pans, crumbs, and bowls of fruit. A few other children stood inside, pawing through cupboards.

"How come you don't use the other one?" I asked Ichiro, thinking the more modern conveniences would be a draw.

"We tried before," said the boy, "but the power kept going off before we were done cooking. It got really annoying. This one has a stove that uses fire." He motioned to a cast-iron stove against the wall. "There's a water pump too. Rob got it going. You have to work at it, but it saves us a trip to the stream."

Our next stop was the library.

"Prepare yourself," said Ichiro. "It's the dirtiest room in the Castillo."

"Not as dirty as your room," piped in Lei.

"Shut up." He swung open the door.

A moldy smell assaulted my nose, mixed with the comforting aroma of old leather. Books were scattered over the floor and along dusty shelves.

"See, there's no glass left in the windows," said Ichiro. "Dirt and dried leaves have gotten everywhere." He pointed to the brown foliage scattered across the floor.

I was about to pull one of the books from the shelf when Ichiro tugged on my arm. "Do you want to finish this tour or not?"

I drew my hand away and made a mental note to return on a book raid when I was alone. "All right," I sighed. "Lead the way, captain."

Ichiro knew which room belonged to each child and said their names as we walked past numerous doors on all five floors. The upper level contained mostly old servant's quarters, and the floor was so creaky I was sometimes worried it would cave in. In the northern wing, I opened a door leading to a small spiral staircase. Ichiro pulled back my arm before I could see where it led.

"Don't go up there," he said.

I laughed in surprise. "Why not?"

"That's the north tower. It's haunted. Everybody knows it."

"Are you sure?" I asked, smiling despite myself. No mansion was complete without a haunted tower.

He nodded. "Keno used to sleep there until the ghosts chased him out. He was so afraid he ran into the jungle and we never saw him again."

"Just like Malia," said Lei.

"Who's Malia?" I asked.

Ichiro gave Lei a look. "She disappeared five days ago. Rodney before her."

"Did the ghost chase them away?" asked Lei.

Ichiro motioned for her to be quiet. "It could have been anything. Maybe they just didn't like us anymore. But I wouldn't push your luck with those ghosts."

I stuck my head into the stairwell. "Hello?" I cried. "Any ghosts up there?" I paused to listen, then turned to Ichiro and Lei. "If there are, they're being pretty secretive." I took a step onto the staircase, but Lei gripped my hand so hard it hurt.

"Please don't go up there," she wailed.

I laughed and unwound her fingers. "Listen. It'll be fine. I just want to take a look. You guys can wait for me here."

She shook her head over and over again.

"They're just ghosts, Lei. They can't hurt me. They're probably getting lonely up there. If I don't say hello, they might wander downstairs for some company." Her eyes widened and she released me.

"Just go fast, OK?" said Ichiro.

"Can you count?"

"I can count to ten."

"Good. Count to ten, ten times. I'll be back before you're done."

He started to count out loud and I hurried through the door.

The winding staircase led to a large circular room with an enormous bed in the middle. There was a fireplace to the left of the entrance, and a little door next to it leading to a small bathroom, complete with one of those porcelain tubs with feet. Long lacy curtains covered a window that still had all its glass intact and offered a remarkable view of the distant ocean.

There was nothing creepy at all about the room. In fact, I'd say it was the most desirable room in the whole Castillo. Whatever kid made up the ghost story must have done so to have it all to himself, which wasn't a bad idea.

I went back down the staircase, interrupting Ichiro's counting.

He and Lei paled when they saw me. "See anything?" Ichiro asked.

"You're right," I said, closing the door behind me. "The room is full of ghosts. But they said they'd be happy there as long as I promised to visit every once in a while." I was fine with the bedroom I already had, but it might be nice to have another area of the Castillo where no one could find me, including Rob.

"Did you promise?" asked Lei, her crescent-moon eyes wide.

"Of course. I don't want them haunting the rest of the house."

They both smiled in relief.

As I let Ichiro lead me to another part of the Castillo, I pushed all thoughts of Rob and the Agency and home into a small corner of my mind. There was a strange new place to explore and two small friends to show it to me. No one was holding a knife to my neck or shooting bullets in my direction. I was safe here.

But for how long?

CHAPTER 22

After the tour came to an end, I decided to do a more extensive search of the kitchen to see if there was any food. The cupboards were picked bare except for a can of black beans that had expired three years ago. Some of the kids flitted around me, hoping I could solve this problem. Others talked about sending someone to scout for fruit in the jungle.

"Stay here," I told them. "And stay away from the jungle. I'm going shopping."

In an instant, they started shouting out requests and begging me to bring them each back something specific.

I assured them that if they were patient, I'd purchase enough food for everyone. Pocketing my bounty money, I headed to the wharf.

The afternoon was hot and sticky. Half a mile into my walk, my clothes were damp with sweat. I'd have to wash them in the stream when I got back, and I mentally added laundry detergent to my growing shopping list.

With a breeze blowing off the ocean, the wharf was cooler, but it smelled fishier than usual. Everywhere, people had decorated their food stands with colorful streamers and banners. Men and women strummed on mandolins and guitars. Others played violins and tiny trumpets. Most were dressed in bright colorful clothing and there were signs all over the place featuring a fatherly man with a neat beard and military uniform. I wondered if the festive mood had something to do with him.

Examining food stands, I was floored by how expensive everything was. I stopped short when I saw an apple with a five-dollar sticker on it. Five dollars for one apple! I was grateful they used American dollars in Cosmar, but clearly, inflation had gotten out of hand. Or perhaps the ridiculous prices had to do with the rarity of imported goods.

I was examining a stand filled with multicolored loaves of dyed bread when a small girl in a leather cap brushed my arm. Her touch was so light I barely felt it when her hand went into my pocket and removed the envelope of cash. I looked over just in time to see her dash through the crowd with the speed of a cat.

"Hey! Stop!" I bolted after her, pushing people aside to keep the girl in view. No one responded to my calls of "thief!" Most barely spared me a glance.

Heart in my throat, I followed her into the skids. As soon as I broke free of the crowds, I pushed myself to a sprint.

The girl glanced back and saw I was gaining on her. She picked up her pace and didn't slow as her cap flew off. Shimmering silver hair spilled out behind her.

A shadowborn!

My stomach lurched as I remembered what Rob had said about them. The really scary ones can stop your heart with the wave of a hand.

Sweat dripped into my eyes. I couldn't let her take that money. I needed it for the kids. I needed it for me.

The alley came to a dead end and the girl stopped. She spun around and stood against the wall, lungs heaving.

Gotcha.

I curled my fingers, ready to pounce. "I'm not going to hurt you," I said. "I just need that envelope back."

Her huge blue eyes only stared at me, and I wondered for a moment if she even understood. No matter. She was probably only twelve years old. As long as she didn't pull any voodoo tricks on me I'd be able to take her out, easy.

As I closed in, the shadows from the sides of the alley darkened and started moving. They flowed onto the road like streams of fog and crept closer to the girl.

Heart hammering, I stopped in my tracks and squinted at the darkness that seemed unusually dense. The shadows rose off the ground, shielding the girl with a black vapor. I took a couple of steps back, my skin cold.

The shadows rose as tall as the buildings on either side of me. They grew, thick as liquid, and came at me. I tried to run, but they moved too fast. Just before the specters could touch me, they collapsed like waves on the shore. I shielded my face as bits of them splattered inky remnants across the road and then writhed back to their proper positions, fading to their normal hues.

When I drew my arms away from my face, everything had returned to normal. Except the girl was gone.

I blinked rapidly. The whole incident felt like one of the hallucinations I'd had while aboard La Ventura. But my envelope of money was still gone, and now I was alone in the skids, which had to be the worst slum I'd ever seen. The garbage-strewn streets were mostly formed of packed dirt. Stray cats prowled everywhere, and apartments were ramshackle hovels stacked over each other. The overpowering smell of sewage made the rotten-fish stench of the wharf seem like a breath of fresh mountain air.

I picked my way around the alley for a few more minutes, but the girl didn't reappear and I saw no sign she'd ever been there, nor how she could have escaped.

I wandered back to the wharf, stomping on my heart with every step. There was no way I could go back to the Castillo and tell all those kids I didn't have their food. They'd never understand, and would never forgive me. Stupid, rotten luck.

I found myself leaning on the rail of La Ventura's dock. Would the ship be making its illegal journey back to California anytime soon? I wished I could climb aboard now and disappear beyond the horizon. But that was impossible.

Even the impossible can be achieved at the right price.

Rob's words rang in my mind. He once mentioned I'd need about twenty thousand dollars to bribe a sailor for their spot on a ship. My trainee's sum for one bounty had cashed in at around three thousand dollars. With enough successful missions, maybe it wouldn't take so long to save the money I needed to escape from this island prison forever.

Right now, I had no better option. Turning toward the road, I started for the Agency.

"This is it, Tey," I whispered to myself as I strove to harness my inner Domino Harvey. "The role of a lifetime." Slipping into the skin of a bounty hunter wasn't exactly something I'd practiced before, but when I put it in acting terms, the prospect became an exciting challenge.

The act would be short-lived, but I'd make sure I'd be remembered for it.

CHAPTER 23

When I arrived at the Agency, Rob's office was empty. I collapsed onto the leather couch and decided to wait. Etched across the blackboard was a web outlining how each of the top Coterie chiefs connected to the other and which connections had been severed now that Nina and Gheisari were out of the picture.

At the center was Ricardo Santos with a line drawn to connect him to Antonio Santos, his cousin and right-hand man. The circle around Antonio's name had been drawn in blue chalk. The only other color on the board.

I must have dozed, because the next thing I knew, Rob and his team were bursting through the door, restraining the same shadowborn girl that had stolen my money.

"Tey?" Rob, said, drawing back. "Sorry, I didn't expect you to be here." He adjusted his grip on the struggling girl's arms and forced her into a chair. Bringing her hands around the back, he secured her wrists with handcuffs.

The small girl growled like a feral cat and pulled wildly at her restraints. She gave me a dark look of recognition.

I went to her, anger buzzing through me. "Where is it?" I demanded.

The girl looked away.

"Don't act stupid. Tell me what you did with it!"

Rob pulled me back. "Whoa, whoa. What are you talking

about?"

"My money!" I cried. "She stole it in the wharf."

"Saints and angels," cursed Damion. He rifled in his pocket and pulled out a thick envelope. "So much for a free handout." He threw the envelope on the table with a plop.

I picked it up, relief washing over me like warm water.

"You should know better than to take all your money with you," Rob said. "Cosmar's a skeevy place."

"I shouldn't know anything. This isn't my home. I'm trying to get off this demented island, remember?"

Rob nodded apologetically and the focus turned back on the girl. Xia crouched down and looked her in the eyes. "What's your name?"

The girl stared back, defiant and silent.

"You better start talking—"

"It's no use, Xia," said Rob, a hand on her shoulder. "None of them know their real names, remember? We don't know if they ever had real names. And that's not what we're here to find out."

He bent close to the girl, his eyes two melancholy pools. "I know you're angry. It's not fair what's happened to you and what's going to happen to you. I'm sorry, but it's for the best. Things won't get worse if you just tell me what your ability is. I don't think you're dangerous or you'd have hurt us already, but you could have a useful talent."

She glared at him. Her mouth was a firm line and she made no move to open it.

"I saw her do something with shadows," I said.

The girl's eyes pivoted toward me, daring me to say more.

Rob leaned forward and his brown eyes widened in hope.

I took a breath. "I cornered her in an alley, but before I could grab her the shadows rose off the ground and shielded her escape. The whole thing looked totally crazy, like I was on drugs or something."

"That's a new one," said Damion, the corner of his mouth rising in a half-smile. "I can see Harrington liking it."

"No kidding," Rob said. He tilted his head to one side as he focused on the girl. "Let's go pay the old man a visit, shall we?" He stood up. "Tey, you're probably tired. You can rest here as long as you want before heading back to the Castillo."

"No, I'm coming with you," I said. "I'm on the team now. I came here to tell you that." I felt something rush through me when I said it, but couldn't tell if it was fear or pride.

His smile was so genuine I had to look away to keep myself from blushing. "That's great, Tey. Glad to have you on board."

Damion gave me a hearty pat on the back. "You're an official trainee now. Lucky girl."

"I wouldn't call my being here, lucky," I said. "If I was back home, this would be my last choice for a career."

Rob gave me a hard look. A look that said he was my boss now. "You're not home. You're here. The other agents have worked hard to get to where they are. If they hear how fast I took you on when you didn't even want it, they might take their concerns to Mr. Corpus."

I looked down. "I understand."

His face softened. "Just be careful, OK?"

I nodded, feeling the brush of his hand against mine as he walked to his prisoner.

"Where are we taking her?" I asked.

He paused, turning. "Somewhere you'd best get familiar with in case you cross paths with another one of these… darling children. Oh, and while we're there, we're not Agency members. Turning in shadowborn to the Coterie is open to the public, but if they ever found out who we worked for, they'd kill us on the spot."

His tone was so casual that he made the threat sound like it was perfectly normal. No big deal. Just a fact of life.

Prisoner in tow, we left the Agency and rode to the skids. On the way, I felt identical chills race down the backs of my arms as I eyed the girl and remembered what she could do. But as her blue eyes met mine, I found myself thinking of the injured boy I'd shared Santos's car with. Was I helping to sentence this girl to his same fate? A fate I'd nearly succumbed to myself? I shook the thought away and followed as Damion led the girl off his bike and toward a small concrete building. There was a symbol of a skull skewered by a trident over the door, and a call box next to it. Rob pressed a button and a robotic voice squawked.

"PLEASE ENTER PASSWORD. PLEASE ENTER PASSWORD"

It continued to repeat the phrase until Rob typed something into the keypad. "For future reference, the password is OPERATION421," he told me.

There was a click and the door opened. Inside, a dark hall ended in a utility elevator. Rob pressed the down button and we stepped inside. Xia and Damion clung to each arm of the shadowborn girl as the elevator door closed and we dropped.

I focused on the floor, noting how the fuzzy outlines of our shadows swayed, even though we stood still. I looked up, wondering if the overhead light was swinging, but it was built into the ceiling.

With a jolt, I turned to the girl. Rob's shadow rose from the floor and flowed up the wall, blotting out the light and plunging the elevator into darkness.

The girl screamed and I could hear the sounds of a struggle.

"Don't let her scare you," shouted Rob. "Hold her tight!"

The door opened, flooding the elevator with fluorescent light. I could see that Xia's and Damion's shadows were now disconnected and swarming around the girl like two mad crows. The shadows then latched onto Xia and Damion and surged up their bodies until they reached their faces. Darkness covered their eyes.

They cried out, and each took one hand off the girl to claw at the formless specters that blinded them.

Rob bent low and lifted the girl by the ankles, holding her upside down. She writhed and screamed as her pale face filled with blood.

"Stop it, now," he cried. "Let them go." He shook her, eyes hot with anger.

I looked down at my shadow, surprised to find that it was the only one still properly attached. Maybe our confrontation in the street had convinced her to leave me alone.

The girl's lungs heaved as she kept struggling. The shadows came at Rob, but he continued to grip her ankles, ignoring the dark film that crept over his eyes.

Her breaths slowed and her face turned beet red. Little by little, the shadows retreated until they returned to their proper places on the floor. Rob held her for another minute, then swung her right side up. She swayed, and Damion and Xia moved in to steady her. The girl's head drooped in defeat, and she didn't resist when they forced her to walk forward.

"I knew we should have given her a Supplicant injection," said Damion.

"Those drugs are expensive," said Rob. "We need to save our store for the big guns." He turned to me. "We surrounded this little scamp in public. She put up quite an impressive fight, but never once moved a shadow. Maybe she needed time to regain her strength after using her abilities on you."

We were in an underground cement hall with low hanging lights. It smelled like metal and the temperature felt twenty degrees cooler than outside. Our footsteps echoed off the walls as we walked.

I kept my eyes on my shadow, not noticing when our scenery changed until I stumbled into a cluttered table and knocked off a box filled with cosmetics. Brand names caught my eye as the items scattered across the floor. Dior. Estee Lauder. MAC. Clinique.

I looked up. The hall had opened to a large open area that resembled the warehouse of a superstore. Random items were stacked everywhere, some laid on tables, others still packed in boxes. Workers dressed in gray jumpsuits sorted through them, distributing them into crates. Their labels caught my eye. Flour. Sugar. Books. Alcohol. Cigarettes. Hair Products. Accessories. All things I was used to seeing daily back home. Valuables here.

My arm brushed some American Apparel cardigans hanging from a rack. They smelled like they'd come straight from a mall, an odor so normal that a wave of homesickness washed over me.

"This is where most illegal imports end up," Rob whispered, examining a box full of electronics. "Shopkeepers have special access to the warehouse and can buy goods they're interested in before the Coterie sells to the general public."

Another inhale brought a whiff of gasoline. I turned my head and saw several large barrels against the wall. I remembered how much Rob had told me each gallon was worth.

"I may be a monarchist," said Rob, "but if there's one thing everyone disagrees with, it's the king's ban on imports. This might be the only good thing about the Coterie."

We entered a connecting hall lined with black doors. One of them had the number 421 in gold paint on the front. Rob knocked, and after an uncomfortable wait, a scraggly man with a balding head opened the door. Height-wise, the man only came to my shoulder and used a cane to support his pronounced limp.

"Rob Stryker is it?" he said in a wheezing voice as he squinted at Rob.

"Harrington! You remembered me this time," said Rob.

"Yes, well, I'd be hard-pressed not to remember the boy who turned in three of the most valuable shadowborn I've ever sold."

I looked at Rob in disbelief, and the reality of what we were doing froze my veins. I searched Rob's face for a trace of guilt, anything to suggest that he regretted what he was about to do, but his face remained impassive, relaxed even.

"Please come in," said Harrington. He coughed as he led the way inside.

The room resembled an antique office similar to the ones at the Agency, except for one strange element. To one side was a chain hanging from the ceiling in front of a padded wall.

Harrington looked over the shadowborn girl. "So this is your newest offering?" He took hold of the girl's chin and turned her head one way and then the other. "She looks healthy enough, but the real question is what can she do?"

"She appears to have the ability to manipulate darkness," said Rob. "We all saw it back there in the elevator. She had some of us blinded by our own shadows."

"Blinded by shadows? I've never heard of such a thing."

"Must be new," said Rob. "My guess is she recently gained awareness. Tey, tell Mr. Harrington what you saw her do earlier today."

I repeated what had happened when I cornered the girl in the alley.

"Well," said Harrington, "that is something special. Could be useful in the event of a quick getaway, or if cover was needed. It's the quiet abilities that are often the most valuable. I will of course have to see proof before we can discuss a price."

"I wouldn't expect otherwise," said Rob.

"Very good; you know what to do." He motioned to the long chain hanging from the ceiling.

My mouth dropped open. They weren't…surely they couldn't consider…

Xia and Damion brought the girl's arms over her head and fastened her handcuffs to the end. She pulled at her bonds, breathing hard.

"Show the man what you can do," Rob said to her. "Please. Then you won't have to get hurt." His voice was so gentle.

The girl hung her head, saying nothing. But her eyes sparkled with unshed tears.

Harrington rolled up his sleeves. "You're right. She must have just gained awareness. Coterie runaways are much more submissive."

He twisted off the bottom of his cane to reveal a sharp metal point, and then circled the girl. "Let me introduce you to my friend. He doesn't like it when little girls don't do what they're told."

A gasp escaped my throat. I stepped forward, but Xia yanked me back with unexpected strength. "It has to be this way," she said.

Harrington touched the point to the girl's arm and her screams deafened me.

CHAPTER 24

Blue zaps shot out of the metal point, each one sending a jolt of electricity through the girl's small frame.

"Stop!" I wailed, but Xia clamped a hand over my mouth.

"Be quiet," she whispered in my ear. "Harrington has to like us, or he'll screw us over."

Harrington stepped back and nodded at Rob. The girl sobbed. Her body looked so frail, her face very young.

"Now that you know the consequences of not complying, I would advise you to make a show of your ability before my friend gets angry again," the old man said.

The girl continued to shake but made no other move.

Harrington raised his cane. "He's getting angry!"

I struggled against Xia, but she held firm. Rob joined her, his voice soft. "Stay calm. This is the only way."

"It's just pain," said Xia, like it was no big deal. "It's not like it's actually damaging her."

When the girl made no move to comply, Harrington stepped up to her and pressed the cane tip against her arm once more. The chain rattled as her screams filled the room. I plugged my ears and shut my eyes. I knew I should hear this. Should watch. If I was joining Rob's team, I needed to understand the consequences that came with it. But this was too much.

The cane struck her again and again. I should never have

lashed out in anger against her. On the street, she would have needed my money way more than I ever did. And as terrible as her life would still have been, at least she wouldn't have to experience this torture. Agonizing minutes passed until the edges of Harrington's shadow quivered. The entire shadow peeled off the floor and stood erect before its owner like a specter, completely obscuring the girl.

Harrington dropped his cane in surprise, then smiled wide. "Good. Very good. You can dismiss the shadow now, my dear, I've seen enough." The shadow liquefied and splattered onto the floor where it wriggled back to normal.

The girl's expression was one of pure hatred, a look that had no place on such a young face.

Harrington turned to Rob. "How about five thousand?"

Rob's eyes narrowed. "Five thousand?"

"She's a bit scrawny."

"They're all scrawny," said Rob, "and I'm not leaving here without fifteen."

"She lacks discipline and submissiveness. I can't sell one like that for more than eight thousand."

"You said yourself she has a new power. That alone makes her worth at least twelve."

"Alright, ten thousand. But you'll be sending me to a pauper's grave."

Rob considered this for a moment. "Add five hundred to that and you've got yourself a deal, old man."

"Insolent whelp. Fine, ten thousand five hundred it is. But don't expect any more favors from me. I'll no doubt die of poverty before you come to me again." Harrington limped to his desk and wrote out a check for the money. "Don't spend it all in one place."

Rob laughed. "The faster I spend, the sooner you'll be seeing my charming face again with another hostage. You're not fooling anyone; I know you'll be counting down the days until our next business transaction."

Harrington waved his hand. "Fine. Fine. Then be sensible and buy yourself a van so you can ferry me a dozen at once. The more shadowborn we have off the streets and put to use, the better our city will be." He unhooked the girl's handcuffs from the chain.

Rob's eyes shone with a determined gleam, and for a split second, he seemed desperate. "You're right about that, old man."

He turned and put his arm around Damion and me, instantly snapping back to normal. "Well done, team. Shall we head out?" He reached toward Xia to add her to the group, but she pulled away, arms crossed. I would have done the same, but his arm was too firmly around me, urging me toward the door.

As we filed out, I glanced back for just a moment. Harrington took the girl through another door in the back of the office. I couldn't see what was beyond it, but there was a look of terror on the girl's face when she turned to look back. She caught my eye, and the coldness in her gaze made me feel like all of this was somehow my fault.

I held my breath, but my anger with Rob smoldered hotter with every step.

As soon as we were off the premises, I pulled on his arm. "How could you let that man do those things? How could you just stand there and watch like it didn't matter? She's only a child!" I grasped for more words, but all that came out were short pants of breath.

Rob stopped walking and grabbed both my arms. "Tey, I need you to listen to me. No matter what happened in there, no matter how bad it was, it's over. And now that girl is better off."

I took a step back, wriggling out of his grip. "Better off? She's being sold as a slave to criminals just like I was."

"It's better than getting executed by the kingsguard, or living on the street where she'd have no choice but to rob people, as you found out today."

"You let orphans live in the Castillo, why not shadow—"

He held up a hand. "Let me finish. Shadowborn don't remember their pasts. They just wake up one day, what we call gaining awareness. They're lost and confused and they don't know who they are, or how they got to be there. It makes them violent. They steal from people and hurt them with their abilities. Often, they hurt themselves because they don't know how to control their powers. I hate the Coterie, but they know how to take care of them, and they're the only ones who can guarantee their protection. Harrington won't cause any lasting harm to that girl. An unhealthy shadowborn won't sell, and most guns don't seriously damage things they paid thousands of dollars for."

I thought of the boy in Nina's mine. Santos hadn't hesitated in beating him unconscious.

"Turning them in is a kindness for everyone," he continued, "and most don't resist like she did. The mere threat of pain will compel the majority to reveal their abilities without a fuss. She was different."

He made a good argument, but I still couldn't erase the image of the girl's shrieking face.

He raised my chin with one finger. "I need you to be on my side and to be OK with this. It's part of what we do as a team. We're trying to make this city a safer place."

I managed a weak nod, but I couldn't meet his gaze.

"Enough moping already," said Damion. "This is making me seriously depressed. We need to celebrate Tey's first day as a trainee. What do you guys think?" His burly arm wrapped around me. "Should we give her the regular initiation celebration?"

Rob's face went slack. "I think Tey's had enough excitement for one day. She's probably exhausted and sick of us three morons."

My mouth tightened. Who was he to tell me what I'd had enough of? I was a team member now; I wouldn't be treated like a weakling. "Actually, I have more energy than I know what to do with." It was true. My mind was fighting a war against itself. I wanted to find a solution to what had just happened, but this was no quick fix. Rob's way really was the only thing we could do without some serious government intervention, and I wouldn't be in Cosmar long enough to have time to instigate that.

"That's what I like to hear!" said Damion. "Did you know that it's King Alden's birthday today? It's a national holiday and there's supposed to be a killer celebration in the city center tonight. Lots of food, drinks, fireworks. Could be fun."

So that's why everyone in the wharf was in such a festive mood. "Will the king be there?"

"Doubtful. The guy hardly ever leaves Santa Isidore where all the royals live safe and sound away from the mass murders and criminal rampages of the Coterie. But every island has its own celebration for his big day." He gave Rob a strange glance. "What do you say, Rob?"

Rob looked somber. "The festivities can get pretty wild."

"That's the whole point!" said Damion. "It's the one time of the year we get to say, 'King Alden, you might be a pretty detached monarch, but if nothing else, you've given us this great party to forget for a few hours how much our lives suck.'"

Despite everything that had happened since encountering Rob and his team, the thought was strangely appealing. I couldn't trust myself to be alone with my thoughts. I didn't just long for a distraction, I needed one. Maybe loud music and a whirlwind of bodies would be enough to erase the nightmare images in my head.

Rob looked at me uncomfortably. "I'm still not sure that's a good idea—"

"It sounds great," I said.

"Ya-yeah!" Damion said, giving me a nudge. "We can finally show Tey that this archipelago isn't just a scary hellhole. She might even grow attached to it."

"Fine. I'm in too," said Xia. "As long as we don't have to work at the same time."

Rob shrugged. "All right. You want to go to the festival, we'll go to the festival. But it will just be the four of us, and we won't stay late. We've got a lot of work to get started on in the morning."

* * *

Back at the Agency, after fingerprints and paperwork were out of the way, Rob presented me with my new trainee ID badge. Now I wouldn't be arrested if the kingsguard caught me going after bounties in areas typically off-limits to civilians.

With the official stuff complete, we still had a few hours before the festival was in full swing. Rob and I opted to return to the Castillo to change, and I asked him to stop by the wharf for groceries on our way home. Ever since my morning shopping excursion had come to an abrupt end, I was eager to bring the kids the food I'd promised them. I picked out everything I could find from the list the orphans had given me, and Rob insisted on buying it all, refusing to let me contribute a cent. "You've got more important things to save for," he told me as he stowed the groceries in the trunk on the back of his bike.

The anger I'd felt toward him went down a few notches at that remark. I was about to mount the bike behind him when a sound from a darkened doorway caught my attention. I took in a breath as an all-too-familiar silver-haired boy materialized on the stoop, his eyes two blue lights in the shadows.

My first thought was gladness that he was OK, but that soon turned to fear when I saw what he carried. A gun: it was pointed at me.

Rob gripped my arm. "Stay calm," he whispered to me. He eased himself off the bike and held his free hand out in front of him to show the boy he meant no harm.

The boy looked down at himself, face a mask of shock. Perhaps he expected to still be invisible. His eyes turned on Rob and me again, and he gritted his teeth, gun held out with both hands. I knew at once that Antonio had sent him to find me and kill me.

"It's OK," I started to say, but Rob cut me off.

"Don't come any closer," he said, stepping in front of me and reaching for his gun.

"I know him," I whispered to Rob. "He belongs to Antonio."

"Just stay behind me," Rob said through clenched teeth. He took a step toward the boy. "Put your weapon down and I won't hurt you," he said.

The boy didn't move.

"Did your master put you up to this?" Rob took another

step. "I can help you get away from him." He took another step, and the boy fired a warning shot at the ground. The bullet hit the cobblestones right in front of Rob's feet. Rob flinched and stopped in his tracks.

The boy vanished.

Rob looked in every direction. "What the—"

I heard a banging sound and looked to see the boy flickering back into focus and scrambling up the fire escape of a brick apartment building.

"There!" Rob pointed. "Let's go." He took my hand and pulled me toward the building. He scaled the fire escape before I could get my foot on the second rung of the flimsy ladder.

We had to climb up five stories before we reached the roof, by the time I'd hauled myself over the top, the boy was way ahead of us. Rob waited for me, but I could tell by his restless feet, how impatient he felt.

On the roof, he dropped to a crouch behind a compressor unit and pulled me down with him to watch in secret. The boy glanced back. He did not seem aware that we had followed him. We watched as he moved to the connecting roof on a bridge made from narrow boards. When he reached the other side, Rob got to his feet and we followed at a safe distance across several more roofs.

We stayed hidden. Soon the boy slowed his pace and looked over his shoulder again. Rob motioned for me to hold still. When the boy didn't see anyone, he fastened a rope to a metal rail and rappelled down.

"That's right," Rob muttered. "Show us your hideout."

We crawled closer and peered over the edge.

The boy made it to the first landing of the fire escape and lowered himself down one more level. From there, he forced open a window and ducked inside.

A light turned on and I could see two silhouettes through lacy curtains. One was the boy, the other a big man. They conversed for a few minutes and then something the boy said made the man roar with anger. His fist smashed into the side of the boy's head. I heard a cry and the boy dropped to the ground.

The half-open window leaked a booming voice. "You stupid little waif. Do you know what happens to shadowborn who fail?" I recognized that voice.

"It's Antonio," I whispered to Rob.

Antonio's foot stomped onto the boy's chest. "I gave you a simple task and you threw away your opportunity. I don't give second chances." He kicked hard. Then kicked again.

My skin heated up. I moved forward, anger surging through me.

Rob grabbed my shoulder and pulled back. "What are you doing?"

"We have to stop him!" I said, my voice louder than I intended.

His mouth tightened. "Do you want to get killed? We can't stop this. Not right this minute. But now that we know where the rat nest is, we can bring the others here. Then Antonio will be ours."

I hesitated, staring at the window, every cell vibrating with hatred.

Rob wrapped his arm around me and pulled my head away. "Come on. Don't watch."

CHAPTER 25

A long time passed before the screams from the room went silent.

I sat, hugging my knees, while Rob dangled his feet from the edge of the roof.

"We need to stay and monitor this place," he said, "and make sure Antonio doesn't leave before we can get to him." His eyes burned as he stared at the apartment. "We were supposed to meet Xia and Damion at eight. I'll have to go tell them what happened when the time gets closer. Then they can join us for the fun part. Until then, we stand guard."

I scooted closer to him, but Rob leaned the other way. He seemed to be keeping as much space between the two of us as possible, as though shying away from my stiff mood. After what had happened today with the shadowborn girl, I should have been happy about that, but one hesitant glance from him melted something inside me. He wasn't a bad person. He was doing the best he could to make a difference in this messed up place. And now that I was a team member, maybe we could develop a better solution: together.

He pulled a small pair of binoculars from his jacket and focused on the window. After shutting the window all the way, Antonio had dragged the boy from the room, but the light was still on, and now and then, silhouettes walked by.

"See anything?" I asked.

"A bedroom. Nothing out of the ordinary."

I looked toward the street and spotted a dark shape coming out the front door. "Someone's leaving," I said, pointing.

Rob's binoculars pivoted down. "It's not him."

"You sure?"

"Yeah. It's a woman. See?" He handed me the binoculars and I saw he was right.

"We need to keep track of everyone who comes and goes," he said. "If Santos is here, chances are there are others. He took out a notepad and scribbled a brief description of the woman.

In the following hours, the temperature continued to drop. It was the first time I'd felt cold since arriving in Cosmar.

I closed the gap between us and pressed my shoulder into his. He radiated heat, and my body itched to be wrapped up in that warmth. It told me I'd be safe there. It was a liar. I'd never be safe with him. I'd never be safe with anyone in this city. I just needed to keep that in the back of my mind always, regardless of the magnetism I felt toward Rob.

He drew away, just an inch, but I followed in closer. His arm came up, then went down again like he wanted to touch me but was afraid. He probably thought I was still angry with him. I was, yet I still found myself putting my hand on his shoulder.

Rob took the cue. His whole body relaxed and drew me in, enveloping me in his warmth. I wrapped my other arm around him while the rest of me sank into his shirt. I was being stupid. I was giving in. But he smelled so good, like sharp mint mixed with an ocean breeze. I breathed him in, not caring that I was weak. For a moment I felt fluttering happiness, as if there was a bird in my chest that had just gotten the hang of flying.

We counted the shadows passing the window. We counted the people that came and went. Santos never made another appearance. In the distance, fireworks whistled over the city, and I could hear the roar of a faraway crowd. The king's birthday festival had begun.

"Damion won't be happy that we'll miss the party," I said.

"But he'll sure be happy when he gets his hands on Antonio's bounty," said Rob.

"So, he and Xia. What's up with them? One minute they're at each other's throats, the next…"

Rob stared back at the apartment and nodded. "They used to be engaged."

I sat up straighter, surprised. "Engaged?"

"For all his flaws, Damion's an amazing agent. If he weren't so reckless, he might be the leader of our team. But there's a reason he's so good. He was once a member of the Coterie. His knowledge of how they operate is some of the most useful intelligence the Agency has collected. But he also worked for the chief responsible for killing Xia's sisters. He was there when it happened and maybe could have stopped it, but was too afraid that they'd turn on his own family if he interfered. He kept the truth quiet for a long time. When she found out, she could never get past it."

"But they stayed on the same team?"

Rob shrugged. "They're super competitive and they knew our team was the best. Neither wanted to be the one to step down. And they're good agents. I'm not going to force anyone to leave."

"How noble of you."

"How infuriating. As much as I'd hate to lose either of them, the tension between them is so tight I'm afraid it'll snap at any moment. If it happens at the wrong time, it could cost us our lives." He brushed a hand through his hair. "As much as I love my team, I'm glad it's just the two of us here right now."

My heart leaped. Why did it keep doing that? I wanted to look away, but I was already caught in his gaze. "Me too," I said, one side of my mouth lifting.

"I'm sorry so many things have gone wrong for you, Tey; I want you to be happy. You remind me of my old life. Things were easier in the states and I want Los Sueños to be like that. So much needs fixing here. I wish there was something I could do to make it right."

"You are doing something," I said. "You're doing something right now."

He smiled, one cheek dimpling. "I know. But for every Coterie gun we take in, another will rise to claim their spot. No matter how hard we try, we can't ever win, Tey."

"Then why do you keep trying?"

He looked toward the window. "Because I have to. I keep telling myself, one day Rob, one day you're gonna find a hole in their wall. You're gonna weaken them long enough to lead the grand charge that will bring them to their knees. Could even start a war."

"Is war what you want?"

"If it would bring about their end."

"Why do I get the feeling there's something else?"

His eyes twinkled. "Getting rid of the Coterie won't fix all this country's problems. It might make things worse for a while. I'd like to go a step further."

"You think you can fix the government?"

He sighed. "I may be a monarchist, but anyone can see that the current monarchy is a joke. King Alden is nothing more than a descendant of the world's biggest play-actor. It's all a game to him, just like Los Sueños was a game to the first people who came here."

"What do you mean?"

"The government the first king established was just an excuse to play at being royalty. Nothing practical. That's what attracted pirates to Los Sueños. It was somewhere they could get away with anything they wanted with little fear of the law. They formed a pirate brotherhood, which eventually became known as the Coterie, and there was little the king or the men he'd gathered as his protectors could do to stop them and their criminal acts. King Alden isn't any different. He was born to the throne but has no real interest in liberating Los Sueños. All he wants is to keep it hidden so other countries won't try to take it from him."

"So you think you could do better?"

"I know I could do better. I have so many ideas. I just need to stop the Coterie first. But some days it feels impossible."

"If anyone can take out the Coterie, it's you. Look at who you've already captured."

Rob's fingers brushed my shoulder. "I had a lot of help. But thanks for your faith in me."

I looked away from him. Away from those brown eyes. He touched my face, sliding one finger along my jaw. Chills ran down the backs of my arms and I hugged my shoulders tighter.

"What's wrong?" he asked. "Are you scared of me?"

"Maybe," I whispered, my heart rising into my throat. But I leaned closer to him anyway, turning my face upward.

He laughed. "Don't be."

And then he was kissing me, warm lips moving over my cold ones, breath tasting of wild berries and mint tea. It felt so natural that I barely registered it was my first kiss. All I could think was how much I didn't want it to end.

CHAPTER 26

Twenty minutes before eight, Rob left to meet up with Xia and Damion, and return to the Agency for supplies. I was supposed to wait on the roof and continue to watch in case Antonio decided to hightail it while he was gone.

My whole body buzzed like I'd had too much caffeine, but whether that was from nerves at the prospect of my first mission as a full-fledged member of Rob's team, or a side effect of Rob's kiss, I wasn't sure.

I'd never had a boyfriend before. All of the men my mom brought home ended up either cheating on her or leeching what little money she had, so the idea of a real relationship had never been a priority for me. Even with Rob, there were things I didn't agree with or understand, but even though we were about to head into a life-threatening situation, being around him made me feel safe, and needed. He wasn't a child like the obnoxious guys I went to school with. He was older, more experienced, and so much stronger than any guy who had ever captured my attention in the past, and for one strange moment, I felt an unfamiliar pang in my chest. It took me a moment before I identified what the feeling was. Fear that I was going to lose him.

A clatter drew my attention to the opposite side of the roof, and for a moment I wondered if the shadowborn boy had awoken from Antonio's beating and had returned to complete his mission. I looked around for a place to hide, but then Damion's muscular form clambered over the edge, followed closely by Xia, then Rob.

Damion grinned when he saw me. "Did ya miss me?"

I turned down my bottom lip. "Terribly. Sorry we won't make the party tonight."

He looked off in the distance to where fireworks were still whistling to the accompaniment of music and far off shouts of merriment, and shrugged. "When we get our hands on Antonio's bounty, we'll be able to pay for an even bigger party—on our own private island."

"Well that gives me something to look forward to," I said.

"This is a far better initiation celebration if you ask me," said Xia. She smirked at me in a way that sent a cold wind sweeping through my chest. "Trial by fire."

"Tey's gonna do great," said Rob. He handed me a gun belt with several small pockets for things like my ID badge, a tiny first aid kit, and extra bullet cartridges. A small loop held a collapsible flashlight and canteen. Rob gave me a heavy black gun that I fitted into the holster at my side.

"Don't get too excited," he said. "It's only a stun gun. We used to have blockier models with neon colors to distinguish them from real firearms, but Mr. Corpus paid quite a sum to a weapons technician to redesign them. Now they look real enough that they might even fool a Coterie chief. They're also much more powerful than any similar self-defense mechanism on the market and have a greater range. Pull the trigger and they shoot out metal tacks containing a concentrated pulse of electricity. They're all you get until I train you how to shoot a real gun."

Rob fiddled in his belt pouch. "The stun gun should incapacitate your opponent long enough to inject him with this."

He handed me a small syringe. "This is called Supplicant. It's a new drug derived from a root found only in Los Sueños. It makes people loopy and open to suggestion. It affects everyone a little differently, but they usually do just about anything you say. Remember, Antonio is much more valuable alive. The kingsguard like to interrogate the Coterie before they execute them. Little good it does. Most Coterie chiefs are trained to withstand any amount of torture, but those roosters still like to try."

I lifted my eyebrows. "Roosters?"

"It's what we like to call the kingsguard because of their ridiculous red jackets. At the Agency, we're much more sensible." He reached into a backpack he'd picked up from the office and took out a black hoodie and pulled it over his shirt. He brought up the hood, shadowing his face so only dark angles showed. There was a black jacket for me, and a beanie, which covered my braided crown. I imagined that I looked like a burglar.

Once outfitted, Rob motioned with his chin to the apartment building. "See anything since I left?"

"There's been little change," I reported. "Five people left the building and two entered, none of which were Antonio. So unless there's a hidden back door, it's likely our man's still inside."

Rob handed syringes of Supplicant to everyone. "All right, here's my plan. Thirty minutes after the lights go out, we move in. The window's closed all the way. If we can't pry it open, we'll have to break the glass. But quietly; it will be a lot easier to take out Antonio if he's asleep. Once we're in there, we'll split and spread out until one of us spots our guy. Stun anyone you come across. When Antonio's location is found, we'll regroup and move in as a team for safety."

"How will we know when to regroup?" I asked.

Rob handed me a small black button. "This is called a locator. If you spot Antonio, push down. It will send us all an alert and lead us to you by flashing a red light. The flash intervals get faster the closer you get to the one who clicked first."

I pocketed the locator and nodded.

His gaze darkened. "Are you ready?"

I nodded, throat dry and tight. "I guess so. I just wish we had a better plan. Storming the castle doesn't seem like the safest approach."

"We're not storming, we're sneaking. Everyone will be asleep. Hopefully. And we like to refer to Coterie hideouts as rat nests, not castles."

I eyed him sideways. "I hate rats."

He laughed. "Good, then the name evokes the right emotion."

"I don't see why we have to go in at all. Can't we just wait and nab him the minute he sets foot outside?"

"This is Antonio Santos we're talking about. He's second only to Ricardo. We need any advantage we can get, even if that means entering his home and catching him while he's asleep. You can stay with me if you don't feel comfortable on your own. You haven't had any training yet—outside of real life. No one would blame you."

I shook my head, reaching into my pocket and gripping my black locator. "I'll be fine." I immediately regretted saying it. The last thing I wanted was to be by myself in that place. But I couldn't bring myself to take back my words. Not with Xia watching me like a cat, silently judging my every movement.

Rob squeezed my hand discretely, and then let go, eyes focused on the window.

Forty minutes later, the lights switched off.

CHAPTER 27

We peered through the window at close quarters. No one seemed to be inside but it was shut tight, and despite all our efforts, we were unable to wriggle it open. Xia made a ring of duct tape on the glass to keep it from shattering out, then put a small piece of cloth over the top to muffle the sound she was about to make. She struck the cloth with her gun and knocked a small hole through the glass, then reached in and lifted the latch. Without making a sound, she pulled the window open and waved us inside.

One by one, we crept through. The bedroom was large and had no furnishings except for an empty bed.

Rob opened the door to a dark hallway and motioned for us to go separate ways. I spotted a wide staircase leading down.

"We'll take the bedrooms," he whispered in my ear. "Antonio shouldn't be too hard to find. Go downstairs. If you see anyone there, stun them so they can't come up. It will be safer that way."

Safer. I watched as he disappeared around a corner, feeling his absence like a cold breeze. My hand went to the silvery pendant I'd found in my room and gripped it tight7.

"It's just a film set," I told myself. "It's not real." Any minute the director was going to call "cut," and I'd come back to the realization that I was surrounded by cameras and lights.

The image helped. I focused inward, my fear closing in on itself until it was a tight knot at my center. I kept it there, willing it not to spread out and overtake my whole body.

The apartment had more rooms than a large house. I took the main staircase to where it stopped two floors down and walked across a spacious black and white tiled foyer. There was a sitting room to my right with couches made of a silky material, pulled so tight, it made the furniture look rock hard. Smoke from a smoldering ashtray hovered around a dangling chandelier.

I stepped inside and froze. Sprawled on one of the uncomfortable-looking loveseats was a listless woman in a black dress. Her eyes were half-open, like she was in a smoky stupor. She straightened a bit when she spotted me but it was too late for her to scream. I stifled a cry of my own as I fired my stun gun. A tiny metal tack was released, surrounded by a blue bolt of electricity.

It struck her face.

Her whole body shook and foam collected in the corner of her mouth before she slid off the couch. She twitched once more and then her eyes closed.

I tried to get a full breath as my chest compressed tighter and tighter. I was just doing what Rob told me to do. I was keeping everyone safe.

Gun out, I searched the room for others, but it was empty.

I entered a large kitchen to my left. The light was on, but there was no one in sight. It had a back door that opened to another staircase not connected to the main one. I recalled a Victorian mansion from a school field trip that had a similar staircase so the servants could come and go unseen.

I checked my locator. Still no alerts from the rest of the team. What was taking them so long?

Curious, I crept down the stairs. They were narrow and creaked under my weight. The lower floor was pitch dark and my skin prickled with goose flesh. I took a deep breath, steadying myself against the wall.

The floor groaned, and I heard two distinct thumps in the darkness. I looked up with a small gasp. Something was moving in front of me. I scrambled for my flashlight and switched it on. The beam illuminated a cruel face.

I stifled a cry. The face belonged to an enormous man in a thick black vest. He stood in front of a door, a rifle held across his chest. I fired out of instinct, heart jumping into my throat. The electric tack hit the man's vest where the current was instantly absorbed. He ran at me, finger on the trigger as he swung the rifle up.

Falling to the ground, I flattened myself the moment he fired. Bullets buried themselves in the stairs behind me. He ran until he was nearly on top of me. I lunged forward, wrapping my arms around his boots. He tripped, but broke his fall with his muscular arms. His gun skittered out of his grip and he leaped to his feet, reaching for it.

I pointed my stun gun and fired again, this time hitting him in the throat. He stumbled against the wall and dropped like a dead fish as waves of electricity coursed through his body.

Sucking in breath after breath, I tried to stand but trembled like an old woman with palsy.

Go back upstairs. Find Rob.

I was on the first step when I stopped and looked back. The man had been guarding something—a door—and he'd been doing it in the dark, perhaps to dissuade anyone from seeing what was down those stairs. It had to be important.

I crept over to the door and pressed my ear against the cold surface, listening for any motion inside.

Except for my pounding heart, all was quiet.

My hand went to the door handle. Locked.

The man I'd zapped was still conscious, fighting his twitching limbs. I knelt beside him and pulled out my syringe of Supplicant. I stuck the needle in his shoulder and pushed down, emptying the drug into his muscle.

His eyes took on a glazed look.

I leaned close, remembering what Rob had said Supplicant could do to someone. "What's behind the door?" I asked.

He tried to speak, but couldn't form the words, probably because of spasms in his throat muscles from where I'd hit him.

"Can you open the door?"

He tried to sit up, but his arms shook and he fell back. After three failed attempts, he reached into his vest and pulled out a chain of keys. With shaking fingers, he found one in particular and handed it to me.

"This will open it?" I asked.

He nodded, his breath coming out in a hiss as he tried to say something. Then he passed out.

I returned to the door and fitted the key into the lock. There was a click and the handle turned the rest of the way. I paused and checked my locator again. Still nothing.

The door was solid and metallic. I pushed it open little by little so it wouldn't make a sound. Inside was pitch dark. I let my flashlight beam illuminate the interior one item at a time. It passed across a Persian carpet and mahogany dresser, then slid up a polished bedpost and onto the figure sleeping under the covers. His body was turned toward me, face relaxed in sleep. Antonio Santos.

My muscles twitched in surprise. I had used my only Supplicant syringe on the guard, so it would be pointless to go after Santos alone, and Rob had forbidden it. I reached into my pocket for my locator and stepped back to go out the door. Before I could hit my button, automatic lights switched on in both the room and the hallway, and a warning alarm blared. Antonio sat up in bed and grabbed for the firearm on his nightstand.

I froze, the locator falling to the floor. Before I could react, Antonio's gun went off.

Fists clenching, I braced for a bullet to enter my skull. Instead, it skimmed my temple and lodged deep into the doorframe. Warm blood trickled down my head as I brought up my stun gun and pulled the trigger.

Antonio dove to the side and the blast struck his sheets with a crackling sound. Another bullet zipped by me, and I dropped to the ground, where I pawed for my locator. Antonio's foot came down on my back, pushing me to my stomach and driving the air from my lungs.

"I've been set on killing you since your little car stunt. But if I'd known you'd come straight to my bedroom, I wouldn't have wasted time looking for you." He pressed the barrel of his gun into my ear.

I squeezed my eyes shut, tears spilling down my cheeks.

I heard a voice. "Please," it said. "Please don't do this." It was my voice, but it sounded disembodied. Like I was already dead.

Antonio laughed and dug his foot harder into my back. "Please? I don't care what I paid Nina. You're not even worth one roll in the sheets." The gun moved to my temple. "Say hello to the devil for me."

Crash!

The pressure of Antonio's foot lifted. I could breathe again.

I turned around in time to see his stocky body collapse, shards of glass covering his hair. Standing over him was the shadowborn boy. The remnants of a broken vase were still clutched in one of the boy's hands.

I grabbed my locator and pushed it; a red light flashed on the front. I struggled to my feet, pointing my gun at the boy who had just saved my life. He stared back, pale eyes wide, body shaking as if I had already pulled the trigger.

"I don't want to hurt you," I said, heart still thrashing like an insane person in a straightjacket. "Why did you save me?"

He took a step back and crumpled to the floor next to his master. His eyelids fluttered, then closed as he lost consciousness.

I fell to my knees beside him. His skin was bruised from where he'd been beaten. His wrist was swollen, probably broken, and his breath rattled in his chest.

I looked over my shoulder. The others would be here soon. They'd come and see him and take him away, just like the girl who could control shadows. I couldn't let them do that. Not after what he just did.

Taking hold of him beneath the arms, I dragged him under the bed. He moaned softly in his sleep and I hoped I wasn't making any other unseen injuries worse. I slipped one of Antonio's pillows under his head and covered him with an extra blanket from the end of the bed. He started coughing violently and I cringed, hoping he'd stop before Rob arrived.

"Listen, I want to help you," I whispered under the bed. "But you need to be quiet. People are coming who will only hurt you."

I wasn't sure if the boy was awake enough to hear me, but his coughing stopped.

"Stay here," I told him. "I'll try to come back for you." I

bit my tongue as a wave of uncertainty swept through me. I couldn't help him. The whole idea was insane.

The door flew open, and I raised my gun, muscles tense. My gaze passed over Rob and Xia's bewildered faces and I lowered my hand.

"Is that Antonio?" Rob asked, pointing at the unconscious man on the ground. "Tey, you disobeyed me! What the hell were you thinking?" He bent over me, wiping blood from the side of my head where it dripped from a hole in my beanie.

"I had no choice," I said. "I triggered an alarm. I had to act fast or be killed." My heart still wouldn't slow down and my words shook.

"I can't believe you weren't," said Rob, his voice softer.

"Why is there glass in his hair?" asked Xia, squatting next to his body.

"I…I dropped my gun, so I threw a vase."

Antonio let out a groan and his eyelids flickered. Xia removed one of the syringes from her belt pouch and stuck it into his arm. He mumbled something, and his eyes came open the rest of the way.

Xia pulled on his hand. "Come on big guy. Let's get moving."

"Hello, gorgeous," said Antonio. His voice slurred as the drug took effect, suppressing all his authoritative cruelty.

"Come on," she said. "Get to your feet."

Antonio obeyed stupidly. "Anything for you, beautiful. Why does my head hurt?"

Xia put his arm around her shoulder. "You drank too much." She led him out the door.

Rob lagged behind, looking around. I prayed he wouldn't peek under the bed.

"What is it?" I asked.

He shrugged. "Just want to make sure there aren't any other valuables here. He opened and closed a dresser drawer.

The boy under the bed coughed again. I hurriedly coughed as loud as I could to cover the sound.

"You OK?" Rob asked.

"Yeah," I said, still coughing. "Must be a lot of dust in here or something. Sorry."

"Let's get you out." He put an arm around my waist and led me into the hall.

Xia stood with Antonio, waiting for further orders.

"There's just one thing I can't figure out," said Rob, head pivoting. "Where's the shadowborn boy we followed here?"

Xia looked Antonio in the eye. "Where's the kid, Toni?"

Antonio's head lolled. "Why should I care? The little waif couldn't do a damn thing right. I taught him a lesson last night, and I don't think he ever woke up again."

"There you have it," said Xia. "The last thing we need is a dead shadowborn. Now let's get out of this rat nest before the Supplicant wears off and he strangles me to death."

"Hang on," said Rob, leaning against the wall. "Damion's not here yet."

"Let the lummox catch up later," she said. "If he's too stupid to notice the alert went off, he deserves to get left behind."

"Not in a place like this," said Rob. "And this isn't like him." He took his locator out of his pocket. It was dark for a moment and then started pulsing all over again with a frantic red light.

CHAPTER 28

Rob and Xia exchanged worried glances.

"Is it supposed to shut off automatically?" I asked, glancing at my flashing locator.

Rob nodded. "It stopped when I reached you. Damion must have just pushed his button."

"Why would he do that?" Xia asked, gripping Santos's arm tighter. "We've got our man."

Rob looked up the stairwell. "Get Antonio out of here."

"I take back everything I said. I'm not leaving without Damion." The tendons in her neck stood out as she spoke.

"Xia," said Rob in a voice that sounded like a scolding father. "You don't have a choice. I need you to do this. I'm not going to let anything happen to Damion. Tey, come with me."

Xia's eyes darted between Rob and Antonio, as though unsure how to act. I gave her an apologetic glance and followed Rob upstairs.

Rob held out the blinking light as we searched the apartment, but it gave off the same steady pulse wherever we went.

"Where is that fool?" Rob muttered.

A choked cry came from upstairs. We both turned.

Rob pushed me behind him and held out his gun as we made our way up the wider staircase. His body was tense and slightly crouched. I followed, trying my best not to make a sound.

At the top, Rob stopped short and straightened against a wall. Slightly turning his head, he peered around the corner.

A door slammed shut.

I felt Rob's body flinch at the sound. He took a step forward and then another, slowly distributing his weight in a hunter's stalk.

He paused in front of the door, holding his breath. The locator blinked rapidly. He gave me one look, then turned the handle.

Rob shoved open the door and stormed into the room, gun arm outstretched. He took a breath to shout, and then released it. The room was empty. Drops of blood trailed to an open window surrounded by billowing curtains. Another cry came from outside. We ran to the window and looked out just in time to see four dark figures scramble down the last fire escape five stories below. They leaped to the ground. One of them landed badly and fell onto his hands and knees. The others pulled him up and half-dragged him to the road. His muscular silhouette was all too familiar. Damion.

"Come on," said Rob in a strained voice. One leg was already out the window.

I watched in amazement as he slid down the connecting ladders with a kind of reckless grace. I followed behind, hoping my foot didn't miss a rung in the dark. By the time I made it to the ground, Rob was already around the corner of the building in pursuit. I stumbled after him, lungs heaving.

Up ahead, I could see Rob catch up with them near the entrance to the building where a clunker car was parked. There was the sound of a gunshot, then the loud warning voices of an argument.

I slowed to a walk and stayed hidden behind the corner of

the building, stun gun gripped in one hand. If Rob needed backup, I'd have the element of surprise on my side.

In front of Rob was Damion, locked between two large Hispanic men who looked like twins. Blood seeped from a bullet wound in his calf, and he looked like he was about to pass out.

A stocky Hispanic woman stood face to face with Rob. Although shorter than him, she had a commanding presence, like one of those moms who could reduce even the most rebellious teenager to a 'yes ma'am.'

"Damion's worthless," Rob was saying. "He hasn't been with the Coterie in four years."

"That only makes his bounty higher," said the woman in a husky accent. "There's been a three percent increase every year he's been missing."

"The Agency was able to get his name cleared. The Monarchy won't pay you a cent."

The woman snorted. "Do I look like I work for your self-righteous Agency? I don't give a damn about the Monarchy or what it wants. Me and my sons take any job that will pay. Damion Hart is a deserter, and the Coterie don't take lightly to deserters."

"You call yourselves Coterie then?"

She gave a sharp laugh. "I don't care about the Coterie any more than I do about the Monarchy. But I'll kiss Ricardo's feet if he'll pay me more than the king."

"You didn't come looking for Damion," said Rob. "Antonio Santos is the real reason you're here. And the king's bounty for him is ten times higher than anything the Coterie can offer."

The woman shrugged. "We've had our suspicions about this building for weeks. Trouble was figuring out what apartment he was in. Tonight was meant to be a scouting mission, nothing more. But when this idiot tried to stop us, we recognized him immediately and had no objections to taking a souvenir for our efforts. We'll be back for Antonio later. When it comes to the High Six, you have to be patient, and absolutely sure."

"We're way ahead of you," said Rob. "Antonio's already ours."

The woman's lips tightened. She glanced at Damion then back at Rob. "You want me to believe that a couple of Agency kids nabbed Antonio Santos? You're even dumber than I thought." She yelled something in Spanish to her sons, and they started dragging Damion away.

"Rob," gasped Damion. "I'm sorry. We always knew this could happen."

"No," said Rob. "Wait." He held up his gun, stopping the woman before she could follow the other men. "We have Antonio. If you give us back Damion, we'll give you a portion of his bounty. Ten percent."

The woman gave a throaty laugh and looked around. "I see no proof. Where is this notorious chief you claim to have captured?"

As if on cue, Xia stepped out of the building, Antonio in tow.

"They're indies, Xia!" called Rob, "and Damion's still got that damn price on his head. We're going to work this out. Civilly."

Xia's face burned. She grabbed Antonio's arm and pointed at the two men holding Damion. "Help me get the tall ones," she commanded him.

Antonio's drugged expression pulled up into a smile. He balled his large hands into fists and ran at one of the men, knocking him off Damion and to the pavement.

The Hispanic woman pointed her gun straight at Antonio, but Rob quickly jammed his weapon into her back.

"Hold it," he said. "We both know he's worth more alive."

She frowned and elbowed him in the gut. He pulled back with a grunt and she spun on him, gun turning.

The other twin threw Damion to the ground and fell on top of Antonio, fist slamming into his head. Antonio cried and swung his arm around the man's neck, pulling him to the ground and squeezing hard.

"Call them off," said the woman, eyes blazing at Rob.

My hand trembled on my stun gun. I looked over at Rob, hoping he'd tell me what to do. He shook his head, urging me to stay put.

The woman fired a warning shot into the air. "Call them off," she commanded in a slow but powerful voice.

Rob motioned for her to remain calm. He took a deep breath and raised his voice so the sound carried over the fight. "Xia, stop Antonio. Now!"

Xia's eyebrows narrowed in anger.

"I said now!" Rob's tone would have made a military general cower.

Eyes blazing, Xia commanded Santos to stand back.

"Luis, Mateo, pull away," said the woman. They obeyed, but they grabbed Damion and jerked him to his feet, holding him secure.

Xia growled, but Rob motioned for her to do the same with Antonio. She gripped his arm and forced him apart from the others, guarding him like a mother lioness.

"I'll make you one deal," said the woman. "It's the only offer you're gonna get, so listen up. You can let your team and my sons kill each other like idiots, or you can agree to an exchange."

I saw Rob's face fall and knew he dreaded what she was going to say next.

The woman motioned with her gun toward the two captives. "Damion Hart, for Antonio Santos."

CHAPTER 29

"Rob, it's not worth it!" shouted Damion. "You know me. I'll get the hell away. I'll take care of these filthy indies for good!"

One of the men kicked Damion's injured leg. He gave a sharp cry of pain and would have collapsed if they hadn't been holding him up.

"That's a show I'd pay to see," the man laughed.

His brother joined in, chuckling softly. "We're taking you straight to the Coterie. They don't draw out executions like the king. They take care of these things quick, and they pay quick too."

I glanced at Xia. She was looking straight at Rob, eyes on fire. "Rob," she said, voice cracking. She didn't have to say any more to convey which course she wanted him to take.

Rob pulled at his hair and took a deep breath. "Your terms aren't fair. Antonio is worth ten times Damion's bounty."

"When it comes to Mr. Hart, money doesn't seem to be the issue," said the woman, eyeing Xia.

Rob looked at Santos and then at Damion.

"I didn't say you could take all night," said the woman, twirling her gun. "What's your choice?"

Rob lowered his hands. "Very well," he said, shoulders slumping. "You have a deal."

They shook hands.

"Luis, Mateo," the woman called. "You can release him."

At her command, they let go of Damion.

Xia pushed Antonio toward the two men, and ran over to Damion, wrapping her arms around him, then abruptly pulling away. "You idiot," she said, slamming the heel of her hand into the side of his head. "You're so stupid. How could you—"

Before she could finish, his lips were on hers. I saw her eyes widen in surprise before they closed, and she melted into the moment.

Rob looked torn up inside. He faced the woman one last time, nodding at her like a defeated rival.

She nodded back, stone-faced in her victory. "We'll take him to the proper place," she said. "I've seen what Antonio can do, and he belongs in Hell." She followed her sons as they dragged Antonio away.

Rob watched after them, limbs as rigid as ice.

I approached him slowly and reached out to take his arm. He didn't move. "I'm sorry," I whispered.

He lowered his head. "Sorry for what? We got Damion back, and if that woman keeps her word, Antonio will be out of the picture for good. We won, Tey."

"But the money."

He shrugged one shoulder. "We'll make out better next time."

"Next time we won't be capturing someone as valuable as Antonio Santos," I said, more for myself. Antonio's bounty would have gone a long way toward my California fund. My mind went to the shadowborn boy I'd left beneath Antonio's bed. Nina had said he was valuable. He might even be worth what I needed. If I turned him in to Harrington alone, I could keep all the pay for myself. I'd never have to tell Rob.

I dug my nails into my arm, hating myself for the thought.

I remembered Rob's words, his justification for what he did. Turning them in is a kindness for everyone. At the time, it had almost made sense. I wanted it to make sense now, but all I could see was the boy's terrified face as Antonio's fist crashed into it.

No. I couldn't do what Rob did. That boy saved my life. I'd find a way to help him.

Damion and Xia finally pulled apart. Damion met Rob's gaze.

"Sweet salvation, Rob, I didn't deserve that. I'm your man for life."

Rob patted him on the back, and Damion enfolded him in a hug. "Seriously, though. I owe you one."

"Did you really think I'd let a couple of lowlife indies drag you away?" Rob asked with a smile.

"Weren't the two of you indies once?" Damion asked.

"A time I'm eager to forget," said Rob. He looked at Xia. "You have to admit, we were pretty pathetic back then."

Xia shrugged. "I don't know. I remember beating you to several big gun busts." She kneeled next to Damion and began to examine the wound in his leg. He yelped and pulled away. "Stop being such a baby," she commanded, and forced him to sit as she took out her first aid kit and stanched the bleeding.

Rob's lips twitched in amusement. "Xia was my greatest rival," he said to me, his mood improving. "It's a good thing I tapped her for the Agency after I was recruited."

"You're lucky I accepted," said Xia, winding gauze around Damion's calf. "Otherwise, I might be the one carting Antonio away tonight."

"At least you have higher standards," said Rob. "Those three only want a paycheck. Exactly the type of immoral bastards the Agency would like to eliminate. I hope that woman keeps her word."

His shoulders slumped in sudden exhaustion. "Let's all go home and get some rest. We'll make a new game plan in the morning." He looked at Damion. "Can you ride?"

Damion tested his bandaged leg. "Think so. Hurts like hell, but the bullet only skimmed me."

"You're lucky it's not embedded in your flesh," said Xia.

Damion swayed. "Yeah, let's not think about that, OK?"

"Just don't let it get infected," said Rob. "I'd hate for something to happen to you after…well, everything."

"I might still swing by that festival on the way out. Saints, I could use a drink right now."

Xia glared at him. "After all the blood you lost?"

"Alcohol is a great antiseptic. I'm only looking out for my health."

We returned to our bikes. Xia and Damion rode off one way, still arguing. Rob and I went the other. We didn't talk much on the ride back to the Castillo, but after we went inside, Rob squeezed my arm. "Good work tonight. You're a natural, Tey."

His praise rushed through my chest and I stood straighter, moving closer to him. He didn't seem to sense my mood. He was in boss mode, and I was only his trainee. I stepped back. "I'm just glad we're safe."

His mouth moved in a not-quite smile, and he patted my arm one last time before disappearing into his room.

I went to my room and waited until I was sure Rob was asleep. For me, the dangers of the night weren't over yet. I'd promised the shadowborn boy I'd come back for him, and I didn't dare wait until daylight.

Adopting Rob's quiet way of walking, I brought blankets

up to the tower room and made the bed in preparation for what would be the Castillo's newest guest. Then I crept down the stairs and out the door, tensing at the thought of what I was about to do. If I brought the boy back here, a thousand things could go wrong. But what else could I do? Without him, my brains would be all over Antonio's floor. Wasn't that enough of a reason to risk everything I could for him?

The night was even cooler now, with a wind gusting from the direction of the ocean. I breathed in the briny smell as I mounted Rob's bike, a shiver running down my spine. It wasn't anything like the bicycle I'd ridden to and from school for the last four years. It was heavy, and I had to push down on the pedals harder than I expected to keep the gears turning and the mechanism upright.

The bike teetered and clicked as I made my way out to the dark road. After about a minute of peddling at a constant pace, the gears took over, turning the wheels on their own. I twisted a knob and a light switched on to illuminate my path.

Going as fast as I dared, I glided through the city, exposed in the quiet streets. This late at night, Cosmar was so different from its crowded and chaotic daytime persona. For the first time, I noticed the beauty of the Victorian architecture as well as the diversity of the ships bobbing in the harbor, little lights glowing inside them. From somewhere nearby, I caught the echoes of laughter and the distant hum of a solo violin—the lingering ghosts of a party that had ended hours ago.

I hid Rob's bike behind a boarded-up fruit stand and returned to Santos's apartment via the still-dangling fire escape. The window Rob and I had crawled out of remained open, curtains rippling in the breeze.

Stun gun at the ready, I tiptoed down the stairs and peered into the sitting room. All but one light was off, and the woman I'd stunned earlier was gone. I paused at the kitchen door, listening. When I heard no sounds, I made my way through it to the staircase leading to Antonio's room. I halted at each step and shone my flashlight into the hall below to assure myself the guard was no longer there. The way was clear.

Slowly, I opened the bedroom door. It was dark and cold inside. I switched on the lights, noticing the drops of blood from Antonio's head that stained the Persian carpet.

"I'm back," I said as I dropped to my knees and looked under the bed. The pillow and blanket I'd given the boy were still there, but he was gone.

Cursing, I stood up again. I had wasted my time. As soon as we took Santos away, the boy had likely gotten up and run for the streets. I should have felt more relieved. He wasn't my problem anymore. Instead, worry gnawed at my stomach. I opened the closet door and peeked behind the drapes just in case he was hiding, but there was no one there.

Drained, I turned and walked toward the door.

The sound of a cough stopped me in my tracks.

I spun around and ducked under the bed. The area was still vacant, but the coughing continued.

The hairs on the back of my arms stood straight. "Are…are you in here somewhere?" I stood up and turned a full circle around the room. "I won't hurt you." I removed the canteen attached to my belt. "Look. I've brought you some water. Bet you could use some."

I looked under the bed again and choked back a cry of surprise as the shadowborn boy appeared. He was lying on top of the blanket, and his body was completely transparent.

I wanted to slap myself in the face for being so thoughtless. "Invisibility! How could I forget?"

The boy gradually filled in until he looked normal again. I

moved closer, and his sky-blue eyes opened to look into mine. "Come with me," I said. "I want to help you."

He was silent for three labored breaths before he spoke. "Why?"

I hesitated, a cacophony of negative answers racing through my head. Because I'm stupid. Because I don't think things through or consider the consequences. "Because what you did to Santos was really brave," I finally said. "You saved me." My reasons hardly mattered anymore. Being here and seeing him like this triggered something inside me—a fury at those who hurt him, and an overwhelming need to make things right.

I crawled out from under the bed and urged him to do the same. It took several minutes, but he eventually followed me, eyebrows knitted together like he didn't believe I was real.

I passed him my canteen. He looked at it suspiciously and then took a sip. When he realized it was safe, he gulped like he had in Antonio's car.

I watched him with a knot in my heart. He could have been a couple of years younger than me, but the bruises on his face made age difficult to pinpoint. Bruises he'd gotten for not killing me.

"Can you stand?"

He grabbed the side of the bed and pulled himself to his feet, clinging to his ribs. I held out a hand to help, but he flinched away.

"I won't hurt you. I want to take you to the place where I live. Are you able to walk?"

He took a shaky breath and put one foot in front of the other. He fell forward, but I caught him and wrapped his skinny arm around my shoulders. He started coughing again and I held him until the spasm ended.

One step at a time, we made our way into the hall and up

the stairs. There was no way I could get him down the fire escape, so I risked taking him out of the front door and down the apartment elevator. Before we left the lobby, I removed my black beanie and put it over his head, hiding his silver hair just in case someone saw us. My blood had dried, and none of his hair showed through the bullet hole. I felt odd asking him to turn invisible, so I didn't suggest it. I didn't want to think about him being anything other than human. Just a boy who needed my help.

I retrieved Rob's bike and had him sit behind me. He lay against my back, arms clinging weakly.

As I pedaled through the city, the remnants of costumed partygoers teetered through the street or were sprawled on the curb, out cold, while vagrants rifled through their pockets for valuables.

I parked the bike next to the entry of the Castillo and helped the boy inside. I looked both ways, searching the darkness for little spies. All was still.

"It's six flights up," I whispered in his ear. "Can you make it?" He was already breathing hard and I worried he would pass out before we reached the tower.

He nodded, gripping his ribs again as he moved forward, eyes squinted in determination.

By the time we got to the last flight, his head was lolling on his neck and he was making small gasping sounds. I tested his forehead. The heat coming off it scalded my palm.

A wave went through my stomach, bringing back all my doubts. I had no idea how sick this kid was. No idea how to take care of anything worse than my mom's hangovers. No idea what I was going to do with him.

I half carried him up the last flight of stairs and deposited him onto the enormous bed, glad I'd brought up blankets earlier. He curled up, quivering feverishly, arms clasped around his ribs. I lit a few old lanterns to illuminate the tower. In the light, I could see that his wrist was still swollen and turning purple. Definitely broken. What else was wrong?

"Let me see where it hurts," I said, trying to make my voice as soft as possible. I separated his arms and gently eased his shirt over his head. He shuddered under my touch and his body became transparent out of instinct, but he couldn't seem to manage going fully invisible.

"It's alright," I said. "I just want to make things better." I brushed his silky hair from his forehead and ran my fingers down his burning face.

He gradually relaxed and came back into full view. I could see his ribs all too clearly, and they were black and yellow with bruises. It looked like at least six were broken, maybe more.

I swallowed hard. Damn you, Antonio. "I wish I had some ice," I said. Helplessness tugged at my heart.

I went into the adjoining bathroom. The water was off, forcing me to go to the pump in the kitchen and fill a bowl, which I set on the nightstand. I searched until I found a rag, then drenched it and spread it over the boy's forehead.

Next, I took some of the ruined material from Xia's old dress and ripped it into long strips. "Hope you like purple," I said, using it to bandage his wrist.

I had no clue what to do about his ribs. Back home, I had relied on the Internet to answer most of my health questions. Within seconds I could have probably found an instructional video on the best method for treating the fractures. Now Google felt like a magic genie of eternal wisdom. One that was far out of reach.

It was hot in the tower, but the boy's teeth were chattering, so I tucked him under the blankets, hoping it was the right thing to do.

"Is the chief dead?" he whispered, speaking for the first time since we left Antonio's apartment.

"No," I said, pulling up a chair beside his bed. "But I'm sure he'll be executed soon."

"Are you going to turn me in too?"

I leaned closer and dabbed at his face. "You can trust me." My words tasted like poison. I couldn't pretend to myself that I hadn't considered it, that a secret part of myself didn't still consider it.

"I shouldn't have come with you," he said, teeth clicking together.

"Not everyone's like Antonio. What's your name?"

No answer.

"You do have a name, don't you?"

"Waif."

"I mean your real—" I stopped, remembering. No shadowborn knew their real name. "It's what Ricky and Antonio used to call you, isn't it? Well, they're gone now. Pick something different if you want."

He only shrugged.

"You're going to be safe here. I won't let anyone hurt you again." As I said the words, they cemented in me, and I knew I could never betray him.

"You can't help me," he said, frowning. "I'm going to die soon."

Prickles of ice formed inside my chest. "You don't know that."

"It will be faster if you throw me out now…save you lots of trouble." His voice was getting farther and farther away.

"Nothing can save me from trouble," I said. "My grandmother used to say it was my middle name. When I was little,

I thought she was serious before I found out my mom never gave me a middle name." I smiled and pulled the covers over his shoulders. "My first name is Tey, in case you wanted to know. It's short for Teylin, but nobody ever calls me that."

Waif's eyes closed all the way, and my name was the last thing he whispered before slipping away.

CHAPTER 30

A shout jerked me awake.

I looked around, trying to orient myself. The sky outside was still dark and I was slumped in the chair next to the bed where Waif was curled into a tight ball. Waif's sleeping face was tense and his closed eyes moved rapidly beneath his lids.

He shouted again, probably reliving one of Antonio's beatings. I patted his cheek. "Hey, Waif, open your eyes. Come on, you'll feel better if you wake up."

His head tossed on the pillow, mouth clenched in pain as he continued to cry out in terror.

"Wake up," I said again, giving his shoulders a gentle shake.

I'd never seen anyone sick enough to be delirious and was surprised how much it frightened me. His eyes finally fluttered halfway open, but his gaze passed right through me, like he was seeing a monster on the other side of the room.

I wished desperately for ice and Tylenol. Two things I could get at any gas station back home. All I had here was a rag and lukewarm water.

I turned his pillow over, cool side up, and took the bowl downstairs to refill it with colder water from the kitchen. When I reached the fifth level, I stopped dead. Lei was standing in the middle of the hall, eyes wide.

"Lei?" I said. "You need to go back to sleep. It's very late."

"I can't." The little girl sniffled. "I heard the ghost in the tower. He was crying."

I set down the bowl and knelt so I could look into her eyes. "You were dreaming. Ghosts don't cry; they don't have any tears left." Just then, I heard Waif give a pained shout and I cringed at how thin the ceilings between the upper levels were. Lei buried her face in my shirt, wailing in fear.

"Shh, shh, shh. It's OK. It's OK."

"Is the ghost sad?" she whimpered.

"Yes," I said. "He's sad because he's all alone up there, and sometimes at night, he gets scared too."

"Ghosts can get scared?"

"Ghosts get more scared than anyone because they have no one to comfort them. But you don't have that problem. Let's get you back to bed."

I left the bowl where it was and let the little girl lead me to her room. It was on the fifth floor, away from most of the other children. No wonder she was so frightened. I crawled in bed with her, and she snuggled against me, clinging to my arm.

I brushed her hair back from her face and tried to think of something to sing. I didn't know any lullabies, so I ended up singing a pop song and changing it so it sounded soft and slow instead of bubbly.

I never finished the song. Somewhere in the middle of it, I fell asleep.

What seemed like only minutes later, my eyes shot open. Daylight streamed through Lei's window. I gasped and unwound the girl's arms from my body. I must have been asleep for hours, and who knew what had become of Waif in that time. If his threat of dying were real—

Pulse hammering, I ran to the tower and flung the door

open.

Waif was so still he looked like a pale statue. I couldn't tell if he was breathing.

My heart shriveled in my chest as I approached the bed. I should have never left him, not while he was delirious.

I touched his cheek; it was still hot. I let out a breath of relief. He was alive.

My heart swelled back to normal size as I tried to give him water from my canteen. Most of it dribbled down his chin, but I thought I saw his throat move up and down a couple of times.

I left the canteen at his bedside, then made my way downstairs to the kitchen where I snagged some fruit for him in case he woke up while I was away. I placed a strange pear-shaped fruit, three giagons, and a bunch of sweet-tasting berries on his nightstand, and then looked over him one last time, my heart sinking at the thought of leaving him alone. But there would be questions if I didn't go to the Agency. Questions I didn't dare answer.

"Stay here," I told him, whether or not he could hear me. "I'll be back as soon as I can." Then I went to find Rob.

I found him in the parlor out of breath and laughing. A small boy clung to his back, another to his arm. More children ran after him, squealing. He stopped when he saw me and let the boy slide to the floor. "I was just about to leave. I came looking for you, but you weren't in your room."

"Lei had nightmares," I explained. "I fell asleep in her bed and woke up late. It's hard to keep track of time without an alarm clock."

"You'll get used to it eventually," he said. "Ready to go?"

I nodded, much to the children's disappointment.

"Don't go, Rob," they wailed in a chorus of distress.

"Stay just a little more."

"Please, Rob."

"Sorry, kids," he said, ruffling a little blond boy's hair. "If I don't work, then there won't be any dinner, and something tells me you won't be happy about that."

They paused and looked at each other.

"Catch any more bad guys, Rob?" asked the blond boy.

"I've caught a few," said Rob, rubbing the back of his neck and grinning. "As for the ones who got away, I need you all to guard the Castillo in case they come looking for me. Can you do that?"

The children nodded in unison. I was surprised at how delighted they seemed. When I was their age, I'd have been terrified at the thought of someone invading my home.

"I expect a full report when I get back. And if I hear that you were really good guards, I may bring you back extra rations."

Whoops of joy followed this news, and at Rob's command, they scattered, running to find posts to defend.

Rob's arm looped around my shoulder. "I'll give them ten minutes before they forget all about it. We best be far away by then." He led me out the door.

I looked back at the tower as we walked toward the bike. The branches of a tall tree stretched out to conceal half of it. I wished more than anything I could tell Rob about Waif, and that he'd want to help me. But every time I blinked, the face of the girl he'd sold to Harrington flashed inside my mind.

Back at the Agency, Rob went to the blackboard and gave us a long lecture, complete with diagrams, about how removing Antonio Santos would affect the rest of the Coterie, particularly Ricardo. He pulled down a rollup map of Cosmar, highlighting all the Coterie rat nests already infiltrated, and drew lines between them to see if they formed a pattern. From what we could tell, there was no correlation.

My leg bounced as I thought of Waif alone in the tower. I wondered if he'd woken up yet, or if he'd taken a turn for the worse. The situation reminded me of a time when I was ten. I'd found a baby robin next to my window that had fallen out of its nest and injured its wing. I kept it hidden in my room and cared for it as best as I could, keeping it warm, even digging up worms and mashing them up for it to eat. The problem was, I had to go to school, and after two days, I came home and discovered it had died while I was away. I remembered how I'd cried myself to sleep that night. Since then, I hadn't been able to keep so much as a plant alive. Why did I think I could succeed with a living, breathing boy?

Without realizing it, I lowered my head into my hands, eyes drooping with the need for sleep.

"What's wrong with you?" Xia asked, interrupting Rob's comment about how Antonio's capture might force Ricardo to take a more active position in Cosmar.

My eyes opened and I thought fast. "Don't feel so good."

"Yeah, me neither," said Damion, rubbing his eyes. His bandaged leg was healing nicely, but he was now clearly suffering from a bad hangover.

Rob glared at him then looked at me, concern in his eyes. "Where do you feel sick?" The urgency in his tone made it clear how serious sickness was in Los Sueños. Without proper medicine, a cold could escalate into something much more deadly.

I pretended to shiver. "Have a killer headache, but my muscles feel achy too, and I'm starting to feel really cold."

The act worked. Rob requested two Asprin from Mr. Corpus, who kept a bottle in a locked case. Corpus was reluctant to hand over the expensive pills, but Rob insisted it was an emergency. I felt bad worrying him, but what else could I do?

"Hey, Tey," said Damion. "I'll split my next bounty with you for one of those pills."

"Ignore him," said Rob.

"No sympathy for the injured," said Damion.

"You said that last night," said Xia. "When you were raving drunk."

"Gotta have something to deaden the pain, don't I? Rob will never go to Corpus for meds on my behalf."

"If it was just your leg that was the problem, I might feel more motivated to help," said Rob. He brought me a glass of water. I pretended to put the pills in my mouth and drink them down, but I covered them with my fingers and slipped them in my pocket at my first opportunity.

"Why don't you go home and lie down?" said Rob.

"Really?"

"Yeah, you look pretty bad. I'll take you back to the Castillo."

Relief flooded through me. Mission: success.

* * *

The bed sheets were tangled around Waif's legs like he'd been tossing. My canteen was still mostly full and the fruit untouched. I straightened the blankets, then refreshed the damp rag with water and spread it over Waif's forehead. He moaned a little in his sleep but didn't wake up.

Now for the hard part.

I took one of the pills out of my pocket and put it on the back of his tongue. Then I filled his mouth with water and clamped it shut, holding his nose the way I'd seen a doctor do it on a TV show. He gagged and tried to cough, his body resisting me, but I held firm.

"Swallow it," I commanded. "Swallow. Swallow." And he did. I let go and he coughed like crazy. I gave him another drink and laid his head back on the pillow. The rag on his forehead was already hot, so I soaked it again, then crawled onto the enormous bed next to him and dabbed at his face. The bed was soft and the warm room full of sunshine. Were it not for the sick boy next to me, I could almost imagine it was a lazy summer day. And I was so tired.

Before I realized it was happening, I drifted off.

CHAPTER 31

Slender fingers touched my forehead. I opened my eyes to see two sky-blue irises staring at me.

I gasped and pulled away, then quickly remembered where I was. "You're awake," I said, smiling to cover my frightened reaction, but Waif's face betrayed no emotion. His metallic hair stuck to his forehead with sweat. A good sign. I felt his cheek, relieved that his fever was down. Now I just needed it to stay down. "How do you feel?"

He didn't answer, just continued to watch me, brow furrowed in what looked like curiosity.

Slowly, I got out of the bed and took a piece of fruit off the nightstand. It was pear-like with bluish skin. "You should eat this," I said. "Food will make you feel better."

He shook his head and turned away from me.

I let out a heavy breath. "Here." I shoved the fruit toward him but he still didn't take it.

"You should have left me to die," he finally said, his voice soft and sad sounding.

"After you saved my life? What kind of person do you think I am?"

"You seem like a smart one, but a smart person wouldn't be helping me, so I'm starting to have doubts."

It was the longest sentence I'd heard him speak, and I was surprised to detect hints of more than a detached personality.

"You're right," I said. "It is stupid of me to help you. But it's more stupid not to accept my help." I tried to hand him the food again, but once more he refused it.

If he wouldn't eat on his own, I'd have to feed it to him. "I'll be right back," I said, and rushed downstairs to grab a knife from the kitchen. When I got back to the tower, I cut the fruit into small pieces and forced one into his mouth. "Chew it," I said.

He obeyed, but I could tell he wasn't happy about it. He swallowed and I pushed in another slice. He flinched every time I drew near, like he was afraid I was going to slap him.

I studied his face; with those high cheekbones and almond eyes, he almost looked like an elf from a story. "Do you have any idea how old you are?" I asked.

"I've had awareness for three years," he said as if that were an answer.

"What's the first thing you remember?"

His eyes were distant, like he was seeing back in time. "An alley."

"What else?"

"It was pouring rain. I was alone."

"Were you scared?"

He picked at a thread coming loose from one of his blankets. "Terrified."

I sat in the chair next to his bed, feeding him another piece of fruit. "At the time, could you remember anything else?"

He stared at the wall and shook his head.

"How long before the Coterie took you?"

He shrugged, and I worried he wouldn't say more. Still, it didn't keep me from asking one more question.

"Did they—" I paused, "did they torture you until you revealed your ability?"

He leaned back into his pillow and nodded. "It would have been better if I'd died on the street." His teeth started to chatter and I worried his fever might be coming back, so I urged him to swallow the other pill. I didn't want to go through another night like last night.

"Don't think about them," I said. "Go back to sleep." I pulled the blankets over his chest. From outside, the setting sun filled the tower with a brilliant orange glow.

He studied me in confusion. I could see something in his gaze. He longed to trust me, but me taking care of him went against everything he'd ever known.

"I'll be here until you fall asleep. If there's anything you need, just ask me, OK?"

I watched the fading sun's reflection in his metallic hair as his eyelids drooped lower and lower. His breathing slowed and he fell asleep.

I went downstairs and found Rob in the parlor trying to light a fire in the hearth. "You're home," I said.

"Yeah. No new leads came, so I sent Xia and Damion to do a sweep of the skids to see if they could spot any new shadowborn prowling about. New ones are the easiest to find. They're usually disoriented and don't know yet that most people want them dead. The trick is to catch them before they realize what their abilities are so they don't fight back. I came back to the Castillo to check on you. How are you feeling?"

"A lot better," I said. "Thanks for getting Mr. Corpus to give me the Aspirin. It helped."

The fire caught and he smiled at me, face lighting up in its glow. "He's a little touchy with medical supplies, but the guy owes me more favors than I can count. Have you eaten yet?"

I shook my head and he got to his feet. "Good. I brought something, but we can't let the kids know."

I pushed his arm. "Rob, we can't stuff our faces while they go hungry."

"They're not hungry. I brought home enough sausage and bread to keep them happy for days, as well as a sack of candy they'll be fighting over the rest of the night." He pulled my arm toward the kitchen where he took a paper bag out of a high cupboard. I tried to peek inside, but he pushed me away. "Not here. There are spies everywhere," he looked back and forth and I thought I heard giggling from various hiding places. He put the bag under his arm and laced his fingers through mine.

"I found something tonight that I want to show you." He led me outside. The air was warm and moist and smelled like every kind of flower in the world. The sky was dark and the night insects had long since begun their frantic chorus.

"Where are we going?"

"Just a little farther." He pulled me into the jungle, breath quick with anticipation. A path had been created by dozens of children's feet heading into the jungle to look for fruit. We followed it to a clearing, and what I saw made me gasp.

Hundreds of silvery orbs fluttered around the open space, twinkling in the air like fallen stars. They were alive. "What are they?" I asked.

"Lunawasps," said Rob, grinning at my expression. "I've never seen so many all at once before. Normally you only find them deeper in the jungle."

"Are they dangerous?"

"No more than fireflies. There must be a pool of earthblood nearby. Miners have used them to find it in the past. The wasps feed off the stuff, then light up like glowing Christmas ornaments."

"They're incredible," I said, my voice laced with laughter.

I ran into the clearing and the lunawasps bobbed around me like spirit orbs. The lights were so bright that I couldn't see the tiny insects concealed within. One of them latched onto the pendant around my neck, and when it finally broke free, another one flew toward me and took its place, as though drawn to my necklace like a moth to a flame.

Rob sat in the middle of the field. "This clearing is my favorite place to watch the stars, but tonight it seems as if the stars have come down to join us." He lashed out with his hands, capturing one of the lunawasps between his palms, and opening them a tiny crack so the glow spilled onto his face. Its reflection caught in his eyes, and when he looked up at me, they sparkled with mischief. "I thought you might like it here." He let the lunawasp flutter away and unrolled the paper sack. "Hungry?"

"Starving." I sat next to him and huddled close. He unloaded a bottle of carbonated cranberry juice and a whole roasted chicken. My mouth instantly watered. In addition to the meat, there were soft buttery rolls, piping potatoes wrapped in foil, and half a coconut cream pie.

I hadn't seen such great food since the Thanksgiving my mom shipped me off to my grandmother's house in Seattle.

"What's all this for?" I asked, pausing to admire it.

He grinned. "You've had it rough these past few days. I don't want you to think living here is a complete nightmare."

"It must have cost a fortune."

He shrugged. "I'm very good at bargaining." He opened the plastic bag containing the chicken, releasing a waft of scents into the air. He pulled off a drumstick and handed it to me. I bit in, juice dribbling down my lip. I could taste herbs and butter on top of the already savory meat. He opened the cranberry bottle and handed it over. I took a long swig and passed it back. The taste mixed perfectly with the meat and made my senses tingle. We finished the meal slowly, savoring every bite.

With a full stomach, I flopped back in the grass and faced the night sky. The lunawasps blinking overhead made the stars look three-dimensional. Rob lay next to me and moved in so our bodies touched side by side. Once again, he wrapped his fingers around mine and I squeezed his hand tightly.

The silvery color of the lunawasps reminded me of Waif. "Rob? What do you think the shadowborn are?"

He let out a long breath. "No one knows."

"Yeah, but you must have a theory."

He shrugged. "Some kind of demented experiment on children? Maybe the result of radioactive exposure? Of course, some people think they came from the stars."

"Like aliens?" I laughed.

"Yeah, something like that."

"Do you believe in that sort of thing?"

His eyes looked up. "There're a heck of a lot of stars up there, so why not?"

He turned toward me, right hand tracing my left shoulder and up to my neck. I faced him with a thudding heart. His skin had a silvery glow in the light of the lunawasps, and his eyes looked as black as the night sky. Pressure built in my chest. I leaned in, brushing his forehead.

He pushed some stray hairs away from my face. "I don't want to think about the shadowborn tonight. I want to think about you."

Blood rushed into my cheeks. I opened my mouth, but no words came out.

"I know you don't like it here," he said, "but a selfish part of me is glad you came. Look how successful our team has been, thanks to you. You're like a four-leafed clover or a lucky rabbit's foot."

I snorted. "If anything, I'm cursed. My whole life has been one bad situation after another. If luck is real, it hates me."

"The old you, maybe. But people change when they come here. Soon, you'll see that you don't need fortune to shine on you. You are fortune itself, and you're the one who's shining." His lips touched mine ever so slightly; more of a caress than a kiss. A warm breath escaped between his teeth before he drew back as though asking for permission.

My heart started to race and I could feel every part of me burn with heat. My lips tingled, longing for a greater contact than the brief touch they'd just experienced. I leaned into him.

Rob's mouth melted over mine, warm and firm. I took a deep breath and pressed harder.

He fell over me, chest crushing mine. I couldn't breathe but didn't want him to draw away. His body grew warmer and my hands moved with a will of their own. They slid under his shirt and up the lean muscles of his back. His lips found my ear, then my neck, then my lips again. My whole body tingled like my blood had become carbonated, and all the anxiety of the day melted into a forgotten corner of my brain.

The pressure lifted off my chest as Rob drew back. "Sorry," he whispered, lips still close enough to tickle mine. "I didn't mean to get carried away like that. We should get back to the house." His cheeks glowed with color and he was out of breath.

I nodded, but my heart sank at the thought of this perfect night coming to an end. He helped me to my feet and we walked with arms clasped around each other the whole way home.

The Castillo was dark and quiet, but the fire still crackled in the hearth. We went to it, letting the heat caress our skin. Our lips met again, and this time, my fingers threaded through Rob's curly hair, pulling him closer to continue what we had started. His mouth was fiercer this time, and I couldn't stop kissing him, couldn't bring myself to draw away.

The front door flew open. We jumped apart and Rob instinctively reached for his gun. In walked Xia and Damion, dragging a small boy between them.

My cheeks burned with embarrassment but quickly cooled when their captive looked at me. It was Ichiro, only it wasn't Ichiro. His hair had turned silver and his brown eyes were now an unnatural sky blue.

He was shadowborn.

CHAPTER 32

"Ichiro!" I gasped, but Rob promptly clamped his hand over my mouth.

"Shh," he said. "The last thing we need is for the other kids to wake up." He looked at Damion and Xia. "Get him upstairs, hurry."

We followed as they hauled the boy up the stairs and into an empty room. Rob shut the door behind us. His face was pale and his arms were trembling. "Where did you find him?"

"In the skids slinking around a gutter," said Xia. "At first I thought he was a stray cat."

Rob took the boy by the shoulders and looked him in the eyes. "Ichiro, do you remember me? It's Rob. Come on kid, give me a sign."

Ichiro stared back, no recognition in his eyes. Rob went to the window and looked out. I approached slowly and touched his shoulder.

"Rob, you don't mean he's one of your kids?" Xia asked.

Rob nodded, face tight. He closed his eyes as though holding back tears.

"Sweet salvation!" said Damion. "This makes no sense."

"What should we do?" asked Xia.

"We could keep him here," I suggested, thinking of Waif. "Rob and I can look after him, and he'll be safe if he stays away from the city."

Rob shook his head. "No. I can't have him around the other kids. They'll start asking questions I can't answer. Besides, we don't know when his ability will manifest. He might be dangerous. One of them could get hurt."

"But I doubt he'd hurt anyone intentionally," I said. "If we show him that we're friends, maybe he'll cooperate."

Rob's hands went to his hair and pulled back. "The Castillo is supposed to be a safe haven for those orphans. I won't compromise that by making a shadowborn part of it. Too many things could go wrong."

My heart sank, not just for Ichiro, but for the boy hidden in the tower. "Ichiro was already a part of it. Is he really so different now?"

"Look at him, Tey, he doesn't remember me. He doesn't remember anyone, not even himself. The little kid we knew is as good as dead."

"So what is he?" I asked, looking at Ichiro who studied me with ice in his eyes.

Rob hesitated and then turned back to the window. "A demon."

I thought of Waif and how soft and human his voice was, and the spark of anger in me ignited into a fireball. "How can you say—"

He cut me off before my voice could escalate into a full shout. "Look, I…I can't deal with this right now. Let's keep him here tonight. I'll decide in the morning."

Damion released the struggling Ichiro. The little boy ran for the door, but I blocked his way. "Ichiro, you need to stay here tonight." He ducked around me, hand pawing at the handle. I held him away. "Please, come back." Like Rob, I wanted him to know me, but it was obvious the little boy who'd given me a tour of the Castillo was gone.

"Tie him to the bed," said Rob, face somber.

"Is that necessary?" I asked in disbelief. I wanted to wrap my arms around the little boy and comfort him, tell him he'd be alright.

"It's for his own safety," said Rob.

"Wait—"

"Tey," Rob scolded. "You haven't had much experience with shadowborn. You don't know how dangerous they can be." He waved for Xia and Damion to proceed.

They pulled Ichiro back. He kicked and yelled until both wrists were fastened to the bedposts.

Rob bowed his head and turned to the door. "Let's go."

I looked back at Ichiro. He cowered on the bed, eyes full of tears. "Rob, he looks scared."

Rob lowered his head. "I'm so tired, Tey." And I could see he was. Dark circles rounded his eyes and his face looked older. He stepped into the hall; the others followed.

I went to where Ichiro lay and touched his shoulder, but he snapped at me with his teeth, and just missed biting my arm. I drew away one step at a time. "You'll be OK," I said, not knowing if I was saying it to Ichiro or myself.

"Let him be," said Rob, motioning for me to leave the room. He took out a long skeleton key and locked the door behind me. He looked so different from the guy who'd kissed me just minutes ago. Now I worried he might topple over.

"Rob?" I began, but he waved me away.

"Tey, go to bed. Xia, Damion, you two can stay here tonight. I'll get you some blankets." He walked off, but I lingered behind, listening at Ichiro's door. The boy was crying: his sobs sounded very young.

I went back to the tower to check on Waif. He was mumbling in his sleep, but it didn't sound like the delirious screams from the night before. I sat with him for a long time, longing for the company of anyone, even if that person was unconscious. As I watched him, I wondered if he too had once been a normal boy like Ichiro. I tried to imagine him without his silver hair and pale eyes. Had something caused him to change? Could it happen to anyone?

I caught myself dozing, so I made sure Waif still had a full canteen of water and went back to my room to sleep.

As my mind slipped into a dream, I found the girl from the photograph waiting for me. We were both dressed in white-ribboned dresses and straw hats like Anne of Green Gables. She took my hand and led me into the jungle. It was filled with fragrant white flowers. We found a clear pool of water and sat beside it, dipping our feet in. Tiny fish with pearly scales nipped at our toes.

"I have a secret," she said, staring at her reflection in the water.

"What is it?"

A tear fell from her eye and splashed into the pool. "I'm dying."

I looked at her. She appeared healthy. Strong. "That can't be true."

The leaves all around us changed into autumn colors and fell off and drifted into the water. "You should leave," she said. "If you're here when it happens, you'll die too."

I shook my head. "No. Tell me how to help you."

"It's too late," she said. "It's coming, Tey."

I came awake with a sharp intake of breath. The girl's voice echoed in my mind. Weak morning sunlight streamed through my window and highlighted her picture on my wall. When I'd first seen her, I thought she looked regal and refined; now she appeared sad.

I rubbed the sleep out of my eyes and grabbed a few bills from my money envelope, which I'd hidden under my mattress. The Castillo was still silent, so it had to be very early.

I slipped outside and made my way down the dirt road to the wharf, where I stocked up on provisions for Waif. He hadn't eaten anything except a little fruit, and I needed to get some real food into him soon.

Sweat plastered my bangs to my forehead by the time I returned to the Castillo, my grocery bags loaded to the brim with food and water bottles. If the showers weren't working, I might have to take a trip to the stream like Rob did every morning.

Waif opened his eyes when I entered, and blinked groggily.

"How are you feeling this morning?" I asked, setting down my bags and going to his bedside. I checked his forehead and cursed. He was burning again. If only I could get my hands on more Aspirin, but the headache excuse probably wouldn't work twice in a row.

He shrugged and closed his eyes halfway. "About how you'd expect a dying person to feel."

When he spoke, he sounded older than he looked, and I wondered if maybe he was closer to my age. "You aren't dying," I said. "Why do you keep saying that?" I took a piece of bread from my grocery sack and held it out to him, but he turned his head away. I gritted my teeth. "But you won't feel better if you don't eat."

"I don't want it," he said.

"Of course you do." I pinched his arm. "You're little more than skin and bone." I pressed it to his lips, and he accepted it grudgingly but took forever to chew the one small piece. When he swallowed, he closed his eyes like the action exhausted him.

"Don't you dare fall asleep," I said, shaking his shoulder. "You're staying awake until you finish every last bite of this." My words were as sharp as my mood.

Waif cracked open one eye. "If you're trying to help me like you say, then why not let me die? It's what I want, you know."

I swallowed hard. "You didn't let me die."

He let out a short laugh. "I don't want payment for that."

"Then why'd you do it?"

"Does it matter?"

"It does to me. It's my life we're talking about."

He shrugged and changed the subject. "If I do somehow recover, what then? Will you hide me here for the rest of my life? Or sell me back to the Coterie? Those are the only options left for me, and neither is worth living for."

I sat on the chair next to his bed. "I don't know, but death isn't one of those options, alright?" I shoved another piece of bread into his mouth.

I couldn't keep my mind from contemplating all the possibilities an ally who could turn invisible afforded me. He probably knew many Coterie secrets, and where countless valuables were stashed away. With his aid, I could easily become rich enough to bribe any Coterie sailor for my passage home.

I tried to block the thoughts out of my head. If all I could think about was how to use and manipulate the shadowborn, then I was no better than the Coterie.

"You shouldn't be so nice to me," Waif said, chewing. "If you knew the things my master made me do—people think because we have no past, we have no conscience, but I know those things were wrong."

I heard Rob shout my name from somewhere below, and leaped to my feet. "Keep eating," I ordered. "I'll be right back." I closed his fingers over the remaining bread and hurried down the stairs.

Rob was knocking on my bedroom door.

I walked up behind him. "What's up?" I asked.

He turned around, surprised, then looked in both directions to make sure no children were listening. "It's Ichiro."

"What about him?"

"He's gone."

CHAPTER 33

I went to Ichiro's room and looked in. Xia and Damion were examining the cords used to tie his wrists.

Rob grabbed my shoulder with a strange intensity. "Tey, you didn't have anything to do with this, did you?"

I opened my mouth, closed it, and started again. "What? No. How could I have gotten in? You're the only one with a key."

He wrung his hands. "Look, I don't know. I just have to cover all bases."

"You can cross me off your list of culprits," I said, folding my arms.

Damion came over. "The ropes are still tied. Maybe he slipped out and jumped from the window."

"That's a three-story drop," said Rob.

"Maybe he floated down then. He must have realized his freaky abilities after we left and made good use of them. It's the only explanation."

Rob rubbed the back of his neck and looked out the window. "I don't have the heart to track him down, even though it would be the kinder thing to do. The old Ichiro was pretty good at finding fruit in the jungle. Maybe this new one has a shot at surviving for a while. And if he turns back up here looking for food, he'll be easy to recapture."

"And if that happens, what then?" I asked.

"Then? He'll go to Harrington. Selling him to the Coterie is the only way to assure his survival."

"You seemed uncertain last night," said Damion.

"I was in shock. Seeing that this…affliction, or whatever you want to call it, can happen to an ordinary kid…it terrifies me."

Damion patted him on the back. "I know what you mean, man. Sweet salvation, this is so messed up. Maybe we should get to the office. I can always think more clearly there."

Rob nodded and let Damion pull him to the door. They left so quickly I didn't have time to come up with an excuse to return to Waif's tower before following them out. But I'd left days worth of food and water in his room, and there was still my canteen and whole fruits from the previous day within easy reach on his nightstand. There wasn't much more I could do for him.

Back at the office, Rob decided all our leads were cold. We'd have to sniff out a new trail if we were going to profit any time soon.

I looked around the Agency. Several teams were gearing up to leave on missions. A few others were gathered around chalkboards planning their next move.

"The other agents seem to be hard at work," I said. "Can't we ask one of them for a tip?"

Xia looked at me like I'd slapped her. "Agents never share information with other teams. Haven't you seen the stats chart?" She pointed out the office door to the large diagram with the names of team leaders hanging on the far wall. "Our team is ranked first, which means we pay a lower percentage of our bounty dues to the Agency than everyone else. And we get the best office in the house. The last thing we need is to butt heads with our own people on a mission. It was bad enough running into those indies."

"Teams form alliances from time to time," said Damion.

"Yeah, but then they have to split the profits," said Rob. "I'll never consider that. For me—for all of us—it's everything or nothing."

"Which is why we're the best," said Damion.

"And yet we have no clue where to go next," I said, sarcasm thick on my tongue. "That's pretty awesome."

"Doesn't mean we're not going to work," said Rob. "Xia, Damion, start making calls to our regular insiders. See if you can bribe them for any information about upcoming Coterie councils or gatherings. Antonio will need to be replaced, and we should learn as soon as possible which chief is going to get the lucky promotion."

I barely heard what he was saying. I kept thinking about Waif, wondering if he was awake or asleep. Isolation couldn't be good for someone who had given up on life, but what else could I do?

I thought again of the baby robin that had died in my room while I was at school and coldness crept through my chest. I didn't want the same thing to happen to Waif. As with the robin, my heart would ache.

Rob noticed my agitation. "Want to go to the roof? It's about time I taught you how to shoot a real gun."

I nodded, grateful for a distraction.

The roof was a spacious plane of cement with targets lined up along one side. Looking back, I could see all the way to the end of the skids.

Rob handed me a pistol. It was heavier than the stun gun, with a narrower barrel.

"We'll start small because it's what we work with more often. Their precision is terrible. We use them more for intimidation than anything, so don't feel too bad if you don't hit any bulls-eyes."

I turned the pistol over in my hand. "How do I disengage the safety?"

Rob snorted. "Safety?"

"Don't all guns have one?"

"We don't have anything that fancy at the Agency."

I'd never considered something like that to be fancy, or even all that brand new. "So a modern gun with a safety is a luxury, but an advanced stun gun that shoots electric tacks isn't? It's like this country can't make up its mind whether to live in the future or the past."

"Think of Los Sueños as one big beach," said Rob. "We claim whatever happens to wash up here, from technology to fashion trends. Every now and then we get something big, but usually, it's just the outdated stuff no one wants anymore. Now let me see your gun."

Several hours and a sore arm later, we rested in the lobby of the Agency, drinking a pair of Cosmar Colas.

"You have a good eye," said Rob. "A few weeks of practice and I might let you take a real gun on a mission."

I smiled. "You were OK, but I expected a seasoned Agency member to have better accuracy."

He lifted one eyebrow. "Better than twenty-five perfect shots in a row?"

"Is that all?"

He finished the rest of his Cola and shrugged. "I'm a re-covery agent, not an assassin. You think you'll be able to top that?"

I snorted. "A few months of training, and I'll top that blindfolded. Easy."

"OK then, Annie Oakley, you've got yourself a challenge." He clinked his bottle against mine. "But before that, we'll have to get some new targets. I'm pretty sure I shot all the bulls-eyes to bits."

"You shot them all to bits? So you're saying I didn't contribute to their destruction at all?"

"I don't know; did you?"

I let a silly smile spread across my face. "Nope. Not even once."

We both burst into laughter, getting looks from other agents.

"I might need an extension on that challenge," I said.

"How much of an extension?"

I shrugged. "A few years maybe?"

We both laughed again and grabbed more Colas from a cooler in the corner of the office.

Rob's arm nudged my shoulder. "Want to head back to the Castillo? Practice is over for today, and I can't see us being much more productive here."

I nodded, trying to hide how happy I was by this news.

When we got home, the showers were working, and Rob went straight for them. I longed to do the same but instead headed for the tower.

I didn't want to wake Waif, but as soon as I entered his room, I saw that he was out of bed and standing at the open window, the orange sunset highlighting his silver hair.

"You're up," I said, a smile spreading across my face. "It's so good to see—"

"It's a long way down," he said in a dreamlike voice, bending far out the window. "But it would be so quick."

My heart slammed into my sternum. I approached him slowly like he was a runaway cat I was trying to recapture.

"Waif? Are you OK?"

He turned to me so abruptly that I froze, holding my hands up to show I meant no harm.

"Don't come any closer!" he cried. He was so different from the listless boy I'd talked to that morning. His eyes were dark and wild, and his trembling hands were clenched into fists.

I kept moving toward him, despite my galloping heart. "It's just me," I said. "I'd never hurt you."

His breathing picked up speed, and he licked his cracked lips. "Did you bring my injection?"

I paused, not sure how to respond. "Injection? What are you talking about?"

"Are you here to kill me, then? If you'd waited a few more minutes, I'd have saved you the trouble." He turned back to the window, quivering.

I ran the rest of the way across the room but found myself afraid to touch him, expecting him to lash out at any moment like a dangerous snake. "Waif, look at me. I think you're having a bad dream."

"Please," he said, his voice now a sob. "I've done everything you asked."

I brushed my hand lightly against his arm, then, gaining courage, took hold of it and pulled. He gripped my shirt, muscles tense, and eyes bloodshot. "Please!"

My heart stood still. "I don't understand."

Tears streamed down his face. "Please," he moaned, and I knew something was very wrong. Even without touching his skin, I could feel the fever heat radiating off him. I took hold of his shoulder and urged him toward the bed.

"You're delirious again," I said, dread frosting my stomach with ice. "You need to sleep this off."

"No!" he said, sending the back of his hand into my cheek

with a crack. I gave a short yelp and released him, nursing my throbbing face. He rushed for the window, but I caught his shirt just in time and dragged him away. Pain from his broken ribs doubled him over, and he gasped in agony. It allowed me to overpower him. I hauled him to the bed and pushed him onto the mattress.

He wilted into his pillow, panting, as I pressed my palm against his forehead. His temperature was climbing to alarming heights.

"Not again." I bit the inside of my cheek. Why wasn't he getting better? What was I doing wrong?

When I was sure he wouldn't try to get up, I strode to the window and reached out to close the glass panels.

By the time I returned, Waif's whole body shivered.

"Are you hurt? Just tell me what's wrong with you and I'll fix it." It was a lie. Whatever caused these terrible symptoms, I couldn't fix it on my own, but maybe if I knew the reason for his suffering I could find a way to help.

My arms trembled as I wrapped them around him, feeling his body quake against my chest. "It's OK," I murmured, using all my willpower to hold it together. I'd never seen anyone this sick before, and it could only mean one thing. He'd been right from the beginning. I was losing him and there was nothing I could do.

* * *

What passed was my worst night since arriving in Los Sueños. Waif was bad. Really bad. I was no doctor, but I could tell he was the kind of sick most people didn't recover from without serious medical help. I stood over him the whole time, mopping his brow and whispering comforting words, but it felt so useless. At last, his eyes fluttered open, confused.

I forced my lips to curve into a smile as I looked down at him. He couldn't know how petrified I was. "Hey there. Rough night?" It was probably the most ridiculous thing I could have said.

His eyelids drooped again and I shook him gently. "No, no. Stay here, right here with me, OK?" My voice sounded hysterical. I debated running to Cosmar and trying to find a doctor or begging someone for help.

Useless. Everything was useless because Waif was shadowborn. After seeing what had happened to Ichiro, I knew being shadowborn wasn't a natural state. Was there something about the alteration that was killing Waif? Maybe it was something you caught like a virus, something that gave you incredible abilities, but slowly ate away at you until you were dead. My mind raced through the possibilities, struggling to make sense of them.

I stood up, thinking of Rob. I had to tell him. Maybe if I explained the truth to him—begged him to understand—he'd somehow change his mind and want to help.

I looked back at Waif as I went to the door. This could be the end of everything, but it was the only way. Waif was dying, and if Rob could do something…

I hurried down the stairs, heart racing as I approached Rob's room. I knocked, feeling my fist tremble against the wood. No answer.

Slowly, I opened the door and looked inside. "Rob?"

His covers were rumpled, but the bed was empty.

I hurriedly searched the Castillo, listening at bedroom doors and exploring every area Rob might be.

When there was nowhere else to look, I ducked outside, calling his name. A trio of lunawasps bobbed out of the trees, illuminating the front drive. Rob's bike was missing. Where could he have possibly gone at this hour? My heart felt cold. His absence seemed wrong, and now I had no hope.

Drained and heavy, I returned to Waif's bedside, prepared for the worst. Outside, the night bloomed into a silvery dawn, further illuminating my hopeless situation.

An hour or so later I leaned forward and straightened Waif's twisted blankets, just to have something to do. My pendant fell out of my shirt, skimming his cheek.

Suddenly, his hand wrapped around the pearly teardrop and he yanked it from my neck. "Where?" he gasped, and for a second his eyes were completely lucid. "Where did you get this?"

I pulled back. "I found it in my room." I looked down at where he held it in his hands and examined it. Silvery with the luster of a hundred different colors. It reminded me of something I'd seen before.

He moaned and held it against his chest, eyes fluttering closed.

I left it with him and went downstairs to see if Rob had returned. None of the orphans had seen him, so I asked a few of them to watch for him to come home, and then tell him I was sick if he came looking.

They absently agreed and I teetered upstairs, wishing I really could spend the day curled beneath my covers and shutting out reality.

When I returned to the tower, I found my pendant hanging around Waif's neck. His free hand still gripped the stone, knuckles white from their tight hold.

"Waif?" I said, but he was deep asleep, his breathing slow and even; so different from the feverish pants of just a few minutes ago. I brushed my fingers across his face and felt sweat dotting his skin. The scalding heat was leaving him, like a fire burning down to its final embers.

All the hours of missed sleep descended on me at that moment. Gravity pulled at every inch of my body, willing me to sink and let the world fade away. I fell into my chair. Maybe he'd get through this after all.

CHAPTER 34

Hours later, I awoke to find Waif looking at me in drowsy recognition.

A laugh hiccupped out of me. "You're awake!" Memories flashed through my mind of me taking care of my mom when she'd decided to go cold turkey. Her week of sweats and shakes. The awful bottle she'd hidden under her bed that had ruined all her efforts in an instant. I shook the thoughts away to focus on Waif.

He lifted my pendant off his shirt and gripped it tighter.

"I see you like my necklace," I said.

He looked down as though surprised to see it there. "This is yours?"

"Don't you remember? You tore it from my neck last night.

Waif reached to take the necklace off, but I waved him away. "It's OK," I said. "Keep it if you like it so much."

The pendant swung in front of him as he held it up to his eyes. "This is earthblood. You must have gotten it from the Coterie. You shouldn't have, Tey. It's dangerous."

"Whoa, wait a sec. I found that in my drawer and had no idea what it was until now—"

"Thank you." He closed his eyes and exhaled.

I took a breath, recollecting myself. Another memory flashed. Seeing Waif for the first time in the rain. Ricky and Nina beating him for running away. Waif had risked everything to escape, but not before stealing a sack full of earthblood.

"Do shadowborn need earthblood?" The thought had never occurred to me before, but Waif's eyes confirmed it. He held the pendant close to his neck and pressed it into his skin.

When I spoke again, my voice shook. "Last night, when you were raving, you said something about getting an injection. Is liquid earthblood what they inject you with?"

He looked away from me, giving the slightest of nods.

Again I thought of my mom and how ill she'd been those times she tried to stop drinking. "And your sickness …it wasn't some kind of deadly virus, was it?" A sharp pain slowly spread out from deep inside my stomach. "It was the side effects of withdrawal."

Waif was silent for a long moment. "It's how the Coterie control us so we don't turn on them. If they stop the injections, we die."

Horror at his words welled up inside me. "You should have told me. I could have gone back to Nina's mine—"

"No," he said. "That's exactly why I didn't tell you. If Nina's gone, the Coterie will be at war over the control of her mine by now." He breathed hard, like the thought deeply upset him. "It's probably the most dangerous place in Los Sueños."

"I saw earthblood drive Nina crazy. How can you stand it?"

"Whatever is in the earthblood, it's in our blood too, like there's iron in your blood. When we get more of it, it gives us energy, sharpens our senses, and makes us more powerful. It's incredibly addicting. If withdrawing from it doesn't kill us, it usually makes us suicidal. If it didn't hurt so much to get out of bed, I'd probably have jumped from that window by now. Guess I have Antonio Santos to thank for that." He stroked his broken ribs and grimaced.

"You really don't remember anything from last night? You almost did just that."

His eyes flicked toward the window, then back at me. "Then I'm in your debt even more than I thought."

"I'd say we're even, assuming you don't relapse. Do you think you'll get better now?"

"I don't know." He fiddled with the chain on his neck. "The pendant is small, but what's here is powerful. It's no blood injection, but it seems to ease the symptoms."

I let out an enormous sigh. I knew my relief was premature, but I latched onto every ounce of hope his words gave me. Then my memories came back and it was like things were happening all over again.

"What's wrong?" he asked.

I tried to shrug it off. "Just thinking about my mom; how she could never get sober. The last time she tried …it was bad. I thought it would kill her." I looked up at him. "I wish there'd been some sort of magic necklace for her."

As soon as I said it, I bit my tongue, wishing I could take it back. "I'm sorry. I shouldn't have compared you to—"

"I'm the one who should be sorry."

"No," I said wiping at my eyes, surprised not to feel any tears. "It doesn't matter anyway. My mom's the reason I ran away. She needed a drink in the middle of the night, but I was so tired of her backsliding that I'd dumped her stash. She was so angry. She pulled me out of bed and…"

My voice trailed off and my hand lifted to my cheek to feel the bruise there, as if it had come from the sting of her palm.

"I know," he said. "You told me about her."

"I did?"

"On La Ventura when you were hallucinating. She doesn't sound much better than Santos."

"Just easier to run away from," I said, looking away from Waif. "Sorry. You need to rest."

"So do you," he said. He reached for my arm instinctively and then drew back.

I gently pulled the blankets over his shoulders. "I can stay longer if you don't want to be alone."

"No. You need sleep."

I nodded but still found myself reluctant to leave him in case something changed. The past couple of days had been like riding a roller-coaster in the dark. I never knew when he'd plunge again.

"I'll be all right, Tey. Promise."

"Ok," I whispered. He looked so helpless lying there that my heart hesitated to trust him, so I gave him a weak smile and promised I wouldn't be gone long. I stumbled to my room and passed out the moment I closed my eyes.

It was dark when I awoke except for a few lunawasps outside my window. The Castillo was graveyard quiet.

I didn't bother to light a candle for myself as I made my way into the hall, feeling the dizziness from sleeping at odd hours. Voices came from below and I leaned over the staircase to look toward the first floor. Rob, Xia, and Damion were in the parlor talking in low voices.

I crept down and found them drinking Cosmar Colas in front of the fireplace.

"You're up," said Rob, his eyes crinkling at me. "One of the kids told me you were feeling sick again. Any better?"

I wanted to ask where he'd been the night before, but now that there was hope for Waif, I was relieved he hadn't been there. Otherwise, I would have told him everything. "Yes, much better," I said. "I think I slept it off."

"What did you have?" asked Damion, drawing back as though afraid he'd catch something from me.

I shrugged. "Just some twenty-four-hour virus. But I feel OK now. How were things at the Agency today?"

Rob smiled. "We patrolled the skids and found a crowd of people gathered around an old movie theater. Apparently, there's going be some sort of Coterie rally there tonight. One man claimed Ricardo was gonna be in Cosmar for the event. This could be the chance we've been waiting for to go after him, or at least to find out what he's planning. The rally will start tonight at midnight, and we're gonna be there. You too, if you're up for it."

My mouth opened. "What if someone recognizes you as Agency members? I'm guessing not every mission has been a success. I bet the guns who got away would love to kill you all."

"We're not so stupid as to go in without disguises," said Xia, holding up a leather bag. "The Agency is stocked with those kinds of things." She pulled out a black wig and threw it at me.

"And Corpus made us supporter badges," said Damion, fishing out some blue leather badges embossed with the Coterie skull and trident symbol I had seen on the door to Harrington's lair.

"There's always the risk it could be a trap," said Rob. "So we've gotta be ready to split at a moment's notice."

"How long until midnight?" I asked.

"About an hour," said Damion. "We should leave now. If we can catch Ricardo early, we won't need to go in."

"Like that's going to happen," said Xia. "The man's not going to reveal himself easily."

"You never know," said Damion, getting to his feet and rifling through the bag of disguises. He pulled out a fake mustache and put it to his lip. "What do you think? Too passé?"

Rob rose and patted Damion on the back. "Looks like you were born with it. You should think about growing a real one."

Xia snorted.

"What's wrong, Xi?" said Damion. "Don't fancy kissing a hairy lip?"

"Not if that lip belongs to you."

I put the black wig over my braided hair, feeling like Uma Thurman in Pulp Fiction.

Xia fitted herself with a blood-red one and a pair of stylish glasses, while Rob settled for a tight beanie over his hair and a scarf to cover his mouth. Damion peeled off the glue covering of the fake mustache and plastered it to his upper lip, instantly looking ten years older. He put a leather jacket over his bulging arms, and a curly wig on his shaved head, giving him a 1970s cop look.

Rob handed me a stun gun and briefed me on the plan.

"The four of us will attend the rally and search for any sign of Ricardo. Once spotted, Damion and me will make a discreet exit to locate and secure Ricardo's getaway car. Meanwhile, you and Xia will continue to watch his movements. When he leaves, follow him. I'll be waiting for you near the exit. If the conditions are right, I'll give a signal, and together we'll move against Ricardo. If all goes well we can use his car to cart him back to the Agency."

This was Ricardo Santos. High Chief of the Coterie. If we messed up, we could lose everything. But if we succeeded, this could be just the opening we needed to wound the Coterie. Fatally.

CHAPTER 35

A light rain fell as we walked toward the Cinema Estrella, a movie theater that hadn't been operational in ten years. I held my breath against the stench of tobacco and urine.

There was a line outside the Estrella with people showing badges to a man at the door with a long cigarette between his teeth. We walked around the perimeter of the building, looking for any back exits. There was one on each side, but only the east side led to a road wide enough for a car.

We got in line, keeping our heads low. When we reached the man with the cigarette, we showed him our fake supporter badges and he waved us inside the dark interior. Our chosen seats were as close to the east exit as possible. I was surprised by how many people were there, and how normal they were. I'd expected the place to be teeming with vicious Coterie thugs, not mothers bouncing toddlers on their laps, or tired old men with grease-stained faces.

Cobwebs drooped from the crumbling ceiling, and an old movie screen hung in shreds. Through the musty smell, I caught a faint whiff of popcorn still lingering after all these years.

"It's sweltering in here," Rob said as he unbuttoned his jacket. He took off his beanie and fanned himself with it, hair damp with sweat.

Damion itched at his wig and eyed the growing crowd.

"Sweet salvation. They better get this over with quick or I'm gonna pass out. The heat makes my claustrophobia ten times worse."

"Next time, let's wear lighter disguises," said Xia rolling up her sleeves.

"When I suggested we go as tranny hookers, you shot me down," said Damion. He winced when Xia elbowed him in the side.

More people crowded in the back, then the doors closed and the lights dimmed. A spotlight highlighted the platform with the ripped movie screen. A tall man dressed in a dark suit stepped through the tatters. I looked at Rob, but he just shrugged.

The man's gaze swept across the audience and he smiled. "Welcome," he said in a Hispanic accent, then paused for dramatic effect.

Cheers erupted around us and we joined in.

He coughed and nodded graciously. "I appreciate everyone's dedication in attending at this late hour. I am ashamed that we have to hide like moles in the dark from the very government that is letting our nation fall to ruin."

Someone shouted an unintelligible agreement and the man smiled sadly.

"When my ancestors came to Los Sueños, they were seeking freedom from tyranny. This is a land of many opportunities. A land where dreams can become realities. But how can we be fully liberated if the man who claims to rule over us isolates us? Shouldn't we be free to come and go like so many people in the rest of the world?"

Shouts of assent.

"Shouldn't we be free to conduct business with foreign lands? Why should the advancements and technologies of our brothers be restricted from us? Why should we have to suffer from infections and illnesses easily cured? It is no secret that our monarch sends ships to America to supply goods for him and his government officials on their elite island, while the rest of us sicken and starve. When we strive to apprehend these ships and distribute these goods fairly, we are labeled as pirates and criminals. How can we obey a man who doesn't follow his own laws? How can we follow someone who keeps raising food taxes when we can't afford the lowliest of sustenance?"

Despite the man's good points, I noticed he was careful not to mention all the bloodshed and terror they also caused in the name of freedom.

"These are just a fraction of the atrocities we face at the hands of a false monarch. A man whose royal ancestor accepted divinity from the original residents of these islands, and then did nothing to protect the ones who had claimed him as their savior. The age we live in doesn't call for dependencies on ancient prophecies and outdated rituals. We are in charge of our destinies. We have the power to change our lives."

I was deafened by cheers.

"The death of our dear monarch will be the sign propelling our cause into action."

I felt Xia flinch next to me, her mouth a tight frown.

"It will be a war of the people!" the man continued. "We will fight together and raise a new leader to bring our nation justice and stability. We will emerge from the shadows as a viable force in this world, and the one who will bring us there is here with us tonight."

Wild applause.

"Would you like to meet him?"

Screams of agreement.

The man stretched out his arm as another stepped through the tatters. Everyone jumped to their feet and applauded like crazy. The four of us joined in, though Rob looked pale.

"That's him," Damion whispered in my ear, "That's Ricardo."

I looked at the man who had taken center stage, taking note of his muscular frame and oily black hair. My mind flashed back to that rain-drenched sidewalk in LA. I knew this man.

It was Ricky.

As the applause continued, a breathless figure in thick-rimmed glasses and a fedora walked down the aisle passing out pamphlets to the attendees. Rob was so focused on Ricardo that he jumped when the man tapped his shoulder and handed him a stack to pass down the aisle.

The man smiled at him. "The high chief's got presence, I'll hand him that," he glanced at the stage. "But wait until you read what he's got in store."

Rob's eyes swiveled from the pile of pamphlets to the man's face, his jaw muscles clenching. "I'm looking forward to it," he mumbled as he reached for his scarf, which he'd strewn over the back of his chair.

The other man patted him on the shoulder. "Have I seen you at one of these things before? You seem…" he leaned closer, eyes squinting behind his glasses and then going wide. Rob tried to pull away, but the man grabbed his arm. "Adrian? My god. I thought—"

Rob immediately pulled his scarf back across his mouth and tried to push his way through the crowd, but the mass of people packed around the door was too thick.

"Adrian!" cried the man, trying to follow. "Stop him! That's Adrian Elder!"

Shouts and whispers echoing the name raced through the crowd, and heads turned away from Ricardo and toward Rob. One of Ricardo's bodyguards jogged down the aisle toward us. He lifted a gun and fired. Rob dove into the aisle and the bullet embedded itself into the back of a chair. Xia and Damion had their guns out in a second and fired back, covering Rob as we tried to retreat through the mob. People pressed in at all sides in a frenzied panic. I brought out my stun gun and pointed at the ones closest to us.

"Move aside," I commanded, but the crowd was too thick. The bodyguard kept coming after us, and the four of us tried to shove through screaming people as they swarmed the door. Someone elbowed me in the side of my chin, and if it weren't for Damion behind me, I'd have fallen to the floor. His big hands steadied me and reached over my shoulders to push aside the men blocking our path. We forced our way outside and ran to the back of the building where a black car with tinted windows waited. Two large, armed men stood beside it.

Rob signaled toward the men and we knew what to do.

Xia and Damion shouted and ran at the men, distracting them so Rob and I could come from behind. We pressed our stun guns against the exposed skin of their necks. The electric darts shot out, and they collapsed in twitching heaps.

Rob opened the front door and threw a strong punch at the driver, then rolled him out onto the curb. He jumped in and started the car while the rest of us hopped in. I buckled myself in front as he stepped on the gas. The car lurched forward.

Twenty seconds later, five motorcycles were on our tail, tires squealing as we left the skids and boarded paved roads. The drivers fired in rapid succession. One bullet struck our back window, which was thankfully bullet resistant. Something punched into the front windshield, creating a web of cracks, and I squinted through it to see if someone was attacking from the front or the side of the road. But I saw nothing but the ramshackle buildings that lined the street.

With a roar, the pavement in front of us split apart, chunks of rock and cobblestone flying in every direction. Rob slammed on the brakes to avoid the destruction and spun the car in a terrifying 180-degree turn.

"They've got shadowborn!" shouted Damion, turning to face the motorcycles. I looked behind me and saw glimpses through the cracks in the glass of silver-haired children sitting in front of riders in black. That explained the explosive road damage.

I held back a scream as Rob pushed hard on the gas pedal and headed straight for them. The riders continued to fire, punching bullet-sized marks in the already ruined windshield. Finally, they had no choice but to pull apart or risk being run over by our larger vehicle. We raced through an alley, running over several abandoned crates, and then pulled a sharp left to an adjoining street.

I forced myself to look straight ahead as we headed for a massive bridge that stretched across the ocean. The bridge had to be over a mile long, but its straight course gave Rob ample opportunity to gain speed. He dug his foot into the pedal and pushed the car faster and faster.

We were almost across when I heard a horrible grinding sound. I fell back as the rear of the car sloped downward and wove back and forth, metal screeching on pavement. The back tires had been shot out.

I squeezed my eyes shut and braced every muscle as the car swerved dangerously to one side, smashing into the guardrail and breaking through. We continued to slide until the back of the car teetered over the edge.

Sweat streamed down Rob's brow as he ground the gas pedal, the front wheels spinning. We leaned forward but the car was too off-balance. We hovered for several seconds, car squealing, and fell backward.

I felt Rob's hand wrap around mine as we plunged into the dark water.

As the car descended, I frantically tried to open my door. It wouldn't budge.

Rob grabbed my arm. "Let's let in some water. When it's up to your chin, the pressure should stabilize."

Xia immediately rolled down her window and the car flooded with freezing water at an alarming rate. Soon it was up to my chest. Then my chin.

My lungs heaved and I sucked in my last bit of oxygen before the water rose over my head. My door came open this time, but I had another problem. My seatbelt wouldn't unbuckle. I pressed the release button over and over again, but the water must have been affecting it because nothing was happening. I started to panic. Drowning was one of the last ways I wanted to go, and if I'd had any breath left, I would have screamed. I tugged and tried to wriggle out, but it was no use, and I was wasting oxygen.

Rob pulled a knife from his jacket and sawed at my restraints, but my heart was pounding in my ears at a frenzied rate. Black spots were already obscuring my vision. I made one last attempt at pressing the release button before my whole world faded away.

CHAPTER 36

Something heavy pressed on my chest. I choked. Salty water came up and I vomited it onto wet sand. When it was over, I coughed for several more minutes, spitting out remnants of seawater before I could breathe normally again. I looked up. Rob was there, hair plastered to his head by seawater, brow crinkled in worry. A little farther down the beach, I spotted Xia and Damion lying exhausted in the sand.

We were no longer on the main island. Cosmar twinkled across a small stretch of ocean and the moonlight illuminated our ruined bridge in the distance.

"Where are we?" I asked.

"Santa Arcadia," said Rob. "If we'd swum back to the main island, they'd have shot us before we reached the shore. I'm hoping they think we all drowned in the plunge."

I sat up suddenly, remembering. "Rob, what happened back there was a mistake, right? That man called you by a different name. Adrian."

Rob's face looked pained. "Come on. Let's find something to get a fire going so we can dry out."

"You're avoiding my question." My chest still heaved, and now I felt frustration welling up inside. After what I'd just gone through, I deserved the truth. We all did.

He groaned. "It was a mistake. He took me for someone I'm not." With a pull, he helped me to my feet and guided me unsteadily to where Xia and Damion lay.

"Keep an eye on her," Rob said to them. He let go and I fell onto the sand, shivering in the night wind.

Damion lifted himself up on his elbows. "Where are you going?"

"To get kindling. We need to dry off." He sounded troubled, and a little angry.

"Wait, I'll come with you." Damion got to his feet and dusted off the sand that stuck to his wet jeans.

"No," said Rob. "I got it."

"But there could be, you know, wild animals in the jungle. It's not safe."

"Just let me do this, OK?" He waved Damion away.

Damion sighed and flopped down again. "You're the boss."

Rob stalked off into the trees.

I put a hand over my mouth as I coughed, smearing sand over my damp lips. "What's wrong with him?"

Xia looked at Damion uneasily and back at me. "That man recognized him."

"Shh," said Damion. "I don't think it's smart to bring up that topic to—" his eyes swiveled toward me and he mouthed something silently to Xia.

"If she's going to stay on our team, then she's going to have to know eventually," said Xia, combing her tangled wet hair with her fingers. "I'm going to tell her."

"Is that smart?"

"Like you would know what's smart and what isn't."

"I'm looking out for Rob."

"Just tell me," I said, frustration clear in my voice.

Xia sighed and looked up at the moon. "Rob's real name is Adrian Elder, but he hasn't gone by it in six years. His father was King Alden's brother."

Something opened up inside my chest, letting in a cold breeze. "So that whole story about coming from New York and his parents getting killed was fake?"

"Oh, his parents are dead, all right," said Damion. "They were never on good terms with the king. They were scientists with no real interest in politics. That's what got them killed. They stumbled onto something big, a huge secret about the islands they were about to expose to the world."

Xia hugged her knees to her chest. "The official record pegs their deaths on a chief named Apollo who was after their research, but I think one of the servants ratted them out to the monarchy."

"There's no proof the king had anything to do with it," said Damion.

"Yeah, but if their research could discredit him like Rob suspects, then he had more reason than anyone to put a stop to it."

"In any case, Rob ran away from the king's care a year later. He did everything he could to change his appearance and vowed revenge. Now, after all this time, his uncle has decided he wants him back. Six months ago, he put an enormous price on Rob's head, and if the truth about him gets out to the other agents, he's done for. So you understand why this needs to stay quiet, right, Tey?"

I nodded as a million thoughts overwhelmed me. Here I was, thinking I was starting to grasp the kind of man Rob was, but it was only a false man Rob had led me to believe was real. I had followed him like a leashed dog, and he had never trusted me, not even now.

"No one else knows?"

Xia shook her head. "Just us. And now you."

"And his parents' research? Do you know what it was?"

"Whatever it might have been was stolen the night they were murdered," Damion said. "My guess is it was destroyed shortly after."

I lowered my head into my hands and desperately tried to make sense of everything. But after spending so much time believing something was a certain way, finding out that things were completely different from anything I could have imagined made me feel betrayed somehow. "Why did he lie to me?"

Damion drew in the sand with his index finger. "He lied to all of us at first. He had to. You can't go around telling something like that to trained bounty hunters, or anyone in need of extra cash," he said eyeing me.

"I don't mean at first, I mean now. On the beach, he said the man who recognized him was mistaken. After everything, does he still not trust me? Haven't I proven myself?"

"You're not just here to take down the Coterie," Xia said. "You have other plans, plans you might do anything to accomplish. Until you give them up, you can never fully be one of us. Not in his eyes."

My lips tightened as I looked at her, but I knew she was right. As much as I hated what was going on here, I wanted to get away from these islands more than anything, and there were few things I wouldn't do to achieve that.

"Don't look so down," said Damion, rubbing my shoulder. "I'd want to leave this mess of a country too if I wasn't so invested in saving it. And I'm sure Rob will get around to telling you the truth soon. It's obvious he's head over heels for you; that's gotta mean he must have some faith in you, right?"

I shrugged. "It's not like it matters now that I already know."

"Know what?" said a voice behind me.

I turned and saw Rob coming through the trees, a bundle of sticks and palm fronds in his arms.

"Nothing," I said. "It doesn't matter."

"Know what?" he repeated, his voice low, almost threatening.

I eyeballed Xia and Damion, but they were staring at the sand, looking ashamed.

Rob's feet crunched as he walked through the line of underbrush and onto the beach. "I asked you a question."

Xia sprang to her feet. "I told her," she said, meeting his eyes.

Rob stopped. "Told her what?"

"Everything. At least, everything important."

Damion stood up beside her and put an arm around her shoulder. "She'd have to know eventually, right? Your plans—"

Rob threw the kindling to the ground, his face dark in the moonlight. "My plans are my own. Not yours, not Xia's, not Tey's. They're mine, and I decide when the time is right to reveal information that could ruin everything I've spent the last six years working toward."

If I couldn't see his mouth moving, I would have thought the angry words were coming from someone else. His voice was the voice of someone much older and angrier than the Rob I knew. The Rob I thought I knew.

"Sweet salvation," said Damion, holding up his hands and walking closer to him. "It's not like Tey's someone we just met on the street."

"It doesn't matter who she is," said Rob. "She knows now, and I can't ever take that knowledge away from her."

"It doesn't change anything," said Xia. "Not really."

"It changes everything! Now every time she looks at me, she'll see the enormous price on my head. She won't be able to help it. And when I look at you two, I'll wonder who else you've told behind my back. Who else will be coming for me in the night."

Xia took a step back. "I would never—"

Damion grabbed Rob's arm. "Saints and angels! Get a hold of yourself. You're just upset that you were recognized tonight. I'd be scared, too."

Rob shoved Damion onto the sand. Then he kicked the kindling on the ground, scattering it everywhere. He frightened me, but I got to my feet.

"Rob, I understand why you'd want to keep this a secret, but I'm glad I know. I just wish you trusted me."

When he spoke, his voice boiled. "After tonight I can't trust anyone. That man who recognized me, he was my bodyguard, the one assigned to me after my parents were murdered. I thought I'd changed enough to be safe from watchers, but you can never be safe from someone you spent nearly every waking hour with for over a year. Someone who became your closest friend. Seems the traitor joined the Coterie. He probably would have killed me if I hadn't run away from Santa Isidore when I did." He let out a half cough half sob and looked from Damion, to Xia, to me. "One of you will probably betray me next. It's only a matter of time, isn't it?"

"Stop it!" shouted Xia, her voice shrill. "What the hell's gotten into you?"

"I can't go back there, Xia. I can't go back to my uncle. He'll lock me up and never let me leave. That would kill me; you know it would. Los Sueños would fall apart around me and I wouldn't be able to do anything to stop it. I can't live like that. I have to fight. It's the only reason I'm still alive."

"Then let us help you!" I cried. "I may have been brought to these islands against my will, but don't think I don't care what happens here. I'm on your side, Rob. We all are."

His eyes stabbed into my own. "You say that now, but for how long? How long until those Coterie bastards claim you all?" He picked up one of the sticks and strode back toward the tree line, swiping at the underbrush.

"Rob, wait!" I shouted after him. I started to follow, but Xia grabbed my arm.

"Let him go," she said. "No one can help him when he's like this." She talked as if this alien Rob was familiar, and I wondered how many other faces I had yet to see him wear.

CHAPTER 37

When I opened my eyes the next morning, light blasted them, and tears streamed down my face. My clothes had dried out and my hair was crusted with salt and sand. I sat up. Next to me, Xia, and Damion roasted fruit over a fire.

Rob was with them. He must have returned sometime while I slept. He smiled at me as if the night before had been nothing more than a bad dream. He offered me a stick skewering various pieces of unfamiliar fruit.

"Breakfast?"

I accepted it warily and turned it over the flames, careful not to get too close to him. Xia and Damion were successfully evading the awkwardness I couldn't help feeling, and lounged next to Rob with their usual laidback ease. A million thoughts raced through my head, but despite what had happened, my thoughts kept returning to the same thing. Waif.

"We should get back to the Castillo," I said. "The kids are probably hungry."

Rob shrugged as casually as if he'd never been angry a day in his life, and for a split second, I almost wondered if his rage had been a dream. "Nah. They're fine. I brought them plenty of groceries yesterday. They'll be OK for a few days." He took a bite of a steaming yellow fruit, wincing as it burned his tongue. "I think we should stay here a couple of nights until the whole incident blows over. If people learn I'm in Cosmar, every Coterie gun and bounty hunter will be looking for me. Let's just hope the Beacon proclaims me dead. Better chance of that if I lie low."

I wrung the end of my shirt. "But you told me that coming to Santa Arcadia was a bad idea."

"Anyone with sense knows the ghost rumors about Santa Arcadia are just a ruse," said Xia, laying back and soaking in the sun. "Think of this as a vacation. I doubt we're gonna get many of those."

I shielded my eyes with my hand and looked toward the water. I was surprised to see a small boat pulling into shore half a mile down the beach. "What's that?" I pointed. I could see men inside wearing red kingsguard jackets.

Rob doused our fire with sand and motioned for us to duck into the jungle foliage. He peered out uneasily. "Those roosters are dropping off some sort of package," he said. A few minutes later, they rowed away. When they were out of sight, we moved to get a better look at what they'd brought.

Ropes bound together large boxes marked with food labels.

"Wait," said Rob, holding his arm out before we could touch anything. "Let's watch it first. Someone might be expecting this shipment." We ducked back into the underbrush and kept our eyes on the prize. When about forty minutes had passed without any sign of trouble, Rob consented to let us explore the contents.

"Jackpot," said Damion, ripping free a can of Cosmar Cola. He popped it open and took a long swig.

He and Xia rifled through the food, taking out cans of beans and rice. "And here I was thinking we'd have nothing to eat but jungle plunder for the next few days," said Damion. "We'll have a regular feast tonight."

A gunshot ripped through the jungle. Damion dropped

the cans and stepped back, hands in the air.

From out of the trees stepped five figures carrying rifles. Swathed head to toe in rags, they looked like mummies out of an Egyptian horror movie.

"Run!" Rob cried as the ragged men fired another round of bullets.

We retreated into the jungle and ducked low. The men, if they were men, didn't pursue. Guns held high, they scanned the area and went to the package. One of them pulled a sled. He loaded the goods onto it and dragged it across the sand.

"What are they?" I whispered.

"Lepers," Rob said, watching them closely.

I suddenly remembered what he had told me about all the lepers being relocated to Santa Arcadia.

"They'll defend their territory to the death," said Rob. "Not the type to mess with, that's for sure."

"They're just protecting their food," said Xia. "Your uncle probably doesn't send them much."

"I'm surprised he sends them anything." Rob kept his eyes fixed on them until they were out of sight. "Now that we're back to searching for jungle plunder, we should split up. Let's go in pairs in case we run into any more trouble. Just don't go too far inland. The leper settlement is a mile northwest of here. Avoid it at all costs."

"How do you know where the settlement is?" I asked.

He blinked, looking startled, then shrugged. "Saw it on a map back when I still lived with my uncle. I doubt it's changed much since then." He motioned for us to move out. "Everyone meet back at the beach in two hours."

I was surprised when Xia offered to go with me, but grateful that I didn't have to go with Rob. I needed to talk to him but couldn't bring myself to confront him just yet.

The two of us set off in one direction, while Rob and Damion went in the other. "He acts like nothing happened," I said when we were alone.

Xia pushed aside some vines and walked in front of me. "He's embarrassed about how he acted and this is his way of apologizing. You'll get used to it."

"I'm not sure I want to."

She shrugged. "It will make your life a hell of a lot easier, especially if you still plan on making eyes at him when this is all over."

"I don't make eyes at him."

She snorted. "Please, Tey. You can hardly be in the same room with him without blushing."

At her words, I felt a blush coming on and willed my face to cool down. "You're one to talk. You pretend anger and annoyance, but anyone can see that's code for I'm still madly in love with Damion."

She stopped walking but didn't turn to face me, probably hiding a blush of her own. But when she spoke, the tone of her voice surprised me. It was low, and ice cold. "I'm not like Rob. I can't forgive overnight. I can't wake up and pretend that things are OK between us." She continued to walk, and I kept my mouth shut as I followed after.

We searched for about thirty minutes before coming upon a tree full of the blue pear-like fruit I'd given to Waif. We climbed it together and knocked some of it off. I noticed a clearing not far away, filled with numerous huts and ramshackle buildings. "Must be where those lepers live," I said, pointing. Sure enough, two bandaged women hobbled out of a hut as the five from the beach came into sight, pulling the goods.

I saw Xia turn to look at a forest green flag whipping in the center of the village. "That's odd," she said.

"What?"

"That banner. It has a black owl on it."

I shrugged. "So?"

"Each member of the royal family has a unique crest. The Owl belonged to Rob's father," she said. "With his death, it's now rightfully Rob's."

Below, someone pushed aside a covering of dead reeds, revealing a round hatch. They opened it and went inside while the others unloaded the sleigh. "What are they up to?" she mumbled, chewing a fingernail.

"Maybe it's just a root cellar," I said.

"Or a prison. Look, they're handing down two cans of food. Why only two?"

We watched them for several more minutes. A woman in a white lab coat emerged. She went into one of the huts and came out with a tiny figure wrapped in a blanket. I couldn't see its face, but it was small enough to be a child. She led it down into the hatch and closed the covering. The reeds were redistributed by one of the lepers, and everyone returned to their huts.

"Maybe they have a doctor on site," I suggested. Although something about that felt off. We kept watch a while longer, but when nothing else happened, we both climbed down from the tree.

We picked up as much of the fruit as we could carry and returned to the beach. Rob and Damion were already there, munching on carrots.

"Where'd you get those?" asked Xia.

Damion took a big bite out of one. "The lepers have a well-stocked garden, and no one was around to stop us, so we took what we wanted."

"I didn't see a garden from the tree," I said to Xia.

"It was hidden farther in the jungle," said Damion. "Rob stumbled upon it by accident."

Xia raised an eyebrow. "We saw the settlement."

"I told you not to go near that place," Rob said, eyes suddenly wild. "Not after the beach incident."

"Calm down; we're not stupid," said Xia. "We saw it from a distance. They were flying your father's crest."

Rob's brows came together and his hands tightened into fists. "Are you sure?"

"Who else uses a black owl crest?" she asked. "Any idea why they'd have it?"

He shrugged like it was no big deal, though I noticed his hands were still clenched. "My parents used to be in charge of sending the colony supplies before they were killed. Maybe the residents think they're still doing it. I doubt lepers are up to date on the latest decade of royal assassinations." He offered her a carrot. "We should clear out of their territory before we're spotted again. Come on."

We hiked several miles down the beach. When Rob thought we'd gone far enough to be safe from the colony, we hunkered down in the sand to spend the rest of the day.

"Keep your eyes sharp for any patrols from Cosmar," said Rob. "They've probably searched the wreckage of our car by now and will be looking for our bodies, dead or alive. The first sign of a boat and we run into the jungle."

Despite his words, no one seemed very afraid. As the day wore on he got an instant tan, while my skin turned bright red. Damion dove into the water and body surfed, while Xia stripped to her bra and underwear and napped in the sun. I paced the shore, feet treading through foam as I tried to come up with an excuse to go back to Cosmar. One that wouldn't give me away.

The day faded into an orange sunset, and the lights from the city twinkled in the distance. "Tey, you're making me nervous," shouted Rob from where he and the others had gathered around a fire. "Come get some food."

Xia and Damion laughed at something, and Rob soon joined in, clearly enjoying himself. I listened from a distance, remembering Xia's words. You have other plans, plans that you might do anything to accomplish. Until you give them up, you can never fully be one of us. As much as I resented being told I didn't belong, she was right, and it was better that way. If I was too invested, I might not have the willpower to escape.

Worry tightened to a knot in my stomach. Waif was probably wondering what had happened to me, if he hadn't relapsed, or worse. I told myself that with all the food and water I'd left in his room, at least he wouldn't starve, but the thought did little to comfort me.

I joined the others by the fire and ate more of the roasted fruit and vegetable kabobs. The sun sank below the horizon and a cool wind swept off the ocean. It felt good on my burnt skin.

"I had the weirdest dream last night," said Damion, throwing a stick in the fire. "It was about the freaky natives all the stories talk about, with the albino skin and white eyes. They were standing over me like they were gonna cut me open or something. Saints, it still gives me the heebie-jeebies."

"Good thing they disappeared like one hundred and fifty years ago," said Xia.

"Do you think it's true what Henry Elder's old reports say? About them having power over all the elements? I hear they could make rocks and trees change shape just by whispering to them."

Xia shrugged. "After seeing what the shadowborn can do, I'll believe anything."

"What are you guys talking about?" I asked. "Who's Henry Elder?"

Damion turned to me. "He was an American sailor and the man who discovered these islands."

"When?" I asked.

He shrugged. "A couple centuries ago. He was trying to sail around the world and got swept off course. Ended up beaching here. But instead of claiming it for the red, white and blue, took it all for himself."

"No one had claimed it yet?"

"There were people here alright, just not the sort good old Henry thought worthy to govern a civilized nation. They were a population of natives with chalk-white skin and hair. They were primitive but could do unexplainable things like bend the laws of gravity and see into the future. It only took them three days to learn his language."

I creased my brow. "That's hard to believe."

He smiled and shrugged. "His reports also mention how the natives believed that Los Sueños was alive. A living, breathing creature that had been asleep for centuries. They thought that when it awoke, it would fly them to their version of Heaven, high in the cosmos. Until then, their spirits were trapped on the islands, forced to live many lives, die many deaths. They were convinced Henry Elder would be the one to wake it."

"Where are they now?" I had to admit, as unlikely as the story was, I was still enthralled.

"Gone. People say they were very sensitive to Western diseases. By the time Henry Elder was an old man, they had all died out. So much for their many lives."

"Was Henry Elder of Spanish descent?"

"Not to my knowledge."

"Then why does this archipelago have a name like Los Sueños?"

"Most of his crewmembers were recruited from South America. They named many of the individual islands after saints, but the archipelago as a whole was named Los Sueños, the place of dreams."

"Too bad the shadowborn won't do for us what the natives did for Henry Elder," Damion continued. "They promised him anything he wanted—riches, a palace sculpted from stone, someone to guide the winds of ships to bring more subjects to populate the islands. That's how he became king, right, Rob?"

Rob poked at the fire with a stick and nodded. "He turned most of Los Sueños into a resort for the impossibly rich. Only the most elite received Henry Elder's invitation to visit. But few who came ever left, and pretty soon, there were shiploads of uninvited guests who didn't fit into Henry's vision of paradise. That's when he secluded himself on one of the northern islands, away from all the riffraff he found increasingly difficult to control."

"Why were the natives so eager to help him?" I asked.

"They thought he fulfilled some archaic prophecy about a stranger coming to wake the sleeping land. They denied him nothing once he promised to try. Not that he intended to do much to help them. It was all just a game to him. One that's been passed down to my uncle. One that I'm going to end."

CHAPTER 38

The next evening, Rob stood up without warning. "Vacation's over," he said, brushing sand off his jeans. "If I don't check in on my kids, they might burn down the Castillo."

Damion let out a long groan and motioned toward him. "Behold, the crusher of dreams."

"As if you didn't have a little brother to take care of," said Xia, frowning.

"You have a brother?" I asked him, surprised by how much I didn't know about him.

Damion raised and lowered one shoulder. "That kid is more self-reliant than I'll ever be. He's used to my absences."

"Well, I for one need to get back to my mom," said Xia. "She's probably freaking out by now. It was stupid of me to stay so long."

Suddenly, I was picturing my mom. Was she freaking out too? More likely drinking herself senseless so she wouldn't have to think about me.

"Let's gather sticks," said Rob. "With the bridge destroyed, we'll need to make small flotation devices to hang on to, unless you're all Olympic swimmers?"

We shook our heads.

"Didn't think so. We'll wait for dark in case any Coterie are still watching for us from the beach, then swim back. Once in Cosmar, we'll continue to lie low until we get a feel for how things have been since the rally, but we'll keep searching for leads on Ricardo. If he's still in the city, we'll get back on his trail."

"I bet those lepers have a boat or two hidden somewhere," said Damion. "Let's hike back to the colony and have a look around first. Might be easier to—"

"No." Rob's tone was harsh. "The colony should be left alone. They're dangerous."

"It's not like we've never been in a dangerous situation before," said Xia.

Rob shook his head. "Doesn't matter. They deserve peace. We're not stealing from them, or going near them. OK?"

Grudgingly, they both nodded.

We each gathered long sticks and did our best to lash them together with vines, a task way harder than movies about people stranded on islands make it out to be. The vines were thick, and most weren't flexible enough to curl around our crude bundles. I searched for slender green ones and tied them carefully so they wouldn't break apart.

The sun was already setting by the time I was finished with mine. I examined my handiwork. It wasn't much bigger than a body pillow, but the sticks floated and would be something to cling to while I made the swim.

When night arrived, we waded into the ocean. The air was cold and the water even colder. I gasped as the frigid waves lapped over my body. Together, we put our bundles in front of us and kicked against the waves as we swam toward the far beach of Santa Delphina.

Three-quarters of the way there, the green vines tying my sticks together split, and the floatation device quickly came apart. My only choice was to do my best breaststroke the rest of the way. My limbs were trembling by the time we reached the other island and my lungs ached. I crawled onto the shore and collapsed until my breath returned.

Drops of water stung my cheek. Rain.

I felt Rob pull me to my feet and guide me to the road. His body felt impossibly warm, and I huddled against it, shivering as we stumbled along in the dark. By the time we reached the Castillo it was pouring, and lightning turned the night to day in ten-second intervals. Damion and Xia joined us to wait out the storm.

"You have some killer instincts," Damion told Rob. "If we hadn't left that beach when we did, we'd have been pummeled by this weather."

Before we even had a chance to grab towels, frightened children poured down the stairs, all running to Rob like he was their long lost father. I wanted to disappear before Lei found me. She'd probably be scared of the storm and want to sleep in my room. I would have loved to let her if I didn't have a bigger problem to worry about.

"I'm going to bed," I announced. "If I can fall asleep with all this thunder."

Rob was too preoccupied to stop me.

I ran all the way up six flights of stairs until I reached the tower. The sound of the rain on the roof was deafening.

"Waif?" I cried. No answer.

It was dark inside and freezing. I'd brought up wood for the fireplace days ago but hadn't needed it. Now I was happy it was still there. Quickly, I set about starting a fire with a book of matches I'd also left beside the hearth. When a steady blaze crackled, I approached Waif's bed, holding my breath. His blankets were covering his head, probably from the cold. Gently, I pulled them back, praying the boy beneath them was still breathing.

Waif shifted his position, the movement relaxing my fears. His eyes opened.

My heart fluttered and I took a breath. I was soaking wet and chilled to the bone, yet to see him awake and seemingly no worse than when I'd left him warmed every part of me.

Waif looked around. He appeared confused, like he was still half in a dream, and didn't seem to see me. His eyes finally turned toward me and he gasped. "Tey?" He blinked rapidly. "You're back. I was starting to think—"

Emotion welled up in me like runoff from the rainstorm. I fell to my knees and wrapped my arms around Waif. He went rigid at my touch, but I didn't let go. "I'm so sorry for leaving you," I said. "I didn't mean to."

Slowly, one muscle at a time, Waif relaxed, his pale face flushing. "I was worried something had happened to you."

"Something did, but it's OK now. I'm just glad you're OK." I pressed the back of my hand against his cheek. "I was so sure you'd relapsed and were dead by now. I worried about so many things."

"You don't have to worry about me," said Waif, his hand going to the pendant at his neck.

"So it's working then, my pendant?"

"Yes."

"But wearing a necklace of earthblood must be so different from getting it injected into your bloodstream. I don't understand how it's helping you."

He held it up, the colors changing as they caught the firelight. "Solidified earthblood can conduct some of the emidion surrounding us."

"Emidion?"

"It's a form of energy like electricity or radiation. It's the main reason they mine for this stuff."

"What does it do?"

"I'm not completely sure. The earthblood is the only substance able to conduct it, sort of like the way metal conducts electricity. And I think it's the reason I can turn invisible."

I knitted my brow. "Why do you say that?"

He shrugged. "Just a hunch. When my ability does work, I can feel myself pulling from the emidion in my surroundings. I was always able to sense that energy better after an injection. It feels similar to the energy emitted by your pendant."

I caught myself rubbing my chest. "When I was in that warehouse in LA, I was hit by a blast of something. Was that emidion?"

He nodded. "A concentrated form. Ricardo and Nina were experimenting with it, but it was only safe to do it off the islands where no other emidion was present. They didn't want to risk triggering a chain explosion."

"Do you know what they were trying to accomplish?"

He nodded. "The Coterie eventually plans on spreading their reach beyond the islands, but they need a powerful tactic. Ricardo and Nina were toying with the idea of manipulating people through controlled climate change."

"Emidion can do that?"

"They thought so."

I shivered thinking of what that could entail. I was glad Nina was no longer around to assist in that endeavor, but now I wanted Rob to find Ricardo more than ever, so he could be taken out before his weapon was fully operational.

There were a million more questions I wanted to ask Waif, but one look at his face made it obvious he still had a long road ahead of him before he was fully well. "You should go back to sleep," I said. "I won't leave you like that again. I promise." I didn't say what I felt in my heart. That he couldn't stay forever. How long before he left me?

CHAPTER 39

We settled back in our office at the Agency a few days later. I looked out the window while Xia and Damion rifled through wanted posters. It was raining and the streets were shiny and metallic.

Rob turned on the radio. The signal was poor, but it was enough to hear the Crime Watch, a fifteen-minute monarchy-sponsored program known for announcing new bounties and any current crime data. Today it was comprised entirely of two men discussing Adrian Elder and the chances he may have survived the crash. Divers had examined the sunken car and hadn't found any bodies, but that didn't mean Adrian hadn't drowned after escaping the vehicle. There was, of course, no proof that it had been the missing royal at all. Information on the case now had a bounty of its own.

The only photograph the king had released of his nephew was of a young, rosy-cheeked boy, with blond curls and wide eyes. Rob's face was much leaner and harder now, and his hair was a dark, unrecognizable color. I wondered if he dyed it, or if it had just darkened with age.

When the rain stopped, Rob told Xia and Damion to head home. I looked forward to returning to the Castillo. After the incident on Santa Arcadia, I hated leaving Waif all day. This was new territory for me, and I feared his withdrawal symptoms would have unpredictable emotional affects. What if he did something crazy again like the night he'd wanted to jump out the window? I couldn't help going over every terrible possibility in my mind and was ready for some reassurance. But when I got on the bike with Rob, I noticed he wasn't headed home.

"Where are we going?"

"It's a surprise."

Although his words were meant to be cheerful, my heart sank. That was the last thing I wanted. "You picked a strange time for surprises."

"Isn't that the point?"

I didn't resist, but my heart still protested.

We rode over damp cobblestones to a part of the city I'd never been to before. It was a tidy sector with clean streets and buildings mimicking Asian architecture. Canals crisscrossed the streets with fancy arching bridges painted in colorful designs.

We pulled up to a nice restaurant with a curved, pagoda-style roof. A well-dressed man immediately came out to take Rob's bike. Rob smiled at me and held out an arm. I took it, but I didn't smile back.

"You should have warned me," I said. "I would have worn something nicer." My clothes were casual close-fitting brown pants and a loose blue shirt with a belt circling my middle; hair, the usual braided halo around my head.

"You couldn't look more perfect," he said, squeezing my arm. "Let's go inside."

We were seated next to a window facing one of the canals. A waitress dressed as a geisha approached and handed us menus and drinks. On a dais was a small musical group playing traditional Japanese instruments. To my left, water spouted out of the mouth of a ruby dragon onto jade stones.

"What do you think?" Rob asked, looking around.

"It's fit for royalty."

His mood immediately darkened. "I don't want you to think of me that way, Tey."

"I didn't mean it like that."

"Yes you did, and I want you to put it out of your head right now."

"Why?"

"Because I wish you could look past it. Ever since you learned the truth, you've been distant. Whenever I think we might have a minute alone, you scuttle upstairs like you're afraid I'll order your beheading."

I flushed. "I've just been distracted with a lot of things."

"What things? Are you still so set on getting home?"

I shrugged. I'd been so preoccupied with Waif that I hadn't thought about home in a while.

"Look, I know working for the Agency isn't ideal. It's a hard life, and it can be terrifying and dangerous. But I believe what we're doing will make a huge difference."

The waitress came back. "Ready to order?"

I scanned the menu for something I recognized, but the names of the dishes were strange to me, so I took a recommendation from Rob and hoped for the best.

After the waitress left, Rob returned his focus on me. "Now that you know the truth about me, I want you to be clear on what I'm trying to do. There is a right time and a wrong time for everything. As crazy as it sounds, war has always been my goal. But it can't happen until the right time. Working for the Agency is allowing me to create that opportune moment."

I toyed with the tablecloth. "I don't see how war could ever be desirable."

"Los Sueños is a deeply flawed nation. War is the only way

to resolve all those problems. The Coterie will never change on their own. Neither will the monarchy. There has to be a revolution." He sipped a carbonated orchid pear beverage from his glass. "Every Coterie gun we take down is weakening them. We've already removed many of the most dangerous chiefs. If we can get to Ricardo, they'll lose direction and they won't recover fast. It will be the perfect hole we need to upturn their criminal network entirely."

"How?"

"That's when I come out of hiding," he said. "Once the Beacon finds out I was with the Agency, they'll give me endless publicity. My exploits won't have to be a secret anymore. To everyone else, I'll look like a man of the people. They'll want to follow me."

"What about your uncle?"

Rob shrugged. "If the Coterie haven't assassinated him by then, I'm sure I can arrange it."

My jaw dropped. "You'd kill a member of your own family?"

He looked at the table. "In war, sacrifices must be made. My cousin, the crown princess Alyah, will have to be dealt with too, so there's no one standing between me and control of the monarchy. I'll give them both ample opportunities to step down. But an assassination at the hands of the Coterie, at the right time, would give us the fuel we need to kick off the revolution full force with me at the head. Neither the kingsguard nor the common people will question following someone with a blood-right to the throne. And they'll finally get someone who knows what to do with it."

The waitress brought us our food. Two plates of thin noodles heaped with roasted vegetables and seasoned meats with a side of egg rolls.

We each took a couple of bites. It was delicious, and the salty seasonings were unlike anything I'd ever tasted before, but Rob's words kept me from fully enjoying it.

Finally, he spoke again. "I want you to understand why I'm doing this so you can be on my side. It would mean everything to me if you stood with me."

"Is this really the best way?" I asked. "After the rally, it sounds like the Coterie want the same thing."

He snorted. "Through crime and murder."

"Will a revolution spare more lives?"

"People will die," he said, staring at his plate. "There's no pretending otherwise. But it will save more lives in the long run. Coterie murder people every day. We have to stop them. This country needs a leader who can change things, and if it doesn't get one soon, it's going to fall apart."

I chewed slowly. "I understand." But I didn't. Not really. So much of Los Sueños was still a mystery to me. Why was it secret from the rest of the world? What was the king hiding from?

There was more at stake than just the Coterie versus the monarchy. There were the islands themselves. Maybe it was the emidion Waif had told me about, maybe it was something deeper, but my emotions were fiercer here than they'd ever been, my mind sharper, my dreams at night as vivid as any reality.

"I know you can feel it," said Rob, as though reading my thoughts. "Like you belong here." His smile suddenly seemed feral. "You can be happy, Tey. When this is all over, we can make this place anything you want it to be."

For a moment I believed him. It was like the islands themselves were speaking to me with his voice. That was the effect this place had. Anything could happen. Any fantasy could be made real.

"There are powers here even I don't understand. Together we'll discover all of the islands' secrets. But first, we must liberate them." He took my hand from across the table. "The things you have done in the short time I've known you have confirmed how much I need you by my side. Are you with me, Tey?"

I looked into his eyes. So earnest. So desperate for me to say yes. Not a killer's eyes. Not a tyrant's either.

"I'm with you," I whispered, but inside I felt myself drawing further and further away.

CHAPTER 40

Needle-like drops poured from the sky as we left the restaurant. Rob pulled me close and we stood under the eaves watching the rain. For some reason, his touch sent an uncomfortable twinge of nerves through my body. I didn't know what I was so afraid of. His methods? His vicious ambition? His body was warm and firm against mine; it should have comforted me. Instead, my heart raced in a way so different from when he last kissed me, and my stomach twisted almost painfully.

Before I knew what was happening, his hand was on the back of my neck, pulling my head closer. His mouth brushed mine, then connected with it.

My nerves electrified. My instinct was to pull away, but I didn't. I wanted these bad feelings to disappear. I wanted to mend the rift growing between us, hollowing me out. But I didn't fill with warmth the way I had hoped. My chest tightened like a vise over my heart until it was difficult to breathe.

Rob's lips softened. "Rain's dying down."

I caught my breath and took a step back, blood hammering in my ears. "Yeah, it's not so bad now."

"We'll still get a little wet," he said, holding his hand out and testing the sky.

I pushed him forward and he stumbled onto the street. "Afraid you'll catch a cold?" I tried to keep my voice casual and flirtatious. Maybe if I acted the part, the old rush of longing would return. The one that had been triggered by Rob Stryker. Not Adrian Elder.

He's still Rob. I told myself. He's always been Rob. But in the restaurant, I had seen something different in his eyes, like a flicker of flame behind glass. Glass that would soon shatter and set the world on fire.

"That depends." He grinned. "Would you still kiss me if I were sick?"

Before I could answer, the valet appeared with Rob's bike. Rob yanked my wrist and swept me onto the seat behind him.

We were soaked by the time we reached the Castillo, but before we went inside, Rob leaned in close. "I'm counting on you. Things are going to be hard for a little while, but when we finally put the Coterie in their place, you're going to be so happy you stayed with me."

I turned to him with narrowed eyes. "I never said I'd stay."

He took a step back and cleared his throat. "I meant, that you're on my side."

A shiver ran up my spine. Was supporting Rob the right thing to do? It worried me how casually he'd talked about killing his uncle. Still, I wasn't so virtuous as to believe this country could be fixed without a few extreme measures. Los Sueños was pretty messed up, and a part of me could see why he believed war was the only way.

I headed for the front door with Rob following. I longed for a warm bath but knew I'd never get one here. Instead, I did what I always did. I disappeared into Waif's tower.

Waif loved to hear my often-exaggerated stories of the daring Rob Stryker and his stalwart team of bounty hunters, and the deadly missions we were preparing for next. I often acted them out for him, channeling my inner Rob, Xia, and

Damion. But tonight, I wasn't sure if I wanted to bring up my dull day at the office or uncomfortable dinner conversation.

He was still pretty weak and often ran a low fever, which spiked if I overexcited him. It kept him in bed most of the time, but he had been showing improvement over the last few days. I'd left him with some crumbly books I'd found in the Castillo's library and a sketchpad I'd bartered off a street artist in the wharf, as well as a few board games and puzzles. Now that he was more alert, I wanted to keep his mind distracted. The last thing I needed was for him to fall into a depression.

He smiled when I came in, sketchbook propped against his knees, and warmth tingled through my middle.

"How do you feel?" I asked like I did every day. The question was becoming somewhat of a joke to him.

He thought for a moment. "What's that story about the girl stuck in the tower?"

"Rapunzel?" I laughed. One of the books I'd given him was an anthology of classic fairytales, which he'd already read three times.

"Yeah, I feel like her. Only with much shorter hair. Guess I can't expect any rescuers."

"So does that make me the witch?" I asked, walking over to his bed.

He squinted as he studied me. "If it does, the story got her all wrong." He flipped through his sketchpad. "I have something for you." He tore out a page and handed it to me, color rising in his cheeks. "It could be much better…"

I took the page and stared at it. It was a drawing of me. My head was slightly inclined, my lips upturned at the ends, eyes wide and glossy. "Did you do this all from memory?" I asked, amazed at his talent.

He nodded and looked away from me. "I can do another

one if you don't like it."

"No," I said, not taking my eyes away from it. "It's incredible. Except it looks about ten times prettier than I do in real life."

Waif's eyes pivoted toward me. "I was thinking just the opposite."

Something melted in my chest. Just like the baby robin, I should have known it would be impossible to nurse Waif to health without feeling close to him. Every day that connection tightened to fill a void inside of me I never knew existed, one that longed to take away someone else's pain to find its own reprieve. I felt a traitor for once considering selling him to the Coterie, or for my part in turning in any other shadowborn for that matter. But when his health was fully restored, what on earth was I going to do with him?

"You look sad," he said.

I shook my head. "Not sad. Just worried about you."

His brows knitted together. "Why?"

The look made my hurt and uncertainty burrow deeper. "In the future, when you're better—"

"You don't have to worry about that. I'll go off on my own. I can take care of myself."

"No," I said. "I don't want that."

Here, he was a criminal, a dangerous thing to be feared or used for the gain of others. There was no road leading him to any kind of a future. Could I change that? If I supported Rob, and his cause was successful, could I convince him to lift the execution order on shadowborn?

"You don't have to be bound to me for the rest of your life, Tey," he said. "You owe me nothing."

That wasn't true. But how could I explain how he was the reason for any real happiness I'd experienced since coming to these islands. How he gave me something—someone—to live for; a reason to be needed for more than hunting criminals. "I owe you everything," I said, my voice choking. Before he could see me break down, I made a flimsy excuse and left the room.

I hung his drawing of me next to the picture of the girl on my wall and stared at it until I fell asleep.

CHAPTER 41

As Waif's strength slowly returned over the next several weeks, his face became less sunken and sallow, and the shadows beneath his eyes disappeared. The transformation made him look older, reminding me that he wasn't the child I sometimes took him for. In fact, he might be closer to my age after all. Standing upright, he was taller than I'd thought—as tall as me, or maybe an inch taller. Had he grown since coming here, or was I just not used to seeing him out of bed?

When he was strong enough to get up, he spent more and more time staring out the window or pacing in front of it. His restlessness made me anxious, and when I hurried home each night, it was no longer to make sure Waif was alive and still healthy: it was to make sure he was still there.

The truth was, I needed him now more than he needed me, but how could I make him understand that? No one had ever needed him the way I did. He'd been a tool for as long as he could remember, not a friend.

"Sorry, I'm late," I said, rushing into his room one evening. I felt exhausted after another long day of work, but happy to see him greet me with a smile.

"What happened today?" he asked, casually setting aside the book he was reading to hear what I could tell he hoped would be a more interesting story.

I didn't know what to say. At the Agency, all of our leads

had gone cold and we were still keeping a low profile after the rally. To keep us occupied, Rob had us hunting for escaped shadowborn, away from the danger of Coterie rat nests where any bystander could be a spy watching for us. So far we'd caught three more of the startled children, and there'd been nothing I could do. No way to help them. It was killing me.

"Not much," I lied. "Rob just took me to the roof and gave me more shooting lessons. He says I'm getting much better."

Waif put his arms behind his head. "You care about him a lot, don't you?"

Something clenched inside me at the question. "What do you mean?"

He shrugged. "You always smile when you talk about him. I figured there must be something between you."

I was silent for a long moment, then plopped down next to him. "I don't know how I feel about him. Sometimes I think I like him; that I could grow to love him, even. Other times I realize how much I don't know about him and it overwhelms me. He has a lot of plans for Los Sueños. Maybe one day he can help you. More than anyone, he has the power to change things here."

Waif's head turned away from me. "Have you told him about me?"

"No. I can't tell anyone about you. Not until I'm sure it's safe."

"Then you don't trust him, do you?"

The reality was, any time I mentioned my disapproval over the treatment of shadowborn, Rob suddenly seemed very uncomfortable, sometimes even responding with outrage. But I couldn't tell Waif that, otherwise he'd despise him. "Look, I'll talk to Rob. I know he only wants what's best for the shadowborn."

"Most people would say killing us is what's best." He sighed. "Maybe they're right."

My heart plunged at his last words. Since he had recovered from the worst of the withdrawal symptoms, he'd been mostly cheerful. But there were still the bad days, ones where he'd sink into a dark and hollow place I didn't know how to reach. Instead of blaming others for his misfortune, he'd agree with them, and in turn, blame himself for being what he was.

"Come with me," I said before thinking it over.

Waif's neck arched in surprise. "What? Where?"

"When I go back to America. Come with me. You'll be safe there."

"Unless you work for some big Coterie chief, it's impossible to leave Los Sueños."

"Maybe we can find a way." It was a long shot to think about earning enough money to get myself off the island, not to mention trying to spirit away a shadowborn, but now that the thought had invaded my mind, it squeezed at my heart.

"I'd like that," he said. "Assuming it's possible."

"Good. Because I don't think I could bring myself to leave without you."

I slid a dusty board game out from under his bed with my foot. It was called Mystery Land—basically a rip-off of Clue and Candy Land that I'd picked up for him in the wharf a few days back. So far, he'd won every round we'd played.

"Wanna play? Bet you can't beat me this time."

He looked down at the game, face relaxing. "Depends what you're betting with."

I cocked my head and thought for a moment. "What would satisfy an expert Mystery Lander like you?"

"Only your eternal soul, of course." I was glad his mood was improving enough for him to joke.

"My soul, you say? Does that make you the devil?"

He sat up straighter in bed, and raised his chin high, emphasizing the sharp angles of his face. "There are many who say we shadowborn are the sons and daughters of Hell. Demons. But as for the devil, his name was Antonio Santos and you liberated me from him long ago. Guess that makes you an angel."

I snorted. "Well then, Mr. Demon, my angelic soul is all yours; if you can beat me two out of three." I spread the game on the floor and motioned for him to join me. He got out of bed.

"And if you win?" he asked. "What shall I offer an angel?"

"Would I lose my standing with Heaven if I demanded your soul as well?"

"That wouldn't be fair."

"Why not?"

"Because you already have it."

Suddenly, I was very conscious of his eyes on mine and I turned my gaze on the game board, positioning my tiny pewter figurine at the start line. "Then I only want a promise."

He leaned closer, face flushed and bright. "What sort of promise?"

I took an unsteady breath, all the humor running out of me. "That you won't leave."

The door swung open.

My heart slammed into my sternum. The fear inside me matched what I saw on Waif's face. He instantly tried to go invisible but only managed to disappear halfway, looking like cloudy glass. With every muscle tense, I turned to look behind me.

It was Lei.

"Lei?" My voice came out as a squeak.

"I saw you come up here," she said. "You never came down."

"I was… I was…" I looked around, searching for an explanation. I settled on Waif. "Just playing games with the ghost."

Lei regarded Waif with wide eyes, more curious than afraid. "I heard you cry one time," she said. "Were you sad?"

Waif nodded at her, maintaining his translucency. "It gets lonely here all alone. That's why Tey comes to visit."

My chest still ached from the fright, but the tightness was starting to subside. I reminded myself that I needed to check the door lock from now on, and hoped no one had seen Lei come up the stairs.

Lei continued to regard Waif with wary eyes. She held out a finger to touch him, then changed her mind. "You're see-through," she said.

Waif looked down at himself, a smile on his lips. "Oh, really? I hadn't noticed."

Lei looked amused, then her lips tightened. "Do you chase kids away?"

"What do you mean?" asked Waif.

"Raquel and Pedro are gone. No one knows where."

My heart sank. Rob had mentioned children sometimes got lost in the jungle or attacked by wild animals. Perhaps more had wandered off recently, but I'd been too concerned about Waif to notice.

Waif shook his head. "I would never chase someone away. All are welcome in my Castillo."

Lei smiled, then her eyes fell to the game on the floor. "What are you playing?"

"It's called Mystery Land," I said. "It's his favorite."

She picked up one of the tiny game pieces and held it to her eye. "Can I play, too?"

"You should get back to bed." I stood and ushered her toward the door.

"Let her play one round," said Waif. "We haven't even started yet."

I sighed. "Fine. But all bets are off." It was too late for Lei to un-see Waif. There was no choice but to make her a coconspirator.

One round turned into two. Two turned into four, and soon my unease was forgotten. Waif and I let Lei win the first couple times, then teamed up to try and take her down. This proved to be harder than we thought. Lei had all the luck. She rolled the best moves and advanced her figure twice as fast as we did. When she made it to the finish line once again, she raised her arms in the air with a triumphant squeal. She smiled. She actually smiled, and we couldn't contain our laughter any more.

Later, I noticed her eyelids drooping and her head nodding. I put my arm around her and helped her to her feet. "Let's get you to bed," I whispered. She didn't protest as I guided her toward the stairs.

"Goodnight, Mr. Ghost," she said, waving a tired hand at Waif.

Waif waved back. "Night, Lei. Visit me again soon."

Lei nodded and we went out the door.

I held Lei's hand and led her down the dark tower stairs. As we reached the fifth level, I heard footsteps pounding up from below. I looked around for a room to hide in, but it was too late. Rob appeared, eyes locking on me. He carried a lantern that cast eerie shadows on the walls and his face. Pale and disheveled, he almost looked like he'd been struck by a sudden flu, but his gaze still held a terrifying strength.

"I heard laughing," he said. "I didn't think anyone ever came up here."

I was wracking my brain for a response when Lei piped up. "We were playing games with the ghost."

Rob crinkled his brow. "The ghost?"

"He lives in the tower," said Lei, turning my insides to gelatin.

I let out a loud laugh and launched into actor mode. "You don't know about the ghost, Rob? He's quite notorious around here."

"I haven't heard of him." Rob's face looked haunted enough to be a ghost himself.

I lowered my voice so only he could hear. "They say he died by leaping out the tower window."

Rob's eyes widened. "I see. What did you guys play?"

"Mystery Land," said Lei. "I beat everyone."

"I've never played that game. Where'd it come from?"

"I picked up a used copy in the wharf awhile back," I said. "You'll have to play with us some time. The kids like it." I nudged Lei. "But now, it's time for this kid to get to bed." I kept my hand around Lei's and tried my best to block Rob's way.

Rob looked over my shoulder, his eyes dark and intent.

"He was a nice ghost," said Lei with a long yawn. "I'm gonna visit him every night."

"He was a nice ghost," I said with a wink at Rob, urging him to play along. "Now come on, sleepyhead." I pulled her forward. "You going to join us, Rob?" I tried to make the question as casual as possible.

He kept looking toward the tower stairs, and the sickness in my stomach spread throughout my whole body, then he nodded and started back down the stairs. I was so relieved that one knee buckled, but I knew in that moment, everything had changed.

As soon as Lei was in bed, I sprinted back to the tower and flung the door aside. "Waif!"

He looked up when I burst in, surprise and confusion on his face. "What's wrong?"

"We have to go," I said, chin quivering. "I ran into Rob in the hall and now he's suspicious."

"Because of the little girl?"

"She told him about you. We have to hurry."

He got to his feet and looked around the room. "Where will we go?" Cold reality had hit him and his body was braced for action.

"I don't know." I pulled the sheet off his bed and gathered his food and belongings into it. "We just need to get you out of here."

He helped me, and soon we had everything wrapped into a transportable package.

"You don't have to come with me," said Waif. "I always knew I'd have to go eventually."

"Don't be stupid. I'm not leaving until I get you somewhere safe."

"I don't want to make things worse for you." His eyes bored into mine like pale-blue icicles. "You're the only person in this world I care about, Tey, I—" his voice broke off as the door flew open. The force of it hitting the wall rattled the old, framed paintings hanging beside it.

My heart froze solid at the sight of Rob.

CHAPTER 42

Waif took another shot at going invisible, but only managed to flicker in and out of focus.

Rob's face was hard as stone. "I've come to take a turn at Mystery Land," he said. "I hear the tower ghost is a worthy opponent."

Waif shrunk back as Rob walked in and looked around the room. "I haven't been up here in ages. I like what you've done with it." He admired Waif's sketches plastered to the wall and a vase of dried flowers I'd put in the window.

"Rob," I said, my voice cracking.

He spun around, his mouth forming a firm downward arch. "Here I was thinking I was the only one with secrets. Turns out you had a pretty big one yourself." He then turned to Waif. "I don't know how long Tey's been keeping you here or what sort of sick delusion is going through her head, but I'm bringing this scheme to an end right now." He took out a stun gun and a pair of handcuffs.

"No!" I cried, latching onto Rob's arm. "His abilities are harmless. Please, Rob. Let him go."

Rob shoved me aside and held up his stun gun. I lunged and hit his wrist hard. His gun fell to the ground and skittered across the floor. We both leaped for it but I was half a second behind him. His hand closed securely around the handle and he pointed it at my chest.

"Don't make me use this on you," he said. His voice lacked any hint of emotion. I could tell that any feelings he had for me would do nothing to get us out of this mess.

I took a step back and looked at Waif. "Run!" I cried. "Go now. Please."

Waif didn't move. His eyes flickered between Rob's gun and me. I wished there was time to explain to him that it was only a stun gun, that Rob wouldn't seriously harm me. But everything happened too fast.

Waif sprang from behind and wrapped his hands around Rob's neck. Rob backed him into the wall and slammed against him until his grip weakened. Waif stumbled to the floor and attempted to regain his feet.

"Just listen to me," I pleaded, but Rob wouldn't have it.

"Get out of here, Tey," he said, raising his gun at Waif.

I jumped forward and pulled him back. Rob twisted around so fast I was knocked to the ground. His gun flashed and electricity surged through me. Pain crackled in every nerve as my body convulsed. I heard Waif calling my name, but then there was another surge of light and he was on the ground next to me, body twitching as crazily as mine.

Gradually, my shaking muscles relaxed and I lay frozen to the floor, gasping for breath. Rob stood over me, face cold and angry.

He pulled me up and draped my limp body over his shoulder like a kidnapped maiden from a romance story. I tried to call out to Waif, but my voice wouldn't work properly. I caught one last glimpse of him as Rob carried me out the door. His frigid stare was my only goodbye.

There was a click as Rob locked my door behind him. I lay crumpled on my bed, reaching for tears that wouldn't come.

Tingling, my body came back to life, one limb at a time. But there was no point. It was too late to help Waif.

For a long time, I stared at his drawing of me where it still hung next to the other girl's photograph. I watched the two images blend together as I faded into something that wasn't quite sleeping and wasn't quite wakefulness—a dark place where the nightmares of dreams and reality both waited to taunt me.

Later, I opened my eyes and squinted in the sunlight coming through my window. Morning.

A dull ache pounded in the back of my head as I rolled out of bed. I tried my doorknob, surprised to find it had been unlocked in the night. I moved like a specter down the hall and up the stairs, all the way to the top.

He was gone.

The flower vase lay in shattered pieces next to the window, and the sheets we'd stripped from the bed had been taken away. My chest felt as empty as the room.

I stumbled to the mattress and collapsed on top of it.

That's when the tears came. A sob shuddered in my throat and broke free in a terrible cry of rage and grief that continued for what felt like hours.

When I'd cried out every ounce of moisture in me, my mind descended into a daze, and I traced patterns along the headboard of the bed.

My thoughts drifted to Rob and something hot welled up inside of me, getting ready to burst out. How dare he take Waif away from me? How dare he pretend like he knew what was best?

I got to my feet, wearing my anger like armor, and went down the stairs as quietly as a ghost in the night. In my room, I retrieved all my remaining money as well as the belt I wore on missions for the Agency. I was going to get Waif back, and then both of us would leave this place forever. I didn't care if we had to swim the whole way to California.

I recalled nothing of my walk to the skids. My feet found their way to the door with the symbol of the skull skewered by a trident over it, following a memory of their own. After typing OPERATION421 into the keypad, the door clicked open and I took the black elevator to the underground Coterie offices. I made my way to number 421 and knocked, surprised that I wasn't nervous or afraid. My anger was like a steady pulse of intense heat; it focused me, burning up all other thoughts.

The knob turned and Mr. Harrington opened the door, one white eyebrow lifting. "Can I help you?"

I pushed the door open and walked past him. "I know Rob came here." My gaze flickered toward the chain hanging from the ceiling. My stomach twisted and I almost faltered when I imagined Waif shackled to it. I turned away and focused all of my emotion on the mission.

"Who?"

"Rob. Rob Stryker."

"You know Mr. Stryker?"

I'd been here multiple times now, and he still didn't remember me. I prayed I'd never get old. "He sold you a shadowborn."

"He's sold me many shadowborn."

"The most recent. A boy who can turn invisible."

Harrington licked his lips. "Oh, yes. Mr. Stryker has a knack for obtaining valuables. The boy from last night is the only one I've seen with that particular ability. Very useful in certain circles."

"That boy wasn't his to sell. Rob stole him from me and I

want him back."

Harrington folded his arms. "If you know the access password to this facility, then you must know our policy on shadowborn. If you're not clever enough to hang on to them, then they deserve a more competent master."

"I'll buy him back," I said, fingering the money in my pocket. "How much?"

Harrington laughed, a dry, gravelly sound.

"How much?" I demanded, jaw trembling.

"You must have one hell of a job ahead of you," he said, obviously taking me for a criminal or Coterie gun. "Are you sure the demon is worth it?"

"What job couldn't benefit from invisible hands?" I forced my voice to remain cool so I could play along. "I'm sure you're aware of the kind of work we both operate in, Mr. Harrington."

Harrington's smile didn't leave his face. "Yes, I am." He hobbled to his desk, leaning heavily on his cane. "I'd like to help you, Miss…?"

"Walker." I probably shouldn't have given him my real last name, but he wouldn't remember it, anyway.

"Miss Walker. But you can put your money away right now. The boy's gone. He went to auction this morning and sold for more money than I've seen in one sitting."

My heart turned into a heavy stone. "Who bought him?"

The old man sat down and poured a shot from a whiskey bottle. "You know that's classified information."

"And we both know nothing's completely classified." I leaned over his desk and spoke slowly. "How much do you want?"

He downed the shot and wiped a gnarled hand across his lips. "A far better question is, how much do you have?"

I smiled and reached into my belt pouch. "Let's take a look."

I pulled out my stun gun and pulled the trigger. An electric tack struck Harrington in the chest and he slid off his chair, convulsing. Some of his recently swallowed whiskey came up and he gurgled on it, turning it to foam. I turned him on his side and it dribbled out of his mouth.

"Who'd you sell him to, Harry?" I asked, my mouth close to his ear.

He struggled to form words. "Ric-c-c....Ric-c-c-cardo Sant-t-t-tos.

CHAPTER 43

I held Harrington's head up. "Ricardo's still in Los Sueños?"
The old man nodded as best he could.

I gripped his collar. "Where is he?"

"I d-d-don't know," he gargled.

"You must have spoken to him," I said. "I bet you two are best buddies. What did he say?"

His body finally relaxed. He took three ragged breaths. "His driver came in." More breaths. "Said they were having car trouble. His agent took the shadowborn away in a bicycle cab to be delivered to Ricardo. The boy was invisible…no one suspected."

"What time?" I asked.

"Ten this morning."

"What color was the cab?"

"Piss yellow."

I smiled and let his head drop to the floor. "Much obliged." I put a single dollar bill on his chest and left the office.

As I walked into Quinto's Transpo, a bell over the door announced my entrance. Mr. Quinto was sipping a Cosmar Cola with his feet on his desk over scattered paperwork. He straightened when he saw me.

"You again. Can I help you?"

"One of your cabbies picked up a friend of mine in the

skids around ten a.m. today. Is it possible to find out which one it was?"

Quinto furrowed his brow. "Was your friend low on cash?"

"No, nothing like that."

"You in some kind of trouble, then?"

"No, but my friend might be. I need to talk with your cabbie. See where they went. It's not against policy, is it?"

"Do you know what my employee looked like?"

I shook my head. "Can't you radio them?"

"I could, but that's an awful lot of work for me. I've got more than twenty cyclers out there right now. I'll have them turn in their reports tonight, and you can come back tomorrow once I've looked them over."

"I can't wait that long," I said. "This is too serious."

"Listen, honey, I'm a busy man. If I did favors for people all day long, my business would fall apart."

I slapped a wad of bills onto his desk.

He picked it up, counted it, and raised an eyebrow. "Come back in an hour."

Within the allotted time, Mr. Quinto had produced a small Indonesian man wearing a New York Yankees baseball cap.

"Meet Bambang," Quinto said, motioning to the driver. "Bambang, this young lady has some questions to ask you."

Bambang nodded, taking off his cap and smoothing back his hair as he approached me. He looked anxious.

"Hello." I smiled. "It's nothing major. At ten a.m., you picked up my friend in the skids. Do you remember where you took him?"

Bambang scratched his chin and then removed a folded time chart from his pocket. "Oh, yes, yes," he nodded rapidly, pointing to a name scribbled in the ten a.m. time slot.

I couldn't read his handwriting, so I just nodded in confirmation. "Can you show me where you dropped him off?"

Bambang nodded again and motioned for me to get in his yellow bicycle cab. He pedaled with surprising speed toward the wharf and stopped in the area where La Ventura was usually docked. He pointed toward the water. "Ship," he said.

I looked over, but there was no ship. "Was it there this morning?" I asked.

"Yes, yes, this morning."

"La Ventura? Did he get on it?"

"Uh, yes. He get on ship. It come and go every day. Leave eleven a.m. Return nine p.m."

A spark of hope appeared inside me. "Thanks for your help." I fished out the last of my bills and handed them to him.

"You be smart to stay clear," he said, pocketing the money. "Ship owned by bad man."

"Ricardo Santos," I said with a nod.

Bambang looked in both directions and lowered his voice. "It not safe to say his name."

"I'll be careful," I said.

He gave me a long look and then rode off.

I found Damion's apartment from the address he had listed in the Agency's roster. It was on the sixth floor of a slightly askew brick building that bordered the skids. There was no elevator, but I was more than used to climbing up six stories by now.

A small boy answered the door. He was about twelve years old and wore only a pair of red shorts. Thick curly hair haloed his head, making his enormous brown eyes pop. "Can I help you?"

"I'm looking for Damion Hart," I said. "Does he live here?"

"He's my brother."

I smiled. "What's your name?"

Before he could answer, another voice called from beyond my line of sight. "Who is it, Toby?"

Damion stepped into view and pulled his little brother away from the door. "Tey? Where have you been? Is Rob with you?"

I stepped inside the small, disorderly apartment, surprised to see Xia lounging on the couch. "Haven't seen him."

Xia groaned. "Why didn't you come to the Agency today?"

I shrugged. "Rob didn't tell you?"

"We haven't seen Rob all day," said Damion. "Neither have the kids at the Castillo. Believe me, we stopped by and asked."

"I don't know where he is," I said.

"Did you two have a fight or something?" Xia crossed her arms.

"Something like that."

Damion glanced out the door and then closed it as though afraid of being watched. "Corpus made an announcement today. The king raised the bounty on Adrian by ten percent, and now it's all over the front page of the Beacon. The other agents are going crazy, and some of those guys are real geniuses. I'm worried about Rob."

"Have a little faith. I'm sure Rob's smarter than all of them," I said. "He's managed to stay undercover for this long. He's probably just avoiding me."

"The fight was that bad?" said Xia.

I looked away from her, the memory of Waif's twitching body flashing into my mind before I could put up a wall. "You know Rob. He just gets angry sometimes. I'm sure he'll feel better tomorrow."

"Then did you come here seeking my love advice?" said

Damion, twitching his eyebrows.

"No," I laughed, sitting next to Xia on the couch. "I have a lead on Ricardo. A good one."

Damion stiffened. "Toby, go to your room for a minute. I need to talk to Tey in private."

The boy paused, staring at me suspiciously.

"Any time now," said Damion, and Toby obeyed.

"You've both got the same eyes," I said.

Damion half-smiled. "Our father's eyes, yeah. They haunt me every time I look at the kid. He's got my old man's smarts too. Luckily, they barely knew each other."

"That's lucky?"

"When you're dad's a level eight Coterie gun and drags his pregnant wife and son into a petty feud over the price regulation of beer, eventually getting one of them killed and the other so entangled in the criminal underground he feels he can't escape, then I'd say Toby's pretty fortunate he was just a baby when the bastard kicked the can."

"I'm sorry," I said, eyes going to the boy's closed door.

Damion looked at me meaningfully. "That doesn't matter right now." He lowered his voice. "Ricardo's still in Los Sueños? You're sure?"

"Fairly sure, and I think I know where he is. This could be our chance to go after him." As I continued to explain, I said nothing of Waif or Harrington, and instead told them a sailor from La Ventura had been the one to mention Ricardo and his possible location.

When I was finished, Xia rubbed her temples like she had a headache. "This ship of yours leaves tomorrow morning?"

I nodded. "I heard eleven a.m. We have to follow it somehow."

"That shouldn't be too hard," said Damion. "I have a small

fishing boat hidden in the brush near the beach east of the Castillo. It hasn't been in the water in almost a year, but I'm sure it'll still float. We can use it to follow behind the bigger ship."

"It better have a motor," said Xia, "or you and Tey will be rowing the whole way.

"It has a motor. What it hasn't got is fuel. But if we put our money together, we could get a few gallons from Mr. Harrington's warehouse."

"Is this a bad time to mention that I'm flat broke?" I asked.

Xia gave me one of her annoyed sighs.

"Hey," I said. "I'll pay you back from my portion of our earnings."

"Assuming we get any earnings."

"We have the chance to chase after the biggest Coterie bounty in Los Sueños and you're worried about a little gas money?"

"Tey's right," said Damion. "We should at least scope it out. We haven't had any good leads in over a month."

Xia got to her feet and headed for the door.

"Where you going?" Damion shouted after her.

"To get ready," she said. "We have work to do."

CHAPTER 44

We met at Damion's boat the next morning. Rob still had not returned, and, when the hulking La Ventura pulled away from the harbor, we decided to leave without him. The lead was too good to wait, and we had to act fast. I for one was grateful for his absence. He'd only interfere with my bigger objective. I could tell that Xia and Damion were nervous, though.

A thin veil of fog hung over the water, and I hoped our rowboat-sized vessel was small enough for the mist to hide us from on-looking sailors. As we circled the island, the fog cleared away, but the sky remained gray, overshadowing the green knolls of Santa Arcadia. La Ventura swung to the north side of the island where the land formed a natural harbor. I could see the outlines of a squat concrete structure on the rocky hilltop. It overlooked a beach on the opposite side of the island as the one where we'd spent three unproductive days, not so long ago.

"That must be where Ricardo's hiding out," Damion whispered.

Xia shielded her eyes with her hand and stared at the stone fort. "Looks dismal. Let's hope we can find him in there."

We pulled into shore and quickly dragged our little boat beyond the tree line.

"It's so weird doing this without Rob," Xia said. "Do you

think he'll be upset we didn't wait for him?"

"Nah," said Damion. "We had a chance and we went for it. He would've done the same. But remember, we need to make sure catching Ricardo is feasible before we put our lives on the line."

We kept to the trees as we made our way closer to where La Ventura sailors were unloading cargo onto the beach. A dirt road slashed through the jungle leading to the fort. Rolling down toward the beach, were several wagons pulled by donkeys.

When the wagons reached them, the sailors filled them with their cargo, and let the donkey handlers lead them back up the hill, one at a time.

We followed the leading wagon as it disappeared into the underbrush that surrounded the dirt road. Maybe it would lead us to an opening and we'd somehow think of a way to get inside unseen.

Before we could formulate a plan, Xia burst from the trees and shot an electric tack at the donkey handler. The man spasmed and then passed out. Xia dragged his body into the trees.

Damion and I watched her, opened mouthed, but she scowled at our expressions and tied the unconscious man's hand around a tree. "Come on," she said, waving us to the wagon. "We have less than five minutes before the next wagon reaches us.

The wagon was mostly full of small equipment boxes, but there was one large wooden crate that looked big enough to hide in. We pried off the lid and found it full to the brim with canned food supplies.

I tried not to look at the road behind me as I helped Xia and Damion unload the food and hide it in the jungle. When it was empty, it was clear that all three of us wouldn't fit.

I turned to Damion and Xia. "Looks like it can only be two of us. Who's in?"

"I am," they both said at the same time. They looked at each other open-mouthed.

"There's no way you're going," said Damion.

Xia folded her arms. "There's no way I'm waiting out here for you freaks to never come back."

"We're coming back," he said reaching out for her arm. "And don't worry. I'll make sure you still get your full portion of the bounty."

She yanked her arm away and shot me a dark glare. "You should be the one to stay behind. Damion and I have years more experience doing this kind of thing."

I had my reasons for getting inside, and I wouldn't let anything stop me now. "Considering you wouldn't be here if it weren't for me, I think I've got more right to go in than both of you put together."

"Can't argue with that, Xi," said Damion. "She did bring us the information, and I think I should be the one to go with her. As a former gun, I'll have better luck talking my way out of a tight situation. Plus, if I'm there, we'll count as four people."

"Four?"

"Yeah. Me, Tey, Pricilla and Antoinette," he said, flexing his biceps.

Xia groaned. "I am ashamed to know you."

"Can we fight about this later?" I said. "I can hear the next wagon coming." I hopped in the crate and crouched with my knees to my chest. "Xia, with the wrangler gone, we'll need you to make sure the donkey makes it up the hill."

"Just don't get seen," said Damion as he scrunched in next

to me. "And keep an eye on my boat."
Xia cussed, but I knew she wouldn't let us down.
We closed the crate and everything went dark.

CHAPTER 45

As the wagon swayed, Damion's breathing turned into ragged pants. I'd never been so close to him before and could imagine our proximity was doing nothing to improve Xia's opinion of me.

"Is it your claustrophobia?" I asked.

He took three breaths before answering me. "Yeah. It's so stupid." He gave a short laugh. "Sweet salvation, I didn't think it would be this bad." He curled up tighter, and I could feel him put his head between his knees. "Sorry you have to see me like this."

"It's too dark to see you," I said. "Besides, we'll be there soon."

"For your sake, I hope you're right," he said. "Enclosed places make me puke."

Great. "Then why were you so eager to be the one to come?"

"To protect Xia, of course. Ricardo's not gonna be easy. The odds of us making it out fully intact are…well they're not good. It's my fault her mother is…the way she is. She needs Xia."

"And what about Toby?" I asked, picturing his clever-eyed little brother.

Damion was silent for a long time. "He's the smartest kid I know. He knows where I go every day and what I'm up against. He's got friends. He'll be fine."

"You don't sound so sure."

"Saints, I can't afford to think about him at a time like this. I might lose my head."

"Seems to me like you can't afford not to."

The wagon slowed to a stop. There was a long moment of silence, and then I heard a male voice call out to someone. Our crate rose into the air and was carried at an angle that sent me squashing into Damion. After a bumpy ride, we were set on solid ground.

I listened as footsteps disappeared up some stairs.

Damion let out a sick moan and started to lift the lid, but I yanked him back down. "Wait. I hear voices." A few seconds later, there were heavy booms as more cargo was deposited around us. Another moment of silence, and then more people entered, repeating the same process over again.

Damion shoved his fist into his mouth and bit down hard.

After about twenty minutes, all was still. I let go of Damion and he forced open the top of the crate, sucking in a welcome breath of air. He crawled out like a newborn colt and vomited all over the floor. When he was done, he looked at me apologetically. "Sorry," he muttered, wiping his mouth.

I climbed out next to him. "You'd only have to be sorry if you'd done it in there," I said pointing at the crate.

He managed a shaky smile. "I nearly did, but I knew we'd attract more attention if you reeked of puke."

"You OK? Can you walk?

"Just give me a sec." He leaned against the cold stone wall and took several deep breaths. "OK, let's get out of here."

He was still a bit unsteady but managed to make it up the stairs. We came out in a dark hallway. Everything was cold and smelled like wet stone. We had to be down pretty deep.

"Do you think Ricardo has prisons down here?" I asked.

An image of Waif lying in a dark cell chained to the wall entered my mind.

Damion shrugged. "I wouldn't put it past him."

"Maybe we should do a quick search. He might have some good people locked up, with information that could help us."

He shook his head. "Where there's a prison, there are guards, and this mission is dangerous enough. We can't risk it. Let's head upstairs and get a feel for what we're up against."

I was suddenly uneasy. How did I ever think I could find Waif in a place like this, let alone get him out alive?

Metal doors lined the corridors, all bolted shut, and at the end of the hall, a dark staircase led to a higher level. We spent the next hour exploring the building. It was cross-shaped with four distinct wings. The higher we went, the more secretive we had to be. Armed men and women patrolled the halls, watching camera monitors and using binoculars to look out windows. They looked more like soldiers than criminal guns, which made me wonder just how strong Ricardo would be when his rebellion began. Did Rob's plan even have a chance?

The upper levels were fancier and less concrete. Dark carpeting muffled our footsteps, and low-hanging lights lit the halls. We walked confidently, like we belonged there, praying that if we ran into a guard we could not avoid, they wouldn't question us.

We ducked in a doorway as two shadowborn in handcuffs were led toward an office numbered twenty-three B. It opened wide enough to admit them. I caught a glimpse of a spacious conference room where several men and women in business attire sat at a large table with half-filled glasses. In a corner of the room, long chains hung from the ceiling, and large men in military style vests lined the walls. The door slammed shut.

"Do you think they're armed?" I asked Damion over my

shoulder.

"Coterie are always armed. With that many bodyguards, Ricardo has to be in there. Let's wait until the meeting ends, then see where Ricardo goes. If we can keep him in sight, maybe we'll find an opportunity to ambush him."

"Are we really going to do this?" I asked Damion, suddenly feeling doubtful.

He tightened his grip around his stun gun. "We shouldn't take unnecessary risks. But let's not pass up a good opportunity if it arises. Who knows if we'll be able to get back in here later, or if Ricardo will still be around? This could be our one golden opportunity."

He made a good point, but my stomach knotted at the thought of Waif. I still hadn't found him and had no idea what to do if I did. "Maybe we should split up for a bit. I can scope out the best escape route for when we nab Ricardo. You can use a locator to alert me when the meeting ends."

"It could end any minute. And if Ricardo's in that room, I'm gonna need all the backup I can get."

Five minutes after he finished speaking, the door opened. Two men carrying assault rifles exited first, followed by the smartly dressed occupants of the room.

Damion and I made ourselves as flat as possible in our doorway, hardly daring to breathe. The last person to leave was Ricardo, looking much the same as he did when I first saw him in LA but cleaner cut.

Ricardo and the two riflemen paused, then headed in the opposite direction of the others. When they'd gone most of the way down the hall, we followed as quietly as possible.

My hand was damp around my stun gun. I gripped it harder so it wouldn't slip, but I couldn't make my hand stop shaking.

Damion led the way, his dark skin and clothes blending in with the shadows of the corridor, despite his muscular form. We darted from doorway to doorway like rabbits trying to make it across an open field. When Ricardo and his guards went down two staircases, we crept behind, watching as he headed for a pair of double doors at the end of an empty hall.

Damion paused and turned to me. "No one else is around. This is the best chance we're gonna get. Let's make our stand before he goes inside." He held out his stun gun. "These things don't have a good range. We'll have to move in quickly and take out the bodyguards first, then stun Ricardo before he has a chance to pull out any weapons he may have hidden in his coat."

I understood, but that didn't mean I was ready. I could feel my heart rate gradually gain speed, like a train leaving the station and heading for an open track. I'd only wanted to come here to find Waif, and now it was very possible I was about to get myself killed. I put my finger on the trigger of my stun gun and bent my knees, preparing to run.

Ricardo paused at the door and fiddled in his pocket for a key. Before he could get it in the lock, Damion tugged my arm and we rushed forward.

The guards turned in unison at the sound of our running footsteps and raised their rifles. It was too late to stop. Damion ducked low and kept running.

Holding back a scream, I did the same, waiting for a bullet to puncture my brain.

Damion head-butted a guard in the stomach and the man's gun smashed into his back. Damion pulled his trigger, sending a surge of energy into the man's leg. The man stumbled and fell on top of him and they both grappled for the rifle.

I shot at the guard nearest me, but he dodged left and my

energy tack struck harmlessly against the wall. I tried to fire again, but the man skillfully grabbed my wrist and pulled my hands behind my back, taking my gun and slamming me into the wall. I felt the barrel of his rifle press against the back of my head.

I squeezed my eyes shut, ready for the blast that would bring on the darkness of oblivion.

"Wait," said Ricardo.

I opened one eye. Damion was unconscious on the ground. The other guard stood over him, gun ready.

"Don't kill them yet," Ricardo continued. "I want to find out who sent them. Throw them in a cell; we'll do an interrogation in the morning, then execute them. In the meantime, get your men to search the complex. There could be others."

"Yes, sir," they said in unison.

The guard yanked me back. I struggled against him and turned to look at Ricardo one more time. His dark eyes studied me with interest. I wondered if he recognized me as the same girl who had followed him into his warehouse in LA. A girl who barely existed anymore.

With a shove, the guard forced me to march.

CHAPTER 46

The guard entered a code into a keypad, and a sliding door opened to reveal metal stairs leading into darkness. A waft of cold air rushed up, bringing the smell of rock fungus and rust. It became stronger as we descended into an underground prison.

Flickering lights illuminated two rows of cells facing each other. My stomach jumped into my chest when I saw the dismal occupants. All but one empty cell was filled with shadowborn, a whole army of them. Ricardo must have been collecting and conditioning them for whatever plans he had to eliminate the monarchy and impose Coterie rule over Los Sueños. Skinny and ragged, they stared back at me, as though sizing me up for a challenge. My eyes searched them desperately as we passed, but I didn't see Waif.

The guard unlocked the empty cell and patted me down. He removed my Agency belt that held my stun gun and Supplicant, as well as a few other practical effects, before shoving me inside. He sneered as he locked the bars behind me. "You must be pretty smart to get in the stronghold undetected, but pretty stupid to try to take out Ricardo. I hope for your sake your smart side wins over in the morning and you tell the chief everything. Otherwise, you and your friend will be squealing like pigs long before your agonizing deaths."

As soon as his footsteps faded into the distance, I peered

through my bars into the cells across from me. It was cold, and the silver-haired children were packed in close for warmth. In the dim light, they looked so similar.

"Waif!" I cried, hoping he could hear me. "Waif! It's me. Are you there?" No answer. Maybe for my sake, he was keeping quiet so I didn't try to do anything rash, like rescue him.

I turned my attention on the others. "Do any of you know Waif? He's shadowborn like you. He can disappear."

Silence.

"I just want to know if he's all right."

Still nothing.

If he wasn't here, where was he?

I sat on a ledge that was supposed to be a bed but had no mattress or pillow. A few minutes later, two guards dumped Damion onto the floor of my cell. He was still unconscious and there was a bloody gash across his forehead. I wasn't strong enough to lift him onto the bed, not that it was much better than the floor, so I just wiped away his blood with my shirt and tried to make him as comfortable as possible. All I could think was that it was a good thing there hadn't been room in the crate for Xia to come along. Now at least one of us would make it off Santa Arcadia alive.

I sat with my head in my hands and shivered like a wet dog. The shadowborn didn't chatter, and their silence was more chilling than the cold.

A long time passed. My stomach growled but we were never brought any food or water. After what seemed like several hours, Damion finally stirred and sat up, clutching his head. He probably had a concussion. Hopefully, it wasn't too serious; I needed him to be able to walk if we were going to get out of here.

Then it hit me: we weren't going to get out of here. We had

no weapons and no way out of this cell. In the morning, we'd be tortured and killed, and there was nothing we could do to change that. It figured that someone with my luck would get the worse imaginable death. What was next? An afterlife of fire and brimstone?

"Saints, I wish Rob was here," said Damion, and despite everything, I did too. Rob was our leader. He'd know what to do. Then again, we wouldn't be in this mess at all if it weren't for what he'd done to Waif. The thought turned my heart cold and I shoved the image of his confident smile out of my mind.

There was the sound of a switch being turned off, and we were plunged into what would have been complete darkness if several shadowborn hadn't possessed the abilities to create silvery lights. They gave the cells an ethereal luminescence that reminded me of lunawasps.

I curled up on the hard bed but couldn't sleep. "I'm sorry about Toby," I whispered to Damion.

Damion rolled over on the floor and wrapped his arms around himself. "It's not your fault."

"Yes, it is. We should have given this more thought, more time."

"He'll be all right."

"And Xia?"

His voice drifted as unconsciousness tugged at him again. "Maybe when this is all over she can finally forgive me."

As he slipped into oblivion, I closed my eyes and tried to slow my breathing, but I had to lower my heart rate first, and that was proving impossible. Damion was snoring softly on the ground below me, but he had a head injury to help him sleep. My mind kept thinking of the inevitable. Torture was something you read about in medieval history books, not something that happened today, in real life. I pictured myself on a rack, arms being stretched out of their sockets; a hot poker searing my bare skin; someone prying off my finger-nails with pliers.

A bright light broke through the darkness, and I jumped. The light came from a flashlight, and its beam silhouetted the tall figure holding it.

Was it morning already? I braced myself against the wall as panic gripped me like a straightjacket.

There was a click and the door to our cell swung open. Damion propped himself up on one arm and shielded his eyes with his free hand.

"I knew you two wouldn't survive without me," said a casual voice.

I smiled so wide my face ached.

"Xi!" cried Damion, getting to his feet. "Sweet salvation, Xi. I love you, you know that?"

She was dressed like one of the sailors from La Ventu-ra, hair pulled tightly back from her face. "Of course you do when I'm saving your hide. Now come on. The guards are un-conscious, but they could wake up any—"

Damion grabbed her head in both hands and pulled her in for a powerful kiss.

To my surprise, she didn't struggle. She kissed him back and let him be the one to finally break away.

"How'd you get in here?" he asked, keeping a hand around her shoulder.

She smiled and motioned to her new clothes. "The sailor uniform should give you a hint, but I'll save the details for later. We need to get moving."

"Wait," I said. "We can't just go up there. They know Da-mion and me. We could get caught and thrown back in here all over again. We need a better plan this time."

"I'm open to suggestions," said Xia.

I looked at the other cages and saw the shadowborn stirring from our commotion. "Let's set them free."

She raised one eyebrow. "Are you kidding me? They're dangerous and we're in enough trouble as it is."

"Exactly. With dangerous shadowborn on the loose, no one's going to care what happened to us. They'll make a perfect distraction to give us a chance to track Ricardo and get him out."

Some of the children moved closer to us and clung to their bars, listening warily.

Xia looked at Damion. "What do you think?"

He raised and lowered one shoulder. "The idea kinda freaks me out, but we could definitely use help. I'm just not sure they'd want to help us or do much more than run away."

Xia nodded, as though making up her mind about something, and turned to the cages. She dangled the keys she had stolen in front of her and raised her voice. "Listen up. I'm gonna let everyone out of here, but I want you to know, the three of us are not your enemies." She passed the flashlight beam across Damion, herself, and me. "Ricardo Santos is the man responsible for your imprisonment. If we take him out, you all have a chance at freedom. It'll be dangerous, and I don't know what sorts of weird abilities the lot of you have, but I'm sure Ricardo paid good money for you, and the guards have orders not to kill you. Right now, we need a distraction. Anything to occupy the other guns while we hunt down your master. Who's in?"

A few murmurs came from their cages but no one answered her directly. Most drew back, frightened.

I stepped forward. "I know you're all terrified. I am too. But I've seen what some of you can do and it's incredible. I think it's a gift these islands have given you; people just don't see it that way yet. I know most of them hurt you and get you addicted to earthblood so you don't run away. It's disgusting. But as Ricardo's property, those guards up there will be hesitant to harm you. If you work together, you can take this stronghold for your own. Then you can start to protect yourselves, not just against Ricardo's men, against all those who want to own you."

Xia dug her nails into my shoulder. "What the hell are you doing?" she hissed. "We've got a Coterie rebellion to quell, a shadowborn uprising on top of that is the last thing we need."

"It's time someone started paying attention to them," I said. "They're only kids, Xia; some will be adults soon. They just want the chance to live normal lives."

"You don't know them, Tey. You haven't been here long enough to see what they can do."

"You're talking about things they were forced to do by the Coterie, or things they did out of instinct to protect themselves. And if you think I don't know them—"

"I'll help you." A boy stepped into Xia's light, blue eyes giving me a pale stare.

All my insides melted. "Ichiro," I gasped, barely able to get the name out of my mouth. It was him. He was here, and he was alive.

He nodded. "You've called me that before."

I fell to my knees in front of him, reaching out to him through the bars. "That's because it was your name. It still is your name, you just can't remember."

"And were we friends in that time I can't remember?"

I smiled. "We only knew each other for a short time, but I hoped we were, and I hope that can continue, even after all of this."

He put his palm on the side of my head and closed his eyes. His touch reached through my skull into a deep place within my mind. I flinched, but it didn't feel unpleasant or threatening, only curious, like a searchlight seeking a lost child in the dark. Finally, he removed his hand, tears in his eyes.

"She's telling the truth," he said to the other children, and several of them murmured among themselves.

He looked at me so intensely that I forgot to breathe. "I saw myself," he said. "The self that you remember. He would have wanted to help you."

I gripped his arm. "What happened to you? That night in the Castillo—you disappeared. I was so worried."

"He didn't tell you?"

"Who?"

"The tall man with the curly brown hair. He came for me in the night and took me away. He gave me to an old man."

My blood turned to ice. Rob. "But, he was worried about you. He…" I stopped myself, knowing Ichiro had no reason to lie. Rob was the liar. I pictured Ichiro tied to Harrington's chain, blue zaps striking him from the old man's cane, and something like hatred burned just below my throat. Rob. He'd answer for this. Sometime, somehow, he would pay.

I turned to Xia and Damion. "Did you know?"

I must have looked pretty threatening because Damion held up his hands as he shook his head, and Xia's frightened, "no" came out an octave higher than normal.

"Get him out of there," I said pointing to the lock on the cage. Wordlessly, Xia complied, then moved on to the other cages and opened the doors wide.

"We're leaving now," I said to the dozens of frightened blue eyes staring at their portals of freedom. "You can join Ichiro and help us with our mission, or you can stay here and be slaves for the rest of your lives; it's your choice. I'm not like Ricardo. I'm not going to force you to do anything." We headed for the stairs, Ichiro's footsteps pattering after us.

There were whispers behind me, then other footsteps. I stopped and looked back. The shadowborn were slinking out into the passageway, hesitant at first, then with increasing vigor. They walked faster; several even ran as they took advantage of their newfound freedom. They passed me, some melting into shadows, others glowing with their silvery light. In vain, I sought one in particular. Maybe he was invisible. Only Ricardo Santos could tell me for sure.

As they hurried up the stairs, Ichiro looked at me as though asking for my permission to follow his comrades. I reached out and squeezed his hand. "Thank you," I said. "And what happened to you…..I'm sorry."

He nodded to me the way a soldier nods to his commanding officer, comprehending and accepting his fate, and took off at a run. He blended in with the sea of silver-haired children and was lost from my sight. I watched them, feeling cold and sick, hoping I hadn't just doomed them all.

Damion's heavy hand on my shoulder brought me back to the present. "Come on," he said. "Let's get this over with."

Xia took out her stun gun and held it ready while Damion and I stole rifles from the unconscious guards.

Damion hefted his gun against his shoulder and looked back at Xia with a sly smile. "You're smoking hot right now. Just thought you should know."

She rolled her eyes. "Say that again after Ricardo's turned in." She pushed him forward and we ran up the stairs after the shadowborn.

CHAPTER 47

The stronghold filled with the eerie hollers of shadow-born as they flooded into the halls. We followed behind, headed in the direction of Ricardo's chamber.

Almost immediately, several armed men and women appeared from around the corner. One of them gave a short scream at the sight of the child army, but they stood their ground, guns held at the ready.

"Stop where you are!" a man shouted. We continued to approach. Surely these guards wouldn't shoot, not when the shadowborn were so valuable.

I was wrong. They were too terrified of the silver-haired children to think rationally. With a ragged cry, a gun went off. The bullet struck a girl so forcefully it knocked her to the ground.

I screamed, shock and guilt racing through me. This was my fault. I had urged her to go to her death.

The rest of the children paused, stunned by what had happened. So did the guards.

The girl on the floor struggled for breath as she reached to where the bullet had pierced her chest. With a grunt, she drew the bullet out of her and let it clink to the floor. Then she sat up and looked around. She should be dead. Instead, the gaping hole in her chest was closing up. Her silvery blood dried to a trickle, then stopped flowing as the wound vanished.

I could see the guns tremble in the guards' shaking hands. Several of the children moved toward them again, looking eerily confident with the girl in the lead.

"Try anything and we'll shoot again!" A guard screamed.

A teenage boy caught up with the girl. He raised one hand out in front of him, gesturing at their guns. The weapons turned orange with heat, and I heard the sizzle of flesh before the guards registered the pain.

At once, they dropped their weapons, crying out in agony from the searing metal. The boy who had caused the heat ran past them with several of the bolder shadowborn on his heels.

Recovering from their pain, one of the guards turned and caught another boy by the ankle and pulled him to the ground. My heart leaped when I saw that it was Ichiro. I raised the gun I'd taken from the comatose guard in the prison, and pointed it level with the guard's back as he slammed Ichiro's head into the ground. My finger hesitated on the trigger and I watched with fascination as Ichiro reached up and held the guard's face with both hands. The man's skin glowed with faint silvery light from the little boy's palms.

"Let me go!" Ichiro commanded. The man immediately released him and pulled away.

"Stop him!" Ichiro pointed to a different guard who had just grabbed an even smaller shadowborn in a chokehold. His guard turned and pounced on the man, pulling him away from the silver-haired child while Ichiro ran ahead down the hall.

It was clear that Ichiro could not only read minds but control them as well.

Xia, Damion, and I held the rest of the guards at bay with our guns, while the remainder of the children kept moving.

We forced the guards to lie face down on the ground. Their weapons still sizzled with heat, so we didn't dare try to get rid of them. Instead, we kept moving. The powers of the shadowborn greatly increased our chances of success, so we needed to catch up with them and work together until we reached Ricardo's quarters.

In the hall to our left, we spotted the silhouette of another group of guards. They had guns out and were crouched at the ready. Behind them, we could see the children disappearing down the hall. Why weren't the guards turning on them or doing anything to stop them? Why weren't they moving at all?

As we drew near, a shudder ran up my spine. The men had a pale, crystalline appearance with horrified expressions frozen on carven faces. They'd been turned into salt.

"Saints!" said Damion as he slid a finger down the rock-solid side of one of the men's arms. "Those kids better stay on our side."

We caught up to the group ahead of us and watched as they divided themselves into packs and spread out. Some took the stairs to higher levels, others led the way down branching corridors.

The whole stronghold was alerted now. A siren blared and red lights flashed from the ceilings, strobe lighting our advance. Metal gates dropped from the ceiling to close off hallways and lock us in. Good thing we were still with the boy who could heat metal. Reaching his hand out to the gates, the bars glowed with heat, then melted and dissolved, leaving wide openings for us to get through.

With such power, these children could have escaped from their prison cells anytime; they had just needed someone to encourage them.

Ahead, about twenty Coterie barricaded the passage, prepared to stand against our attack. I looked over my shoulder and saw others running to block off the space behind us.

Several of the older shadowborn encircled Xia, Damion, and me. Then a girl around my age lifted her hand toward a light hanging from the ceiling. The bulb ruptured, and somehow its light was transferred to her hand. It sizzled and sparked there in a ball of yellow energy. She threw it at the oncoming attackers who were overwhelmed by the blast of electricity. She raised both hands this time, and bulbs erupted in quick succession as she took their electricity, one after the other, and used it to clear our way forward.

I managed to look back as we kept moving. Behind us the shadows were separating from the walls, filling the hall like dark mist and cloaking the attacking shadowborn from the oncoming guards. My heart leaped as I connected with the icy blue stare of a familiar girl before the darkness swallowed her whole. Despite myself, I smiled.

In battle formation, we reached Ricardo's room. The doors were locked, but one of our shadowborn escorts, a tall boy with Indian features, took care of that by pressing his body against them and squeezing his eyes shut in apparent concentration. The wood turned into white ash and crumbled to the floor.

We entered with caution, remembering all too well the bodyguards that had put Damion and me to shame. The room turned out to be a large bedroom with tinted windows that looked toward the ocean. It was spotless, with no sign of Ricardo. We searched it anyway, checking under the bed and inside the closet, but found nothing.

"Come on." Damion waved for us to leave. "He was probably evacuated at the first sign of trouble, but we should search the halls just in case."

That's when I noticed that a painting on the wall was slightly askew; the only thing out of place in the orderly room. I tipped it to the side and exposed a lever. I pulled it and a wall panel turned in, revealing a dark opening. Inside was a metal staircase leading down.

"Sweet Salvation!" said Damion. "Those are some sharp eyes, Tey." He peered inside. "Think our man got out this way?"

"Don't go any further!" shouted a commanding voice. I turned to see guards overwhelming the doorway. One had a gun pointed to the head of the boy who had destroyed the door.

"Go," the boy said. "The others will cover you."

I broke away from Xia and Damion and raised my gun at his captor.

BANG.

The boy dropped to the ground with the guard's bullet in his skull. My heart arrested as I stared in shock at his cold dead face. He didn't heal like the girl in the hall.

"Don't come any closer!" commanded the guard. "I'll kill everyone in this room."

This couldn't be happening. This wasn't real. I stood speechless, unable to react.

In a rage, the rest of our shadowborn escorts ran at the guards.

Damion's muscular arms wrapped around me and pulled me back. I struggled against him, even though I knew there was little I could do to help the other shadowborn in the room. They were risking themselves for us, dying for us. The least we could do was escape.

I let Damion pull me through the doorway after Xia. I

heard a child's scream that vibrated loud enough to shatter glass, followed by two gunshots and someone I hoped was a guard pleading for mercy. I forced myself not to turn to see what was happening. Instead, I plunged down the stairs after my comrades.

At the bottom was a small room with a floor of metal grating. On the far side was an elevator. I pushed the button next to it and the door slid open. When we were all inside, I pressed the only other button on the panel and braced myself against the wall as it dropped fast, and then lurched to a stop. A gust of cool air greeted me when the door slid open, and the elevator's light spilled into the darkness beyond.

This time Damion took the lead at a slight crouch. We were in a passageway smelling of soil and wet stone. The ceiling was uneven rock, as if the tunnel had been blasted into existence. As Xia fumbled for her flashlight, I saw another small beam of light far ahead. I pointed and we crept forward, keeping our light off for the time being.

We followed for some time. The beam was like an elusive will-o-the-wisp, always the same distance ahead of us. The passageway split in two several times, and sloped up or down dramatically. After about half an hour, we were out of breath. Next to me, Damion tried to stifle a cough on his arm, but that didn't stop it from echoing on the stone walls around us. He winced apologetically, and the light in front of us went dark.

We stopped in our tracks, unsure of how to proceed. Three breaths later, guns fired.

We dropped to the ground and rolled to the side of the tunnel where small outcroppings of rock partially shielded our bodies. I covered my ears at the reverberating sound and gulped back a cry of horror as bullets showered over us. Next to me, I heard Damion pull his rifle out from under him and fire rapidly into the dark.

I followed his lead and lifted my gun at a forty-five-degree angle. I closed my eyes to focus on the direction the shots were coming from then shot blindly ahead. The butt of the rifle slammed into my diaphragm as it engaged. There was the sound of bullets hitting the tunnel walls and ricocheting off, followed by round after round of fresh gunshots from whoever was at the other end of the tunnel.

I felt a slice of fire across my shoulder as one of the bullets grazed me, and another across the side of my head. Hot blood seeped from the wounds, but I barely noticed. All I could think about was how much I didn't want to die. Even lying in that cell preparing for torture and execution hadn't brought out my will to live quite like this terrible moment. Every muscle clenched, every nerve engaged. Sweat coated my body in a matter of seconds and my heart felt like it was about to combust.

Above the gunfire, someone cried out, and the shower of bullets coming at us decreased by half. A few seconds later, there was another strangled cry. Then everything went silent.

I lay shaking on the cold ground. Tears I hadn't felt until now streamed down my face. Pain awakened like burning coals in my wounds, and next to me, I could hear groans from Damion and Xia.

"Is everyone still alive?" Damion croaked, a half-formed sob in his throat.

There was a click, and Xia's flashlight illuminated her blood-streaked face. Like me, she had been grazed a few times in the head, and there were bad gashes in her right arm, but nothing looked deadly. Lines of blood striped Damion's bulky shoulders and the sides of his collarbone, but by some miracle, we'd all survived.

Xia's flashlight beam passed across us, then toward our attackers. Two men lay motionless on the ground several yards away.

We helped each other to our feet. I could walk, but my legs were like rubber. We approached the fallen men, who lay in widening pools of blood. There was a grunt, and we saw a third man farther in the tunnel struggling to sit up.

Guns ready, we approached the lone survivor.

Ricardo.

I swallowed, tasting blood. Here was the same man who'd tried to kill me in California. Now he was the one who looked afraid. One of his legs was riddled with bullet holes, and blood seeped between his fingers from where he clutched his side.

Damion raised his gun and pointed it at his head. "I could do it. You're wanted dead or alive."

Ricardo closed his eyes and leaned against the cavern wall. "Go ahead, but you'll never find your way out of these tunnels."

I looked behind me. My eyes were greeted with pitch darkness. Had the last turn in the tunnel been a left or a right? The passage had branched off so many times I couldn't remember anything.

"Do you have a map?" Xia asked, searching his pockets.

Ricardo pointed to his head. "In here."

"Damn you!" Xia kicked him in his wounded side. Ricardo flinched and spat out a wad of blood.

Damion pulled Xia away before she could strike again. "It's alright, Xi. We'll just go back the way we came."

Ricardo smiled. Through clenched teeth, he said, "These tunnels are programed. Every twenty minutes, grates come down, blocking off different passages. The way you came is already impassable."

Xia let out a growl and had to be restrained by Damion again.

"He could be lying to distract us," I suggested.

"You're welcome to check for yourselves," said Ricardo, "but you'll only be wasting time."

Sweat beaded Damion's brow and his breathing sped up, reminding me of the short time we'd spent together in the box.

He leaned in close to Ricardo. "I doubt you want to die today any more than we do. Tell us how to get out of here and we won't hurt you. I swear."

"And what then?" said Ricardo. "You'll spirit me away to some kingsguard post and give me up to the monarchy like they did with Antonio? That's the same as death."

Damion put his hands to either side of his head and took several deep breaths. "So you'd rather just die in the dark like a worm?"

Ricardo closed his eyes and pressed into his side, blood oozing around his hand like water from a sponge. "It's going to happen whether I want it to or not. At least this way, I can ensure your company when I pass to the other side." He tried to laugh but ended up choking on another wad of blood that he spit out on the ground.

Xia bent and examined the man's wound. When she looked up, her eyes were grave. "He's right. He's not going to last long."

"We can't wait around for someone to rescue us," said Damion, curling his hands into fists. "We need to get moving."

"I agree," I said. "We might be down here a long time. Any waiting will just add to our hunger and thirst."

Xia stooped and lifted Ricardo's arm around her shoulders. Damion quickly supported the other side.

Ricardo gave a short cry as he was lifted, one leg dragging behind him.

"I thought you monsters didn't feel pain," Xia said.

He grunted. "We are taught not to yield to pain. Blocking it out entirely is an art we've yet to master."

With an injured man in tow, our progress was unbearably slow. I clenched my hands into fists, suppressing the urge to scout ahead. We passed several blocked passages and occasionally heard the echoes of closing grates.

Damion's breathing grew heavier, and I could see him gritting his teeth.

"I can take a turn," I said, motioning to Ricardo. My wounds had stopped gushing blood and were now itching like mad. I felt I could use a distraction from them.

Damion shook his head. "I'm fine."

"Please," said Xia, "you look like hell."

"Not as bad as he does."

Ricardo's head was down, oily hair falling into his eyes. He was semiconscious and his leg dripped blood with every step.

Just then, Damion gagged and vomited all over the ground.

I pushed him away from Ricardo and lifted the man's arm around my shoulders. His weight slumped against me. Damion fell to his knees and threw up again, his whole body trembling. When he was done, he couldn't catch his breath.

"Damion?" said Xia. She handed off Ricardo to me alone and kneeled beside Damion. I braced myself against the tunnel wall to support Ricardo's full weight. He moaned softly.

Xia's hand stroked Damion's back. "Hey there. You OK?" Her voice was gentle in a way I'd never heard it before.

Damion's breathing only picked up speed. "Sweet salvation, I have to get out of here, Xi. I'm gonna die. I'm gonna die." He put his head between his hands and rocked back and forth. It sounded like he was hyperventilating.

"Hey, look at me. You're going to be fine, OK? We're gonna find a way out of here, but I need your help."

I lowered Ricardo to the ground and propped him against the cavern wall. Xia continued to comfort Damion while I faced the dying man. The bloodstain on his shirt now covered the entire front of his torso.

I held his head between my two hands and looked him in the eyes. "I don't expect you to remember me, Ricky, and I don't expect you to tell me the way out of here. I just want to know one thing."

He looked at me through half-lidded eyes. "And what's that, girly?" Blood dribbled from the corners of his mouth and made me want to retch myself.

I took a breath to steady my voice. "Where's Waif?"

He coughed and spat again. After catching his breath, he said, "Who?"

"He's the shadowborn who can turn invisible. Harrington said he's the only one he's seen with that kind of ability. He belonged to you once before, and you bought him back two days ago."

Ricardo coughed, turning the blood into foam. "Why? Did you think I'd sell him to you?"

"No. He was my friend. I just want to find him."

"Aww," said Ricardo. "As sweet as that is, I have no idea who you're talking about. I have a whole army of shadowborn, one that will soon bring about the end of our pathetic monarchy once they're brought back into order. Do you think I keep track of them all? Even if I did, there's no reason to tell you. I'm already dying."

It was true; I had nothing to barter with. "I can't give you a reason," I said. "Except that maybe the knowledge you helped someone might give you a bit of peace. I would always remember it, and always be grateful." It was the first thing that came to my mind, and also the stupidest.

"You're a sentimental thing aren't you?" said Ricardo. "I never had much room for those particular emotions. They don't go well with the business, you understand." His eyes rolled back and his head drooped. For a minute, I thought he was dead, but then I heard the ragged sound of his breathing and knew there was still time.

CHAPTER 48

After much coaxing, Xia got Damion to stand up again. He looked like a crazed animal, teeth gritted and eyes darting in every direction, but he somehow managed to keep going.

We had to completely carry Ricardo now, and tried our best to distribute his weight between the three of us; Damion and Xia took his arms, me his ankles.

The passage twisted and turned, sometimes leading to dead ends, other times branching off in confusing directions. Hunger gnawed at my gut, but it wasn't as bad as the thirst. The thirst dried up all the saliva left in my mouth until I could no longer swallow.

Exhaustion dragged us to the ground and we deposited Ricardo against the cavern wall. He was still breathing, but his breaths were getting shallower. We collapsed nearby, sleep drowning us the moment we shut our eyes.

Ricardo's moaning pulled me to the surface. I wasn't sure how long I'd slept, but my eyes were gritty and my mouth even more sandpaper dry. It felt like we'd been in the tunnels for days. Xia and Damion gave no signs of life, so I grabbed the flashlight and crawled next to Ricardo, touching his shoulder. His head tipped to one side as if he was having trouble supporting its weight.

"Are you in a lot of pain?" I asked.

"Death is coming," he said, relief in his voice. It hit me for the first time that one of my bullets might be buried inside him, draining his life away. There was no way to know for sure.

"I'm sorry you have to die in here," I said, although I didn't mean it. I couldn't afford to waste any feelings on a man who'd caused so much terror, but if I appeared sympathetic, perhaps he'd still tell me the one thing I wanted most.

The corner of his lips twitched. "You're sorry? For me?" His laughter brought up more blood and he coughed and spat. "If I'd wanted to see daylight again, I'd have told you the way out."

"It might not be too late," I said, keeping my voice soft and hopeful. He could still change his mind. He could still help.

He shook his head and leaned it back. "It is for me. You? You've still got time." His chest wheezed and he closed his eyes, all tension leaving him. "Will you shepherd me to Hell, girly?"

"I'm not going anywhere if that's what you mean." I kept my hand on his arm so he could feel me there, trying my best not to cringe at the contact.

"The weapon," he whispered. "The one in Los Angeles. I could never get it to work again. Seems you were its only victim." He wheezed. "And it sure did a poor job killing you."

My heart stuttered in my chest. He remembered who I was. "So did you," I said.

He didn't answer. A long time passed, and the rise and fall of his chest became less frequent, leeching away whatever hope remained in me. Here lay a terrible man—a king among criminals. He had caused the deaths of hundreds, maybe thousands. Why should I expect his last moments to change him?

The breath I released shook like a sob. I was never going to see Waif again, and I was never going to get out of here alive. The truth fell on me like loose rubble and I was suddenly hyperaware how much the wounds in my head and shoulders burned, and how my throat ached with the need for water.

To my surprise, Ricardo opened his eyes again, but they were glazed and distant. "Lazar," he said, his voice little more than a whisper.

"What?" I leaned in, straining to hear him.

"Lazar. That's where I sent him."

"Who?"

Three more breaths passed. "Your precious Waif."

Suddenly I was alive again. "Where is Lazar? Is it an island? A town?"

Ricardo did not answer. His eyes had stopped blinking.

I let out a shaky breath and closed his eyelids with two fingers, unable to bear their glassy stare. Beside me, Xia and Damion were stirring.

"Ricardo's dead," I said. They sat up fast and rushed over.

Xia checked his pulse then stood, wiping her hand on her pants. "Let's get him out of here before he starts to reek."

"Ever heard of a place called Lazar?" I asked as we hauled up Ricardo's body and distributed the weight. He seemed heavier now that he was dead, and the limp feel of his corpse made me want to puke.

Xia and Damion both shook their heads. "Why do you want to know?" Xia asked.

"It was the last thing he said. Maybe it was important."

She shrugged. "To him, maybe, but it's meaningless to us. We've got our man, and now we're going to get the hell out of here." She cleared her throat and shouted into the dark. "Did you hear that? We're getting out of here! You can do what you want with Ricardo, but you're not taking the rest of us!" Perhaps she was losing her mind as quickly as Damion.

We pressed on but made no visual progress. Tunnels opened and closed, leading us in an endless deadly circle.

Damion was reduced to tears. His shoulders shook with sobs as he carried Ricardo's dead weight.

"Stop blubbering," said Xia. "You're wasting water."

"I can't help it," he said. "Saints! This is …this is the last way I wanted to die." It was strange to hear a guy unafraid of sneaking into an armed Coterie fortress to capture the most dangerous criminal in Los Sueños terrified of a dark tunnel.

"Maybe if you focused on something other than death, you would have an easier time," said Xia. I could tell that she was scared too; she just held the fear inside, every muscle tense, skin pasty.

Frustration had more of a hold on me. I wanted to breathe fresh air; I wanted to feel the sun on my face. Most of all I wanted a drink of water.

Time kept ticking and we kept walking, seeing no logic or strategy to the way the tunnels branched off. We tried shouting for help, hoping someone might hear us, even if they were an enemy. Only our echoing voices answered.

My mind started to wander. I kept thinking I glimpsed shapes in the dark just beyond the range of the flashlight. I stopped feeling my exhaustion and became nothing but a head floating above my body.

Maybe Damion was right and we were going to die trapped in the darkness. One day, some archeologist might stumble across our skeletons and wonder what poor fools we'd been to traverse the tunnels without a map. Or maybe they'd be lost too and see our remains as a sign that death was coming for them soon. After all we'd been through, this seemed like such a stupid way to go.

We stopped to rest again, easily finding sleep despite the hardness of the tunnel floor. Would I ever wake again? Did I want to? The thought barely brushed my mind as unconsciousness wrapped around me.

For a while, I saw only blackness, my dreams reflecting the darkness of my waking world. Then there was a light. I looked up. A ghost? No, an angel. So I had died. It wasn't as terrible as I'd thought it would be.

"Hello, Tey." The angel spoke my name, only she wasn't an angel. I knew her. The girl from the photograph.

"What are you doing here?" I asked.

Her white dress swirled around her as she turned and danced down the passage. "I came to find you."

My heart jumped. "But this is a dream. It isn't real. You're not real."

"You disappoint me, Tey. I'd thought you would have learned by now."

"But you're just a photograph on my wall."

"The useful thing about dreams is that I can appear however I wish."

I swallowed hard. "Are you alive in the real world too?"

"Not for much longer," she said, eyes downcast. "And you won't be either if you do not follow what I am about to show you." She put her hand on my face, the way Ichiro had done, but instead of reading my mind, she projected something into it, a vision of me rushing through branches of the tunnel. Left, right, right, left, left, right. The vision continued until I saw an opening up ahead. The way out.

She pulled away. "I have imprinted the path in your memory. When you are free, come and find me. I'll be waiting for you."

"Wait, how will I find you?"

"I'm all around you."

"I don't understand."

"I am the dirt. I am the trees. I am these cavern walls."

"Who are you?" I said, still not understanding her nonsense.

She touched my forehead, eyes locking with mine. At that moment, I saw that her irises were crescent moons. Suddenly I knew the truth about her. The truth about everything.

"I am Los Sueños."

My eyes snapped open.

I sucked in a breath. A thousand images rushed into my mind and out of it just as fast. The islands weren't islands. They were alive just like I was alive, and they wanted me to stay that way.

I roused Xia and Damion and they peered at me, blurry-eyed. "We should keep going." I felt energized after my dream, the dream that was so much more than a dream, and didn't want it to go to waste. Xia and Damion grumbled, but followed my lead with bowed heads, and pulled Ricardo's corpse off the ground. I didn't tell them what I'd seen, but they followed without question. What did the way matter to a lost person?

The tunnel branched left, then right, then right again. Then, the next tunnel was blocked off by a grate. Ricardo had said they changed every twenty minutes. We'd have to wait.

"Can we take a short break?" I asked, pretending to be more tired than I felt.

Xia shook her head. "If we stop, I'm not sure I can get up again. Let's go a bit farther."

"I think we should wait for this passage to open."

"Why?" croaked Damion. "Does it matter?"

"I think I feel a draft coming from this one," I lied. "It could mean we're getting close."

Xia licked her finger and held it out, testing the air. "I don't feel anything."

"I swear I felt something, and we have nothing else to go on. Why not try?" I debated explaining the dream, but worried they'd think I was hallucinating.

They shrugged and lowered Ricardo to the ground. The time we waited felt like an eternity. Every second my heart beat faster, filling with worry that I was wrong, then there was a rusty squeal and the grate lifted. I helped Xia and Damion with Ricardo's limp body and we continued.

I had to convince them to wait at three more grates, each time, praying we were making progress. I remembered the vision from the dream with incredible clarity, immediately knowing which tunnel to choose when we came across a fork in the path, but I couldn't recall how much farther we had to go.

I wiped my brow and found that I was sweating, but how could I be sweating when I was so parched? The air was warmer. Much warmer. The tunnel sloped upward and I could see without the aid of the flashlight. Ahead was a small patch of gray from which poured sweet-smelling air.

"Look!" I cried, surprised by how hoarse my voice had become. Despite my fatigue, I ran, arms pumping madly, desperate for the relief of the outside. The mouth of the tunnel was narrow and covered by weeds. Outside it was pouring rain. The most beautiful rain I'd ever seen. I stepped into freedom, spreading my arms wide, mouth open to the falling droplets.

Xia and Damion came out behind me. They dropped Ricardo and collapsed in the mud, lying on their backs and drinking in the bounty from the sky.

CHAPTER 49

We walked for a few hours and tried to get our bearings in the thick jungle that surrounded the tunnel opening. With the rain, we were nearly up to our knees in mud, which made travel that much more exhausting, not to mention the added burden of Ricardo's corpse.

"Where do you think all those tunnels came from," I asked, shivering when I thought of how they'd nearly claimed us.

"The Coterie were probably mining for earthblood," said Damion. "But if they ever got lucky, they cleaned it out years ago." He used his free arm like a machete, lashing away any weeds that stood in our way. "Say, Xi, you never did tell us how you got inside the fort."

Xia shrugged. "It's not much of a story. I just used the front door."

Damion raised his eyebrows. "The front door?"

"Yep. I stunned one of the sailors, stole his uniform, then told the guards at the entrance that I was the ship's cook. They bought it and escorted me to the dining hall for a free meal and everything."

"Saints and angels," said Damion. "What if they'd questioned you? Or asked for your Coterie clearance?"

"Then you'd be dead by now."

She repositioned Ricardo's limp arm around her shoulder. The sight of his pale and lifeless form in daylight made me nauseous. I brought up the rear and continued to carry his ankles as best I could while ignoring all the dried blood on his pant legs.

"How did you find us once you were inside?" I asked.

"Sailors in the dining hall gossiped. They told me all about your capture and where you were being held. Finding you two ended up being my easiest mission yet."

The rain let up and we stopped to rest on a dry patch of ground we discovered under a leafy tree. I sank against the gnarled trunk. Every muscle ached and my stomach felt like it had been hollowed out with a shovel. I closed my eyes, wanting nothing more than to drift off and awaken back in my bed in the Castillo, or better yet, back in my bed in Washington. But my stomach growled with a dull ache I could no longer ignore.

I looked back at Xia and Damion. "I'm going to look for fruit," I said. "I won't go far."

"Stay in shouting distance," he said, leaning against the tree, "and if you see any giagons, bring me back an armload."

"You got it," I said. "Any requests, Xia?"

"Something edible," she said, laying back and throwing an arm across her eyes. "I'm almost hungry enough to eat grubs."

"I'll make sure to find you some fruit with worms in it, then," I said with a smile.

I made my way through the thick trees, picking up any fallen fruits I found along the way and filling the front of my shirt with them.

It eventually occurred to me that I'd been walking along a footpath for the last few minutes. Up ahead I saw several ramshackle buildings with dim lights glowing from open-air windows. A sense of familiarity washed over me. I knew where I was.

The leper settlement.

I drew back at the sound of rustling in the underbrush. My skin prickled and I looked around. It was nearly dark, and lots of nocturnal creatures probably prowled the island.

Something tore through the underbrush, running at top speed. I stifled a cry as a heavy form fell on top of me, pinning me to the ground. I screamed and tried to fight back, but a bandaged hand clasped over my mouth. "Who are you? What are you doing here?" asked a male voice.

My mind scrambled for an explanation as the hand lifted away. "My boat got a leak," I said. "I didn't want to swim back to Cosmar at night so I decided to stay on Santa Arcadia until morning."

"You're a little far from the beach," my captor said.

"I went looking for fruit."

"This deep in? There are plenty of well-stocked trees closer to the shore."

"I'm sorry. I've never been here before. It's getting dark and I couldn't find anything." I pretended to cry and managed to get my eyes to tear up a little. Such a performance wasn't a stretch from how I really felt.

"Get up," said the man. "You're coming with me."

I thought about trying to break away and run into the trees, but then I remembered the lepers shooting at us from the beach. I couldn't be sure if this one was armed.

He grabbed my wrists and held them tightly behind my back as he forced me to walk at a brisk pace. Lantern light illuminated our way, and we walked through the muddy roads between the huts.

People looked out of windows as we passed. Some wore bandages, others left their deformities exposed—missing limbs, deteriorating faces. I tried not to look anyone in the eye or give any sign of discomfort as I passed by.

An old woman hobbled outside, blocking our way. Her feet were bare and she was missing all but one of her toes. "Who's this?" she asked, coming uncomfortably close.

The man who captured me stopped. "I found her on the path. I think she's another Coterie spy."

I shook my head. "I swear I'm not. If you just let me explain—"

The woman silenced me with a wave. "We've been ordered to shoot anyone who gets near Lazar. You're lucky Lorenzo didn't have a gun."

My heart screamed at her words. "Lazar? This is Lazar?" I could feel my body warming as hope surged through my veins.

She looked at me like I was crazy. "You've heard the name of our village before?" Her voice sounded much younger than I would have expected. I squinted. She wasn't old at all, but her face was so disfigured that all signs of youth had been stripped from it. "You must be a spy."

My enthusiasm vanished. "No, I mean, yes I know the name, but I didn't know it was this village. It was just a story I heard. I promise not to tell anyone about it."

"The master will decide," said the woman, and I was grateful she didn't try to question me further. "I'll take her to him."

She led me to one of the larger and sturdier huts and rapped on the door. There was the patter of bare feet and it swung open. My heart stopped when my eyes met Rob's.

CHAPTER 50

I couldn't speak. I couldn't move. Rob? How could he be here?

His face was pale and unshaven, his normally perfect curls, disheveled. He blinked twice when he saw me as though to clear a haze. "Tey?"

"You know this girl?" the woman asked.

"Of course I know her," said Rob. "She's one of my—friends." He dragged me inside. "You can leave us, Neya. She won't hurt me."

I nearly laughed. If only he knew how much I wanted to do just that.

The leper woman bowed her head and walked off.

Rob closed the door and untied my bonds. "It's really you."

"Yes," I said bitterly.

"You look terrible; are you OK?"

I itched unconsciously at a wound on my shoulder where a bullet had skimmed me and looked down at the crusted blood and mud caking my clothes. I was a mess, but so was he. Dark circles rimmed his eyes, and his clothes were rumpled and dirty, giving him a wild look. "Fine."

"What are you doing here?"

I stood rigid and clasped my shaking hands together to steady them. "I could ask you the same thing."

He pulled away and poured something into a clay mug.

"Want some coffee?"

I shook my head. I wouldn't take anything from him ever again.

He took a sip and sat at a round table in the middle of the hut. "Some agents caught on to me. I knew it was only a matter of time. I had to hide until I decided what my next move was."

"And you knew the lepers would give you a royal welcome."

He shrugged. "Remember how you and Xia saw them flying my father's crest? I figured it was a good bet they still thought my parents sent their supplies. I was right. They practically kissed my feet when they found out who I was."

"How convenient."

"Are the kids all right?" he asked, abruptly changing the subject.

"Last I checked. But I haven't been to the Castillo for a couple of days. At least, it feels like a couple of days." I had no concept as to how much time had passed in those tunnels.

He sat up straighter. "Why not? What have you been up to?"

My mouth wanted to form a wicked smile, but I kept it composed as I sat across from him. "Oh, nothing much. Just tracking down Ricardo and snatching him from his own hideout."

Rob dropped his mug and coffee spilled all over the table. "Ricardo Santos? You got him? You got Ricardo?"

I let the smile show, pleased that he had no part in our victory. "He's dead, but yes, we got him."

"We? You mean Xia and Damion were there too?"

I nodded.

"You're not serious."

"You don't have to believe me. I'm sure it will be all over

the front page of the Beacon by morning.”

He shook his head, a smile forming on his lips. “I knew my hunch about you was right. You’ll make the greatest agent of us yet.”

Despite everything, it was hard not to blush under his praise, but I didn’t want to give him the satisfaction of seeing that, so I said, “It’s not my fault some poor coward was hiding away, leaving us with all the work. While we nearly got our heads shot off and died in an underground maze, you were sitting here drinking coffee and getting your feet kissed.”

He ignored the comment and stood up. “If you’re telling the truth this could mean…This means we can finally start our campaign. I want you there with me, Tey. If you can find Ricardo, you can help me with what’s coming next.”

I drew back from him, coldness sweeping over me. “I don’t want to be part of it anymore.”

His face dropped. “You’re still mad at me.” He sat down again and put his head in his hands. “I did the best thing for that kid; you know that, right?”

Anger burned away the cold. “Torture, starvation, and slavery are the best things?”

“He could have hurt you. You saw how he attacked me that night.”

“He was protecting me from you.”

Rob made a fist and stared at the table. “He couldn’t have stayed in that tower forever. You should have told me about him.”

“So you could have turned him in before he had time to recover? He would have died.”

“I’m sorry,” he said, his voice choking. “I was scared. I didn’t know what else to do.”

“You’re so concerned with changing this place, and yet you

can't even see how you're making things worse."

He looked up at me. "If you let me tell you what's happening here, you'll see why it has to be this way."

"And you think I'll believe you, after all your lies? I know what you did to Ichiro."

He looked at me, surprise evident in his face, then resolve. "It was the right thing to do. He'd have never made it on his own."

"I was once a Coterie prisoner too. Do you think it was right what Arun Gheisari was about to do to me?"

My argument was interrupted by a child's scream that rippled through the colony. I stood up and ran to the door.

Rob grabbed my wrist and yanked me back. "Tey, wait. You don't want to go out there."

He held firm, but I spun around and twisted my wrist sharply. I came free and hurried outside.

"Tey stop!" Rob cried, running after me. He was too late. I saw what I needed to see.

The hatch in the ground was open and one of the lepers carried down a little girl. Lei.

Her eyes found mine and she screamed my name. I ran after her, arms outstretched. "Lei! I'm coming!"

The top closed, muting her cries.

Fire swept through my veins. Rob. He'd brought her here. Why?

I could hear his voice behind me. "Tey, I can explain; just listen to me," but I kept running for the hole.

Something hard struck the back of my head and my anger was snuffed out like a candle in the wind.

The return of consciousness brought a dull ache to my skull. My body was strapped to a hard surface and I could sense the distant pressure of earthblood like a bass drum in a far off parade.

Voices spoke from somewhere close to my head. One came from Rob, the other from an unfamiliar woman with a slight accent.

"She might be too old," said the woman. "The process could have adverse effects on her brain."

I felt Rob's cold fingers stroke my brow and I tried not to flinch. "I hate to risk it. She was a valuable teammate, but I can't cover this up. You know as well as I do, there was a good reason I ordered the lepers to kill anyone who got too close."

"Then why not kill her? That would be the kinder thing to do."

"I've told you many times, I'm not a killer. You don't kill people you care about, even when they go too far."

"Fine. But you need to bring me more children," said the woman. "We both know the little girl isn't likely to survive and we're running out of time. I've been monitoring energy levels on multiple islands. They're getting stronger. Much more could be harmful to humans. It's already affecting the ecosystem."

Rob exhaled loudly. "How long do we have?"

The woman hesitated. "A year. Maybe two."

"And then we're all dead?"

"The sickness is progressing. When the islands die, the emidion wells beneath them will be released. The results will be catastrophic, not just for us, but also for the rest of the world. If people do manage to survive, everything will be changed. Seasons, climates, life as we know it. Only the shadowborn have a chance of stopping it."

I could hear Rob pacing and imagined him pulling at his hair like he always did when he was worried. "I'm counting on you to figure this out!"

"Research is improving," said the woman, her voice emanating an icy calm. "Like the little girl, I've had a few come out white, but they died before the islands could take them. Other subjects are emerging with multiple abilities. Allow me to show you the statistics I've gathered in my office."

The two voices got quieter as they moved out of the room. I dared to open my eyes for the first time. I was lying on a hard rolling bed, the kind they strapped corpses to before an autopsy. My heart hammered as I struggled. All around me were surgical items, sharp edges glinting in the dim fluorescent light.

A scream wanted to push out of my throat, but I held it back, focusing on trying to wriggle one hand out of my bonds. It was useless. I was held down too tight, and the effort of trying to free myself was exhausting. I could still hear Rob's voice talking to the other woman in the next room. They'd probably be coming back soon, and when they did, I had a hunch that everything would be over for me.

Something pressed on my arm and one of my straps came loose. I gasped and craned my neck in search of an explanation. Another strap came apart with a snap, then another. I was free. I sat up slowly, my heart pounding crazier than ever.

"Who's there?" I hissed.

A hand clasped over my mouth, muffling my cry. I tried to pull away, but someone whispered in my ear. "You have to keep quiet."

The hand lifted away and relief flooded me to the tips of my fingers. "Waif," I gasped, tears springing to my eyes. "Is that you?" I hadn't even heard his footsteps.

"It's me," his comforting voice affirmed. "Let's go before they come back."

I looked for him, searching for a sign that he wasn't a hallucination. "Where are you?"

"Right next to you. Come on."

He was invisible. Of course. I itched to wrap my arms around him and pull him close. Instead, I slid off the bed.

His slender hand took mine and he flickered into visibility as if my touch were a light switch.

"What's going on?" I whispered as we exited into a long corridor lit by dim lights. "Where are we?"

"There's a hatch in the leper colony that leads below ground," said Waif. "We're inside it."

"Did Ricardo send you here alone?"

"Some of his guards brought me. They assumed I was still dependent on earthblood injections like the others. If I hoped to get another one, I'd have to do what he asked then return to where they waited for me. Thanks to you, injections are no longer necessary."

"What was the mission?"

"Ricardo thought the monarchy was hiding something in Lazar. Since I can turn invisible, he sent me to find out what it was. He suspected valuables—brand name items from America, antibiotics, weapons maybe. He never came close to the truth."

Waif opened a metal door and I felt an instant change, like the vibrational frequency of the air was stronger now. Inside was a laboratory. There were three enormous glass tanks filled with liquid earthblood. Strange tubes connected them to various dials and equipment, all monitored by flickering computer screens.

"What is this place?" I whispered.

Waif's voice was frigid. "It's where shadowborn are made."

CHAPTER 51

Sweat broke out across my forehead. "Waif, I—" I didn't know what to say.

He answered my unspoken question.

"This whole place is familiar. When I first came inside, I thought I was going crazy. There were these flashbacks where I'd get glimpses of memories, and then they'd be gone." He grasped my hand tighter. "The look of it. The smell of it. Everything feels wrong."

"How long have you been here?"

"Ricardo sent me here right after he retrieved me from Harrington. I hoped I'd find a way to shut it down. I pulled some plugs, pushed some buttons, but I think I just messed things up. Now I'm worried she won't make it."

"She?"

That's when I saw her, a small body in one of the earth-blood tanks. Lei.

I let go of Waif's hand and ran to her. Her hair had turned completely white and there was a breathing mask over her face. Her eyes were closed and she looked as pale as death. I pounded on the glass and called her name. When nothing happened, I looked around for something to shatter it with. Waif handed me a chair, and I prepared to slam the legs into the glass wall of the tank.

"If you interrupt the process she will die," a female voice

said from behind me.

Waif instantly went invisible, and I spun around to face whoever had come in. There was Rob, with a tall, olive-skinned woman at his side.

The woman wore a white lab coat and carried a leather bag. I realized I'd seen her before from a tree while gathering fruit with Xia. She smiled at me like a doctor examining a child at a check-up. "Her death will not be swift, or painless. Is that what you want?"

My gaze turned to Rob, and my emotions burned into hot coals inside my chest. "You did this. You weren't raising those orphans out of the goodness of your heart. All that time they were just subjects for you to kidnap and experiment on. The bounty money, it was just something to fund your demented research, or whatever…whatever this is." I gestured at Lei then pointed the chair in my hands at him.

"You don't understand. What we're doing here is necessary. I wouldn't have allowed it if I wasn't convinced we might have a chance to save Los Sueños. To save the world."

"You're lying. You were always lying." My voice shook; every word a sob. "Nothing you ever told me was real."

"I never wanted it to be like this. The islands are sick, Tey. They're dying. The shadowborn are all castoffs, failures of an experiment started by my parents to keep that from happening. Most of their abilities are unpredictable and defective. They can't yet do what we need them to."

I wanted to fling the chair at him and shatter bones. The memory of his lips on mine suddenly made my skin crawl. "If you brought them here, then why hunt them down later?"

"Once the process is complete, the earthblood absorbs them. We don't yet know why or how, but each child is somehow transported elsewhere, only to be reborn by the islands.

They turn up in different locations, so I made it my mission to find and rescue them from my uncle's kill order, and then sell them to the Coterie where they'd be safe. The money we get from them is vital if we're going to make more progress here. Soon, it won't have to be like that."

"Why?" was all I could say. "Why children?"

He sighed and started to pace. "They were mostly street orphans with terrible lives who I welcomed in to the Castillo for protection. No one would miss them, and they're better off now than they ever were on the streets. Besides, children are the only ones the procedure works on. We don't know why. If you immerse an adult in earthblood, they just end up a babbling psycho. But with a child, something miraculous happens. It's as if Los Sueños can sense their purity. She imprints on their developing brains and grants them a link to her emidion. They're like ghosts of what the native dwellers of these islands once were. Beautiful. Powerful."

"Tortured and abused," I spat.

He took a deep breath. "Don't think I don't care about those kids, Tey. I'm doing this so there can be a future."

"Not for them," I said, eyes lowering to the floor. He was a much better actor than I could ever hope to be. Every one of his performances since I'd met him had been Oscar-worthy.

"It may not seem that way right now," he said, "but if things go as planned, we'll change that."

The woman nodded at him in agreement. "Every child brings us closer to perfecting the process. Soon, they'll be able to do everything the native dwellers once could."

Rob nodded at her. "Vashti is one of the most brilliant scientists in the country. My parents studied with her at the Royal University on Santa Isidore. When they were killed, I brought their research to her so we could continue their legacy. Together, we've stumbled on secrets about this country you'd never think possible. Secrets that would help us when the time for fighting came. And it's here, Tey. Ricardo's dead, thanks to you. With the disorder that will cause, I can finally come out of hiding. I'll rally the people around me and get rid of the filth on these islands forever. That's going to help save them. Support us, and I promise I won't turn you into a shadowborn. If I know you're with me, there'll be no reason to make you forget."

I lowered the chair. Support him? I'd agreed to it before, back when I thought he had some noble solution for eliminating the nation's criminal underground. But how were these methods any better than the Coterie's? "I'd rather be one of them."

He pulled a syringe of Supplicant from his pocket and fiddled with it. "And here I was thinking I was truly starting to care about you," he said. "You and I worked so well together; I hoped you'd stand with me when I told you the truth. I've wanted to tell you for a long time, but I had to make sure you'd be on my side. Now it's too late for regrets. I'm going to miss you, Tey."

And there were those eyes. Those eyes that told me he really would miss me. That he was sorry. I glared into them, willing them to break character and show what Rob truly was. They never did.

I was cornered against Lei's tank as he moved forward. I tried to keep my breathing calm. I wasn't going to go down without a fight. If he eventually overpowered me, he'd have some permanent scars to show for it.

Rob raised the syringe. "Vashti, prepare the tank next to Lei."

The woman entered a code onto a keyboard but was interrupted by a flashing light and a blaring alarm. "Rob!" she shouted.

He lowered his hand, annoyed at the interruption. "What's happening?"

"The emidion levels in the little girl are the highest I've ever seen. They—"

Lei opened her eyes inside the tank. They were milky white and looked angry. She struggled against the tubes connected to her body.

"Can't you pump something in there to sedate her?" Rob asked, his hand rising to his hair in panic.

"I'm trying," said Vashti, frantically entering commands into the computer, "but the emidion is burning up anything besides the earthblood entering her body."

Lei's pale figure glowed the way earthblood glowed, only getting brighter every second. The air around me vibrated faster and my heart raced to keep up.

I could see Rob's eyes squinted against the life-sucking force that still had little power over me. "Shut it down," he said. "Just abort everything."

Cracks appeared in the glass in a growing web.

"That will certainly kill her."

His face twisted and filled with heat. "Fine. If it's the only way, just do it. If that emidion escapes the tank, it could destroy this place."

Sweat dripped down Vashti's brow as she tried to do what Rob asked. The earthblood drained away from around Lei into valves in the wall, but that did nothing to stop the emidion meters on the sides of the tank from rising.

I tried to run for the door, hoping Waif—wherever he was—would follow. But Rob came at me and reached for my arm. I bashed the chair into his side and he was knocked to the floor. He reached out his arm and I tripped over it, sprawling on the ground.

Rob's hand caught hold of my pant leg before I could crawl away. I flipped onto my back and kicked at him as he tried to inject the syringe into my calf. My free foot struck his face and the syringe fell from his hand and rolled away. For a moment, I was free, and then he was on top of me, hands pressing down on my throat. My energy drained away with the oxygen in my lungs, and my flailing limbs fell useless to my sides.

"I want you to live, Tey," Rob said, tears forming in his eyes. "But I can't let you ruin everything. I have to make you forget. Then we can start over."

I still heard the blaring alarm, still saw the flashing light, but they were distant now and getting farther and farther away. I mouthed words but no sound would come from my closed-off throat, and no air would enter either. Blackness ringed my vision and my body burned as I tried to make my limbs work. He let up one hand so he could reach for the syringe. I sucked in a burning breath, but it wasn't enough to restore my lungs. The needle flashed as it came for me.

Something moved in the corner of my eye. I saw a small microscope rise from a lab table and float over Rob.

Rob's tears dripped onto my face the same moment the microscope connected with his head. He collapsed onto the floor.

Vashti looked up from her screen at the sound of the impact. Fear widened her eyes. "What just happened?"

I drank in air, rubbing my throat and silently thanking Waif with every restoring breath. I stumbled to my feet and searched the floor for Rob's syringe. I found it and turned on the woman.

Vashti reached into her leather bag and pulled out a gun. She swiveled the aim between my forehead and the microscope that still seemed to hover in the air where Waif's invisible hands held it. "Someone had better explain what's going on."

There wasn't time. The microscope rose higher and flew at her. She twisted and ducked just in time, and the object slammed into the computer behind her, shattering the screen.

"No!" she shouted. "You don't know what you've just done!"

Lei's scream made me forget anything else. She glowed so brightly I could see nothing inside her tank but intense whiteness. There was a sound like ice breaking over a lake, and then the glass shattered in an explosion of light.

The last thing I felt was Waif pushing me to the floor before my consciousness winked out.

CHAPTER 52

"Tey?"

I tried to open my eyes, but my lids felt weighted down. "Tey?"

The voice was gentle and familiar, and there was the sensation of a hand on my shoulder. I reached up to touch it. It was warm, and I didn't want to let go.

The voice gave a relieved sigh. "We need to get you out of here," it said. An arm slipped around my shoulders and lifted me into a sitting position.

I attempted to open my eyes again, and this time succeeded. Waif peered down at me, skin bloodied where fragments of glass had struck him, but illuminated by light.

"You're glowing," I whispered. I blinked, thinking the aura must be a trick of the eye, but it didn't disappear.

"So are you."

I looked down at myself, shocked to see a pale glow coming from my skin.

"It's the emidion that came from Lei," Waif said, eyes sparkling with uncontained energy. "I think we somehow absorbed it." He paused. "It doesn't make sense. I'm shadowborn, so it's in my blood. But you…"

I sat up straighter, suddenly remembering what had just happened. Vashti was lying in front of the shattered tank in a pool of blood, her body pierced by large shards. I didn't have to go to her to know she was dead.

I still gripped the syringe of Supplicant in my hand. I put it in my pocket; it would be useless now.

The glass from the other tanks had also shattered in the explosion, filling the room with crystalline debris. I looked at the ruined computers and saw a small electrical fire flickering between the wires.

My gaze passed across a limp figure next to the broken tank. "Lei!" I got to my feet and would have fallen over if Waif hadn't supported me.

"She's alive, I think," he said, helping me stumble to where the little girl lay. To say she looked pale would be an understatement. Every part of her was as white as powdered sugar. Vashti's words rang in my mind, sending a chill through me. I've had a few come out white, but they died before the islands could take them.

Lei's body hummed like a harp string, and when I passed my hand over her mouth, I felt a hint of warm breath. I tried to pick her up, but my arms were as useful as ropes of licorice.

"I'll do it," Waif said, and he bent down and scooped her up. She responded to his touch, clinging to him weakly. A good sign.

We turned for the door.

"Stop!" The voice was frail and raspy, but it was Rob's and he was definitely alive.

I froze, not wanting to look at him, but I did anyway. Blood ran down his face from the shards of glass impaling his skin, and he'd somehow gotten hold of Vashti's gun.

I went numb. Too numb to feel fear or even anger anymore. I stared at him, and this time glimpsed the flickers of insanity growing behind those deceitful eyes. Perhaps the emidion blast had caused it, or maybe it had always been there and I'd just never allowed myself to see it.

"Put the gun down, Rob," I said, keeping my voice low and even.

I couldn't tell if his shoulders shook with silent laughter or tears. "I should have known this would happen. All you ever cared about was yourself. You think getting back to your stupid country is somehow going to save you. But when Los Sueños falls, nothing that follows the destruction will be spared. And when it happens, you'll know that you had a chance to make things right, and you threw it away. And for what? Brats like him?"

He pointed with the gun at Waif. "When I found him wandering the skids three years ago, he was suffering from a fatal infection he'd picked up after his mother tried to kill him with a kitchen knife. The transformation saved his pathetic life."

Waif looked away and gripped Lei tighter. "I'd rather have died."

Every muscle in Rob's face contracted and his finger twitched on the trigger of the gun. "Then you can die now."

I stepped in front of Waif. "Put the gun down," I said again, surprised at how calm I sounded.

"So you can both run away and tell the world what I've done here?" He motioned to the destroyed lab.

"So I can come over there," I said, not letting my confidence waver.

Rob's forehead knotted in confusion. "Why?"

I let emotion that I didn't feel leek into my voice. "Because I'm sorry, and I think you might be right."

"Tey?" said Waif from behind me, but I waved for him to be silent.

I could have brought up the king's kill order, and all the

hundreds of other children whose lives Rob had destroyed, but I knew it would be pointless. If Rob was crazy enough to do those things, there would be no reasoning with him. He'd already justified his actions a thousand times in his mind.

"You don't want to kill me or him," I said. "You never wanted to kill anyone."

He nodded, hand trembling, and suddenly he seemed very young. "I was supposed to save people."

"It's what your parents would have wanted you to do."

His teeth chattered and he wiped away some of the blood that flowed into his eyes. I took a step toward him, cautious but deliberate, then another. He didn't shoot, but he didn't lower the gun either. I kept inching closer and kept talking.

"Let Waif and Lei go," I said, "and we can talk about this. I'll listen this time."

He shuddered and looked at the shattered glass. "It's too late."

"No," I said. "We'll find a way to fix this."

I was close enough to touch his arm. He flinched when my fingers connected but didn't pull away.

"Please, tell me what you know," I said, and drew him into an embrace. He stared away from me, gun still pointed at Waif, but he let my arms encircle him and my head press into his shoulder.

His chest moved against me in fitful breaths. "Why should I trust you now?"

Because it's easy to trust someone when they tell you what you want to hear. You should know; it worked so well on me. I didn't say the words. Instead, I reached into my back pocket, fingers wrapping around the tubular object there. "You don't need to trust me."

I pulled out the syringe and launched it at his shoulder.

His hand shot up and grabbed my wrist just before the needle struck home.

I cried out as he twisted my arm around behind my back and forced the syringe from my fingers. I would have screamed for Waif to run, but he and Lei were already gone. At least they would escape, even if it was the end of the line for me.

"I know what you're thinking," said Rob, into my ear. "You think your friend is safe. But once the Supplicant is inside you, you and I are going to hunt him down like the teammates we are. And once we find him—and you know we will—you're putting a bullet through his head."

"Why?" was all I could get out. "What has he ever done to you?"

Rob twisted harder, sending jolts of pain surging up my arm. "He stole your faith in me."

The needle was against my skin when Rob let out a ragged cry. He lost his grip on my arm and spun around. I saw a large piece of glass sticking out from his shoulder. Fresh blood pooled around it and ran down his back. His face turned the color of magma as he shoved the syringe into his coat pocket and struggled against something I couldn't see.

"You should have run away," I shouted at the invisible Waif, feeling both grateful and afraid. Waif didn't answer me.

More glass rose from the floor and flew at Rob. Rob dodged to the left and drew out his gun, firing aimlessly in its direction. I winced, praying Waif wasn't in the line of fire. I yanked on Rob's arm, trying to upset his aim, but he twisted around so fast, I was knocked off balance. With a shove to my stomach, he pushed me to the shard-littered ground.

I fell hard, feeling my ribs and shoulder bruise as the breath was knocked out of me. I looked up, dazed, and saw Rob fire again and again as more objects were hurled in his direction from invisible hands. Waif, please get away. I wanted to scream but had no breath to manage anything more than a dry hiss.

"Show yourself, little coward," cried Rob, his whole body shaking with anger. "You'll never get Tey back. You can die now, or you can die being hunted like an animal."

A piece of machinery was wrenched from inside the shattered tank and flew straight at Rob's head. Rob ducked, lashing out with his hands. I heard Waif grunt as Rob caught hold of him. Rob's bloody face curled into a smile of triumph. "Got you."

I knew I had to act. Wincing, I pushed myself to my feet and dove for Rob's pocket, hand scrambling for the syringe inside. Rob threw Waif into me and we toppled together onto the floor. I bit back a shriek as a shard of glass pierced my palm and blood gushed out at an alarming rate.

Rob didn't seem to notice. His eyes were fixed on the ground next to me, the ground where Waif lay catching his breath. Waif was fully visible again, and there was a darkness in his eyes I'd never seen before.

Rob's gun came forward again, his finger on the trigger.

I heard glass crack under Waif as he climbed to his feet. He slammed into Rob's legs and threw him to the ground. Rob's gun went off in a succession of three identical cracks as he fell.

There was only one thing I could think to do. On the third blast, I let out a strangled yelp and pressed my wounded hand to my side, the blood soaking my shirt in dark red. I fell forward, hearing Rob and Waif go still at my cry. They were both at my side the next moment, Waif looking shocked and concerned, Rob pushing Waif away and cradling my head.

I gasped for breath, curling up tighter and tighter, but Rob forced me to look in his eyes. Those eyes.

"You weren't supposed to get hit," he said, voice flat as if all his emotions had run dry. "I never wanted to hurt you, Tey, you know that right?" My whole body shuddered as I tried to pull away, but he held my face between his hands. "I wanted you with me when the fighting started. I wanted you to trust me." He squeezed his eyes shut and leaned closer to me, the emotion that hadn't been there a moment ago, flooding him to bursting. "Why couldn't you have just listened to me?"

"You were…going to…turn me…into a shadowborn," I rasped. I could see Waif peering over Rob's shoulder, tears streaming down his face. At some point, the glowing aura had left him, as it had left me when I wasn't paying attention. For a brief moment, I wondered if it had ever been there at all. I looked away from Waif, wishing he would escape. I could feel the blood beneath my palm spreading out, warm and sticky against my side.

Rob glanced at it, his face turning whiter than Lei's. "I only wanted to make you forget. You'd never trust me if you didn't forget."

I coughed and trembled in his arms, and then allowed the muscles in my neck to go limp and my head to fall back. Rob caught it, stroking the damp hair away from my face. "I wouldn't have sold you to the Coterie, I wanted you to stay with me."

I reached out to him with my unwounded hand, my shaking fingers running from his lean shoulders down to his side, where I could feel his abdominal muscles clench in grief. I blinked twice and then let my eyes close all the way, my final breath leaving me in a long sigh.

"Tey?" said Rob, holding my head up, willing me to respond. "Tey!" His voice was a hideous shout, but I didn't move or breathe. "You were only going to forget." He held my body closer, lowering his blood-streaked face into my chest. That's when I dropped my hand into his coat pocket and wrapped my fingers around the syringe.

As the first tears spilled from his eyes, I brought the needle down hard. He gasped in pain, and I opened my eyes, seeing for a moment the full knowledge of my betrayal in his gaze. But as the drug entered his bloodstream, that gaze lost its focus, and his eyes became the eyes of a stranger.

CHAPTER 53

I was nearly crushed by Waif's arms. Waif had never been comfortable with physical touch, so his sudden affection surprised me.

"You're alive!" he said, pulling back to look at my bloody side.

"I'm not hit." I held up my wounded palm. "The blood is from my hand." I lifted my shirt so he could see the unblemished skin of my side, assuring him there was no bullet wound there.

He hugged me again until I was sure he'd never let me go. "I have no one but you, Tey. If you had died, I would have too."

I leaned back and gave him a harsh look. "You'd have just given up? After all the work I did to keep you alive? I'd never have forgiven you in the next life."

He lowered his head. "You have to know how much I care about you."

I reached up with my uninjured hand to ruffle his silver hair, the way I would a child, but stopped myself; he wasn't a child at all. At that moment, I could see an ageless maturity in his eyes that made me take in a breath. The helpless boy I'd rescued from Antonio was gone, and here was someone I didn't know at all.

I pulled back my hand and touched his arm instead. "I care

about you too." I felt both sad and excited by the words. Back home I was used to being alone and looking out for myself, but when I'd met Waif, for the first time I didn't care what happened to me as long as he was happy and safe. Could an entire family be wrapped up in one person? If so, he was everything I'd never had.

Suddenly I felt very heavy. "We should leave this place."

Waif peered over my shoulder at Rob's listless form. "What about him? Will you kill him?"

I drew back and turned to look. Rob propped himself up on one arm and watched us, a drugged smile spreading across his face.

He probably deserved to die, and maybe he still would after I told the king about the treachery he was planning, but I knew it wouldn't be by my hand. I still had one problem left and had a hunch that keeping him alive might lead me to the prize I so desperately sought. I had become too much the agent he had made me, and when his uncle carted him away, Rob would see that better than anyone.

I shook my head at Waif and smiled sadly. "I'm a recovery agent, not an assassin."

* * *

I would always remember the next few days like a collage of pictures in my mind. A moment here and there, but never a continuous scene—Waif bandaging my hand; Lei's arms around my shoulders as I carried her out of the underground lab; Rob taking my arm as I led him to the beach.

I was just starting to worry how we'd get back to Cosmar when a small ship full of red-jacketed kingsguard rowed to the shore with their supply drop for Lazar. With Lei comatose in my arms and Waif invisible, I approached them and explained Rob's true identity. After receiving that news, they were more than willing to take us back to Santa Delphina.

At the kingsguard station in Cosmar, Rob's identity was verified, and the king quickly contacted.

My next memory was of me in the king's office, staring into his tan, fatherly face as he prepared to offer me the bounty for Rob's return.

I'd held up my hand. "If it's possible," I said, heart picking up speed, "there's something I want more than money."

He folded his large hands and raised one eyebrow in anticipation of what I was going to ask.

"There are two things, actually."

He nodded for me to continue, and I took a breath, preparing to make my requests. I explained to him about the children in the Castillo and asked if they could be given a proper orphanage. My second request was that I be granted passage home.

The king looked into my eyes for a long moment, as though searching for anything that would discredit me. For a moment, I could see the family resemblance he shared with Rob. He sat up straighter and smiled, looking as regal as a lion despite the dimples in his cheeks. "Miss Walker, by turning in my nephew, you have done the monarchy a great service. It will not go unrewarded. If money is not what you seek, then I will do as you ask. A monarchy-sponsored orphanage will be immediately constructed on Santa Delphina. In addition, I will grant you passage to wherever you wish."

It was the true bounty I'd longed for since setting foot in Cosmar, but now it sent a pang through my chest. Home. I was finally going home. But where was home exactly? A mother who didn't care? A dream that no longer existed? Or was it a boy with silver hair and eyes like the sky, and a little girl the color of new snow? As long as they were safe; that would be home.

I glimpsed Xia and Damion one last time as they left the Agency hand in hand. Xia smiled and leaned her head against Damion's muscular shoulder. I'd come to say goodbye to them, but saying goodbye meant telling them about Rob, and they looked too happy to be burdened with that news just yet. The Beacon would learn of it soon enough, and so, in turn, would they. I'd let them have one last good night together before their world came crashing down.

I watched after them sadly until they were out of sight, and then took the elevator up to the seventh floor. Rob's name was still in the number one spot on the score chart against the far wall. How long would it be before another agent rose to take his place and Rob was forgotten like one of the criminals with a red X across their wanted poster?

In the office, I wrote a letter for Xia and Damion to find in the morning. I let them know I was safe and that I was going home. I thanked them for their friendship and for accepting me onto their team, realizing with a pang how much I was going to miss them. Damion's encouraging words had always lifted me when I needed it most, and Xia had made me want to be braver and stronger. I hoped my words conveyed that.

At the bottom, I wrote one final line. Rob is where he needs to be. I prayed that one day they'd understand what I meant and would find it in them to forgive me.

The king had promised me a cabin aboard one of the royal supply ships that sailed to California. The next one wasn't scheduled to leave for another week, so Waif and I chose to spend our final days in the Castillo. The children had all been taken away by the kingsguard to a safe house where they'd be looked after until the orphanage was built. Now the mansion seemed too quiet. Only the ghosts of their yelps and laughter remained to haunt the dark hallways.

When we finally slept, I dreamed one last time of the girl on my wall.

"I'm leaving," I told her in a voice that was neither happy nor sad.

"No," she said from the confines of her tarnished frame. "You are not finished yet."

"It's too late," I said. "I'm going home."

"But I know where you belong."

"Oh yeah? Where's that?"

"Santa Eurosia. Go there, Tey." She looked into my eyes and I saw a vision in her gaze. The crescent moons of her irises blended into one and became a small curved island surrounded by rough waves.

I shook my head. "No. I promised Waif I'd take him somewhere he'd be safe. And Lei still hasn't woken up yet. She needs a doctor."

"The little girl is safe," she said. "She's with me, waiting for you."

I was taken aback. "No, she's here in the Castillo. In a coma."

"Only on the outside," said the girl.

The dream shifted to a vision of Lei. She was awake and running through tall grass as Waif chased her with outstretched hands. They were both laughing. Waif caught her in his arms and spun her around while she squealed with delight.

"How long do you think they'll last off the islands?" the girl asked me. She stood beside me now and put her hand on my shoulder.

Coldness crept into my heart. "What do you mean?"

"Without emidion, their bodies will sicken and die."

"But Waif has the pendant."

"It only channels what is around it. It will be useless in a place where there is no emidion to absorb. He can't survive in your world, Tey."

I opened my mouth to speak, but nothing came out. The truth of her words settled over me like a cold blanket. It was a fear I had never dared voice aloud, but it had always lurked somewhere deep in my heart. Here, earthblood flowed through the very veins of the islands. It was always there, even if you couldn't feel it. But I'd never seen anything like it back home.

I knew the girl was right, but that didn't make it any less painful. Tears welled in my eyes. "How do I find you?"

"Go north. My island is at the end of the chain."

Sunlight streamed through my window and pulled me into full wakefulness. With a start, I realized that this was the day we were scheduled to depart. A deep sickness gnawed at my stomach as I stared up at the ceiling. I had so many questions. Questions about Rob's research, the islands, and my unusual resistance to the crippling effects of earthblood. If I went to Santa Eurosia, would I finally get answers? Could I somehow do something to fix this place? Or was I acting as crazy as Rob?

I dressed and walked downstairs, feeling hollow and un-certain. At the harbor, a ship waited to take me home, but now I would never go aboard.

Waif greeted me in the dining room. His smile melted into a look of concern when he saw my face. "What's wrong?"

I took a deep breath and sat next to him, folding my hands

on the table. "There's been a change of plans."

* * *

Damion had left his boat hidden on the same beach as before. Together, Waif and I pulled it out of the weeds and pushed it into the water. Damion said the small craft hadn't been used for a year before our trip to Santa Arcadia, so I doubted he'd come looking for it before I had the chance to return it.

"What do you think will happen to Rob now that he's in the king's custody?" asked Waif as we set sail for an island I'd only dreamed about.

I thought for a moment. Rob had gone with the kings-guard willingly; He'd even held the door open for me when I'd led him into the guard office. The Supplicant made him as chivalrous as a medieval knight. I'd been sad to see him that way. He reminded me of the person he could have been if things were different—a great leader and instructor, and perhaps someone more than a friend.

"The King was angry with him," I said, recalling the short time I'd spent there after King Alden's arrival. "Rob may be his nephew, but I was assured that he would be brought to trial for his crimes, just like everyone else." I pictured Ghesari, Nina, Antonio. It felt strange to add Rob's name to that list. I wanted to believe I had done the right thing, but Rob's talk of the need for revolution and the dying islands still worried me. I assured myself that if it took hurting children to accomplish his goals, I wanted no part of them.

I looked at Lei, still unconscious on the seat next to mine. Her vitals seemed strong, but I couldn't get her to wake up. I could only hope the strange girl I was following would be able to help her.

As we got further away from Santa Delphina, the wind picked up, carrying the scent of wild gardenias, and I breathed in deeply. The smell was gone with my next breath.

Waif's hand brushed mine hesitantly, then gripped hard as we watched Santa Delphina fade from view. In that moment, I flashed back to our first encounter on that warped sidewalk in the rain, and suddenly, any doubt I still had vanished. Maybe, just maybe, all my bad moments were what led to the good ones. Because even if it took an entire childhood of misfortune just to be here with him, then perhaps my life had been lucky after all.